SHATTERED APPARITIONS

Rebecca Jose

FREE DOWNLOAD!

https://mymeshara.wixsite.com/nethersouls

OTHER BOOKS BY REBECCA JOSE

THE NETHER SOULS (BOOK ONE OF THE NETHER SOULS SERIES)

TIME AND TIME AGAIN (BOOK TWO OF THE NETHER SOULS SERIES)

THE LAND IN BETWEEN (BOOK THREE OF THE NETHER SOULS SERIES) ***COMING SOON***

FOR THE LOVE OF DAWN (BOOK ONE OF THE PRODIGIUM MORTEM SERIES)

SHARDS OF DUSK (BOOK TWO OF THE PRODIGIUM MORTEM SERIES) ***COMING SOON***

FORCE OF THE IMMORTALS (BOOK ONE OF THE DRAGONS OF DESTINY TRILOGY) ***COMING SOON***

WITCHBALL
WITCHBALL II ***COMING SOON***

This book is dedicated to Margaret Daugherty.

You helped awaken my inspiration and desire to write once more. I had all but given up on being a writer. My life had fallen apart, and I was concentrating so much on being a mother to my children that I forgot to take care of myself.

You welcomed me into your home and helped me through the darkest of times, and then awoke that spark in me once more with our talks and time together. You pulled that desire back out, where I had buried it deep inside of me.

Thank you for that and for everything you have done, and continue to do, for me and my family.

This is why you will always be "Gran Gran"

We love you. xoxoxo

Contents

OTHER BOOKS BY REBECCA JOSE ____________________ iv

PROLOGUE ____________________ 1

PART ONE ____________________ 4

CHAPTER 1: Lucy ____________________ 5

CHAPTER 2: Birthday Trip ____________________ 15

CHAPTER 3: Mountains of Madness ____________________ 32

CHAPTER 4: The Long Drive ____________________ 45

CHAPTER 5: Deja vu ____________________ 61

PART TWO ____________________ 73

CHAPTER 6: Dreamscape ____________________ 74

CHAPTER 7: Home ____________________ 89

CHAPTER 8: Running ____________________ 100

CHAPTER 9: Shattered memories ____________________ 110

CHAPTER 10: Restoration ____________________ 123

PART THREE ____________________ 132

CHAPTER 11: Hidden ____________________ 133

CHAPTER 12: The Doctor ____________________ 146

CHAPTER 13: The Organization ____________________ 158

CHAPTER 14: The Great Escape ____________________ 171

CHAPTER 15: Taken ____________________ 184

PART FOUR ____________________ 193

CHAPTER 16: Memories ____________________ 194

CHAPTER 17: Lily ____________________ 205

CHAPTER 18: The Mountain ____________________ 212

CHAPTER 19: Awake _______________________________________ 225

CHAPTER 20: Safe ____ 231

PART FIVE ____ 242

CHAPTER 21: Greg's return _______________________________ 243

CHAPTER 22: Kidnapped ___________________________________ 253

CHAPTER 23: Betrayed ____________________________________ 262

CHAPTER 24: Lily's Reign ________________________________ 273

CHAPTER 25: Preparations ________________________________ 281

PART SIX ____ 291

CHAPTER 26: The Confrontation ___________________________ 292

CHAPTER 27: Secrets Revealed PART ONE____________________ 304

CHAPTER 28: The Takedown ________________________________ 313

CHAPTER 29: The Chase ___________________________________ 328

CHAPTER 30: Secrets Revealed PART TWO ___________________ 337

PART SEVEN ____ 349

CHAPTER 31: Lucy's Return _______________________________ 350

CHAPTER 32: The Plan ____________________________________ 363

CHAPTER 33: New Beginnings ______________________________ 375

CHAPTER 34: Separation __________________________________ 386

CHAPTER 35: Hope ____ 396

PART EIGHT____ 404

CHAPTER 36: Henry _______________________________________ 405

CHAPTER 37: Lost Boys____________________________________ 418

CHAPTER 38: Coming Together _____________________________ 426

CHAPTER 39: Free Time ___________________________________ 438

CHAPTER 40: Preparations _______________ 451

PART NINE _______________ 466

CHAPTER 41: Doctor Sheppard _______________ 467

CHAPTER 42: The Rescue _______________ 476

CHAPTER 43: Hiram _______________ 489

CHAPTER 44: Hell's Bells _______________ 502

CHAPTER 45: Hell Hath No Fury _______________ 512

EPILOGUE _______________ 524

ABOUT THE AUTHOR _______________ 530

PROLOGUE

The first-grade class of Daisville, Kentucky Independent Schools filed out of the yellow school bus and lined up along the side in a neat row. Two teachers and three chaperones stood and waited for the children to quiet as they each did a headcount of the students.

Twenty students in all calmed at the stern faces of the teachers and stood at attention, waiting for their instructions and eager to see a new piece of the world. The children were learning geography, and here in Pikesburg, Kentucky, the mountains loomed like giants over the city. The teachers had taken the students to one of the many lookouts so that they could see the majesty of the mountains.

The female teacher stepped forward, raising her voice above the drone of the children's voices as they excitedly whispered to each other.

"Students, pay attention, please," She called out sternly.

The cacophony of voices stopped abruptly, and twenty chubby faces focused on the teacher. She glanced up and down the line, ensuring that she had everyone's attention before continuing.

"We will split you up into groups of four. Be sure that you stay with your group and that your group stays with your assigned chaperone or teacher. When I call your name, you will go and stand with your group."

She commenced assigning groups to each chaperone and the other teacher. Six-year-old Lucy stood at the end of the line waiting to hear her name. She had just turned six years old that very day, so this field trip was a birthday treat for her.

She was the youngest and most intelligent in the first-grade class, but being the smartest did not make her the most popular. On the contrary, it made her a loner in class. The games and shenanigans that the other children participated in held no interest for Lucy, and the other students did not understand Lucy when she wanted to discuss the meanings of life instead of playing with dolls and running away from the disgusting boys.

"Lucy Montgomery," The teacher called, and Lucy snapped to attention. "You will be in group three with Mr. Halcomb."

'Great,' Lucy thought to herself as she made her way over to the group. *'My least favorite teacher…curse my luck. Why couldn't they have put me with one of the chaperones?'*

Lucy joined the group but kept her distance as much as the teacher would allow. She trailed behind as her group made its way toward the fenced-off, concrete structure that looked out over the mountains of Pikesburg, Kentucky.

The large, concreted lookout was enclosed in a tight, chain-link fence to prevent anyone from falling, and the students up and linked their fingers into the holes of the fence as they stared out over the side of the mountain in wonder.

Whispered "oohs" and "ahhs" filled the air around Lucy's group, and Lucy sucked in an awed breath as she caught her first glimpse of the land beyond the fence. The pictures she had seen of mountains on the computer did little to capture the wonder and fascination that came with the actual live viewing.

The land sprawled far below her, so far below that even the trees looked tiny and insignificant. She could see tiny dots resembling houses surrounded by minuscule trees and miniature lines along the land that had to be roads weaving through them.

Lucy looked straight in front of her and was surprised to find clouds that looked so close that she thought she could reach out and touch them. The sky, which seemed to loom closely above her head, was dotted with cottony white billows all around her.

She stood at the very end of the line of students, a little ways apart from them but still within shouting distance so that she felt as if she were in her own little world surrounded by sky and clouds with the world below so far away.

Lucy was awestruck at the sight, so much so that she failed to register that little prick of anxiety that shivered its way up her spine.

Lucy had always been a little sensitive to changes in her environment and always seemed to know when things were wrong. She could sense when bad things were about to happen, and sometimes she could even reach into a person's mind and calm their fears and anxieties or make them tell the truth.

It was not only a sense of wrongness or a feeling deep inside the pit of her stomach that she experienced but a tingling sensation that started in the tips of her fingers and filled her arms. She only saw the pictures or heard the voices in someone else's mind if she concentrated on the buzzing energy in her arms and sent it out to the other person, but she could sense dangers to herself without any concentration.

However, Lucy was too enthralled in the sight before her to pay attention to it just now, so she was unaware when the dark figure snuck up behind her, so quiet in his treading that no one noticed its presence. She did not turn to look behind her, even though the feeling squeezed her gut and screamed for her to turn around.

Lucy was caught unaware as the figure grabbed her, wrapping her up tightly into solid arms with a hand over her mouth so she could not scream. She had a fleeting sense of danger as an acrid smell filled her nostrils, and then her world went black around her.

There was no sense of movement or indication that little Lucy was gone. One second she was there, staring over the lookout with the rest of the class, and the next second she was just gone. It was as if she had vanished into thin air, leaving the space where she had been empty and void of her presence.

It was too late when it was finally discovered that Lucy was gone. Lucy had been taken, and by the time the police organized a search and rescue, Lucy was far away from the mountains of Kentucky.

PART ONE

ASLEEP

CHAPTER 1: Lucy

Bright lights pierced the darkness, causing my eyes to water. I squinted and whimpered as tears filled my burning eyes and streamed down the sides of my face. I was lying on my back staring up into the bright lights but I could not turn my head away from the stabbing, painful lights.

"Look, I think she is waking up," a strange female voice said from beside me.

"She couldn't be," said another voice. "She is not scheduled to wake up yet. Her brain is still healing from the trauma."

"I don't know about that," said the first voice. "I know the chip can cause random bouts of muscular spasms, but her eyes are opening."

"Is this some kind of April Fool's joke? Because it is not funny," the other voice said condescendingly.

The first voice responded, "No, Megan, I am being serious. Doctor Sheppard is not going to like it if she wakes up early. My job is to watch them and make sure she stays asleep by administering the proper medications."

"Well," said the one called Megan. "My job is to monitor her brain chip and her medication dosages. The chip has been deactivated and she has had her limit of sleeping meds today, so you will have to do something else to make her sleep."

"Fine," said the other woman. "If she wakes up fully, then it is on you. I will tell them that you would not give me the meds."

"And, I will tell them that she has had her maximum levels." Megan paused for a moment, and then asked, "Debbie, are you sure she is waking up, or is she just dreaming? Sometimes that can cause random eye flutters too."

"Come see for yourself," Debbie answered.

I tried once again to turn my head and scream out that I was indeed awake, but it was no use. I could not move or speak, and fear began to make my heart pound.

Who were these women, and where was I? The fuzziness in my brain was so overwhelming that I did not even know who I was.

I could not remember who I was!

I began to gasp as my heart beat even faster. I squeezed my eyes shut and began to cry, but it was a silent cry. For some reason, my muscles were not responding. I could not move, could not speak, and could only lay there and cry silently.

I heard monitors beeping wildly and the two women gasped.

"She is going into cardiac arrest!" Debbie shouted out in panic.

"Call the paramedic team, quickly!" Megan said sternly, but her tone was calmer than Debbie's.

My chest felt like it was going to explode as I cried even harder, and the lights above me faded as I closed my eyes to the brightness. I felt something stab into my chest, and pain exploded through my tiny body. My heart quivered momentarily before it began beating hard and firm once more.

It beat so hard against my small, frail chest that I thought it would break through my skin, but it was no longer racing. It beat steadily at a calmer pace, hard and rhythmic, and the pain eased throughout my body.

My panic and sadness subsided and the hard pounding of my heart eased to a lighter thump. I heard voices around me, felt hands all over my body, and the beeping of the monitors steadied to a rhythmic 'beep…beep…beep'.

Sleepiness overtook me and my eyes grew so heavy, but I did not want to go to sleep. I swallowed hard and tried to open my eyes to stay awake. I almost started to panic again, but a calm, sure voice made serene little shushing sounds and began to sing to me.

Her tone was tranquil and soothing, almost hypnotizing, and sleep pulled at me harder. I could not resist any longer so I gave in to the sweet oblivion.

***MARCH 26, FOURTEEN YEARS AGO ***

"How is my favorite girl this morning on her birthday?" Megan's cheerful voice cut through the horrible dream I had just had, and I was glad that she had woken me up.

That had been a horrible dream, and I did not want to dream like that again.

"I have good news today," Megan said as she pulled open the drapes of the window.

Sunlight streamed through the open curtains as she came around the bed and sat down beside me. Her brown hair was put up in its usual bun and she had on her nurse's clothes. Her green eyes sparkled in the sunlight as she smiled down at me.

I struggled to sit up, flinging the covers off of me and bouncing excitedly on the bouncy mattress. I loved Megan's surprises. It was usually cookies or sweet cakes, small little outings to the park outside of the hospital where I had been for the past year, or she would bring the hospital cat into my room for me to play with.

My name was Lucy, and I was sick. Doctor Sheppard said that my brain had been hurt in an accident. My brain had been sick for a whole year and he had fixed it, but he said that I would not remember anything from before I had woken up.

All of my memories were gone.

But that was a year ago, and now I was better. I would go home to my mommy and daddy and everything would be normal again, or as normal as it could be when I did not know mommy or daddy and would have to get to know them again. I would have to get to know all of my friends again too, since I would not remember having known them either.

Luckily, I did not have a big family. My mommy and daddy were all I had. They had both been only children, and their parents had passed away long ago. It was just the three of us.

It all seemed strange to not have memories of myself before the sickness. I did not remember my first day of school or Christmases or birthdays. I did not remember having friends or playdates, even though mommy said I did. Strangest of all was that my mommy did not feel like my mommy. I could not explain it, but something always seemed off about her during her visits, and my daddy had only visited once because he worked at home and was always busy.

Doctor Sheppard said that this was all normal because it was my brain that had been sick and my brain is what helps me remember things and feel emotions. He said that I would never remember my life before I was sick and that I would have to adapt and grow new memories and emotions with my friends and family.

Even so, I did not feel comfortable or safe when my mommy was here. I did not feel love radiating from her when she held me. I did not feel huge love coming from my heart for her. Wasn't I supposed to feel those things for my mommy, or was that just made up on television?

I liked to watch the television, but Megan said nothing I watched on there was real, that it was just made-up stories and people that pretended the stories, so maybe the big mommy love that the little girls on television felt was not real and they were just pretending.

Or, maybe it was because I did not remember her. Maybe, because I did not remember my life before my brain got sick, I just needed to get to know her better before I could have huge mommy love again.

'Yeah,' I told myself. *'That's it. You just have to grow to know and love her again. Most babies do not forget their first seven years of life because their brains got sick.'*

"Lucy, are you listening to me?" Nurse Megan asked.

I had stopped bouncing and was motionless on my bed with my feet curled under me. I was staring out the window, lost in thought about the past year of my life here in the hospital. I flinched and looked up at Megan.

"I'm sorry, miss Megan. I had a bad dream last night and was just thinking about it," I said. It was not a total lie. I had been thinking about the dream before my mind was flooded with other things.

Megan sighed and smiled softly. "Another bad dream?"

I just nodded.

"Well, I will talk to the doctor and see what we can do about that. Bad dreams are normal. Your subconscious mind may remember some things about your accident that caused your brain to be sick." Megan patted my leg as she spoke, which was comforting.

My nose wrinkled in confusion as I tried to process what she said. "What kind of mind?"

Megan chuckled and said, "Sorry, Lucy. Sometimes I forget you are just a child because you are so smart."

I smiled and giggled at her compliment.

"Your subconscious mind is a part of your brain that holds emotions and memories that are locked away from the front of your brain. Sometimes, it is because those things may be too painful for you to think about, so it keeps them hidden from you to protect you." Megan paused, giving me a quizzical look before asking, "do you understand?"

I thought about it for a moment and nodded. "I think so. Will my sib…sub…dontis…"

Megan snickered and interrupted me. "Subconscious mind."

"Yeah that," I said in relief that I did not have to remember that big word. "Will it ever allow me to remember what it has hidden?"

Megan looked away in thought for a moment before answering. "Sometimes, when the brain is sleeping, the thoughts escape from that part of your mind and come out in your dreams. However, they get jumbled up with other things that your brain thinks of or imagines, so you can't rely on them to be true."

"Like a television show? It isn't really real?" I asked, trying to understand and piece together what she was telling me.

"Exactly," Megan answered with a bright smile. "You are so smart, Lucy."

I returned her smile, feeling proud of myself and pleased by her approval. I thought momentarily about the dream, about the pain and the lights and the voices.

"You were in the dream," I said softly. "You and Nurse Debbie were taking care of me while I slept, but I tried to wake up and got sick again. Then, something stabbed me in the chest and I went back to sleep."

Megan eyed me warily for a moment, and I swore she looked like she was scared. Then, her eyes cleared and she took a deep breath.

"That was a scary dream I would imagine. But the part about Debbie and me taking care of you while you were sick is real." Megan smiled and winked at me, causing me to giggle.

"You and Debbie still take care of me," I said.

Megan's bright green eyes became sad for a moment as she stood up from the bed. "For now we do, but that is part of what I came to tell you."

I frowned and stared up at Megan with curiosity and a little bit of dread. Was she not going to take care of me anymore? I bit my lip to keep from panicking as I waited for an explanation.

"Today is your birthday, and we are going to have you a birthday party. Your mommy and daddy and all of your old friends will be there. We thought it would be a good opportunity for you to meet them all and start to get to know them again."

My heart began to pound and I became excited. In my year in the hospital, I had not seen another child. There were, strangely, no other patients on this floor, no children on the playground when I had gone out with the nurses, and no children came to visit me.

I had longed for a playmate and companion during my stay. I liked Megan and Debbie, and even the doctor that came to see me twice a week, but it was not the same. I was nervous about meeting the friends that I no longer knew, but I would finally have people my age to play with.

I jumped up and down on the bed, still on my knees, and could not keep the excitement inside. I yelled, "Yay! Yay! Yay!" as I jumped and clapped my hands.

Megan laughed and clapped her hands with me, and then her eyes became serious once more. "We have to get you dressed. Your mommy has bought you some clothes to wear to your party, and I have a little gift for you too, from Debbie and me. You can open it now if you want so you can have it for your party."

I widened my eyes in anticipation and curiosity as Megan reached into the pocket of her nurse's smock and lifted out a small, wrapped box. The pretty paper was pink with white hearts all over it and a big white bow was taped to it. The bow was bigger than the box.

I reached out my hands, grasping for the pretty box as Megan handed it to me. I jerked the box from her outstretched hand, but she only laughed delightedly. I tore at the ribbon, ripping it away, and began working on the paper.

When I finally had all the paper off I opened the box and my breath froze in my chest.

Nestled inside a bed of cotton was the prettiest silver bracelet that I had ever seen. It was small and delicate and had several little charms connected to the chain.

A small silver heart, a silver nurse's cap, a tiny silver stethoscope, and a silver star dangled from the bracelet as I lifted it from the box. I marveled at the sparkles that came off of it as I held it up in the sunlight that streamed in from the window.

"Each of the charms represents something special," Megan said as she sat back down and jangled the charms with her fingers. She touched each one as she explained their meanings to me.

"The star is for the shining star that you are. You came through a horrible accident and survived. The nurse cap is for Debbie and me, the nurses who have taken care of you during your stay here, the stethoscope is from Doctor Sheppard, and finally, the heart is for the love we have grown for you and how much we will miss you when you are gone." Megan's voice was tinged with sadness as she described the heart charm.

Suddenly, I felt as if I wanted to cry. I could not tell if I was sad or happy, or maybe both, but tears spilled down my cheeks as I watched the silver heart dangle from the chain.

Megan lifted the bracelet from me gently, smiling as she said softly, "would you like for me to put it on you?"

I smiled through my tears and nodded. My voice was strained and scratchy as I said, "I will wear it forever and never forget you and Debbie."

Megan put the small chain around my wrist and attached the clasp. "You may have to get a bigger chain when you grow up if you want to wear it forever," she said laughing.

When she had released my wrist with the chain around it, I jumped up and wrapped my arms around her neck, hugging her tightly to me.

I was excited to meet my friends and finally see my home, but I was also sad to leave Megan and Debbie. I was even a little sad to leave Doctor Sheppard.

"Come on, Lucy. Let's get you ready for your party," Megan said as she unwrapped my arms from her neck.

I gave her a quick kiss on her soft cheek before I released her and fell back onto the bed. I swung my legs over the side of the bed and hopped down to the floor. Megan walked to the door leading to my private bathroom, and I followed with a skip.

I was happier and more excited than I had been in a long time, and I could not wait to meet all my friends and get to know them again. I wondered if anyone else had gotten me presents. I sat on the stool in front of the floor-length mirror hanging on the wall beside my little sink and watched as Megan moved behind me with a hairbrush.

I stared at my reflection in the mirror as Megan worked on my hair. She ran the brush through my straight, black tresses, parting and pulling them into two pigtails on either side of my head. My bright blue eyes sparkled as I watched Megan fasten two bow clips on top of each pigtail.

My full pink lips turned up in a smile, causing my slightly upturned nose to wrinkle. "I love the bows," I said.

"The color is the same as the dress that your parents got you to wear," Megan said, returning my smile.

The bows were a soft baby blue which looked very good in my ebony hair and brought out the vibrant blue of my eyes. Megan turned and sat the brush down on the top of the sink. She reached around the other side of the small bathroom and opened the linen closet door.

The bathroom was so small that she did not even have to move from behind me to reach it, so I could watch her and see the soft blue bundle she pulled from the closet. She was right. The color was the same as the bows in my hair.

Megan carefully unfolded the dress and held it behind me so I could see it in the mirror. I gasped in delight. It was a beautiful dress trimmed with white bows around the hem and a big white bow on the waist.

I pulled off my nightgown excitedly and held up my arms so that Megan could slip it over my head. Then, when the dress was in place and Megan had zipped up the back, I looked at my reflection again.

The color made the blue of my eyes shine, and my ivory skin almost glowed in contrast to my raven black hair. My cheeks held a rosiness that matched my full, pink lips as I flushed with happiness and wonder at how pretty the dress looked.

"I look like Snow White," I said with wonder, causing Megan to laugh aloud.

"You are so much prettier than Snow White," Megan said as she hoisted me off the stool.

She gave me a pair of white shoes that looked like my baby doll's shoes and a pair of blue socks with lacy trim that matched the dress. I put them on, proud of myself that I could put on my own shoes and socks.

I checked myself in the mirror and was happy with what I saw. Megan smiled down at me and held out her hand to me. I took it, and she led me out of the bathroom, through my hospital room, and down the corridor leading to the cafeteria.

My eyes widened in delighted surprise when the cafeteria doors opened to a room full of people that yelled "SURPRISE" as I walked in. I jumped up and down excitedly and giggled as I clapped my hands.

The day went by quickly, but I savored every minute of it. I promised myself I would never forget this day, no matter what kind of accident I had or how sick my brain got.

I met my friend Dianna who had red hair and startling green eyes, just like Nurse Megan's. She was very spunky and energetic like me, and she loved my blue dress and bows.

My friend Blake was dark and broody with black hair like mine and dark brown eyes. He did not say much, but I could tell that he was happy to see me by the soft smile on his face.

Chris was more talkative than Blake, but he talked to Dianna more than he did me. He had brown hair and sparkling gray eyes that lit up when he smiled.

I liked my friends each in their own way, and they seemed to accept the fact that I could not remember them, and I would have to get to know them all over again. None of them even talked about it or asked me any questions at all, and they answered my questions patiently just as if we were meeting for the first time.

It was the greatest day of my new life.

CHAPTER 2: Birthday Trip

*** March 26, PRESENT DAY ***

"Lucy!" The voice called, yelling over the fading sound of the dream I had just been having. "Lucy, come on get up! We are going to be late!"

I moaned as I rolled over in my bed, pulling the sheet up over my head. "Just five more minutes!" I called back sleepily.

I had not been sleeping well because of the dreams. I had been having them a lot lately. The one I had just awoken from had not been that bad. That had been the day that I had come home from the hospital after my accident.

I had only been seven years old.

However, the one I had had before, the one with the mountain, that one was bad. It scared me and woke me up every time, and I would usually fall back asleep and have the good dream.

That day of my seventh birthday was my fondest and earliest memory of my childhood. The rest of them had been wiped away due to the accident on the mountain.

Why was I having these dreams now? Maybe the reason had something to do with where we were going.

"We only have ten minutes before we have to leave!" My roommate and life-long friend Dianna replied with a frustrated edge to her voice. "Come on, Lucy, this is your birthday trip after all. You are the one who has been harping about this trip forever. If we don't leave in ten minutes, we could miss our flight. We have to get through baggage check and security. Come on girl!"

"Alright, I'm getting up," I answered, cutting off her ranting.

I flipped the sheet off me and rolled to a sitting position with my legs hanging off the side of the bed. Dianna stood by her bed on the other side of the large room, tapping her foot with her hands set on her ample hips.

Her red curls bounced as she shook her head at me in exasperation. She rolled her emerald eyes as she sauntered her hourglass figure over to her side of the room.

I gave her an encouraging smile as I sat for a few seconds, allowing my brain time to click on for the day before I rose and shuffled into our en-suite bathroom.

I picked up my brush off the sink counter and began running it through my straight, black hair. I glanced in the mirror at my reflection and noticed the dark smudges under my bright blue eyes. My usually pale skin seemed even paler under the bright lights of the lighted mirror, causing the dark smudges to seem even darker. My small nose and full lips curled into a disgusted look at my reflection.

I did not have the hourglass figure Dianna had. My figure was more slender, but I did have a nice butt and nice breasts. I wanted to put on makeup to make my face look more presentable, but I would not have time. The best I could do would be to quickly apply concealer to the dark smudges and brush some bronzer over my round forehead and high cheekbones to get rid of the paleness.

It had been the bad dream again that had kept me up half the night. The other half of the night had been the other dream, but I still had not gotten enough sleep.

I was sure that the reason for the dreams was that we were going to the place where my accident had taken place. I had picked that place to visit the mountains, even though there were many other mountainous locations that I could have chosen from.

I really did love looking at pictures of mountains, and I really did want to see them in person. It was simply morbid curiosity that had awakened the desire inside me to visit the scene of my childhood accident.

I had been talking about this trip since the beginning of school, telling my friends about it and showing them the brochures, well what little brochures I could find. It was not a very touristy place, but the brochures made it seem beautiful.

I had not told my friends the reason I had picked that particular location, and they had not questioned it.

Right after I learned that my friends had arranged for me to take the trip I had been harping about for 'an eternity' (as my friends said), the bad dream had started.

I should not have been able to remember anything about the accident or before it, but my subconscious remembered some of it. I was sure it was about the accident, but I could never tell which parts of the dream were factual and which were constructed from my imagination.

I knew that I had fallen and had not been kidnapped, so I knew that part of the dream was not real.

Maybe it was symbolic.

Maybe it signified me being taken away from my life since the accident had caused me to lose my memories. I did not know the answers, but the dream always chilled me to the bone.

I remember the stories the doctor and nurses told me about my accident. The chain link fence had a weak spot, and when I had leaned on just the right area, the fence had given way, and I fell through it and down the mountain.

I fell a long way before a tree branch latched onto my backpack and held me there until rescue workers found me and pulled me to safety. However, I had hit my head pretty hard on something on the way down, and I had had a severe brain injury that caused me to forget my entire life up to that point.

The doctor said I was lucky to be alive and could suffer some side effects for years. I had never experienced any side effects, but maybe that was what was happening now.

Maybe that is what the dreams were.

Could they be some weird overly-delayed side effects from my accident? Dammit, I hoped not. I did not need this type of drama in my life, and I definitely did not want to start remembering the accident.

"Don't take forever in there," Dianna called out through the closed bathroom door, startling me and causing me to jump. "The tickets are non-refundable, and we will all be angry with you if we lose all that money. You are the one who wanted this trip, so you have no one to blame but yourself for having to get up early."

I placed a hand over my rapidly beating heart and said in irritation, "Alright, alright! I will be out in no time."

Dianna was right.

Dianna and the others had wanted to visit home, hang out at the beach all day, and order drinks from the Tiki Lounge, the little walk-up outdoor bar that sat right on the beach's edge close to our apartment building.

I was turning twenty-one today, so I could finally legally drink, and my friends wanted to celebrate that with me. However, I had seen the beach almost every day of my life, or at least as long as I could remember.

My friends and I lived in the apartment building only a block from Hoss Beach in our small Floridian town, so we frequented the beach during our free time. It had been the only thing to do in the small town where we had all grown up together.

It was not a popular tourist location, so most days, the beach was not crowded. We would go shopping afterward in the only tiny strip mall our town had and then veg out on the couch and watch television for the rest of the day.

It was not as if I did not like hanging out with my friends every day, but I was in kind of a funk.

My life was boring.

I did not mind boring, but it was beginning to grate on my nerves.

I had always wanted to see other places, especially the mountains. But, other than that fateful first field trip, I had not traveled at all during my childhood.

Maybe my parents feared something happening to me again, or perhaps it was something else. Whatever the reason, my family did not travel much, and I was never allowed to participate in field trips again.

My parents did not leave our apartment much at all. My father had an online job working from home, and my mother cooked and cleaned and took care of me, her only child.

I always found it strange that they were content to sit and waste away inside when the outdoors were much more fun and exciting. I would have gone crazy if I had to sit and stare at the same walls daily. I needed variety; I needed change. I was not a consistent daily schedule kind of girl.

I was in college now and was not bound to stay home with my parents and waste away. I was an adult now, and I was free to travel where I wanted when I wanted.

I lived in a dorm room during school, even though the university was only in the next town over. It gave me a chance to experience independence. Dianna had come with me, even though she had thought it was crazy to pay for a dorm room when we only lived thirty miles from school.

My mother came to my dorm once a week to help me with my laundry and bring me a dozen of my favorite jelly doughnuts so I could have them for breakfast every morning. My mother had just brought me a batch yesterday so I could take them on my trip.

There would only be five of us going on my birthday trip: me, my roommate Dianna, my boyfriend Greg, whom I had met just this year, my lifelong friend and now Dianna's boyfriend Chris, and of course, Blake.

I was sure that Blake had paid for most of the trip. He had been trying to get me to go away with him for the entire school year, but I had been too focused on my studies and keeping my grades up to leave. Then, I started dating Greg, and Blake did not mention it again.

A loud banging on the bathroom door drew me out of my thoughts.

"Lucy, come on! Are you getting ready or what?" Dianna's voice sounded more panicked than angry.

I answered consolingly, "I am almost ready, Dianna. My bags are already packed, so we can leave as soon as I get out of the bathroom. We still have plenty of time."

I could hear Dianna's loud sigh, even through the closed bathroom door. "We have five minutes."

"We have more than five minutes," I said in a huff of irritation. "You always insist on being hours early for everything."

"You can never be too early. It is better to be early than late, especially when catching a plane. If you are late for a plane, then you are screwed."

I shrugged at myself in the mirror. She had a point.

However, I was out of the bathroom by the time the conversation ended. It only took two minutes to put on my bra and panties, slip on a pair of jeans, and slide a light blue t-shirt over my head. Finally, I pulled my silver charm bracelet from my bedside table drawer and placed it around my wrist.

I smiled at the still beautiful charms that dangled from it and gently touched the three newest additions.

On my sixteenth birthday, my three oldest friends got me a larger chain and three new charms that represented them to add to the chain.

Dianna had gotten me a tiny silver pair of shoes to signify our shared love of shoes. Chris had gotten me a pair of silver smiling lips to represent his ability to make me laugh and smile.

I sighed as I touched the last newest charm and the only gold one on the chain. It was a gold heart from Blake, dangling next to the silver one. Blake said it signified his hope that we would be more than friends someday.

I had turned him down before and would continue to turn him down.

It was not as if I did not love Blake because I did. I loved him with an intensity that scared me, and that was why I did not want our friendship to grow into something else.

I knew that if I gave in to Blake and it did not work out, I would lose Blake forever and destroy us both. I was not willing to take that chance.

I quickly cast the thoughts aside as I pulled my hair into a high ponytail and secured it with a hair band. Then, finally, I was ready to go.

"Oh, thank god!" Dianna exclaimed when I announced that I was ready.

I rolled my eyes at her dramatics.

"Let's grab our luggage and get out of here," she said.

"Did you call the cab already?" I asked as I grabbed my two suitcases, carry-on bag, and purse.

"Of course I did," Dianna answered in a tone that said I should have known better than to ask. "It is waiting downstairs."

Dianna grabbed up her luggage as well as I headed for the door. I held the door open for Dianna and sat one of my suitcases down in the hallway so that I could lock and secure the door. Then, I picked up my suitcase again and followed Dianna down the hallway toward the elevator.

"We should have invested in one of those roller carts for our suitcases," Dianna complained as she dragged her suitcases, one in each hand, down the hallway. Her carry-on bag and purse were slung over her shoulder, and they became entwined and slid off her shoulder as she walked.

"Dammit!" Dianna cursed loudly as the bag and purse slid down her arm to the suitcase. The straps wrapped around her hand and caused the suitcase to slide from her grasp.

The suitcase, her bag, and her purse hit the hallway floor with a loud THUD, and Dianna dropped her other suitcase so she could pick up her bag and purse. She slung them back over her shoulder, picked up the suitcases, and started back down the hallway.

"Yes, a roller cart would have come in handy," I answered as I struggled with my own suitcases. I had slung my bag on one shoulder and my purse on the other to even out the load, so I did not have the same problems as Dianna. However, the bags were heavy, and I was breathing hard from the strain and effort it took to carry everything.

The ride down the elevator provided a short relief, but even so, once we reached the lobby of our dorm building, I struggled to breathe, and my heart threatened to burst from my chest. I took a deep, relieved breath when we exited the building and found the taxi cab waiting for us.

The driver helped us load our luggage into the trunk, and Dianna and I sank gratefully into the cab's back seat. As the cab drove through the streets, I stared out the window, and a soft smile lifted my lips as I anticipated the trip ahead.

Suddenly, I realized with a groan of disappointment that I had forgotten to grab the box of jelly doughnuts from my mother. They still sat on the tiny island counter in our dorm room's mini-kitchen. I sighed and shrugged my shoulders in defeat. There was nothing I could do about it now.

The boys were waiting for us when Dianna and I arrived at the airport. They stood in the waiting area in the front of the airport, watching everyone who entered the door. Smiles lit their faces as we entered, and they waved their arms wildly to get our attention.

There was no need. I saw Blake as soon as we walked through the door.

"Over there," Dianna said, pointing to where the boys stood still, waving their arms in the air.

We weaved our way through the crowd clutching our cumbersome loads until we finally made it to the waiting men.

Chris stood closest to us, smiling at Dianna with sparkling gray eyes. His dark brown hair was tousled, and he ran a hand through it to calm the unruly locks. His medium, muscular frame was shoved into a tight-fitting t-shirt, baggy jeans, and his favorite sneakers.

Dianna preened under his scrutiny, her cute nose scrunching up with her dazzling smile. She tossed her scarlet curls over her shoulder with a flick of her head as she sauntered up to him, giving him a wink as her emerald eyes sparkled with mischief.

Her legs looked stunning in the short black skirt that she was wearing, her calves emphasized by the strappy black heels on her dainty feet. A cute, forest-green camisole top completed the look and brought out the fiery color of her hair.

Chris smiled hungrily and gathered her into his arms, kissing her with a spicy kiss that could melt all the plastic chairs in the waiting area. Her bag and purse slid down her arm again, and this time she let them fall to the floor along with her luggage so she could wrap her arms around his neck.

I shook my head and looked away, and my eyes caught the gaze of Greg, my boyfriend. He smiled broadly as he brushed past the kissing couple and walked towards me.

My heart fluttered as I watched his muscles bulge under his black tank top. He gave me a heated look through the bangs of his sandy blonde hair, his hazel eyes turning a molten gold as he looked me up and down.

"Hey gorgeous," he said in his soft voice, the sultry tone evident as he reached down and took one of the suitcases from my hand, setting it down with his load.

I smiled at his handsome face with its chiseled features and strong jawline and sighed in relief as the weight of my suitcase left my hand.

"Thanks. That was getting heavy," I said.

I could feel Blake's presence coming up behind me, and I whirled around to face him.

"We need to get to the baggage check," Blake said as he grabbed my other suitcase and Dianna's luggage. He had only brought one duffle bag, which he had slung over his broad shoulders and turned so that it rested on his back.

"It is this way," he said as he gave me a quick smile and gestured with his head for us to follow.

His medium-length, straight black hair flowed around his head with the movement. His dark brown gaze flicked momentarily to Greg as Greg put an arm around my shoulder, and Blake turned quickly and walked away.

I watched his large muscular frame glide along with the grace of a predator stalking its prey as he led us through the crowd toward the baggage check-in counter. His bright yellow t-shirt was not hard to follow through the crowd, but it looked good with his black hair and pale skin.

Greg gathered his luggage and my one remaining suitcase and moved to follow Blake, and I slung my carry-on and purse over my shoulder and followed behind him. I turned and whistled to Dianna, and she and Chris pulled away from each other. Chris gathered up his luggage, Dianna's carry-on bag and purse, and they both moved to catch up to us.

One hour later, we had checked in our luggage, made it through security, and sat in the waiting area in front of the departure gate for our two-hour flight to Kentucky. I was amazed that we had made it through so quickly.

"Why Kentucky?" Chris asked for about the hundredth time. "I mean, many other locations have more mountains with more tourism. Why would you pick a location where we could be kidnapped or shot by some backwoods hills-have-eyes people?"

Dianna rolled her green eyes. "Come on, Chris. That's just a movie. Things like that do not happen in real life."

"Actually," Blake cut in. "Hills Have Eyes was based on a true story."

Dianna's eyes widened in fear and surprise. "Really?" she squeaked.

Blake nodded, his serious brown eyes piercing her with a dark stare. She shuddered and cuddled into Chris's side.

Chris chuckled and shot Blake a mock irritated look. "Stop it, man. You're scaring her."

Blake's full lips quirked up into a half smile. "Why should she be afraid? She has you to protect her."

"Damn right," Chris said, sitting forward slightly and puffing out his chest. He looked over at Dianna and winked as he said, "I got you, baby. No one is going to kidnap you while I'm around."

Dianna flashed him a sultry smile and said, "my hero."

I rolled my eyes and made a retching sound, which made Greg and Blake laugh aloud. Dianna shot me a dirty look, but there was a smile on her lips as she turned back to Chris.

"Seriously, Lucy," Greg said, bending his head close to me as I lay my head on his muscular arm. "Why do you want to go to Kentucky?"

I swallowed hard.

I had not told my friends that it had been the location of my accident. My friends and I had never talked about my accident. Even after that wonderful birthday party on my last day in the hospital, none of them asked what had happened. We had just started over as if we had only first met, and none of us had talked about it since.

Greg had come into my life just recently. He had moved to our small town from New York, and I met him this past semester on the first day of classes. We had our second class of the day together. He asked me out one day, and we have been going out since.

I had never told him about my accident and never talked about it to my friends whom I have known most of my life, so how was I supposed to answer his question?

The truth was that I had picked that location as my first traveling spot because of its significance. It was the first place I had ever visited and was where the first six years of my life had been taken from me by the accident. So it would be perfect to begin my new life of freedom and travel in the same spot that had taken away the first part of my old life.

Plus, I really wanted to see if those mountains were as beautiful in person as they were in my dreams and pictures.

I raised my head from Greg's arm and looked up into his soft, hazel eyes. He was looking down at me expectantly; one sandy blond eyebrow raised quizzically.

I sighed and answered softly, "I have been to that spot before, long ago, but I did not get to enjoy it and do not remember it. I want to see what I missed."

Silence fell around me. The conversation about Texas Chainsaw Massacre that had ensued between Blake, Dianna, and Chris stopped abruptly. They all turned and stared at me with different looks on their faces.

Dianna's green eyes held a strange look that I could not read, but she quickly averted her gaze when I looked at her.

Chris's gray eyes were serious as he held my gaze. "I did not know that you remembered the location of your…."He paused for a moment as if looking for the right word. "Incident," he finally said so quietly that I almost didn't hear him.

"I don't remember," I said just as softly. "I asked Doctor Sheppard about it one day during a routine check-up, and he told me about the mountain and showed me pictures. I have wanted to visit the place since."

"What incident?" Greg asked.

I started to open my mouth to answer, but Blake's dark brown gaze caught my attention. It held intense anger, and I jerked back in surprise at the darkness of his stare.

However, Blake's look was directed at Greg, and his tone was menacing as he said in a low voice, "We do not talk about that, so don't ask her that again."

Greg looked confused for a moment before he chuckled nervously and replied, "All right, man. Don't get your panties in a bunch. I was just being curious."

"You cannot be curious about that. None of us can," came Blake's ominous reply.

He turned his gaze to me. "Why did you pick that spot, Lucy?" he asked in a softer, gentler tone.

I shrugged and said, "There are a few reasons, but I think it just boils down to simple curiosity."

Blake nodded in apparent understanding, but his eyes held a haunted look that I did not understand. Chris and Dianna had the same look, and Greg just looked confused.

I frowned at my friends' worried looks. I knew we had never mentioned my accident, but I had not known that they considered it taboo. Was this their way of protecting me from horrid memories that could be uncovered if triggered? Was it possible that the right trigger could bring the memories back?

I had continued to see Doctor Sheppard up into my early teens, and he had always assured me that my memory loss was permanent as far as he could tell, but he had also explained that the brain was a wonderful and tricky thing. The memories were there; they were just damaged beyond repair.

Did I want to remember?

The revelation hit me, and I almost doubled over in my chair with its force. Was that the real reason I wanted to go to this particular location? Was I hoping to trigger my memories of my early childhood?

I did want to remember my early childhood. I wanted to remember my friends and family and how I felt about each of them.

Did I want to remember the accident?

No, but…

I thought about Blake, who I had always known felt more than friendship for me since I could remember. Had he always felt that way about me? Had he loved me the way children can hold love for one another when they are small, like the kids in the movies that grew up together and ended up together as adults?

Had Dianna always been stuck to my side everywhere I went and bossed me around as if she were my mother?

Had Chris always joked around, made me smile when I was sad and made me feel better about everything?

I wanted to remember how I felt about my parents when I was small. Did I love my momma with all my heart? Had I been a daddy's girl that wanted to marry a man just like him when I grew up, as most little girls did?

I had never felt close to my parents after the accident, and I had always wondered why. Had I ever been close to them?

The most important question was; would I ever remember these things, or were they lost to me forever?

I hoped not. If I had to endure the trauma of remembering a horrifying, grueling accident, I would if I could only have my precious memories back.

I glanced around at all the faces still staring at me with that faraway haunted look in their eyes, and suddenly I felt so alone. Tears pricked the backs of my eyes, and I blinked rapidly to keep them from falling. Why was I so emotional all of a sudden?

I took a deep breath and focused my gaze on Greg. "I had an accident. It was long ago when I was small, and I don't remember it. So we have never talked about it."

"I think it best that we keep it that way," Blake said, but his voice had gone soft, and his eyes had lost their darkness. "It could trigger memories that Lucy's mind may not be able to deal with."

Aha! So I had been right. However, my friends did not know how much I wanted that trigger, how much I wanted to remember.

Greg shifted his gaze to each of us, and then his hazel eyes landed on me. He smiled kindly and touched my cheek gently with one finger.

"You do not have to talk about anything you do not want to, Lucy. It was not my intent to force you to tell me anything. I did not know it was that serious, or I would not have even asked."

I smiled as my sadness drained away just as suddenly as it had come. "Maybe I will tell you about it someday," I whispered to him.

He nodded as he ran his finger down my cheek and tweaked my chin between his rough fingers, causing a fluttering sensation to churn in the pit of my stomach.

His smile turned devilish as he said, "I would be happy to listen to anything that comes from those sexy lips."

I felt a blush start up my neck and spread into my cheeks at his words. A quick chill went up my spine, and I shivered as Greg's face drew closer to mine. It was not a shiver of pleasure.

For some reason that I could not understand, I did not want him to kiss me just now. Whether it was because my friends were watching or because the subject was so profound, I did not know.

The fluttering in my stomach grew stronger, and I realized that it was the churning sensation of nervousness, not the stirring of passion as I had first assumed.

I did not want Greg to touch me. What was wrong with me?

I did not want to draw back and risk hurting Greg's feelings because I was an emotional idiot, so I stiffened and let him pull me to him. His lips were inches from mine when an echoing voice boomed over the speakers in the room.

Greg jerked back with a chuckle before he could kiss me as the voice announced that our flight was boarding our row. I sighed quietly with relief and rushed to grab my carry-on bag and purse. I pulled my boarding pass from the front pocket of my purse and got in line behind the other passengers.

Greg followed close behind me, and I could feel his presence at my back. Guilt squeezed my heart as I thought about our almost kiss. Why had my body reacted that way? Greg had kissed me many times, even though we had never gone any further, and I had never felt like that. His kisses were always sweet, and I felt safe and comfortable in his arms.

'Maybe you are just tired,' I told myself. *'You have creeped yourself out by talking about the accident and thinking about that horrible dream, and you are nervous about visiting that place again.'*

Yes, that must be it. Not to mention that I had never been on a plane before and was also nervous about that.

The line moved quickly, and before I could creep myself out even more with more dark thoughts, I was walking through the terminal to board the plane. I found my seat with Greg's help, which I was glad to discover was a window seat, and placed my carry-on in the overhead baggage area as everyone else had done. Then, I sat in my seat with my purse in my lap, strapped myself in, and prepared to fly for the first time.

I stared out of my window at the sunny Florida runway, and a sense of ominous foreboding filled me. Frowning, I shook my head and scolded myself once more. I would never relax if I kept feeling this way, and I wanted to enjoy my vacation, not spend the entire time driving myself crazy.

I took a deep breath, laid my head back against my seat, and closed my eyes. I felt a hand cover mine, and I opened my eyes and turned my head to find Blake's dark brown irises filling my vision. I focused on his face, smiling softly as he patted my hand comfortingly.

His fingers brushed over the gold heart on my bracelet, and his smile widened. My heart lurched at the intensity of his gaze, and butterflies played around in the pit of my stomach.

This time it was not from nerves.

I swallowed hard and gasped softly as Blake's fingers caressed the skin of my wrist, sending tendrils of sensation running up my arm and down my body.

Blake's smile became something more, something darkly sensual, as his fingers continued to play on my wrist under the bracelet. My eyes widened and I shook my head, pleading with my eyes for him to stop his assault on my senses.

As he drew his hand away, the hurt in his eyes sent a stabbing sensation of guilt through my chest. I smiled a weak apology and darted my eyes behind him to Greg, who sat in the aisle seat.

Greg noticed me watching him and shrugged. "I can never sit in the middle. It makes me feel as if I'm suffocating. You gonna be alright without me?"

He smiled jokingly and gave me a wink.

I returned his smile and said, "I guess I will have to make due." My tone was mockingly dramatic, and I sighed loudly, which made Greg laugh and shake his head.

I laughed and turned back toward the window, ignoring the guilt that shot through me at Blake's sullen look. Greg made me feel safe, it was true, but Blake was the one that had always calmed me when I was upset and made me feel steady and grounded; that is when he was not setting my nerves on fire with his light, flirty touches.

Even though he was slightly hurt at my rejection of his touch, I knew he would never let anything happen to me. Blake was my rock, my solid foundation in a world of turmoil.

It had always been Blake.

His presence at my side comforted me as I heard the plane's engines grow louder and louder, preparing for take-off.

My eyes stayed plastered to the window, but a small smile lifted the corners of my lips when I felt Blake's hand on mine once more. He covered my hand with his, not pushing or giving more than I wanted to take, comforting my torn nerves.

That was just what I needed right now.

Takeoff was not as scary as I thought it would be, though. The plane's engines were loud, but I was not scared of loud noises, so it was fine. My head was thrown onto the back of the soft seat as the plane took off at high speed, and then we were lifting into the air. Watching the ground grow further and further away was a fascinating sight, and I watched out my window in awe.

I watched the world pass by with a bird's eye view, and then my eyelids began to grow heavy. The loud, constant thrum of the plane's engines became strangely soothing as I lay my head back and closed my eyes, finally relaxing in my seat.

"See, I told you that flying was relaxing," Blake's sultry, deep voice whispered into my ear.

His hand still lay on mine, and he stroked the back of my hand softly with his before taking his touch away. I felt cold without his touch, and I shivered inwardly but kept my eyes closed tightly.

"It seems you were right," I answered groggily.

31

I heard his soft chuckle that sent a thrill through me, and I smiled softly at the sensation. Sleep tugged at me gently, enclosing me in its comforting embrace, and I gave in and let myself drift off to dreamland.

CHAPTER 3: Mountains of Madness

I got off the bus, and my heart pounded with excitement. The teacher said something about everyone staying with their group, but I was not paying attention. I was too busy staring in wonder at the sight in front of me.

I did not have to walk out to the overlook to see how high we were. The sky was so close that I thought I could reach out and touch it. I could see the tiny trees far below from here, but I wanted a closer look.

"Lucy Spears," The teacher called, and I snapped to attention. "You will be in group three with Mr. Halcomb."

'*Great*,' I thought to myself. '*My least favorite teacher…curse my luck. Why couldn't they have put me with one of the chaperones?*'

It did not matter to me anymore, however, when my group stepped up onto the fenced-off concrete platform, and I found myself looking out over the mountains. I was so amazed that I did not notice how the fence shuddered when I leaned into it to get a better look. I was caught unaware as I felt the fence give way under my insignificant weight.

I fell.

My stomach lurched, and my body filled with horror. I was so high up in the air that I could not see the ground. Instead, I could see the tops of tiny trees far away and the blue sky spinning in my vision as I flipped head over heels in a free-fall. My arms flailed wildly, my legs kicked uncontrollably, and I opened my mouth to scream.

I screamed…

*** THE PLANE TO KENTUCKY ***

"Lucy! Lucy, wake up!" Blake's voice sounded frightened and concerned.

Why was Blake scared? What was going on? Who was screaming? Then, I realized it was me.

I gasped and awoke to his face hovering over mine. His dark, worried eyes searched my face as he stroked a hand through my hair. I was half lying in his arms over the plane seats.

"You were screaming out in terror," Blake said when he saw my eyes open. "Are you ok?"

My heart beat violently in my chest, and my breathing was coming hard and fast. Sweat beaded on my forehead, and my eyes blinked rapidly as I tried to pull myself from the dream and focus on Blake's words.

I had been falling.

The stomach-lurching sensation still fluttered inside me, and I felt as if I was going to be sick. I rose suddenly, grabbing for the little plastic bag that was in the pocket of every seat. I took deep, even breaths to try to keep from throwing up.

I hated to throw up. The sensation always left me weak and vulnerable, and the taste lingered in my mouth forever, no matter how many times I brushed my teeth or rinsed with mouthwash.

I held on to the bag, gripping it tightly in both hands, as I hovered my face over the opening and breathed slowly in…then out…then in. Finally, the nausea began to fade, and my stomach calmed somewhat. I wiped a sleeve over my forehead, wiping away the cold sweat that had collected there.

Blake rubbed circles along my back gently, and I heard Greg's voice asking if I was okay. Blake turned, and I heard him mumble something to Greg, but my still fuzzy brain could not make out the words. I tried to pull myself back to the present.

I did not want to remember the rest of the dream.

The cacophony of voices around me began to form inside my brain, and I could finally make out individual voices and words. People were whispering about the crazy screaming woman in the seats in front of us, but I was too sick to be embarrassed.

I could hear Dianna asking, "what happened over there? Is Lucy alright?"

"She is fine," Blake answered comfortingly. "I believe she just had a nightmare."

"That must have been some nightmare," Greg said. "Are you okay, baby?"

"Mmm?" I said, still a bit nauseous and dizzy.

"She is trying not to vomit," said Blake calmly. "Give her a minute. She cannot speak yet."

"Maybe we should take her somewhere else besides Pikesburg," Chris said so low that I almost could not hear him. "It may trigger her, and we don't want that, especially now."

"Hush," Blake said sharply. "Now is not the time to discuss such things."

"Why is this accident such a big deal?" Greg asked confusedly.

No one answered him.

I did not say anything, either. I was still trying to breathe around the threat of vomiting up my breakfast of gummy snacks and chips that Greg had bought me at the airport. My stomach had settled, but the queasiness still threatened to burst forth if I moved too fast or let down my guard.

"Everyone, please return to your seats to prepare for landing," a voice said over the plane's intercom. The voice continued droning on, continuing the landing speech.

I did not listen to the rest. All I heard was that we were landing, and I breathed a sigh of relief at the news. I wanted out of this plane and away from the suffocating closeness of everyone. I needed air, I needed to breathe, and I needed to move.

My entire body tensed with nervousness and frustration as I watched the ground get closer. My stomach did another nauseous tumble inside, and I clutched the bag I still held between my two hands. I took in a deep, gulping breath of air and closed my eyes, willing the sensation to pass peacefully.

It did, and I felt the gentle jolt of the plane's wheels touching the ground as I opened my eyes and saw my first glimpse of Kentucky…well, technically, my second glimpse…I did not remember the first.

All I could see at the moment was the runway.

I waited impatiently for the plane to stop and prepare for our departure. It seemed as if it took forever for the crew to get the aircraft ready for us to get off. I continued to sit with my hands gripping the bag, waiting for that voice to tell us we could start de-boarding.

When it did, I grabbed my purse and jumped from my seat, not waiting to hear the entire speech. I practically climbed over Blake and Greg in my haste to get off the plane. I squeezed through the aisle before anyone else could even get up from their seats. Finally, I reached the door where the stewardess was waiting to thank everyone with a wide smile.

I glanced at her and gave her a slight smile as I dashed down the terminal and into the airport waiting area. I had no clue where I was or where I was going. I followed the exit signs until I came to the front of the building and hurried out of the glass exit doors.

I stopped outside the doors and bent down, placing my hands on my knees. My long black hair fell down either side of my face as I let my head fall forward. I stood like that for a few minutes, breathing deep breaths of the cool, fresh air. It was much cooler here than it had been in Florida. I finally felt better, more like myself again, so I rose and glanced around at my surroundings.

The airport where we had landed was not a large one. The pick-up area where I stood only had a few cars waiting in line. No one besides me had come out of the exit doors yet. The parking area for long-term parking did not have many cars either.

It was nothing like the buzzing and busy airports I had seen on television, and I was glad of that. I did not want to be in a crowd of people right now. I needed to be out in the open, away from people, and breathe in the fresh air. I needed to clear my foggy head.

I wondered if I had claustrophobia. I had never experienced a bout of claustrophobia before, but I had never been on a plane before, so I had no way of knowing whether this feeling was normal.

"Lucy, are you sure you are alright?" I recognized Blake's deep, smooth voice behind me, and my nerves calmed drastically at the sound.

I took a deep breath and plastered a smile on my face before turning around to face him.

"I am fine, Blake," I said as I turned around. "You should all stop worrying...." I stopped speaking abruptly as I came around and saw his face.

The look in his eyes had me frozen on the spot. His raven bangs had fallen into his face, partially hiding the agonizing worry in his dark brown gaze. There was an intense sadness mixed with the concern that had what I could see of his black brows raised over his almond-shaped eyes. His strong jawline was bulging with tension, and he pressed his full lips together tightly.

He ran a hand through his tousled hair, pulling his bangs back from his face, and the full intensity of his gaze hit me like a punch to the gut. My breath caught in my throat, and I brought a hand to my lips to stifle the compulsion to sob.

"Oh, Blake," I said softly. "Why are you looking at me that way? You make me want to cry when you look like that."

"I would never want to make you cry, Lucy," Blake said, and I could hear the tightness in his tone. "I am sorry, but I am very worried for you. Had I known this place would trigger you this way, I would never have let you come."

The sorrow and compassion I felt for my best friend quickly turned to irritation at his words. "Let me?" I seethed.

Realizing that he had made me angry, his eyes widened, and the worried look became even more intense. "Lucy, I did not mean it that way. I only meant...."

I cut him off, not wanting to hear his explanation right now. "It's fine, Blake. Let's get our luggage and find our rental car. It is scheduled to be dropped off here in twenty minutes."

"Lucy, please," he whispered, but I ignored him. I brushed past him as I went back into the airport and looked around for the signs for baggage claim.

A pang of guilt slid through me as I felt Blake's presence at my back. I did not want to make him feel sad or lead him to believe that I was angry at him. Truthfully, I was angrier at myself than I was at him.

I was beginning to have second thoughts about my choice to come here. I had no idea that it would affect me so intensely. Blake had said something about my mind not being able to handle the trigger, which frightened him.

It frightened me too.

Did I want to go through with this? Was it too late?

Sighing, I stopped just feet from the baggage claim area, where my other friends looked through the baggage coming around on the baggage carousel.

I turned to Blake and said, "Look, Blake, I'm sorry. I think my nerves are still frazzled from the nightmare I had. I did not mean to take it out on you."

The tension in Blake's eyes eased with his soft smile. "You have nothing to apologize for, Lucy. It's me that should apologize. I just worry about you so much…."

He stopped mid-sentence, closing his eyes and taking a deep breath. Then, after a few seconds, he continued, "Look, let's just forget this and enjoy your vacation, alright?"

I smiled and nodded my head. "That would be lovely," I responded with a smile.

I turned back to the baggage claim area and caught Greg's eyes. He smiled at me, but there was tension in his eyes as they flicked to Blake following behind me. A flash of possessive anger went through his gaze, and I shuddered inwardly.

What had that been about?

I had never been afraid of Greg's possessive little looks before. On the contrary, I found it flattering and even amusing at times, but he had never given me a reason to be afraid. So, why was my body responding as if I were suddenly scared of Greg?

Chills were still moving up and down my spine as I moved closer to Greg and the unsettling look in his hazel eyes. His gaze turned back to me, and his features softened, easing my anxieties and calming my rapidly beating heart.

"There's my girl," he said, sounding relieved and happy, and the sound of his smooth voice made me smile.

"I just needed some fresh air. I think I may be afraid of flying." I let out a small laugh as I moved closer to Greg.

Greg chuckled, and the lovely sound cut through the fear and anxiety that had gathered inside my chest. I had not paid attention to how hard it had been for me to breathe before now. I took a few relieved breaths as oxygen filled my lungs, and my heart began to calm to a steady beat.

My nervousness dissipated as I reached Greg's side, and he wrapped an arm around my shoulders. "I think you may be right. You nearly gave me a heart attack from worrying about you."

I leaned into him and took a deep breath. I closed my eyes as I relaxed into him for just a moment. "I'm sorry. I am fine now."

He bent and kissed the top of my head, released me from his hold, and then bent down to continue looking for our luggage on the carousel.

Why had I been so afraid of him before?

I felt a pang of regret for the little white lie I had told.

I had actually enjoyed flying; it was the nightmare that had scared the hell out of me. I did not want to talk about the nightmare, though. Greg would not understand, and the others would freak out and insist we get back on the plane and go home.

I just hoped the nightmares would stop so I could finally get some sleep and not be so jumpy and nervous. I wanted to enjoy my vacation, but I also wanted to feel normal again, and I had not felt normal in weeks.

Not since I discovered that we were coming to Kentucky for my birthday.

Once again, I was seriously doubting my decision and wondering if it were too late to change our destination when a man on the other side of the carousel caught my eye.

He narrowed his eyes at me in a searching manner as if he were trying to figure me out, as if he knew me. I had never seen the man as far as I could remember. Nevertheless, he continued to stare at me as if he knew me. It made me nervous, especially the eyes. There was something familiar about those eyes.

I shivered apprehensively as his cold, gray eyes wandered over my face. He was huge and intimidating with a bald head, slightly handsome chiseled features, and substantial bulking muscles. A snake tattoo curled from the neckline of his shirt, ran up his neck, and then disappeared behind his ear.

I swallowed hard and backed away from his daunting presence even though he was on the other side of the carousel. I wanted to put some distance between myself and his unnerving stare. My breathing quickened as fear raced along my body, and my heart began to beat faster.

I could not take my eyes away from the man. I began to tremble as his searching look became dark and menacing. I widened my eyes in confusion. What had I done to upset this stranger, and who in the hell was he?

I could see Greg in my periphery, still searching the carousel for our belongings. He had not noticed me backing away, nor did he seem to notice me drifting further away now. He was too focused on searching through the piles of luggage that came around to notice anything.

I swallowed hard and tried averting my gaze. Maybe if I looked away as if I had not noticed him, he would stop looking at me and leave me alone. Instead, his cold, gray stare hardened, and I gasped. He began to move forward, and terror gripped my heart in its icy fingers.

I turned to run and opened my mouth to scream, but I was stopped by a pair of strong hands gripping my shoulders. The scream died in my throat, and the only thing that came out was a slight squeal. I began to struggle but froze when I heard the soothing, deep voice.

"Lucy, what is wrong with you?" Blake said in concern. I looked at his face to see his searching eyes darting around the room.

"There was this man," I answered weakly, turning my head to look over my shoulder where the man had been standing.

He was gone.

Had he even been there?

I took a deep, calming breath as my body began to shiver. The moment's adrenaline was fading, leaving me weak and shaky. Tears threatened to burst from my eyes, and I sniffled as I turned my attention back to Blake.

"A man? What man? Did someone try to hurt you?" Blake's voice had become cold as his dark eyes scanned the room more intensely.

I glanced over my shoulder again, but there was no sign of the frightening bald guy with the creepy eyes and snake tattoo. Had he just been a figment of my imagination?

What was wrong with me?

'Alright, Lucy, you need to get a grip,' I told myself as I took another deep breath. My heart slowed, and my breathing evened out as the fear drained away to be replaced by confusion and an overwhelming sense of bleakness.

Maybe I just needed to rest. It had been a trying day already. I looked into Blake's face and said, "I saw this man, and he was scary looking, but he is gone now. At first, I thought he had been staring me down, but now I think I was just scaring myself. I think I need to rest. Maybe I have jetlag."

Blake's worried gaze stopped scanning the room and landed on me. "You're trembling, Lucy. Are you sure you're alright?"

I closed my eyes tightly and tried to control the shakiness I felt all over my body. I did not respond and only nodded weakly as I opened my eyes and gave Blake a small smile.

Blake took a deep breath and released my shoulders. I felt vulnerable and exposed without his touch, and I nervously glanced one more time over my shoulder. The man was nowhere to be seen, but I saw Greg loaded with our luggage, smiling brightly as he walked toward me with his cumbersome load.

"I am pretty sure I found all of our stuff. Chris is getting his and Dianna's stuff." His voice was normal and cherry, so I knew he had not noticed anything of what had just happened.

I plastered a smile on my face, even though I felt like screaming and running away. I wanted to return home, but I could not tell my friends that. They had already spent their money on this vacation, so I decided to force myself to enjoy it.

"Great. Thank you so much for fetching my luggage," I said, forcing a happy tone into my voice.

Greg smiled, clueless that my smile and tone were fake, and glanced behind me at Blake. He frowned. "Where's your luggage, Blake?"

Blake pulled the duffle bag he had slung over his shoulder toward the front of his body. "Right here," he answered with a smile. He pulled another smaller bag around as well and handed it to me.

"That reminds me," Blake said. "I grabbed this for you when you ran from the plane."

He handed me my carry-on bag with a smile. "Oh," I said in relief. "Thank you. I had forgotten about that."

Greg's eyebrows rose as he stared at the duffle bag draped over Blake's shoulder. "That really is all you brought?"

Blake shrugged nonchalantly. "I don't need much."

Greg's surprised look remained on his face as he said, "Alright, man. If you say so."

His face relaxed as he turned his attention back to me and smiled. "Are you ready to find that rental van and get the heck out of this airport?"

The fake smile still plastered on my face became genuine as I answered, "Yes, let's get out of here."

Greg lifted the load of our luggage effortlessly and motioned with his head for me to follow. I slung my carry-on bag over my shoulder with my purse and quickly glanced back at Blake. His dark brown eyes regarded me with a knowing look. My fake smile had not fooled him.

I turned away to avoid meeting his gaze and followed Greg down the hallway toward the front of the building, glancing around for signs that would lead to the car rental area.

By the time we had found the rest of our group, got the van keys from the rental counter, and were loading our luggage into the van, my encounter with the strange man was the furthest thing from my mind.

As we pulled away from the airport and merged into the traffic on Man O' War Boulevard in Lexington, I focused my attention out of my window. Greg was driving, which automatically put me in the front with him. Dianna and Chris were cuddled in the shorter middle-row seat, and Blake stretched his large frame out on the long back seat.

I watched the scenery silently. It mainly was traffic and stores as Greg maneuvered the van through the heavy traffic and onto Nicholasville Road. We passed a small mall on the left, and Dianna squealed that we should stop and go shopping.

"I would rather find a hotel and get some rest," I said, turning in my seat to see her. "We still have a three-hour drive before we get to Pikesburg."

"Alright," Dianna conceded. "But it will be more like six hours because we must go shopping first."

I rolled my eyes playfully and, in a huffing tone, said, "fine, we will go shopping tomorrow before we head out. We have ten days to kill, after all."

Dianna gave me a happy little smile, and I turned back around in my seat.

"Pikesburg is right on the border of Virginia," Greg said. "Remind me why we didn't land at the Tri-City Airport, which is only an hour and a half from Pikesburg and has a much bigger mall?"

"I know," Dianna said in a pouty voice. "It also has more shopping centers."

"That is true," Blake answered, raising his voice slightly to be heard from the back. "However, there were no direct flights to Tri-City. We would have had a two-hour layover in Georgia before reaching Tri-City.

There were cheaper direct flights here, so I figured we could drive the rest of the way instead of waiting two hours and then getting on another plane. Plus, I thought Lucy would like the scenery if we drove."

"Yeah," Dianna said, still pouting. "So we have to put up with the smaller shops here."

Chris chuckled. "Look on the bright side, babe. We have more money to shop with the money we saved on the plane tickets."

Dianna's tone instantly brightened. "You do have a point. You always know the right things to say to make it all better."

I chuckled and rolled my eyes, although she couldn't see me since she was behind me.

"Well, I guess that means we have to find a place close by to stay the night so we can go to the mall in the morning," Greg said as he swerved into another lane.

"That would probably be best," I said. "There are a lot of outlet stores around this area too, and I love the outlet stores."

"The map system on my cell phone says there is a motel about a mile from here," Blake shouted from the back.

"A motel? Can't we find a hotel instead?" Dianna whined.

"Dianna," Chris said frustratingly. "A motel will be cheaper, and we do not need all the amenities of a hotel just for one night's sleep."

"Fine," Dianna huffed.

Blake handed his phone to the front of the van so we could follow the map's GPS location to the hotel. Luckily, the hotel had two empty rooms next to each other, one with two double beds and one with a single bed.

We left most of our luggage in the van, parking it right in front of our rooms and locking it securely before making our way into the hotel. Blake caught my eye as he unlocked the door to his room. He smiled softly, his dark brown eyes twinkling, as he opened the door to his room and slipped inside.

I returned his smile before he slipped from view and then hurried to catch up with Dianna and Chris. Greg had hung back at the van to rummage through my luggage. I asked him to find my blue suitcase with my pajamas, and he happily complied.

I smiled as I thought about how sweetly accommodating Greg was. He always did everything I asked of him without complaint. I was not that hard to please, so it was not a cumbersome task, but it was nice to have someone so compliant. I was not too fond of emotionally overloading situations.

I thought about Blake in the room beside us as I sat down on the bed and knew I was lying to myself. If I was being honest, I had to admit that I liked the intense feelings I sometimes felt at his touch or certain looks that he would shoot my way.

His touch brought out sensations and feelings that scared me when I was younger, and I had not known how to deal with the heat that his touch lit through my veins. I had not known how to cope with the intense need that burned through me when he would come close to kissing me. I was scared to go down in his flames. I had been too young for that kind of intense passion.

Now that I was older, I wanted a burning passion to consume me, but not with Blake. I would always hold Blake close to my heart, but I could never let him in. Those kinds of consuming romances never lasted, and I would rather have Blake as my friend than lose him forever.

Greg broke my concentration when he entered the room with my blue suitcase and dropped it on the bed beside me. I rummaged around in the case until I found my flannel pajamas and then went into the bathroom to shower and dress for bed.

I turned on the water and adjusted it as hot as my body could stand. I undressed and stepped inside the shower when the water was fully heated. Sadness poured into my soul while the steaming water ran over my body as I thought about never having Blake in my arms.

As the hot water eased the stiffness in my muscles, I tried to ease the sadness in my heart by thinking about the other man in my life. Greg was sexy and compassionate; someday, I might experience that burning passion in his arms. Maybe after we had dated for a while, I could have that with him and forget my obsession with Blake.

My brain may have accepted the words as I said them, but my heart knew it was a lie. My chest heaved as tears fell from my eyes and mixed with the water pouring down the drain.

My heart will never forget Blake.

CHAPTER 4: The Long Drive

I was standing in the hospital cafeteria, wearing my blue dress with the white bows. My mommy seemed happy that she could take me home today after the party, and she told me that it would be a long trip back home. However, since we all lived in the same apartment building, my friends and I would ride together, so I was happy about that.

The boy with black hair like mine…Blake was it?...came up to me with a shy look. His dark brown eyes were serious as he stopped in front of me.

"Hey, Lucy. Do you wanna sit beside me when they give us cake?" he asked hopefully.

I liked this boy. His voice made me smile. I nodded my head in consent. His quick smile lit up his sad face at my confirming nod, and he reached out to me as the smile faded.

"I saved us a seat," he said somberly.

I wondered why he always seemed so sad.

I took his hand, and it felt warm and safe. He pulled me over to one of the tables with the bench seats and pulled me down beside him.

I turned my head to look at his sad little face, and recognition hit me full force, taking me back to a memory…or perhaps a dream?... of before that day in the cafeteria.

The day I had fallen…

I was stepping off the bus again, but this time Blake was there. He was looking for me, but I did not want him to find me for some reason, so I stood still and hoped he did not notice me.

I huffed when they called my name and put me in a group with my least favorite teacher. I crossed my arms over my chest as I stomped off toward my group, but I kept my distance as much as the teacher would allow.

I trailed behind as my group made its way toward the fenced-off, concrete structure that looked out over the mountains of Pikesburg Kentucky, taking quick peeks over my shoulder to try to see where Blake was. I hoped he had not seen me.

The large, concreted lookout was enclosed in a tight, chain-link fence to prevent anyone from falling, and the students up and linked their fingers into the holes of the fence as they stared out over the side of the mountain in wonder.

Whispered "oohs" and "ahhs" filled the air around my group, and I sucked in an awed breath as I caught my first glimpse of the land beyond the fence. The pictures I had seen of mountains on the computer did little to capture the wonder and fascination that came with the actual live viewing.

The land sprawled far below, so far below that even the trees looked tiny and insignificant. I could see tiny dots resembling houses surrounded by minuscule trees and miniature lines along the land that had to be roads weaving through them.

I looked straight in front of me and was surprised to find clouds that looked so close that I thought I could reach out and touch them. Blake was forgotten in my mind as I stood and stared out at the wondrous sights in front of me. I felt as if I were in my own little world, surrounded by sky and clouds with the world below so far away.

I was so awestruck at the sight that I failed to register that little prick of anxiety that shivered its way up my spine. I had always been sensitive to changes in my environment, but I was too enthralled with the sight to pay attention to it now.

I did not pay attention when the dark figure snuck up behind me, so quiet in his treading that no one, not even the teachers, noticed its presence.

I was caught unaware as the figure grabbed me, wrapping me up tightly into strong arms with a hand over my mouth so I could not scream. I heard Blake's little-boy voice calling my name, and the rest of the memory faded away…

"Lucy, what is wrong?" Blake asked me in his sullen voice.

I jumped and focused my attention on his face. He was frowning worriedly at me. Someone had put slices of cake in front of us, and Blake was eating his.

"I'm alright," I said as I picked up my little plastic fork. "I think I may have had a brain spasm. The doctor said I would have those sometimes."

Blake did not answer. He only nodded and looked down at his cake with that worried frown.

I patted his hand on the seat between us and said, "Don't worry. I am much better now, and the doctor said they would eventually go away."

Blake looked at me and smiled softly, easing the frown just a bit. "I don't want to talk about you getting hurt ever again, okay?"

I smiled and said, "Okay. We will never talk about it again."

Blake's smile brightened, and his hand turned over to grasp mine. "I will keep you safe, Lucy. I will never let you get hurt again."

I returned his bright smile as I pulled my hand from his to take a bite of my birthday cake…

I was suddenly torn from the moment, caught up in a whirlwind of darkness, smoke, and smog. I tumbled head over heels in a void of flashing voices, pictures, and places in time.

Now I knew I was dreaming.

I flew further into the past as the fabric of space and time rippled before me, and suddenly I was in a strange classroom, standing in the front of the class.…

"Students, pay attention," The teacher called out. "We have two new students with us today."

I was nervous, my heart beating wildly in my chest. I was too little to go to school. I was only three years old, but mommy said it would be okay. I was much smarter than most three-year-olds.

My sister was like me. It would not have been as bad if she had been with me. They had taken her from me.

They all looked at me as if I were crazy when I asked for my sister. I had called out to her in my mind when I first arrived and woken up from my first procedure, but she had never answered.

I wish I had never been brought to this place.

I remembered my mommy and daddy crying hard when the men came to take us. They had said not to worry, that we would go to a special school and that we could see our parents again someday. We just needed to learn to control our minds first.

They had lied.

They had taken my sister, and now my world had fallen apart. I was devastated and wanted to go home, but everything in my mind calmed when I first saw him sitting at his desk. His brown gaze caressed me with a tender look, and when I looked back at him, he smiled brightly.

His smile repaired my torn heart and world in just an instant. His face changed from the little boy he was now to a very handsome adult with black hair and deep brown eyes…

I was pulled from the dream again and instantly transported to freefalling in the beautiful blue sky after falling from the mountain.

NO!

I did not want to dream of that again. That would be too much.

I began to scream

"Please, No," I said repeatedly, fighting against the force that held me in its grasp, begging it not to take me to that moment.

Darkness fell as my screams echoed through my mind.

*** THE MOTEL ***

"Lucy!" Blake's voice called out over the fogginess in my brain. "Lucy, wake up!" He called again.

Something was wrong. I could feel a heaviness inside me that prevented me from waking fully. I tried to open my eyes, but I could not. I tried to move my arms, but I could not. I was frozen.

My heart beat with terror, and my breathing came in short, rapid gasps. I opened my mouth to call for help, but nothing came out but a squeaking sob.

"I got you, Lucy. You are safe. I got you." Blake's deep, soothing voice cut through the heaviness and the fog, calming my heart to a more even pace. I began to breathe easier when I felt his hand lightly brush strands of hair from my face.

I was lying on a soft bed with my head propped on an even softer pillow. It was very comfortable, and I snuggled under the blanket thrown over me when I felt a chill run through my body.

The blanket did not help.

I tried once more to open my eyes, and this time, they opened. Blake's vexed face filled my vision. His full lips were stretched out with worry, his eyebrows pinched over his almond-shaped eyes, and his strong jaw was tensed with anxiety.

I smiled up at him. I did not like to see that look on his face.

He let out a long, slow breath and visibly relaxed, taking my hand into his as he returned my smile.

"Lucy," he whispered my name in relief.

"I'm okay. I must have fallen asleep after I got out of the shower. It was just another nightmare. You were in it this time."

"Yeah," Greg's irritated voice cut in. "We know. You kept calling out his name and would not answer anyone else."

The hurt in Greg's hazel eyes and the sullenness of his tone sent shards of guilt piercing my heart. I struggled to sit up, pulling my hand from Blake's and reaching out to Greg for help.

Greg's face relaxed, and he smiled softly at me as he pushed Blake out of the way to come to my side. He grasped my hand and pulled me to a sitting position. My gaze flickered to Blake, and he gave me a knowing look as he backed away and gave up his spot to Greg.

"I cannot control my dreams," I said as I grasped Greg's hand and pulled him to me. "Stop being so possessive."

My tone was playful as I gave Greg a mischievous smile, and the tension and anger drained away from his face and shoulders. He returned my smile as he allowed me to pull him to me, and I wrapped my arms around his shoulders when he got close enough.

"I'm sorry," I whispered into his ear. "I don't even remember what the dream was about. I only remember Blake's face and that I was in danger, so I called out to him."

Greg's arms wrapped around my waist as he sat down and pulled me closer. "I forgive you," he whispered playfully.

He pulled me practically into his lap as he nipped at my earlobe and kissed my neck. I unwrapped my arms from his neck and pressed my hands to his chest, holding some distance between us as he tried to pull me entirely onto his lap.

"Greg, we are not alone," I said as I pushed away from his kisses.

"No, you are not," came Blake's snarling tone. I looked up into his angry face and sighed.

I was not in the mood for this.

Greg looked irritably over his shoulder and then turned his attention back to me.

He smiled softly as he said, "It's fine for now. We will have our own room at the hotel, so we can pick up where we left off later." He waggled his eyebrows up and down suggestively as he released me and stood, grabbing my hands and pulling me up with him.

I frowned.

"When was someone going to tell me I was sharing a room with Greg?" I said sternly, shooting an irritated look at Dianna, who sat on the bed on the other side of the room.

"I told you to book her a separate room," Blake said with a snarl. "I knew she would not like sharing a room."

"Well," Dianna stammered. "I…I just assumed that…well…Chris and I have been….well, you know…for a while now, so I thought…."

My eyes widened in horror, and my face flamed with embarrassment. I did not want to know about Dianna and Chris's sex life, and I certainly did not want to have my own sex life.

"Greg and I are not having sex," I spat angrily at Dianna. "Nor do I want to. I am not ready for that kind of commitment yet."

I shot Greg an apologetic look, but he only smiled as he ran a hand through his sandy blonde hair and said, "That's fine, Lucy. I would never force you into something you are not ready for. I will sleep on the couch in the sitting room at the hotel, alright?"

I breathed a relieved sigh and gave him a thankful smile and a nod. Blake stood over to the side, but I caught his satisfied smirk out of the corner of my eye as he walked to the door and left, closing the door behind him.

I sighed, shaking my head as I turned my attention back to the room. "As far as tonight goes, can we have girls in one bed and boys in the other, please?"

Dianna nodded. "Of course, Lucy, but you have to forgive me. I hate it when you're mad at me."

I smiled and held my arms out to her as I said, "I am not mad at you."

She came into my arms with a sigh of relief and hugged me tightly.

"I'm the worst friend ever," she said against my shoulder.

I hugged her and said, "No, you are not."

"Alright," Chris's triumphant tone rang across the small room. "Girl-on-girl action tonight!"

He pumped his fist in the air and gave a whoop as Greg doubled over in laughter.

Dianna and I glared at him and said in unison, "Absolutely not!"

"Well, I can tell when I am not wanted," Chris huffed playfully, throwing his chin up in mock indignation. "Come on, Greg. We will build a boy's only fort and then see how they feel about leaving us out of all their fun."

Dianna and I pulled away from each other, giggling, and Dianna threw a pillow at Chris's head, which began a massive pillow fight that caused Blake to burst into the room to find out what was happening.

Several pillows flew at his face as he stepped in the door, and we knew we were all in trouble.

Blake had been the pillow-fighting champion when we were younger, and he still held the championship by the time we were ready for bed.

I felt better when I laid down next to Dianna to sleep, but there was still a dull heaviness in my heart. It was as if my mind were caught in a perpetual state of fogginess that was slowly lifting, and my heart did not want to see what lay inside the fog.

A sense of eerie dread settled over me as my eyes grew heavy. I did not want another nightmare, but I desperately needed sleep. I wanted to let myself drift off and take my chances, but my mind was buzzing with anxiety and would not let me relax.

I turned to my side so I could see from the one large window in the room to the lit parking lot outside. There was not much out there other than a few cars. I sighed loudly and closed my eyes, trying to force myself to sleep. I took deep, even breaths in my nose and out my mouth and pictured a blank wall in my head.

I had learned this technique from my mother, who loved to research things, one of which was different forms of meditation. I did not know about meditation, but I knew this exercise helped me fall asleep.

I finally fell asleep, and I did not dream.

Thank the universe.

The next morning Dianna was in high spirits, ranting about shopping. Finally, we all dressed for the day and piled into the rental van. Blake double-checked both rooms to ensure we had gotten all of our stuff.

I felt much better this morning and more like myself than I had in weeks. I was hungry, though, and as I got into the van, I thought about the jelly doughnut I could have had if I had remembered to bring them. My mouth watered for one, and I sighed in disappointment.

"Can we go to a doughnut shop for breakfast?" I asked, turning in my seat to address everyone in the van.

Dianna's emerald eyes turned to me. She had piled her red curls into a messy bun and dusted some bronze shadow over her eyes. She wore a bronze-colored camisole tank that matched her eyeshadow, blue jean shorts, and bronze-colored Viking sandals.

"Where are the doughnuts from your mom that you love so much?" she asked.

"I left them on the counter in the mini-kitchen," I answered, wrinkling up my nose in disappointment.

My black hair was piled into a messy bun, but my straight, fine hair never looked as good as Dianna's curly locks. I had not bothered with make-up this morning since I had gotten some decent sleep, and the bags under my sapphire blue eyes were gone.

I had opted for my orange gypsy top with cut-out sleeves, my favorite pair of jeans, and my black ballet flats. The orange color of the top made my eyes pop and made my pale skin look more tanned.

"So, did you at least get to eat one before we left yesterday?" Dianna asked.

I shrugged. "No, remember? You woke me up just in time to get dressed and rush out the door."

"Oh, yeah," Dianna said with a sheepish smile.

I caught Blake's stare from the back of the van. His almond-shaped dark brown eyes locked on my bright blue ones with a worried frown. I gave him a confused look back, quirking one eyebrow.

"What?" I asked.

He did not respond and only shook his head as he turned his gaze out the window. Still frowning, I turned back in my seat and focused out the front window. The traffic was horrible here, almost as bad as when we would drive into the city back home.

Home…

The word seemed so foreign to me as I repeated it over and over in my head. Had home ever really felt like home to me?

No…no, it had not, but the fact that I had my friends had made it bearable over the years.

I smiled as I listened to them bickering in the back. They were discussing the difference between jelly doughnuts and cream-filled ones and which ones were better. Of course, they already knew my opinion, so I opted out of the discussion.

We made it to the mall and piled out of the van. I shook my head as I watched the men pile out and noticed that they all wore jeans and t-shirts this morning. Had they all coordinated their outfits?

Greg wore a forest green t-shirt that brought out the green color of his hazel eyes. His sandy blonde hair was unruly, and he had stubble growing on his strong chin. He had on faded blue jeans and his favorite pair of sneakers.

Chris climbed out behind Dianna, wearing a gray t-shirt that matched his eyes, baggy blue jeans, and sneakers. He had spiked his dark brown hair on top of his head in a short spike.

Blake climbed out of the back of the van, and my heart dropped when I saw him.

His white t-shirt was tight fitting across his broad chest, showcasing the rippling muscles of his chest and stomach. His black jeans were tight in the back and clung to his perfectly round ass nicely as he climbed backward out of the back of the van.

He turned my way and caught my gaze. His black hair fell into his dark brown eyes like it always did, and he brushed his hand through it and pushed it to the side. It fell in an unruly mass, revealing his almond-shaped eyes as they focused on me.

My stomach flipped as I watched his tongue dart out from his mouth and slide across his full, sensual lips. He stalked toward me with a hungry look in his dark eyes as if he was a predator stalking his prey, and I was the prey.

My lips parted as my breath became ragged, and my heart fluttered in my chest. I felt the heat rise up my neck and color my cheeks as electric desire coursed through my veins. I watched his lips curl into a sensual smile, and a malicious little sparkle twinkled in his come-hither eyes.

I swallowed hard and darted my eyes away from the sight. I turned to find Greg coming around the van to my side, and I schooled my features so he would not see how affected I was by Blake. I prayed that the coloring in my cheeks would be gone by the time Greg made his way to me.

I had to do this a lot, and I knew that if I turned around, I would find Blake smirking at me with that knowing look. He knew how he affected me when he looked at me like that, and I knew that he did it on purpose whenever he had the chance.

Stupid traitorous body!

It was becoming more and more difficult to resist my intense feelings for Blake.

I took a deep, cleansing breath as I felt Greg's presence at my side. I looked up into his smiling face and plastered a smile on my own face. He draped his arm around my shoulders and walked with me as we made our way toward the entrance to the mall.

We found the food court and had breakfast before braving the stores. We shopped for a bit, returned to the van with our purchases, hit a few discount outlet stores where I wanted to shop, and then began our three-hour drive toward Pikesburg.

It was late afternoon by the time we finished shopping.

Chris wanted to drive this time, so Chris and Dianna sat up front, leaving Greg and me sitting in the middle seat in front of Blake. The shopping had worn me out again, and I wondered if I would get any sleep during the trip. We traveled for almost an hour when my eyelids began drifting shut. I struggled to keep them open since I had nowhere to lay my head.

Greg had opted for the window seat and was staring out the window with his back to me. I had been playing games on my cell phone to keep myself awake, but now my neck was stiff, and I felt I needed to stretch and move before my whole body stiffened up.

"Can we stop for a restroom break?" I called up to Dianna in the front passenger's seat.

"Already on it," she answered in a chipper voice. "There's a rest area coming up in two miles."

I breathed a sigh of relief as I responded, "oh, that's great. I so need to stretch."

I would stretch out my muscles, use the restroom, walk around a bit, and then nap. Maybe if I asked Blake, he would change seats with me so I could stretch out on the long backseat and rest comfortably.

I asked Greg if he minded and heard a soft snoring noise. He had already fallen asleep with his head leaned against the window at an awkward angle. I shook his shoulder gently, and he startled awake suddenly.

"What…where…I'm awake!" he stuttered as he turned his startled hazel eyes toward me.

I giggled and responded, "Yeah, you are now. We are getting ready to stop for a restroom break."

"Oh, yeah, alright," he said as he straightened up in his seat. His eyes fluttered sleepily before his body slumped down in the seat again.

I snickered. Poor guy. Maybe he should be the one to change seats with Blake so that he could take a nap. He seemed to need it worse than me right now.

I heard Blake chuckling in the seat behind us, and I turned to see him leaning casually in the back bench seat with his arm slung up and resting on the back of the seat. He watched me, his dark brown eyes twinkling with mirth as I tried again to rouse my sleeping boyfriend.

"Alright, I'm up," he mumbled groggily as I shook him again when we stopped at the rest area.

I was able to wake him long enough for us to visit the restrooms. I emerged from the ladies' room with Dianna to find Greg curled up on the back bench seat sleeping again.

So much for my nap.

"Looks like you're gonna have to sit beside me," a dark, sultry voice said in my ear.

My senses instantly became highly alert as I felt Blake at my back. His breath tickled my neck as he spoke into my ear, causing delicious little tendrils of desire to curl through my stomach.

"Are you going to be able to stand being close to me for another two hours?" he asked huskily.

I swallowed hard and turned to face Blake. "As long as you behave yourself," I said, trying and failing to sound stern.

Blake chuckled sinisterly. "I make no promises."

I huffed and climbed up into the seat next to the window. The afternoon sun was hidden behind tall hills dotted with evergreen trees. I looked off into the distance at the mountains that had begun to loom closer as we drove across the interstate. They looked so small and insignificant from this viewpoint, but my dreams of how they had looked standing at the top flashed through my mind, and I knew that they were far from paltry.

They were breathtakingly beautiful, vast and majestic, and darkly dangerous, and I was about to see them in person. My heart fluttered in excitement at the thought as I watched the scenery fly by my window. It was mostly trees and an occasional grassy clearing, and then there were buildings and random houses as we would pass by an exit, which were few and far between.

I was constantly aware of Blake's presence sitting beside me. I glanced over at him several times to find him sitting straight in the seat. His back was rigid, and his eyes were fastened to the front of the van. He stared straight ahead with a stony expression, and his gaze never moved.

The silence became monotonous as I stared out of my window, and just when I thought I could no longer take it, I felt Blake move beside me. I stiffened as I felt his hand brush my arm, and I turned to face him.

His brown eyes pierced me with a serious look, and his voice was so low that only I could hear it. "Why won't you ever give me a chance, Lucy? I know you want me, so why?"

I cringed inwardly. Blake had never been verbal about the issue. He would tease me with looks or 'accidental' brushes of his hand, but it was not his way to talk about it. I had known the conversation would come up eventually. Still, I was not expecting it to be now, here in this enclosed space, with my boyfriend sleeping behind us and my other two friends silently engaged in their own conversation in front of us.

"Have you forgotten that I have a boyfriend?" I whispered back, slanting my eyes toward the back seat where I could hear Greg snoring away.

Blake's eyes darted that way, and a dark look came over his features. "You have not even known him that long. He will never be good enough for you."

I raised my eyebrows. "I thought you liked Greg."

"I tolerate him," Blake said, pausing before adding, "for your sake."

"He's a good guy, Blake," I said consolingly. "He has been good for me so far."

"He bores you, Lucy," Blake said, rolling his eyes. "I can tell you hold no passion for him the way you do for me. You deserve to be worshipped as I worship you. Your body tells me so."

Blake's fingers slid inside the opening of my cut-out sleeves and stroked the bare skin of my arm. Goose bumps broke out along my skin, and I shuddered with desire. Tendrils of hot need awoke inside my veins, and I gasped at the powerful sensation.

"See?" Blake whispered, his voice deep and sensual as he leaned closer to me. "Just one touch, and you tremble for me. One brush of my fingers along your bare skin, and your heart beats faster. Just one seductive glance and your breathing becomes quicker. Greg has never affected you this way."

He was right, and it was not only his touch. Just the sound of his voice had me panting before he had even touched me. Had I not told myself these same things just yesterday?

My heart was pounding inside my chest, and I was breathing in short, fast gasps. My body burned with desire and lust, and the intense need to fist my hands into Blake's dark locks and pull him to me became too much for me to bear. This was the fire that I had been afraid of, the one that threatened to consume me.

I clenched my hands into fists and shoved them into my lap, pulling my arm away from Blake's touch. "Why are you doing this to me?" I hissed. "You know I only want us to be friends."

Blake leaned into me, placing his lips just above my ear as he whispered, "Liar. I can taste your heat."

He licked the top of my ear, and I quivered as a gasp of longing escaped me.

I swallowed hard, my voice husky with need as I said, "Blake, please."

Blake's breath blew along my skin as his lips drifted from my ear and down to my neck, sending coils of fire licking through my veins. My body burned with need as my brain became fuzzy, and all I could think about was what it would feel like if he placed those full, kissable lips against my neck and suckled lightly.

I let out a soft, lustful moan at the thought and shut my eyes tightly as I felt him draw closer. Then, I felt his breath against my neck travel up the side of my face as he said huskily, "Please, what?"

Please what? I could not think. What had I been trying to say? The only thing that kept going through my mind was, 'please kiss me, take me, touch me.'

I shook my head to clear it from the foggy desire that held me prisoner. The slight movement caused my face to brush against his lips, and I froze.

The touch of his lips against my cheek sent a sensation of fiery ecstasy through me so strong that I thought I would melt away right there in my seat. Blake brought his hand up to my face and turned my head toward him. I kept my eyes squeezed shut.

"Look at me, Lucy," he whispered, his breath hot against my lips.

I opened my eyes slowly to see his face inches from mine. The tortured expression in his dark brown eyes tore at my heart, and the sadness in his tone almost brought me to my knees.

"Why, Lucy? Why won't you let me in? I know you want to."

He drew even closer, so close that our noses were touching. I wanted to close that distance, capture that kissable mouth with mine, suck on that full bottom lip, and run my tongue across it. I wanted to pull his body against mine so close that I could feel every ripple of his gorgeous muscles against my softness.

He was right. I did want him. I wanted him with an intensity that frightened the hell out of me, and that was why I could not let him have me. That was why I could not give in to my desire for him.

I wanted him with me always, but if I gave in to my desire, I could lose him. I could be content to have him forever as my friend rather than give in and lose him later when the relationship failed.

I took a deep breath and said in a strained whisper, "I can't, Blake. I don't ever want to lose you."

Blake's eyes frowned in confusion. "Why would you lose me, Lucy? You will never lose me."

"You can't know that, Blake," I said.

The desirable sensations were fading to be replaced with a cold dread that curled along the pit of my stomach, causing me to shiver for other reasons.

"If it didn't work out and I lost you, I would never forgive myself."

Blake moved even closer, his hot breath brushing along my lips and cheeks. His lips were so close that they brushed against mine in a feathery light touch, so light that I thought I might be imagining it.

"That will never happen. You will always have me by your side as long as I am alive. That I can promise you."

His voice had grown deep and husky, almost as if it were silk brushing along the inside of my body. His lips pressed closer, pressing ever so gently against mine in the beginning of a kiss, but then he pulled back suddenly, leaving me cold and confused.

A light rustling of clothing came from the back of the van, and I jerked my head around to see Greg stirring in the seat behind us. He turned over, released a stuttering snore, and settled into sleep again. Guilt overtook me, and I buried my face in my hands.

My voice echoed through my fingers as I said, "please, can you stop pressuring me? I have a boyfriend, and that is the end of it."

I heard Blake sigh and whisper, "fine. I will stop for now."

He paused and then added, so low I almost did not hear, "but someday I will have you."

I kept my face hidden in my hands for a long time after that, wondering if my shivering was from the sudden cold in the van or the anticipation of feeling Blake's lips against mine again someday.

CHAPTER 5: Deja vu

We stopped once more for a break, and I finally got to stretch out on the bench seat in the back as much as I could. I drifted on the edge of unconsciousness but could not fall asleep. I was still aware of the soft voices of my friends and the sound of the tires along the road.

The swaying of the van as it drifted along the highway finally lulled me to some semblance of a sleep state, and I dozed in this state until I felt the van slow down.

I opened my eyes and slowly rose into a sitting position.

"Why are we slowing down?" I asked sleepily.

Greg turned around in the seat in front of me and smiled. "We are leaving the parkway. The roads are only two lanes here."

I glanced forward curiously, straining to see out the front window. The sunlight had dimmed immensely, but it was still daylight. I glanced out of the window beside me and gasped.

I could see nothing but a large rocky cliff that rose to a tree-covered hill high above us. I turned to glance out the opposite window to see a valley falling away below us, with a large town nestled at the bottom.

A sense of familiarity rose inside me as if I had been here before. Of course, I had long ago, but I was not supposed to be able to remember it. However, there was no mistaking the eerie feeling of déjà vu that spread throughout my body.

"I've been here before," I whispered.

No one answered me, but I had spoken so low that they probably had not heard me.

Blake turned and glanced at me over his shoulder. "Did you have a nice nap?"

His dark brown eyes pierced me with a devilish look, and I narrowed my eyes at him as if daring him to start his games again.

"Yes, as a matter of fact, I did," I shot back with a snarky tone.

Greg turned, frowning as he darted his gaze between Blake and me. "Are you two mad at each other?"

Blake chuckled and answered, "That's not the word I would use to describe it."

I shot Blake an irritated look and said, "We just had a small misunderstanding, but it is fine now."

Greg's frown deepened as he replied, "You look like you want to tear each other apart."

Blake laughed aloud and said, "You could say that."

I groaned, shaking my head and snarling at Blake, which only made him laugh louder. Greg climbed over the arm of the seat and plopped down next to me in the backseat.

He draped his arm over my shoulders and said, "Don't worry, babe. I'll back you up. I believe we should be able to take him out if he keeps messing with you."

I groaned again, peeking at Blake's expression. He was laughing so hard that tears formed in the corners of his eyes as he doubled over in his seat.

Greg pierced Blake with a mock angry stare, clearly believing this was all a big joke.

"Please, just stop," I ground out between clenched teeth as I ran my hand down my face.

My face flamed with mortification as I sat there and listened to Blake's laughter, rich and deep and…absolutely beautiful.

It made me smile despite myself, even though I wanted to punch him in his perfectly handsome face.

The van stopped, and I scrambled over Greg to reach the door. The door opened from the outside, and I darted out of it. Seeing that it had been Dianna who had opened the door, I grabbed her hand and hauled her with me. I lifted my gaze to check our surroundings and realized we had stopped at a gas station.

"Girl, slow down. What in the world is wrong with you?"
Dianna gasped as I dragged her into the gas station with me,
scanning the area for the restroom.

Spotting the restroom, I turned in that direction as I responded, "I
just needed to get away from those irritating boys."

Dianna stopped and pulled at me, causing me to stop and turn
toward her. I lifted my eyebrows questioningly when I met her
piercing green gaze.

"What?" I asked.

"Blake got to you, didn't he?"

My eyes widened in surprise, and my stomach fluttered
nervously. "What do you mean?" I asked weakly.

"I know that he is head over heels for you. You can see it all over
his face every time he looks at you, and I have seen you look at him
too. Don't try to deny it." Dianna placed her hands on her hips and
glared at me, but it was not an angry glare. It was more of a
challenge, daring me to deny what she was saying.

I closed my eyes and took a deep breath before responding. "I
adore Blake, Dianna, and that is the problem. I am not willing to
ruin our friendship to pursue a relationship that may not even work
out. Plus, I already have a boyfriend."

Dianna scrunched her nose as she said, "You have only been
seeing Greg for a few months. You do not even know him that well
yet."

"And yet you thought I was having sex with him," I huffed and
crossed my arms over my chest. I raised my eyebrows and gave her
an exasperated look.

"Well, we are in college now. So I figured you were 'sowing
your oats' as they say." Dianna shrugged nonchalantly.

"No, Dianna, I am not sowing my oats, nor have I sowed
anything yet," I said, throwing my arms up in the air in exasperation.

Dianna's eyebrows shot up so high that I thought they would
disappear into her hairline. Her mouth gaped open, and her arms
dropped to her side.

She looked at me in disbelief for a moment before leaning closer
to me and whispering, "Are you still a virgin?"

"Of course I am!" I cried a little too loudly.

I glanced around quickly to see if we had attracted any attention. Blake was at the counter handing some money to the attendant behind the register, a plastic bag dangling from his hand. Greg was nowhere to be seen, and Chris was walking out of the exit door. There was not anyone else in the store.

Blake caught my eye as he turned from the counter and shot us a questioning look. Dianna pointed toward the restrooms, grabbed my hand, and hauled me inside. I saw Blake nod before I turned and let Dianna pull me into the women's room.

Dianna turned back to me after checking under each stall for feet. "I cannot believe this. I thought you and Blake had fooled around at least once in high school. Why did I not know that my best friend was still a virgin?"

I shrugged. "We just never talk about boys like most girls do. We always talk about clothes, what shows we like to watch, and stuff like that. You have always been with Chris and never talk to me about your relationship or ask me about any of mine, not that I have any."

Dianna looked sad for a moment before responding, "Well, I should have asked. I always thought you would end up with Blake."

She shrugged and added, "I have been a shitty friend, haven't I? All wrapped up in my own shit and just assuming that you're okay."

I frowned in confusion. "But I am alright. Why would you assume otherwise?"

"Because you have been having nightmares and panic attacks. Why would you want to return to this place if it triggers you this badly? Girl, what were you thinking?" Dianna's green eyes swirled with worry as her scrutinizing gaze roamed over my face.

"Why does everyone keep asking me that?" I asked. "How was I supposed to know that I would be triggered?"

I paused, huffed in frustration, and added, "I just thought it would be symbolic, you know? Like visiting the place where I lost my early childhood to start my new adulthood…does that make sense?"

Dianna sighed and nodded. "I can understand that. But, Lucy, if the nightmares and panic attacks get any worse, we leave and find another vacation destination, okay? We are all worried about you."

I looked into Dianna's anxious green eyes and nodded. "Alright. We will go to the lookout, and if it gets too difficult, we leave."

Dianna smiled in relief. "Good. Also, give Blake a chance, eh? Greg is alright, but you will never be happy with him."

I let out a small chuckle and shook my head. "Dianna, I am happy with him."

Dianna gave me a skeptical look and said, "No, you are comfortable. There is a difference."

Before I could respond, Dianna turned and left the bathroom. I sighed, running a hand down my face as I followed her back to the van.

"We only have thirty minutes left before we get to Pikesburg," Blake said as he climbed into the driver's seat. "Where do you want to go first?"

Everyone looked at me, and I looked at each of their faces. Greg smiled softly at me, and I noticed his eyes were still red-rimmed and droopy. Chris yawned and stretched before climbing into the van and collapsing on the back bench seat. Dianna shook her head and climbed into the front passenger seat.

"I guess I'm riding up here with you," she said to Blake. "It looks like my man is tired of me already."

Chris raised his head and said, "I'll never be tired of you, baby, but I need my beauty sleep if I want to stay sexy for you."

His head flopped back down onto the seat as I giggled and climbed into the tiny middle seat next to the window. Greg climbed up and sat in the seat beside me.

Blake turned around in his seat and looked at me expectantly. "This is your trip, Lucy. Where are we going first?"

"I want to see the mountain," I said without hesitation. "Just a few minutes, and then we can go to the hotel and rest for the night."

Blake darted a look at Dianna and then back to me, and I could see the worry in his eyes. "Are you sure?"

Dianna chimed in. "Lucy and I already talked about it. She agrees that we leave if it gets too intense."

Blake nodded and turned back around. He tossed me a plastic bag before starting the van. "Here, I got you some snacks. We will have some dinner later after we see the mountain."

Smiling my thanks, I looked in the bag to find a gas station cheeseburger, a bag of my favorite chips, and a soda. Unfortunately, the cheeseburger was cold, the cheese tasted like plastic, and the bun was stale. I wrinkled my nose at the bite I had already taken and tossed the rest back in the bag before opening my chips and popping a few in my mouth.

I opened my soda and took a drink, noticing Greg staring at me from the corner of my eye. His gaze was scrutinizing and wary. I turned my full attention to him, and the look vanished, replaced by a bright smile that had his hazel eyes twinkling.

Confused, I returned his smile with a quirk of one eyebrow and said, "Why were you looking at me that way?"

"I was trying to decide whether or not to ask you to tell me about your accident. It seems to be such a big deal." He gauged my reaction carefully.

I gave him a comforting smile and rolled my eyes playfully. "That's because I have dramatic friends."

"I heard that," slurred a sleepy voice from the back seat.

I laughed and turned my head to see Chris lying in the seat with his arm draped over his eyes.

Greg was not laughing. His serious hazel eyes bore into me as he said, "Lucy, I'm serious. There must be a reason why everyone is so worried about you."

I sighed in defeat. Turning back around, I saw Blake's eyes peer at me through the rearview mirror. His intense gaze flicked to Greg, and he narrowed his eyes before focusing back on the road. Dianna glanced at me over her shoulder, and her eyebrows raised questioningly. I could hear her silent question playing in my mind.

Was I willing to share that part of my life with Greg, a man I had only been dating for about four months? Hell, I had not even talked about it to my friends until they had found out that the location I had picked for my vacation was ground zero of my accident.

"So, you remember this morning at the airport?" I began, turning to Greg with a pleading look, begging him silently to understand.

He only frowned and nodded, so I continued. "When Blake said that we never talk about it, he was right. None of my friends have ever talked to or asked me about it. Ever."

I said the last part sternly, pausing for emphasis before continuing. "Not even they know my version of what happened because they have never asked."

I paused as Greg's frown deepened. He looked at Dianna, who was still looking at us. She nodded at him in confirmation. Greg turned his frown back to me.

"But why?" Greg asked, confusion coloring his tone.

Dianna answered, "It was too horrific to talk about for us, and Lucy does not remember much. I would imagine that what she does remember would be too difficult for her to share, so we never asked her to tell us. We would not want to put her through that pain."

Her tone was low and sad, and her eyes zoned out in a faraway look as she continued, "It was so long ago. We were just kids, but I can clearly remember how Lucy looked so fragile with the bandages wrapped around her head and the adults talking about how she might not remember us."

Dianna shuddered and turned back around. The intense grief in her voice surprised me. Blake's eyes caught mine in the mirror again, laced with sorrow so fierce that a jolt of distress shot through my heart.

I turned away from his look and lowered my eyes to my hands clenched tightly in my lap. I took a deep, shuddering breath and said, "I don't remember anything about the accident, but I get glimpses sometimes of being in the hospital afterward. The only thing I remember clearly is the day I was allowed to come home, and that was a happy memory. I'm not sure I would want to remember the bad ones."

I raised my gaze to meet Greg's hazel eyes and smiled sadly. "If it is too painful for my friends to remember, then it is best that we not speak of it."

I could see Greg's throat work as he swallowed hard, and his features changed to one of acceptance and understanding with a tinge of regret.

He nodded and responded, "I'm sorry. I will not speak of it again."

"Thank you," I whispered, and Greg gently brushed his lips against mine.

I felt nothing. No spark, no flutter in my stomach. There was only a slight patter of my heart and a feeling of comfort and safety. Isn't that what everyone wants, though?

'*No,*' a tiny voice in my head said. '*Safety and comfort are satisfactory, but what about passion, heat, desire, those things that consume you and take you away from the world, if even for a moment?*

Judging by how my body practically melted at one touch from Blake, I was sure I could have those things with him, but those things were fleeting and did not last. What would happen once the heat had cooled and the passion and desire had waned? I was not willing to lose Blake, even if I had to keep him at arm's length for the rest of our lives.

Greg was safe. If I lost him, it would not destroy me.

I laid my head on his shoulder and relaxed into him when he draped his arm around me. But my eyes kept flickering to the rearview mirror, where Blake's intense, brown gaze became increasingly livid every time he looked back.

I closed my eyes to avoid the mirror and found myself drifting off to sleep, lulled by the comforting sway of the van and Greg's arm around my shoulders.

"We're here!" Dianna's excited shout aroused me from my slumber.

Greg pulled his arm off my shoulders and turned toward me. "Wake up, sleeping beauty. You are going to want to see this."

I opened my eyes slowly and was surprised that it had darkened drastically. I blinked rapidly, blinking the sleep from my eyes, and tried to focus on my surroundings. It took a few moments for my eyes to adjust to the darkness.

Greg turned, opened the sliding door, slid from the seat, and stepped out. He turned to me and offered me his hand. I slid my hand into his, and he pulled me to him, catching me in his embrace as I practically fell out of the door.

I steadied myself against Greg's chest and stood up straight. I heard Chris slide out behind me and shut the sliding door, and then I heard him gasp.

Frowning, I turned to see what had caused Chris to react that way and noticed him looking up at the sky. I followed his gaze, and my breath caught in my throat at the sight.

We had parked in a tiny parking lot on the side of the road. It was not a busy road, and there were no other cars in the lot, at least not as far as I could see. There were no lamps in the lot, and it was darker than I had ever seen it.

The small Florida town where we grew up never got this dark. The lights from the various tiki bars along the beach and lamps that lined the city streets lit up the night enough to chase away the complete darkness.

There were no such lights here. Instead, the lights that lit up the night here were above us, stretched out across the night sky in glittering wonder. A half-moon hung in the sky, along with millions of twinkling lights that littered the heavens everywhere I could see.

I had never seen the stars in this brilliance except on television and in pictures, and I could only stare up in wonder at what my eyes beheld. A sense of surprise and delight filled me as I gazed up at the incredible night sky, and a satisfied smile spread across my face.

"It is so…so…I have no words," Dianna said in a low, strained voice.

I glanced her way with a smile of agreement, but she was not looking up at the sky. Instead, she was staring straight ahead, standing a little before me with Blake at her side. Chris was behind me, and I looked over my shoulder at him. He was also gazing at the sky, so I poked him softly with my elbow and motioned my head toward Dianna and Blake.

"I wonder what they are looking at that could be anything more beautiful than what is up there?" I asked him.

Greg also pulled his gaze away from the sky and said, "Let us go see."

Greg began walking toward Blake and Dianna, and Chris and I followed. I stepped up beside Dianna and followed her fascinated gaze.

The lights that shone from the night sky were far above, but the lights that Dianna was staring at were far below. I could barely make out shadows of treetops surrounding the twinkling lights. It was hard to tell how far away those lights were in the darkness.

It was a breathtaking sight. It was as if we were standing in the middle of a fantasy land of twinkling lights and fiery stars, and I carefully stepped closer to get a better look at the lights far below.

Three steps led up to a large concrete slab enclosed with a chain link fence. The sight triggered something in my mind, but I could not place it immediately. Instead, pictures and images flickered through my brain as I stepped onto the concrete, and suddenly my nightmare played bright and loud in my head.

The concrete slab with the chain link fence, the vision of the mountains before me and the sky so close I could touch it, the strange man that had taken me away from my friends, and the sensation of falling all hit me at once, stealing my breath from my lungs and ceasing my heart from beating.

A feeling of miasma rushed over me, and I suddenly did not know where I was or how I had gotten here. Intense pain shot through my head, and I cried out in agony, crumpling to the hard ground onto my hands and knees.

I heard voices shouting, calling my name in fear and worry, and strong hands came around my shoulders and pulled me up from the ground. I panicked, remembering the strong hands coming around my small body and dragging me away from my friends, and I screamed and flailed at the hands holding me.

"Let me go! Let me go!" I screamed repeatedly, but they did not let me go.

Instead, strong arms encircled my waist and pulled me back against a solid chest, holding me tightly with my arms pinned to my sides. I struggled, but it was no use. The arms that held me were too strong.

"I got you, Lucy. You are safe. I got you." A deep soothing voice cut through the fog in my brain, swirling through the panic and releasing me from its freezing embrace.

Warm breath on my neck caused me to shiver, an automatic response, and the words bounced around in my mind until they settled into my thoughts in recognition.

"I got you, Lucy. You are safe," Blake repeated, holding my back tightly to his chest as my heart beat against his arms.

I stopped struggling and concentrated on the feel of his arms and the sound of his soothing voice, reaching through the fog in my brain and begging him to pull me free.

"That's it, baby. Come back to me," Blake whispered in my ear, and his hot breath on my neck caused me to shudder again.

My lungs felt constricted, and I could not breathe, and for a moment, the seizing panic threatened to return. Then, when I wanted to struggle and scream again, Blake's arms loosened, and I could draw a deep, cleansing breath.

My lungs expanded with sweet oxygen, and my heart stuttered to a steady beat. Sobs escaped my mouth with each exhale, and I felt the first hot tears scorch down my cheeks.

"Breathe, baby. Just breathe. That's right. Cry it out if you need to. I won't let you go." Blake's soothing voice slowly brought me back to reality, and the fear and panic drifted back into the dark recesses of my mind.

I stood in Blake's hold for what seemed like an eternity. Finally, my breathing slowed to normal, and my heart beat steadily. I took one more deep, shuddering breath and slowly opened my eyes.

Chris and Dianna were looking at me with intense worry on their faces. When I opened my eyes, I could hear Chris's thankful sigh.

Dianna muttered, "Thank God," and let out a long, relieved breath as if she had been holding it in until I calmed down.

Greg took a tentative step toward me, holding his hand as he said, "Lucy, what happened to you? Are you alright?"

I felt Blake stiffen and his arms tighten around me. "Answer him, Lucy. I am right here. No one will hurt you." he breathed against my neck.

My voice was thick from crying as I answered, "I think so…I'm not sure."

Greg stepped closer, his hand extended, and a sudden chill of fear ran up my spine. My breath caught in my throat as I met Greg's hazel eyes, and the panic that had fled my mind threatened to return. His eyes held a softness that I did not trust for reasons I could not fathom, and I did not want his touch anywhere near me.

I was confused by this, but I did not want the panic and fear to return. As Greg advanced, I shook my head slowly and met his gaze apologetically.

"I can't right now, Greg. I'm sorry," I whispered.

I turned in Blake's hold and buried my face into his chest, bringing my arms up to grab handfuls of his t-shirt and clinging to him for dear life. I breathed in Blake's scent, and it calmed me once more.

"Blake was always the one to calm her down when we were little," I heard Dianna saying. "Don't take it personally, Greg. Blake is her safe haven and always has been."

Greg did not respond, and guilt pierced my heart. What must Greg be thinking right now? I would have to talk to him later and explain if I could. However, right now, all I wanted to do was stay right here, where the memories that had tried to break free could not find me or hurt me. Here in Blake's arms, I was safe. He would never let anything hurt me if it were in his power to stop it.

Blake's hold never left me. He bent down and wrapped an arm under my knees, lifting me into his arms like a baby and carrying me to the van. I still had a death grip on his t-shirt, but he never complained. Instead, he climbed into the van's back seat with me in his arms and pulled me into his lap as he sat down.

I heard the van's engine start and felt it pull away. I did not know who was driving or where anyone was sitting, nor did I care. I curled up into a ball as tight as possible and drifted off to nothingness in the safety of Blake's arms.

PART TWO

73

DREAMING

CHAPTER 6: Dreamscape

Bright, intense light cut through the darkness and fuzziness in my mind. I was lying in a cloud of softness with solid arms wrapped around me, holding me close to a hard body that was breathing deeply and steadily.

I felt safe and comfortable and did not want to leave the protective shell I found myself in upon awakening.

I loved waking up like this.

Sometimes, I would pretend to have a nightmare just so mommy and daddy would let me sleep with them so I could wake up in my daddy's arms.

"Lucy, honey! Breakfast!" my mommy called out.

The smell of freshly cooked bacon hit me, and I stretched my arms up over my head, careful not to accidentally punch my daddy in the face.

He hated it when I did that.

My tiny fist fit right in his eye socket, and he would usually end up with a black eye. I never meant to do it, and I had learned to be more careful.

My stirring must have awoken him because he chuckled humorously and said, "Good morning, beautiful."

I smiled up at my daddy sleepily.

Something was definitely not right with this.

This was not my daddy. I did not know that face.

"Daddy?" I said weakly.

The man frowned in confusion and asked, "Lucy, what is wrong, baby girl?"

My little heart pounded rapidly in my chest. "You are not my daddy!" I yelled loudly, but I knew that was not right.

This stranger felt more like my daddy than my real daddy.

I cried out in terror as the man's face changed to the man from the airport. "You are mine now, little girl," he said in a menacing tone.

I opened my mouth to scream, but no sound came out. I whimpered helplessly, but another voice cut through my mind.

"You are safe, Lucy. I got you."

It was not my dream daddy. It was my Blake. He was here, and I was safe. It was his arms that I had been curled up in.

I breathed a sigh of relief and tried to open my eyes to look at him, but they would not open. I was still floating in a dream state as if a weight were pulling me into an endless abyss, and I was fighting to stay afloat.

I was not afraid, however, because Blake's soothing voice was still speaking, cutting through the nightmarish fog, and calming my senses. I focused on his smooth, deep voice, and other voices began to penetrate the fuzziness of my dream state.

"She just needs to sleep it off," Blake was saying. "She is fighting it, which is making it worse."

"You heard her, Blake." That was Dianna's worried tone. She sounded as if she had been crying. Why had she been crying?

"She has not had her meds, and you know what that means."

"Would you hush before Greg hears you?" Blake said, his tone becoming irritated.

"Greg is gone," Dianna said with a hiccup. "He said he would call his mom to come and get him. I tried to tell him not to take it personally, but he was livid. He said to tell you and Lucy that he hoped you two were happy together and that she should not have played him like that when she was clearly in love with you."

Greg was gone? For some reason, that did not bother me. Instead, the words floated through my mind like dust motes in the air, unnoticed and scattered in the wind.

"Maybe you need to call your mom," Chris's voice piped in. He sounded worried too. "She will know what to do and maybe give us more meds."

"No!" Blake exclaimed, and the angry tone of his voice made me cringe and whimper. His muscles tensed, and my heart pounded with anguish. What was wrong with Blake?

I tried to move and open my eyes, but it was no use. The most I could manage was to clench my hands into fists and let out a slight, squeaky sound of utter helplessness.

Instantly, Blake's body relaxed, and his arms folded more tightly around me.

"Shhh," he soothed. "I am sorry, Lucy. I did not mean to scare you. I am here. You are safe."

The dulcet sounds of his soothing voice eased my frustrations, and I relaxed, curling into him tighter and relishing the feel of his hands around my body.

My hands relaxed when I realized I had clutched his shirt in my fists. My fingers splayed over the hardness of his rippling pectorals, causing tingles of pleasure to spread down my arms and into the most intimate parts of my body. I sighed with pleasure at the intense sensation as I shuddered in his arms.

When Blake next spoke, his voice was lower and his tone less angry. "We cannot call your mother," he said. "If she gets involved, Lucy will end up at the Institution again."

"Well, maybe that is what she needs," Dianna said.

"Dianna, you know as well as I do that if I take her there, then she could end up like those other walking corpses that your mother takes care of. I risked too much for us for Lucy to end up like that. I already lost parts of her. I will not lose her completely." Blake's composure began to slip again as he spoke, and I wondered what the hell he was talking about.

He had not lost me. I was right here. Also, what was this about sending me to an institution? Did they think I was crazy? I did not want to go into an institution.

I tried to pull myself from the haze and wake up. I fought the darkness around me and tried to open my eyes again, but it was no use. The harder I fought, the deeper I sank until I was dragged under again, falling even further into the void of dreams...

I was angry. The little girl had taken away Lily's doll, and I wanted it back. I did not remember what the teacher had said her name was, but it did not matter. She was going to learn that she could not touch that doll.

The others knew, so she needed to learn too.

I darted her an angry glare and stalked toward her with my hand held out. I was going to take it back from her, and if she tried to stop me, she would see what I could do.

She cuddled the doll close and sniffled. "I only wanted to play with her for a minute. The teacher says we are supposed to share."

"I do not share her," I seethed. "Everyone else knows that. It is time you learn that."

The tingling sensation started in my fingertips and spread down my arms. I held out my hand, palm facing her, willing the tingling to flow out of my hand toward her.

I saw recognition in her eyes as I took control of her mind, willing her muscles to hand over the doll to me. Her jade-green eyes filled with confusion and widened in fear when she looked at my face, and she shakily handed me the doll as her muscles obeyed my commands.

Good. I was happy that she was afraid of me. She would not want to play with my doll anymore. I snatched the doll from her and dropped my hand. The tingling stopped, and the little girl fell at my feet and began to cry.

"Lucy!" the teacher's angry voice shouted. "How many times do I have to tell you that you are not allowed to use your gifts? Do you want to be decommissioned?"

The dreaded word sent terror down my spine, and I cringed. I turned to face my teacher, shaking my head as I stared at the floor. I held my precious baby doll in one arm, cradled to my chest like the other girl had held it.

"Why did you do that, Lucy?" Miss Megan asked in a calmer tone.

I began to cry. The sadness that came whenever I had to explain the doll to anyone wracked my tiny body, and my voice was thick with tears as I answered, "she had my baby doll, the one that belonged to Lily."

Miss Megan did not comment, so I raised my face to meet hers with tears streaming down my chubby cheeks. Understanding lit her emerald green eyes.

"Oh," she said softly and knelt. She was at my eye level when she was on her knees, which made me feel more connected to her. I liked Miss Megan and did not want her to be angry with me.

"Honey, I know that you miss her. What happened to Lily was awful, but you cannot keep this up. I do not want the same to happen to you."

I took a deep, shaky breath and nodded my understanding. Then, I turned to the little girl still huddled on the floor, crying. Guilt shot through me as I handed the precious doll to her with a smile.

Why had I made her cry? I was not a mean girl. I had to make this right. I had overreacted over missing Lily again.

"Here, take her. I am sorry," I said to the crying girl.

The girl sniffled and looked up into my eyes. Her cheeks were wet from her tears, and her red, curly hair was plastered to her face. "Really?" she squeaked.

I widened my smile encouragingly and said, "yes, really. I should not have treated you that way, and I am sorry. My name is Lucy."

She reached up tentatively and gingerly took the doll from my hands. She cradled it as if it were precious, and it was. "Thank you," she said in a whispered voice. "I'm Dianna."

"Well, Dianna, take excellent care of her. She belonged to someone extraordinary," I said and turned back to Miss Megan.

Miss Megan was smiling at us approvingly. "That was very nice of you, Lucy, and you did a wonderful job with your vocabulary."

I smiled and blushed at the compliment, but my joy was short-lived.

The door to the classroom opened with a bang, causing Miss Megan and me to flinch in surprise. The huge, bald man with the snake tattoo curled around his neck came into the room. Miss Megan reached out slowly and grabbed my arm. She pulled me to her and wrapped me in her protective embrace.

"Lucy Spears!" the man called out.

"What do you want with Lucy?" asked a tiny yet intensely angry voice.

"Don't worry about it, boy. This does not concern you," the scary bald man said with a sneer. His tattoo bulged out on his neck as he stepped further into the room.

The man was trying to be scary, but I knew he was not always this way. He only acted this way when coming to collect someone to be decommissioned. The thought made me whimper.

Was he really going to let them decommission me?

Blake stepped forward with his arms crossed over his chest like a grown-up. He had been my protector for as long as I could remember, but I doubted he could protect me from them.

No one could.

Miss Megan's hold tightened on me with one arm, and she put a hand out to stop Blake's advancement. "Blake, stop," she said softly.

But Blake did not stop. Instead, his hands clenched into tiny fists, and he uncurled his arms and dropped them to his sides. I knew his body language, knew what he intended to do, and was powerless to stop it.

The army men that came with the bald man when they came to take away the unruly children for decommissioning wore protective charms that made them immune to gifts such as mine, but Blake's skills were more physical, and their charms did not protect them from that.

When they had to come for a child with Blake's abilities, they usually wore protective suits and gear, but they had not come for Blake.

They had come for me.

Therefore, they wore army gear and protective bands around their wrists, but their army clothes were no protection from Blake's magic.

"Lucy, when I do this, you must run, okay?" he whispered, too low for anyone else to hear except for Miss Megan, who gave an imperceptible nod of her head and loosened her grip on me.

"Get the others out, too," she whispered to me.

I nodded and prepared myself. I knew what I had to do. I felt the tingling in my hands and pulled myself from Miss Megan's arms. I looked at Blake and nodded, and Blake thrust his hands out suddenly, unclenching his fists and releasing a spray of fire that shot out toward the men.

The bald man dodged out of the way just before the fire hit him, but the men behind him were not so lucky.

"You're not immune to fire, you bastards!" Blake shouted, surprising me with his use of the b-word. He must have been livid to curse that way. Then again, he usually was when I was being threatened.

He shot another spray of fire, which caught one of the bookcases and sent it into a raging inferno. Kids began to scream.

I concentrated on the tingling in my arm and sucked in a huge breath. Then, I shot my gift out with all my might, aiming it at every mind in the room.

'*Calm down and get out,*' I said in my mind, willing all the other brains to follow my commands.

It was too hard. There was too much fear, and I could not get them to listen.

"I can help," said a small voice beside me. It was the red-headed little girl, still cradling the doll in her arms.

Dianna, was it?

"How can you help?" I asked her, raising my eyebrows.

She smirked and said, "watch this."

She raised her free hand to her head and squeezed her eyes shut. She looked as if she had a headache. Then, a few seconds later, a flock of birds flew in through the open window and began flying around the room, going toward the men and pecking at their eyes and heads.

They threw their arms up in defense and began shouting at the birds, and Dianna giggled at the commotion. The fear in all the brains that I still had my mental clutches in turned to humor, and I was able to gain control of them all.

I smiled menacingly. "Thanks, Dianna. Now I have them all."

"Good, then let's get out of here," my friend Chris said, coming up behind us.

He smiled shyly at Dianna and said, "Shall I make a door for you, my lady?"

I made a gagging noise and rolled my eyes, which made Dianna laugh. The minds under my control were melded into mine so completely that they laughed too. I had to get them out and release my hold on them so we could all escape.

"Do it, Chris," Miss Megan shouted over the din of the shouting men and the crazy birds.

Chris pointed his finger at the outside wall of the metal building we were in, and a large hole melted into the metal. The hot molten metal melted all the other materials that made up the wall, revealing the playground as the hole opened up to the outside world.

Blake shot another bought of fire around the room, igniting the other bookshelves and holding off two more of the army men that had come into the room, stepping over the burnt corpses of the other three.

I urged all of the minds under my control to run through the hole that Chris had made, and Dianna, Chris, and Miss Megan followed. Miss Megan turned back after getting out.

"Lucy, Blake, come on!" she called into the burning room.

The fire had spread to all the walls except the one with the hole. The men were still pouring into the room, but this time it was men in yellow suits holding fire extinguishers. They were slowly putting out the fires.

"Blake, come on!" I called out.

Blake turned to look at me, and his eyes glowed a burnished gold, lighting up his face with his power. "Go, Lucy," he said sternly.

"I'm not going without you," I said. There was no way I was going to leave him here.

"Lucy, Blake!" Miss Megan called out.

I turned to see the hole slowly closing and frowned in confusion. I knew Chris would never let that hole close until Blake and I came out of it.

Maniacal laughter caused the hairs on the back of my neck to stand on end. I turned toward the sound to see a man pointing his hands toward the wall. His eyes glowed with power, much as Blake's had.

He was a null!

The hole got smaller, and the smoke, which had nowhere to go now that the gap was closing, filled the room. I could no longer see the man and could no longer see Blake. Panic gripped me as the smoke went up my nose, filling my lungs and causing me to choke.

I fell to the floor, remembering our fire drills and what we were supposed to do in a fire. Stay close to the floor, crawl under the smoke, and stay calm. So I did.

The smoke was thinner on the floor, but it was still seeping into my nose, and I could not breathe. I tried to stay calm, but my heart skittered with fear causing me to breathe in short, quick gasps that filled my lungs with smoke.

I started coughing, deep wracking coughs that weakened my body and brought tears to my already stinging eyes. I could feel heat from the fire lapping at my back as I crawled on the floor, fumbling around with my hands for any sign of Blake.

"Blake, where are you?" I choked out, coughing up smoke and inhaling more with each breath I took.

"I'm here," came his deep, smooth voice from somewhere above me.

Only, it wasn't his voice. Well, it was…but it was his adult voice.

I had been dreaming again.

I tried to pull myself out of this horrid nightmare and breathe in actual oxygen instead of smoke-filled dream air. The air became clearer as I came up out of the cloud of the nightmare, but still, I floated in a semi-unconscious state.

"Lucy, please come back to me," Blake's adult voice said. It was broken and rough with emotion.

Was he crying?

I struggled to break free of the murkiness that still gripped me. I was breathing easier now, but I could still smell the smoke from that burning room and feel the heat of the flames on my back.

Or was it the heat from Blake at my back? Slowly, I realized that I was still in Blake's arms, still held tightly in his strong embrace.

"Please, baby, please come back to me," he said, and I could hear a broken sob escape on the last word.

He was crying. I did not want him to cry. I struggled to speak through the misty haze that still surrounded me.

"Blake?" I managed to squeak out past my raw, sore throat. My voice was scratchy and weak, but I had spoken. It was a start.

"Lucy?" Blake said, a hopefulness in his tortured tone that set my heart pattering in my chest. "Lucy, are you awake?"

Was I awake?

I did not feel as fuzzy as before, but I still could not open my eyes. I tried to move, but my muscles remained frozen. The only thing that seemed to work was my hands, which clenched and unclenched as I tried to move the rest of my body.

I could not smell the smoke anymore, and the heat I was feeling was from Blake. I felt as if I was awake, but my body would not respond. I had spoken before. Could I do it again?

"Why can't I open my eyes?" I asked weakly. "Why can't I move?"

"It's the medicine. You are safe, Lucy." Blake tightened his hold on me, and I felt his head touch the back of mine. His voice sounded relieved and tired.

Even though I could not move, I could feel every touch, every inch of my body pressed close to Blake's, his fingers kneading my stomach and sending delicious tendrils of pleasure through me.

"What kind of medicine?" I croaked feebly.

"It doesn't matter. You will be fine in a few hours, and then I am taking you back home." His breath blew against the top of my head, and I heard him inhale deeply as if he were breathing me in. "I just needed you to wake up for just a moment to be sure you were alright."

"Blake…," I began, but he cut me off.

"Shhh, Lucy. Just rest a bit longer, and everything will be fine. I promise."

I believed him. Blake had never lied to me before and never let anything bad happen to me. I trusted him and always had, but he could not protect me from dreams.

"I don't want to sleep anymore," I said. "I cannot take another nightmare."

"I know," Blake said, and he sounded miserable. "But you won't sleep much longer. When you wake up and can move, we will go home, and the dreams will go away."

"How can you be sure?" I asked, but I did not hear the answer he gave. Instead, my eyes fluttered inside my eyelids as the persistent pull of unconsciousness reached me again.

I tried to fight it, but I could not. Whether it was the medicine or simply fatigue, I was too weak to resist the pull. So I was captured once more and dragged into the void…

"Stop fighting, kid, and hold still. It won't hurt if you don't fight," the bald man said.

It was the man from the airport, I realized. In the dream before this one, I was too caught up to realize that it was a dream. This time, however, I was aware that I was dreaming.

Strangely, I felt as if I had known the bald man and had even liked him to some extent, but my now alert-to-dreaming mind did not know this man.

I knew I was safe in Blake's arms and sleeping, so I felt more like an observer than a participant. However, it still did not stop the fear from making my heart beat hard inside my chest.

I was still in a little girl's body, and I had no idea why I was dreaming about a stranger that I knew in my dreams. Maybe, because he had freaked me out a little when I saw him staring at me with that creepy look at the airport, the recognition in his eyes when he looked at me as if he had known me somehow.

Maybe, my dreaming brain was reflecting on that.

I was small again, maybe five years old, and I was buckled down to a bed with Blake buckled down on another bed beside me. I turned my head to look over at him squirming and fighting to break free from the restraints.

They had his hands bound with some contraption that covered his whole hands. I supposed it was so that he could not use his abilities, but I knew he could probably break free if he wanted to. I knew a secret that these dumb adults did not know.

His black hair had fallen into his eyes in his struggles, and his brown gaze kept shooting my way in desperation. He knew that I knew his secret. He knew he could get out, but it would hurt.

I could see the fear in his gaze as he looked my way, which scared me too. But, I did not understand his fear. Why didn't he get away? I knew he could.

A man in a doctor's outfit was trying to hold down his arms with one hand, and he had a syringe full of a milky white liquid in his other hand.

"Leave him alone!" I shouted and was surprised at the strength of my tiny girl's voice.

"A little help here?" the doctor ground out as he struggled to hold Blake's arm down.

"You can't handle one tiny boy?" the bald man said derisively, and he smirked as he looked over at me.

"Maybe you would have better luck with the girl." He added, and I swallowed hard at his menacing tone.

"Fine, I will call a nurse to help with the boy. We can start with the girl." The doctor released Blake and started toward me.

"No! Leave her alone! I'll be still this time, I promise!" Blake's voice was panicked as he ceased his struggles and squeezed his eyes tightly shut.

"Lucy, can you hear me?" Blake asked, but he did not speak out loud. Instead, I heard his voice in my mind, and the power in my body instantly latched onto it.

In this dream, my ability to communicate telepathically was not new, but the observer part of me was startled by Blake's boy voice in my head. I was also surprised at the feeling of energy surging through me as I used my ability.

I was instantly struck with a sense of déjà vu again, the feeling that had brought me to my knees when I had stepped up onto the platform on the mountain earlier.

How long ago had that been? How long had I been stuck in this dream state?

I did not crumple this time, however. This time I was riding the dream, and the little girl me was calm as she communicated with Blake in her mind.

"Yes, I hear you," I said silently.

"Get away if you can. I will distract them, but you have to run."

"I told you before that I am not leaving you," I answered stubbornly.

"Lucy, you have to get away. I can't stand to see you get hurt." Blake's tiny voice was sad and pleading, and I turned my head and gave him a steady look.

"Blake, listen to me. Let the doctor decommission me, and you get away."

"What?" his voice was incredulous, and he started shaking his head rapidly.

The doctor paused. "I thought you said you were not going to fight."

Blake instantly stilled, and I strengthened my telepathic voice and said, *"Blake, listen to me! There is not much time. My abilities cannot touch them with their protection bands on, but yours is a physical ability, and you can get around their shields. You can get away. You can protect the others and get me back somehow. I know you can. I trust you."*

Blake's breathing was coming in fast, rapid gasps as he listened to my voice in his head, and his wide, scared eyes were focused on my face. Then, slowly, I watched the understanding resolve fill his eyes, and they began to glow a molten gold color as his power filled him.

"I will bring you back, I promise. I will find a way."

"I know," I said as I gave him a sad look. *"Find me. Save me. I love you."*

"I love you too," I heard him say as his features set into a determined look.

The doctor had just reached his side and grasped his arm when Blake let out a high-pitched scream and began flailing his limbs again.

"Oh, for fuck's sake, just do the girl first!" the bald man roared in frustration. "You are going to need help with that one."

"You could help me, you know!" the doctor shot back angrily.

"I will not have anything to do with this," the man answered sternly. "I am forced to guard you while you work, but I will not help you decommission them."

I shivered at the threatening tone of his voice as he gave me a flat, emotionless look. I turned away from his stormy gray eyes and saw the doctor turning to come toward my bed.

I began to whimper as he grasped my arm and held it down. He rubbed my arm with an alcohol swab to ready the spot, then shot the needle into my upper arm right below my shoulder.

I let out a tiny whimper of pain as I felt the liquid enter my body. It burned.

When the doctor began to lean away from me, I heard a scream of pain from across the room. The doctor jumped violently and turned toward the source of the sound.

I turned my head to see Blake's hands free, his wrists and hands covered with blood. He had bloodied himself by pulling his hands free from the restraints while the man and doctor had been distracted.

I didn't have to ask how he had done it. I already knew. I knew his secret.

Blake could control the elements, earth, air, fire, and water, with his entire body. He did not need only his hands as most mutants did. Well, except for mentals. Mentals used their minds. Physicals used their hands most of the time, but Blake was unique.

I knew Blake had taken control of the water in his body, specifically in his hands. He shrunk his hands by sucking the water from them, making his hands smaller than his wrists, and then yanked them free from the cuffs.

He could not pull all the water because that could damage him internally, but he could draw enough to make them small enough to yank free with some damage to the outside. That would heal, though. It was only scratches and raw flesh.

I watched as Blake used his hands-free ability, but this time he used air. He would not risk burning the room down again. Instead, he blew the doctor and the man down with a gale-force wind that knocked the glass from the room's door and blew it open.

He used his hands to create a blast of molten fire to melt the metal restraints on his ankles, but his magic fire would not burn him. Finally, he broke the contraptions apart and jumped from the bed.

With a last, longing look at me, he fled from the room before the doctor or the man could recover and catch him. I smiled. I knew Blake would be okay. He would get out of this place and find the others, and then he would be back for me.

A sudden pain shot through my head, and I screamed. I had never felt pain like that in my life. It raged through my head so forcefully that I could only close my eyes and scream.

Darkness swirled around me, thick and heavy, and stars floated around the inside of my eyelids. Thoughts and emotions were ripped from my mind as the decommissioning serum took hold and tore me away from myself.

A welcoming void stretched before me, beckoning me into its blissful, painless embrace. I reached for it with a smile, welcoming the darkness, welcoming the abyss, and the release from this pain.

My old life fell away as the serum took hold, but there was one thing that I hung onto that I would never let go of. I refused to let go of the memories of my friends, especially Blake. I fought against the forgetful void pushing into the corners of my mind, and held onto the moments that were special to me of my friends and Blake.

I refused to let them go.

CHAPTER 7: Home

I was warm, warmer than I had been in a long time. Brightness entered my eyelids as I emerged from the dragging sleep that had held me prisoner. It felt like forever, but I could not be sure how long I had been unconscious. Time worked differently in the dream world.

I lay with my eyes closed for a time, trying to process everything. Had it all been dreams? Were parts of it real? I was sure that Blake pulling me from unconsciousness and holding me while I slept had been real because I could still feel him now, curled up at my back with his arm resting over my side.

I was sure I was awake now because my senses were instantly on high alert. I knew this familiar feeling I always got when Blake touched me.

The more awake I became, the more the dreams drifted away. I tried to hold onto the memory of them, but they drifted from my thoughts the more I tried to remember. Finally, I sighed and concentrated on Blake; his body pressed tightly to my back.

His breathing was steady and even, so I knew he was still asleep. I slowly opened my eyes to the brightness burning my lids and squinted at the sun coming in through the open curtains of the window.

We were at another motel, I guessed. Those thick motel curtains that were similar to the ones at the last motel we stayed at greeted me as my eyes adjusted to the brightness. They were a different pattern than the other ones, but they were the same style.

The same kind of small, wooden round table sat under the window with two leather armchairs on each side of the table. They were the same style as well, only a different color.

Were all motel rooms the same, only different colors? I had nothing to compare it to since I did not travel; this was my first experience with motels.

I lay very still, not wanting to disturb Blake, as I wondered if anyone else was in the room with us.

"Hello," I called out very softly, so quietly that I wondered if anyone could even hear me if they were here.

"Lucy?" Dianna's soft voice answered, and I could hear her straining not to cry out in relief.

"Shhh," I said urgently. "Blake is still asleep."

"He will want to know you are awake," Chris whispered.

I was so happy to hear their voices. They were behind me, probably in the other bed, if we were in a room with double beds like the last room we had stayed in.

"I don't want to wake him," I said softly.

Truthfully, I enjoyed being curled up in his arms and did not want it to end. I knew that when it ended, I would not allow him to be close to me like this again, so I wanted to enjoy this while I could. I could not let Blake get too close, but just this once would be okay.

"I'll do it, then," Chris said, and before I could say no, I felt Blake's body move against mine as Chris shook him gently.

"Blake, wake up, man," Chris said, but he did not shout.

He did not have to. Blake was a light sleeper.

Blake's arms tightened around me, and I heard him suck in a breath. "What? What's happened?"

His voice, which was thick from sleep, sounded urgent and panicked. I did not like to hear him so freaked, so I caressed the arm across my stomach comfortably.

"It's alright, Blake," I said softly.

I felt Blake stiffen as the muscles in his forearm bulged with tension, and the disbelief in his voice melted my heart.

"Lucy?"

I smiled, and you could hear it in my voice as I answered, "Yes, I'm awake, and I am fine."

I felt Blake shift on the bed behind me, rolling slightly away from me, and gently grab the arm I was lying on to roll me onto my back. He moved back toward me, and then he was suddenly over me, staring down into my eyes with his worried brown gaze.

His eyes were wide with disbelief and lit up with relieved happiness when I smiled at him. Then, his bright, wonderful smile spread over his face, and before I could say anything, he leaned closer to me. His hands came up to cup my face tenderly, stroking my cheeks with his thumbs. His hands were soft against my face as he smiled down at me.

"Lucy," he whispered in relief, and suddenly he was kissing me.

His lips were soft and gentle against mine, and I released a startled gasp at the sudden jolt of electric desire that shot through my body at their touch. My hands were against his hard chest as he leaned over me, and my traitorous fingers curled into his t-shirt, pulling him closer to me.

I heard him moan softly, and then he deepened the kiss. He opened his mouth and sucked my bottom lip into his, licking it with his tongue before releasing it and then darting his tongue into my mouth. My tongue danced with his, and I suddenly realized I was kissing him back.

His lips pressed into mine gently, moving over mine in a passionate dance that had me curling my toes under the blankets. I released his shirt to run my hands up his arms and down his back. He still held my face between his hands, stroking my cheeks with his thumbs as he kissed me.

I came alive under his kiss. His touch had always affected me, but I was not ready for the intensity that the touch of his lips against mine would bring. It was as if my entire body was alight with electricity and heat. A hunger I had never felt before throbbed from my very soul, and my desire to be filled by him ignited inside my secret core.

I had never felt these sensations with anyone, and I never wanted it to stop. A soft moan escaped from my lips, vibrating against Blake's as he moved his lips against mine in an electric dance that had me arching my back to press myself against his hard body.

"Ahem," Dianna cleared her throat loudly. "I would say get a room, but you have a room. Might I remind you, however, that you are sharing that room with two other people?"

I gasped at the sound of Dianna's voice, and I felt a slow blush creep up my neck and fill my cheeks as Blake broke the kiss and pulled up from me with a startled laugh. His breathing was ragged, and I could see the pulse in his neck throbbing rapidly. He let go of my face and smiled down at me apologetically.

"I'm sorry, Lucy. I just got carried away because I was so happy to see you awake," he said breathlessly.

I felt the loss of his touch deep in my soul, and I tried to push the sensation away. I was also breathing hard, and my heart threatened to beat out of my chest. I gave no response because I did not know how to respond. My brain refused to process what had just happened.

I swallowed hard and stayed silent as he rolled away from me and sat up on the side of the bed, but I saw his eyes flinch slightly with a hurt look before he turned away. I hated to see that look in his eyes.

"Blake," I said in a whispered voice. "I just need a minute to process."

He turned to me with a spark of optimism in his gaze, and I gave him a weak smile. It was the best I could do at this moment. He nodded, stood up, and walked toward a door on the other side of the room.

"I'm going to take a shower. Does anyone else need the bathroom first?" Blake asked.

Dianna shook her head, and Chris gestured toward the door with his hand as he said, "Go right ahead. We will fill Lucy in on everything."

Blake nodded, gave me one final hopeful gaze, and then turned and went into the bathroom.

I took a deep, calming breath and draped my arm over my eyes. I lay there silent for a moment catching my breath and letting my heart calm to a more normal pace.

"Lucy, please don't leave us again," I heard Dianna's panicked voice say.

I moved my arm and opened my eyes. "I'm just trying to gather myself for a moment," I answered comfortingly. "I have been living in a dream world for what seems like forever."

"Yeah, you screamed out and talked a lot in your sleep," Chris said sullenly. "We were beginning to worry that you would never wake up."

I took in one final deep breath and sat up on the bed. I scooted to the side away from the window, facing the other bed, and swung my legs over the side. I ran my hands through my sleep-tousled hair and finally met my friends' worried gazes.

"I had a lot of bad dreams," I said in a low tone. My throat was sore, and my voice was scratchy.

I placed a hand to my throat and said, "Can someone get me something to drink?"

Chris rose from the bed where he was sitting and walked over to the table under the window. He grabbed a bottle of water that was sitting on it and tossed it to me. I caught it easily, took off the top, and took a long, cool drink. The wetness relieved the pain in my throat.

"What kind of bad dreams?" Dianna asked curiously.

My voice was slightly better as I answered, "You were in one of them. We were little, and you had taken my doll...."

I trailed off, squinting my eyes in frustration as I tried to remember the dream. I could not remember any of them. I could recall bits and pieces of each dream, but most of the dreams had faded into the recess of my mind when I had awakened.

"I did what?" Dianna asked humorously.

"I can't remember now," I answered as I opened my eyes and gave her an apologetic look.

I shrugged and continued, "I don't remember any of my dreams. There are bits and pieces that I can recall if I try hard, but most of it is gone."

"Hmm," Chris said, giving me a contemplating look. "Maybe it is a good thing that you can't remember. You seemed awfully scared while you were dreaming."

Suddenly, my brain came fully awake, and I remembered something. Guilt slid through my heart as I remembered the one person I should have asked for as soon as I had woken up, but instead, I had kissed Blake. Of course, I was relieved that he had not been here to see the kiss I had shared with Blake, but at the same time, I was ashamed and laden with guilt that I had acted in that manner.

"Where is Greg?" I asked as the embarrassment and remorse burned through me. I tried to keep it off my face as I looked toward my friends for an answer.

Dianna glanced toward Chris with a sullen look, and Chris gave her a worried look back.

I looked from one and then the other, my gaze shooting back and forth between them, and asked, "What? What is wrong?"

"Well…umm…he…," Dianna stuttered and gave Chris a pleading look. "Help me out here," she said to him.

Chris sighed and ran a hand over his face. "Lucy, after you collapsed back at the mountain lookout, Blake picked you up and carried you back to the van. He would not let anyone help or touch you. Greg was alright with it when Dianna explained that Blake had always been the person that could calm you down when you were over-emotional."

He paused, and I looked at him expectantly, waiting for him to finish. Instead, Dianna patted his hand and finished for him.

"When we found this motel and got a room, Blake carried you in and laid down with you, holding you to him. He fell asleep with you in his arms, and then you started calling for Blake in your sleep.

Greg got upset and said he could not stand to see you in Blake's arms or hear you cry out for Blake any longer. He told us to tell you that he no longer wanted to see you. He said you should have told him from the start that you were in love with Blake, and then he left."

I stared at Dianna in disbelief. "So, he broke up with me while I was unconscious over a stupid dream?"

Dianna frowned in irritation and said, "No, Lucy. He broke up with you because you are in love with Blake. When are you going to own up to it?"

Was it that obvious to everyone? It was not as if I had not acknowledged it to myself because I had, but my fear of losing Blake overrode any desire I had to let him in. How could they see my feelings for Blake but not understand my reasons for pushing him away?

I sighed deeply and ran a hand over my eyes. "Look, what is between Blake and me…well…it's complicated. I don't know how to explain it to you."

Dianna's frown deepened. "Lucy, love is always complicated. But that doesn't mean you shouldn't try. How will you ever be happy if you don't take a chance?"

"I don't want to take that chance with Blake. Besides, I was happy with Greg," I mumbled as I moved my gaze down to my hands in my lap.

"No, you were comfortable with Greg. There is a difference between comfortable and happy," Dianna said. "I think I told you that at the gas station the night Blake begged you to give him a chance."

Startled, I glanced up to meet her green gaze. "Were you listening to us in the back seat?" I asked incredulously.

Dianna shrugged with a mischievous smile and said, "Maybe just a little."

I rolled my eyes and shook my head. "Do you mind letting me handle my own love life?"

"Well," she said, and the mischievousness had entered her voice. "You no longer have a love life since your boyfriend just broke up with you."

"Jeesh, Dianna, that was harsh," Chris said in a scolding tone.

"No, it's okay," I said to Chris before he could get angry with Dianna. "She's right. I did not love him. He was just a comfort to me, like a close friend. When we get back to school, I will speak with him. I still want to be friends if he would be alright with that."

Chris shook his head as he said, "I don't know, Lucy. He seemed really torn up about you."

I shrugged. "Well, I will miss him, but it won't destroy me." Then, giving them each a direct look, I added, "not like it would if it were Blake that had broken up with me."

Dianna's gaze filled with understanding, and she came over to sit next to me. She gathered me in her arms, hugging me sideways, and said, "I don't think you could ever lose Blake, no matter what happened between the two of you. That boy would follow you to the ends of the earth and back whether you wanted him to or not."

I laughed a sad little laugh and cuddled into Dianna's side. If only I could believe that myself.

The bathroom door opened suddenly, and I jerked my gaze up to see Blake walking out of the bathroom wearing nothing but a towel around his waist.

The sight of his naked, muscular chest and abs sent shockwaves of electric desire through every nerve ending in my body. I sucked in a breath as I watched droplets of water drip from his wet, black hair and travel down those muscles. My eyes followed the water trail as it slithered past his stomach to the line of dark hair that led down into the cover of the towel. Then, my eyes went lower, past the towel, to below his knees and the bulging muscles of his calves. He had great legs. Hell, even his feet were sexy!

I swallowed hard and averted my gaze, trying to calm my frayed nerves as the pleasurable sensations coursed through my body. Dianna released me and rose from the bed, leaving me alone and cold, fighting for control over myself.

"Sorry," Blake's deep, rich voice rang through the room. "I forgot to grab my clothes before I went into the bathroom."

I slowly brought my gaze back up to his face. His brown eyes were watching me, and he had a sheepish grin across his chiseled features. His grin faded as he looked into my blue gaze to be replaced with a longing heat that had me blushing furiously. I turned away from his gaze, realizing I had been staring lustfully at his body. My face was on fire as I gazed down at my hands.

I was utterly mortified.

I heard Chris snicker, and I shot him an irritated glare. He winked at me, and I stuck my tongue out at him and looked back down at my lap. The bathroom door closed solidly, and I jumped at the sound.

I caught Dianna's emerald gaze when I glanced back up from my lap. She had a triumphant smirk on her face with her arms crossed over her chest. I rolled my eyes and looked away, rising from the bed and busying myself with looking for my suitcase.

I found my suitcase and rummaged through it for an outfit for the day. I wondered if Blake was taking me home as he had said he would or if that had been part of a dream. I would have to ask him later.

I found a simple sweetheart neckline top with long sleeves, a pair of faded-out denim jeans, simple white cotton panties, and a bra. I also dug out a pair of white socks and sat on the bed to wait for Blake to reemerge from the bathroom.

"Are we going home?" I asked, looking to Dianna for an answer.

"Well, yeah. Blake said he was taking you home, so Chris and I are going too. We wouldn't let you celebrate your birthday alone."

I sighed guiltily. "I am sorry about all of this. I know you all spent a lot of money on this trip, and I don't know if I can ever repay you."

Dianna waved her hand in a dismissive motion and responded, "Don't worry about it. The trip isn't a total loss. We got a lot of shopping out of it."

Her smile was humorous, but I did not feel much like laughing.

Dianna's expression was more serious as she added, "Besides, you are more important than all the money in the world."

My heart exploded with emotion. This may not have been the best trip in the world, but I had the best friends. I smiled gratefully at her.

"I love you all," I said, my tone full of emotion.

Dianna smiled her brightest smile and said, "We love you too."

"The bathroom is free," Blake announced as he came striding into the room wearing a black polo shirt, jeans, and sneakers. Even in such simple attire, he was stunning to look at.

The shirt was a bit tight and showed off the muscular stature of his chest and arms. His towel-dried black hair stuck out all over his head, making him look more adorable. His dark, exotic eyes were so brown that they were almost black, like the shirt. His high cheekbones, muscular jaw, and strong nose gave his face a bad-boy look that would bring any woman to her knees.

I took a deep breath and looked away, not wanting to get caught lustfully staring at him again. I stood and went to the bathroom to shower and get dressed. Blake stopped me with a hand on my arm, his touch sending the now familiar sparks of desire flowing through my body.

I looked up into his eyes and gasped at the emotion I saw on his face when he gazed down at me. "I am taking you home today. Chris called the airline and got the return dates on our tickets moved up, so we are going straight to the airport." His voice was soft as he spoke.

I nodded slightly as I said, "Yes, okay."

His eyes hardened, and his tone became more serious as he added, "And you are not to come to this location again."

That pissed me off. Who did he think he was? Blake had never spoken to me like that, and I was not about to let him bully me now. Did he think he owned me now just because we had shared one kiss?

Hell, no.

I narrowed my eyes at him and said, "You have no control over where I go. Are you going to start acting as if you were my father suddenly?"

Blake did not seem to be moved at all by my courageous stand. Instead, he smirked sardonically and moved closer to me. I automatically took a step back, and my back hit the closed bathroom door.

He leaned in so close that I could see the tiny flecks of gold deep in his brown irises. His breath hit my face as he spoke low and deep, almost with a growl. "If you would like to start calling me daddy, you will get no complaints from me."

My face flamed with fury and, I had to admit, a bit of desire.

I poked my finger into his chest. "That is not even close to funny, Blake Montgomery."

His smile never left his face, even though he knew he had royally pissed me off, as he said, "Who said I was joking?"

My mouth dropped open, but I could not think of a retort. Instead, I huffed indignantly and pushed against his chest, wanting to push him away from me. He was solid and powerful, so I knew his stumbling back was on purpose. He let me push him away.

Snarling, I turned, opened the bathroom door, and stomped into the bathroom. I turned back and saw Blake still staring after me with that annoying smirk on his face. I slammed the door with a resounding boom and then crumpled to the floor with a groan.

I sat with my knees up, resting my elbows on them with my head in my hands. What was wrong with me? I had never been this easy to anger before. Blake always teased me, but I always laughed it off. It took a lot to anger me.

That was before he had kissed me.

The memory of that sensation-ridden kiss was still burning in the back of my mind, and I did not think I would ever get it out of there. It was not just the kiss that had my nerves raging, either.

It was everything.

The dreams, or memories, had me on edge all the time…or, at least, the bits and pieces I could remember. It was all so confusing. Then there was my guilt at hurting Greg and causing him to run off, which was burning a hole in my gut. And, finally, the irresistible draw of the mountains had me wanting to run back there, even though I knew it might trigger me again.

I wanted to brave that lookout and see if I could go back there without having an emotionally déjà vu-ridden breakdown. I wanted to know if my dreams were really dreams or memories coming back from long ago.

Taking a deep, cleansing breath, I drew myself up from the floor and turned on the shower. Thirty minutes later, I emerged from the bathroom, clean and ready for the trip back home.

The trip home was boring and uneventful. We did not speak much during the drive. It was the same on the two-hour plane ride back home and after departing the airport. Blake said a short and quick goodbye and stalked to his car.

He would not even look my way as he left.

That night as I lay in my bed in our dorm, I thought about Blake and wondered why he was so angry with me when I was the one that should be angry, then I decided I did not care. But as I drifted to sleep, I heard that voice in my head again calling me a liar.

CHAPTER 8: Running

I did not want to go back to class. The vacation was almost over. For the last week of break, we had stuck to our original plan of hanging out at the beach and ordering drinks from the Tiki Lounge. We had fun, and I had to admit that I enjoyed it much better than my short trip to the mountains.

There were no dreams to keep me awake at night. Blake no longer pushed me to mental insanity and was dark and broody again. Dianna and Chris made out like animals all the time, which made me want to barf, except when he was making me laugh. Everything was back to normal.

Except for one thing…

I did not see Greg for the rest of our break.

I was nervous about facing him again. I knew we would have at least one class together in the next semester since we were both working on the same business major. I wanted to talk to him and try to rectify our situation. I wanted us to remain friends because I did hold some affection for him, even though it was nowhere near as intense as my feelings for Blake.

I awoke two hours early for the first day of my classes, having gotten my schedule and picked up all of my syllabuses from my professors the day before. I had just gotten out of the shower and was wrapped in a towel. I went to the closet to pick out my outfit for the day when Dianna's sleepy tone distracted me.

"Why are you up so early?" Dianna grumbled from under her covers.

"I want to look nice on my first day," I answered. "Maybe I'll meet a cute guy, and he will ask me out for coffee."

Dianna raised her head from her pillow and rolled her eyes at me. "Yeah, and then Blake will have another guy to run off," she said sardonically.

"Blake did not run Greg off," I said. "That was my fault for acting like a drama queen over a silly mountain."

Dianna sat up in bed, scrutinizing me with a severe expression on her cute, sleep-ridden face. "That was not your fault, Lucy. You went through a huge trauma at such a young age, and it is not your fault that your brain was broken by it."

I turned from my closet and looked at Dianna with narrowed eyes. "My brain was not broken. I don't know what was wrong exactly, but the dreams have stopped, and I am no longer an emotional mess."

Dianna's serious expression vanished, and she laughed sardonically, a touch of humor in her tone when she replied, "Honey, you are a girl. You will forever be an emotional mess."

That made me laugh, and I shook my head at her as I turned back to my closet. "What should I wear today?" I asked.

"You are seriously not going to address the situation between you and Blake?" Dianna said in a grumpy tone. "Lucy, the man is mad over you, and you can't keep your feelings for him locked away forever."

I knew Dianna would bring this up eventually. Blake had not pushed the issue since we returned home, but Dianna and Chris always made sly comments that I had ignored or pretended I did not hear.

Maybe I should do that now, keep getting dressed and pretend I did not hear what Dianna had just said, but I knew she would not let it go this time.

I was right in my assumption.

"Lucy, did you hear me? You cannot date other guys when you are in love with Blake. It is not fair to him, and it is not fair to the men whose hearts you break."

I swung around as sudden rage gripped me in its clutches. My hands were fisted at my side, and my voice came out low and menacing.

"What do you mean by that, Dianna? Just what are you trying to say?"

Dianna flinched in surprise at the anger in my tone. I was also surprised. I had never spoken like that to her or anyone before. Where was all this anger coming from?

Dianna's eyes widened, and her mouth dropped open as she shrank back on her bed. "Jeesh, Lucy, get a grip. I'm sorry. I won't mention it again," Dianna said in a whispered tone, and I thought I heard the tiniest bit of fear in her voice.

A sly, vindictive smirk spread across my face, and I liked the tiny bit of power I felt at making someone fear me. My mind swirled with possibilities of what I could make her do. My fingers began to tingle slightly, and the prickling sensation ran up my arms and shoulders.

What was I thinking? This was not me at all. It was as if another person were speaking through me and controlling me. I tried to snap myself out of this funk that I was sinking into, but icy fingers dragged me down into my mind's recesses. I was powerless to stop it.

I could only watch as a part of my brain that I did not even know existed took over my mind and thoughts, even as I held on to some semblance of who I was. The part that was still me was being buried deep within and watching the entire scene play out.

Dianna's wide eyes grew even wider, and the surprise on her face became terror as she watched me stalk toward her. I saw tears well up in her bright green eyes, and her voice was shaky as she said, "Lucy, what is wrong with you?"

I laughed, a low malicious sound that I did not recognize coming from my own mouth, and my voice was deep with spitefulness as I replied, "Everything is wrong with me, and it is all your fault. You and everyone around me have broken me."

Where had that come from? I began digging from the grave my mind was trying to bury me in.

What was I saying? Why was I treating my best friend as if she were my enemy? What was this tingling sensation swirling up and down my arms?

My breathing was steady and even, and my heartbeat remained calm despite the whirlwind of thoughts and emotions swirling around in the back of my mind, the part that was me trying to fight whatever this was.

The front of my mind was still focusing on Dianna, and the horrible image I saw of what I wanted to make her mind do had me fighting even harder through the haze.

A single tear fell down Dianna's face as I stopped at the foot of her bed. My tone was cruel as I said, "If I were you, I would kill myself. If I were you, I would not be able to live with what you, all of you, have done to me. You should jump out of that window."

I opened my hands and pointed them at Dianna with my palms facing her. The tingling sensation grew warm, then hot, and fire lit up my veins as the power slid from my palms toward Dianna.

"Lucy, please. We had no choice. We only did it to protect you." Dianna's voice came out in a terrified squeak, and she fisted the sheets into her hands as she shrank away from me.

My inner self frowned. I did not understand the words coming from my mouth, and I did not understand what Dianna was saying either. I struggled to regain control of my body even as I swam in a sea of confusion and dread at what the force that had taken over me was about to make me do.

I could feel my mind connect with Dianna's when the sensation from my palms hit her. I felt it lock into place in the most inner recesses of her brain and fill it up, rendering her powerless to stop the control it had over her.

I saw the picture in my mind of Dianna rising from the bed and walking slowly to the window and then heard my mind command hers to obey. I watched in horror as Dianna followed the commands, her body moving in jerky movements as if she were fighting it every step of the way.

Our dorm was on the sixth floor of the building. The fall would kill her if she fell out of that window. Tears burned the backs of my eyes as I watched Dianna move even closer and felt the force that had me in its control urge her to move faster.

I fought myself even harder. The fear of seeing Dianna move even closer to the window lent me strength that I did not even know I had, and when I heard his voice, I came completely out of the trance that my inner mind had locked me in and took back my control.

"Lucy, what are you doing?" Blake yelled as he burst into the room.

His bass tone was panicked with alarm as he ran toward me. I turned my head slowly and watched him come. His shocked brown gaze pierced through my soul as I dropped my hands to the floor.

The tingling sensation left me suddenly, and I felt empty and cold. Dianna stopped walking toward the window as I felt my brain release hers, and she turned from the window and flung herself back onto the bed with a terrified sob.

What in hell had just happened?

I raised my hands and stared at my palms in disbelief, switching my gaze from my hands to Blake's face over and over. Finally, I stopped on Blake's gaze, and my heart fell to my feet.

Blake had never looked at me that way before. The heated fury on his face broke me, and I sank to the ground with a wail of utter helplessness. I brought my knees up and wrapped my arms around them, burying my face in my arms and resting my forehead on my knees. I began to sob, great wracking cries that shook my entire body.

"What is happening to me?" I sobbed loudly. "What is happening to me?"

The words left my mouth on repeat between sobs, and my body began to rock back and forth on the ground. Tiny hands gripped my shoulders from behind, and I could feel them trembling as the fingers squeezed gently. I felt Dianna at my back, kneeling behind me as she held my shoulders.

"Lucy," Dianna's soft voice broke through my mind, quacking with the release of adrenaline. "Lucy, I'm here. I am not mad. I'm here. It wasn't your fault."

Another pair of hands, large and strong, gripped my forearms and shook me gently. I could feel him in front of me, and his heat burned through me. Blake's deep, gentle voice sent shivers through my body as he stopped my rocking motion and held me firmly but gently.

"Lucy, calm down. It was not your fault. Just sit for a moment and calm yourself, and then we can talk about what just happened."

A talk? What could they possibly say to make this any better? I had lost control of my body and mind and tried to kill my best friend with some freaky power. What was there to talk about?

"Blake, we have got to take her to mom. No more delays," I heard Dianna say from behind me.

Blake answered menacingly, "No. I trusted your mother and my father with her, and it did no good."

Dianna huffed in frustration and said, "Yes, but that was a long time ago. They have come a long way in their research, and the new serum has had some successes."

Blake's loud, sardonic scoff made me flinch, and his hands tightened on my arms. "You call those walking zombies a success?"

"I am not speaking of those," Dianna began. "The procedure has been improved drastically since the first subjects. There are others…."

Blake cut her off with a snarl and said, "I said no, Dianna. She is not your personal lab rat. Now, let her go and let me take her out of here. It is time she learned the truth."

I had no clue what they were talking about, but my wracked nerves were too raw to allow me to raise my head and ask. Instead, I sat silently and listened to every word, absorbing everything and storing it away for later. Did this relate to the nightmares and my breakdown on the mountain? What had happened to me on the mountain that day?

I felt Dianna's grip leave my shoulders reluctantly as she said in a defeated tone, "Fine, Blake. Take her and hide her away as you have done her entire life. You can't run forever, though. They will find you."

Dianna's voice drifted further away as she walked to the other side of the room.

In an icy tone, she added, "And when they find her, you know what they will do."

"Have I not done my job and kept us safe?" Blake asked defensively.

"Yes, Blake, you have, but Chris and I are tired of lying to her to protect her, and we are tired of being afraid all the time. If we allow mom and your father to complete their research, then maybe this could all be over, and we could live a normal life."

I raised my head and opened my eyes to see Blake kneeling in front of me. He looked over his shoulder at Dianna as he spoke with her, giving me a view of the back of his head.

Blake sighed and released my arm to run his hand through his tousled black hair, causing it to stand up slightly on top and lay down in the back. I kept staring at those dark locks as I listened to the conversation.

"I understand that you are tired, Dianna. But don't you think that I am tired too? Don't you think I live in fear every minute of the day, wondering if and when they will find us and take her from me? We should never have taken her to that mountain." Blake's voice was low and defeated, and my heart twisted at the sadness hidden under the surface of his tone.

Dianna sighed and did not answer. I glanced at her and saw her face scrunched up in thought. Blake bowed his head and stared at the floor.

Blake's tortured voice tore my heart when he finally broke the silence. "What are we going to do now? She used her ability, which means they are tracking us as we speak."

Dianna's tone was apologetic as she replied, "Your dad assured us that it would be fine to take her to the mountain, but he was wrong. I must concede that if he was wrong about that, he could be wrong about the serum. So we will not take her to mom."

Dianna's voice was laced with determination as he added, "That leaves us with two choices. We run, or we fight."

"We are not strong enough to fight," Blake said in a whispered voice. "We run."

He turned his gaze back to mine, and defeat shone in his eyes when they locked on mine.

My voice was thick with emotion as I asked, "What is going on, Blake?"

Quiet resolve overtook his features and reflected in his bass tone as he answered, "It is time that I tell you everything. It is time that you know the truth even if you cannot remember."

"Remember what?" I asked.

Blake opened his mouth to speak, but a sudden pounding on the dorm door caused him to jump up, grasping my forearms tightly and bringing me up with him. He pulled me tight against him and held me, looking toward Dianna questioningly.

"Were you expecting company today?" he asked worriedly.

Dianna's eyes were filled with fear as she answered in a whisper, "No."

The pounding resumed again, more forcefully this time, and we all relaxed in relief as Chris's voice yelled through the closed door.

"Dianna, Lucy, let me in quickly." His tone was urgent, and Dianna walked quickly to the door, unlocked it, and opened it just a crack. She peered through the gap and sighed in relief as she opened it wide enough to let Chris through.

"I am so glad it is you," she said as he hugged her.

"I saw the WAMB trucks. What is happening?" Chris asked, looking toward Blake for an answer.

"Lucy unknowingly used her ability. I think the chip may be malfunctioning again," Blake answered, giving Chris a knowing look.

"Chip…ability…Blake, what is going on?" I asked as I pulled out of Blake's embrace.

"Lucy, we will explain everything later. Right now, we have to get somewhere safe." Blake sounded scared, which caused my own heart to race with fear.

"If the chip malfunctions completely, it could be bad," Dianna's shaky voice said.

"What chip?" I asked more forcefully this time.

Blake made an irritated noise and said, "We don't have time for this right now!" Then, he turned his attention to Chris and asked, "Where did you see the trucks?"

"They were pulling into campus as I came out of my trig class. I ran all the way here across campus, but they will have to stick to the roads, and the student crossings will delay them a bit. We have a few minutes at best." Chris released Dianna and turned to close and lock the door.

Dianna moved quickly, darting across the room to the closet and pulling out our suitcases, which we had just finished unpacking days ago. Blake moved to help her, heaving mine onto my bed and opening the lid.

"Pack only what you need," he told me as he maneuvered me toward my dresser. "We cannot afford to be dragging a bunch of useless things with us."

I moved on autopilot, still hazy and confused about what was happening. The urgency in everyone else's movements made me hurry, and I blindly tossed some underwear, pajamas, a few outfits, and a pair of sneakers into my suitcase.

Suddenly, I realized I was still wearing my shorts and t-shirt, which I had slept in, and my hair was a mess.

"I have to get dressed," I said to Blake, who still hovered over me protectively.

"What you have on is fine," Blake said softly, stroking my cheek with the back of his hand. "Just put on some good running shoes. You can get cleaned up when it is safe for us to stop."

Something was wrong. Blake's touch did not stir any emotions inside me as it usually did. I was numb.

My voice was flat and monotone as I asked, "Where are we going?"

"Somewhere safe," he answered. "We will figure it out on the road."

He bent down, picked up a shirt that had fallen to the floor, put it back into my suitcase, pushed down the scattered pile of clothes I had thrown in, and closed the suitcase. His movements were quick and hurried, and he gave me a questioning look as he moved past me.

"Lucy, we need to hurry," he said, but his tone was gentle and soothing.

Automatically, I moved to my closet and pulled out my running shoes. The only thought running through my mind was the sight of my messed up clothes as Blake had stuffed them into my suitcase. I had not folded my clothes. It bothered me.

Suddenly, I remembered something very important to me that had been with me since I left the hospital when I was small.

My charm bracelet.

I walked hurriedly to my bedside table, opened the drawer, and pulled it out gently. I wrapped it onto my wrist and fumbled with the clasp, dropping it several times. I made a frustrated sound, and Blake was suddenly there, gently taking the chain from me and clasping it around my wrist.

"There you go," he said softly. "Now, hurry and put your shoes on, okay?"

I nodded automatically and hurried back over to my closet. I put my shoes on quickly and returned to Blake's side as he picked up my suitcase and grabbed my hand with his other hand. "Just follow me and do everything I say," he said.

I just gave that automatic nod, still obsessing about my stupid clothes not being folded. They were going to get wrinkled.

Blake's hand was warm in mine, but that was it. There were no sparks of longing, no tendrils of desire, nothing. I was not afraid that we were getting ready to leave everything behind and run to who knows where. I was following the movements and accepting my fate without question.

Was I in shock?

There was no longer time for me to wonder about it as we stepped out into the hallway and made our way toward the elevator. I was behind Blake, Blake was behind Chris, and Dianna was behind me as we cautiously walked down the hallway.

Chris stopped suddenly, and I almost crashed into Blake as he stopped behind Chris. I saw his back muscles stiffen, but I could not see around his huge bulk to find the source of his worry.

I did not have to look to know.

The chilling voice came down the hall, echoing against the empty walls. Trepidation seized me, chasing away the numbness and awakening my terrified brain.

"WAMB has finally come for you. You will have to come with me, Lucy." I knew that voice.

It was the voice of the man who had been so familiar to me in my childhood dreams. I swallowed hard and peeked around Blake's body. The man's bald head gleamed in the hallway lights and caused the snake tattoo curled around his neck to seem darker. He was older than I remembered him in my dreams and the same as he had been at the airport, but the terror-evoking spark in his stormy gray eyes had not changed.

His eyes found mine, and a malicious smile spread over his thin lips as he said, "Hello, Lucy."

I screamed.

CHAPTER 9: Shattered memories

My scream reverberated along the empty hallway, loud and piercing. Several doors began to open, and the bald man stiffened as girls started to peek their heads out of the rooms and look up and down the hallway.

I felt a buzz of energy pass over me, alerting that part of me deep inside that threatened to come to the surface again. I gasped and clamped down on the sensation, forcing it back into the recesses of my mind.

I saw Blake with his hands held palms up in front of him, and suddenly the fire alarm went off, and the lights in the hallway blinked and went off. Then, everything went dark, and I could smell smoke.

Startled screams erupted from the entire floor, coming from closed and open doors. I could not see anything in the pitch-blackness. I felt a hand grab my arm, and I started to scream, but Blake's voice cut through the darkness and eased my fear.

"It's only me," he whispered into my ear. "Follow me and keep up."

I turned my head even though I knew I would not be able to see his face, and I almost pulled my arm free from him when I saw his eyes glowing. The glow only lasted a second, and I wondered if I had only imagined it. I shook my head to clear it and followed the pull of his hand on my arm. Then, We were running, and the freaky glow of Blake's eyes were forgotten as the chaos of startled screams followed us on our escape down the hall.

Excited voices began to rise above the screams…

"What's going on?"

"Where is the fire?"

"Someone hit the lights! Why aren't the emergency lights coming on?"

The shouts and screams continued, and finally, Blake stopped and pulled me to a halt beside him. I felt the buzz of energy in the air around me again, and the fire alarm went silent as emergency lights began to flicker around us.

The lights came on suddenly, and cries of relief filled the air. I looked up into Blake's face, and there it was again…that glow that changed his eyes from dark brown to molten gold…and then it was gone as quickly as it had come. The triumphant smirk that turned up the corners of his full lips confused me until I turned my head to follow his gaze over my shoulder.

We had made it into the elevator, and the doors were rapidly closing. As the doors slid shut, I saw the bald man staring back at us with surprised anger on his sharp features. In the confusion and tumult of the fire alarm buzzing and the lights going out, we had managed to slip right past him and into the elevator.

The man's gray, evil gaze narrowed at us as the doors slid shut and the elevator began to move rapidly down, pulling my stomach up into my chest as a bought of nausea overtook me. I wrapped my arms around my stomach and bent over, but I did not have a long reprieve. Blake's hand was pulling me up again, and we ran out of the elevator and toward the front doors.

Blake slid to a stop causing me to stumble. He caught me and brought me back up, but Dianna and Chris bumping into me in their haste to stop had me stumbling again. This time, Dianna captured my arm and kept me from falling. I looked back at her with startled eyes, and she gazed back at me calmly.

"It will be alright, Lucy. Blake has gotten us out of closer scrapes than this," she said.

I turned to Blake questioningly as he motioned toward the front doors. "The trucks are outside."

I turned to follow his gaze and saw three black SUVs with black tinted windows sitting right outside the doors. Several men were standing at attention on the sidewalk, guarding the 'trucks' with serious gazes. They were all dressed in sleek black suits with black ties and white shirts under their black jackets.

A shiver went up my spine at the sight of them, and I turned my attention back to Blake. "Who are these people, and why are they chasing us?"

Blake glanced down at me with a serious expression. "They belong to the agency. I will explain everything when we are safe."

I wanted to ask more questions, but before I could, Blake turned us around suddenly and began to walk away from the doors. He led us toward the back of the first floor, which I knew had a back door that led out into the alleyway behind the dorm.

The only problem was that the door set off an alarm when it was opened. I supposed it did not matter now, however, since we had already set off one alarm.

The alleyway led to several other back entrances to other buildings, one of which was the campus library, which was usually busy this time of day. If we could make it there, we may be able to blend into the crowd and get away.

"We need to get to the library," I said as Blake led us toward the back door. "It will be full of students at this time of day."

"What if there are more trucks?" Chris asked urgently.

Dianna answered, "There won't be. The alley is too narrow for vehicles, but there might be soldiers."

"We can deal with soldiers," Blake said, and there was a darkness to his tone that made me shiver.

"What if the library's back door is locked?" I asked as I hurried along at Blake's side, with him still holding firmly onto my hand.

Blake chuckled. "That isn't going to be a problem. These emergency doors are metal."

I pondered Blake's enigmatic words, but I had no time to sort them out. We barreled through the emergency door, and the alarm blared, startling several men outside the door.

My heart fell to my feet. They were dressed the same as the men standing in front of the SUVs outside the main entrance, and they were all pointing guns at us.

I felt that energy pull wash over me again, and, this time, I saw Chris hold his hands up much as Blake had done just before the lights had gone out in the hallway upstairs. I gasped in amazement as Chris's eyes began to glow as Blake's had earlier, changing them from gray to a bright, burnished silver.

I heard the men's horrified yelps and turned my attention to them. I watched in stunned wonder as their guns melted away, pouring into liquefied metal puddles at the men's feet. The men seemed shocked for only a moment before quickly recovering and moving toward us threateningly.

A sudden bought of remembrance hit me like a punch to the gut, and I doubled over. The guns had melted away, just as the wall had in my dream. The details of the dream came flooding back to me. Six-year-old Chris had melted a metal wall just as he had done to the guns, and his eyes had glowed the same.

I shook my head to clear it and felt Blake's hand guiding me back upright. I clung to Blake's arm, and he patted my hand soothingly. I looked up at his face and was stunned to see that he was smiling. It was a cold, calculating smile that he had aimed at the men as they approached us cautiously.

The one in front spoke.

"Come with us quietly. We do not want any trouble."

Chris scoffed and replied sarcastically, "Sure, you just want to take us on a nice little walk, right?"

I glanced toward Dianna, who stood behind Chris, and she had her eyes squeezed shut with her fingers pressed to her temple. It looked as if she had a sudden headache.

Another memory shot through my mind, but this time it came gently, and I stayed standing. Dianna looked this way in my dream just before the birds attacked the men who had come to take me away. I looked up to the sky and sure enough, birds began to pour into the alley, pecking at the men's heads and eyes just as they had done in the classroom.

In my dream, the birds had been black crows, but now the birds were pigeons. Lots and lots of them. They seemed to ignore us and only focus on the men.

"Move, now!" Blake shouted, and we all darted around the distracted men and ran down the alley.

"Which door is the library?" Chris called out as we ran.

"This way," Dianna shouted as Chris hung back and let Dianna take the lead.

She ran toward the library's emergency door, and Dianna pointed at it and yelled, "It's that one!"

Chris held out his hand, and that now familiar buzzing sensation brushed across my body as Chris's eyes began to glow again. I was getting used to the feeling and the glowing eyes, so I ignored it and kept running, clinging to Blake's arm as he ran beside me.

The door's lock and handle melted away before we reached it, and Dianna crashed into the door, slamming it open without the alarm going off. We piled into the library's silence, and Blake gently closed the now-ruined door behind us.

As he turned, Chris's hand was still held out, and I watched in stunned amazement as the door's lock and handle reformed before my eyes. I turned my stunned gaze to Chris, and he smiled and winked one glowing eye at me. He turned and motioned for us to follow, moving quietly into the silent library.

The back door was hidden behind several rows of bookshelves, so no one had noticed when we had come barreling into the back door. We made our way down the back row of bookshelves and reached the central aisle leading to the library's front.

Students were sitting at tables here and there, just as predicted. Many were reading, but some huddled together, talking in hushed tones to avoid disturbing the others around them.

We cautiously made our way closer to the front door. Unfortunately, there were no large windows in the front of the library as there were in our dorm building, so we could not see if the SUVs were out there or not.

The library sat opposite the alleyway from our dorm, so the SUVs would have to circle the block to get to the front of these buildings, and then they would have had to know which building the door we had entered led. Therefore, there was a high possibility that no SUVs would be waiting outside.

The sidewalk in front of the campus library led to classroom buildings, the science lab, and the arts center, which meant the sidewalk would abound with students at this hour. If we were lucky, we could exit the library and blend in with the crowd. Blake and Chris's dorm building was only a block away, and if we could make it there, we could get in Blake's car and drive away.

If we were lucky.

As we headed to the front door, no one seemed to pay special attention. The librarian glanced up from her large desk on the far wall as we passed, but it was only a momentary glance. Others gave a quick cursory look but then turned back to what they had been doing before we passed.

Every eye that glanced our way made my nerves cringe, and I was startled several times when someone would rise from their seat and come our way. Then, a sigh of relief would escape me when that person's focus would stray away from us, and they would head down an aisle away from us.

It was like walking through a minefield, tense and ready to be blown up at the slightest wrong step. I wanted to scream and run, but I could not. I wanted just to barge out the front doors and get this over with, but we had to be careful.

Tension and frustration overrode the fear that had clung to me since the bald man had come at us in the hallway earlier. Every muscle in my body was coiled and ready to act at any second. The buzzing sensation I had begun to ignore still curled through every nerve in my body.

Everything that had happened in my dreams seemed to be proving true, leaving me wondering if the dreams were actually lost memories. The mysterious abilities that my friends appeared to have, the bald man chasing us, and my crazy mind powers had all happened, even though I had been in sort of a trance when I had used them. Just the thought that superpowers existed had me wanting to scream and run to the nearest mental facility and check myself in.

I could not seem to process all this information, and I could feel myself slipping again into a shocky state. I needed to get a grip on myself. Whatever was happening was seriously messed up, and I could not afford to be an emotionally broken child.

We finally came to the front door after what seemed like an agonizing forever, but it had only been a few seconds. Still in the lead, Dianna cracked open the door and peered outside.

She pulled her head back in and whispered, "All clear."

We followed her outside, and I took in a great gulp of fresh air and blew it out slowly. Then, we merged into the multitude of students hustling and bustling along the busy sidewalk, walking casually as if we had been there all along.

I tried to walk normally, tried not to take off running and never look back. My muscles twitched with the effort of holding them back at a steady pace when all I wanted to do was run away.

Every person that bumped into me made me jump, and every loud noise brought a small, frightened squeak from my lips. Finally, Blake leaned down and put his lips next to my ear.

"Relax, Lucy. We are safe for the moment." His breath tickled along my neck and sent warm tendrils of desire coiling through me.

I took another deep, cleansing breath and tried to relax and slow my pace. I walked hand-in-hand with Blake down the sidewalk, following Chris and Dianna, who were also holding hands as they walked. They seemed at ease and carefree, but I knew it was just a ruse. I knew they were just as alert as I was, and I could feel the tension in Blake's hand that clung to mine as well.

"We are almost to the dorm," Blake said as he squeezed my hand reassuringly.

I plastered on a fake smile as I glanced up at him and said brightly, "Okay."

Blake chuckled. "You are good at pretending to be calm."

"So are you," I replied, arching an eyebrow.

He chuckled and swung our clasped hands between us as if we were on an ordinary afternoon stroll. Blake's dorm came into view, and I could see his red sedan sitting in the parking lot. It took all of my will to stop myself from running the rest of the way to the car.

Screeching tires and horns came from behind us, and we all swung around to see two black SUVs drifting around the corner of the block.

"Run!" Blake yelled, pulling me with him as he broke into a full-out run down the sidewalk.

I kept running, surprised that I was keeping up with Blake, as I listened to the SUVs roar closer and closer. We pushed through the crowd, earning us dirty looks and curses from some people, but we did not stop. This was nuts. We would never be able to outrun a vehicle through this crowd.

I heard a loud BANG behind us, and something hit me in the shoulder hard. It knocked me down and tore Blake's hand from my grasp. Pain blossomed in my shoulder and ran down my arm, burning through my veins like lava.

The crowd went wild.

Panicked students began screaming and running in a tightly packed flow of bodies, flowing around my still, prone form as I lay on the sidewalk and wondered what had happened to my arm. A few people stepped on me, knocking the air from my lungs and making it impossible for me to yell for help.

"Lucy!" Blake cried out in alarm. "Lucy!"

His voice drifted further and further away as the crowd pushed him away from me, and I lay there and tried to catch my breath against the unbearable pain. I tried to get back up, but the pain in my arm was excruciating. I heard the loud bangs again and suddenly realized that it was gunshots. They were shooting at us!

Horror clutched its frozen fingers around my heart, and I tried again to get up against the push of the hurrying bodies, using the other arm to lift myself from the ground. I cradled my hurt arm to my chest and looked wildly around for Blake, Chris, or Dianna.

The crowd was pushing at me even as I tried to stay in place, and I cringed every time someone bumped my shoulder. I could not see Blake or the others anywhere.

My shirt became heavy and sticky, and I looked down at my burning arm. My sleeve was wet with what could only be blood. Pain washed over me in waves, and my vision became spotty. I looked around once more for my friends, but I could not see any of them through the rushing crowd. I could not hear Blake calling out my name anymore, either.

"Blake!" I screamed out over the crowd. "Blake, where are you?"

There was no answer. I looked up at Blake's dorm building in the distance and the red sedan in the parking lot. We had all been heading that way. If I followed the flow of the crowd and ran that way, I would eventually catch up to them.

I glanced over my shoulder to see the SUVs barreling down the road toward me with men leaning out the windows. They had guns pointing toward the crowd. I ducked beneath the running people hoping that the bodies would hide me from their searching gazes.

I scurried as fast as possible, bent over and hiding as my shoulder burned in agony. The spots in my vision became more prominent, and I began to feel dizzy. I could not pass out now!

I forced my eyes to stay open and my body to keep moving even as my peripheral vision became fuzzy and distorted. I could barely see where I was going, especially since I was bent over slightly and could only see a few inches in front of me.

I noticed the running feet becoming fewer and fewer, and I dared to stand up straight for a split second to gauge how far away from Blake's car I was.

Another gunshot rang out in the air, and then more screams and brakes screeching. Something hit me again, this time in my leg, and I crumpled to the ground as pain seared up my thigh and into my stomach. I lay there gasping for breath, with my fuzzy vision worsening. Finally, darkness began to close in as great waves of tormenting pain wracked my entire body. I screamed in agony as pain tore through my shoulder and leg when I tried to turn over and sit up.

I heard the passing engines of the SUVS roaring past my location, and I sighed with relief. I took a deep, preparing breath, held it as I fought the pain, and pulled myself up to a sitting position. Then, I saw a hand reach for me from the corner of my eye, and I flinched away.

Instinctually, I brought a hand up to protect myself, swiping out with the other hand. I curled my fingers and scratched at the arm, and I heard an angered growl of pain as I fell back to the ground.

I ignored the pain shooting through my arm and leg as I turned and scrambled across the ground to escape. I dared a look over my shoulder, and my heart jumped to my throat.

The bald man stood over me, a menacing gleam in his evil gray eyes, holding his arm as blood dripped steadily from where I had scratched him. I swallowed hard and narrowed my eyes at him, smirking in triumph at the blood.

I had bloodied him.

It gave me a sense of empowerment to know that, and I felt that niggling little force nudging at me in the back of my brain. This time I welcomed it, allowing it to come forth and take over, hoping it would be as cruel to this man as it had been to Dianna.

The pain in my body vanished, and I slowly rose from the ground. The bald man towered over me, a good foot and a half taller than I was, glaring at me with his malicious features.

I glared back, unafraid and calm, as I felt the now familiar tingle of power race up my arms and through my body. Somehow, I knew I would not be able to take his mind, but two of his minions were coming up behind him, and I could take those.

I narrowed my gaze at one of them and pointed my palms out, letting the buzzing energy fly from my hands and into the unsuspecting man. It hit him, and he stopped as if stunned, turning wide, surprised eyes toward me.

It was easy to take him, latch into his mind and make him my slave. I pictured what I wanted him to do in my mind, then watched in satisfaction as a look of horror overcame his features.

His body shook with the effort to fight my command, but he could not stop himself. He was not strong enough to fight me. Shaking violently and darting the bald man a look of terror, the man pulled his gun from his holster and pointed it toward the bald man.

My voice was deep, calm, and menacing as I looked toward the man and asked, "Why do you keep following me?"

The man did not seem affected by my tone, nor was he frightened that his man was pointing a gun at him. Instead, he stood calmly and watched me with narrowed eyes.

"You know why I am following you, Lily." His voice was cold and cruel, and I wondered why he had called me Lily.

"She does not remember Lily because you decommissioned her, Waller," Blake's steady, angry voice came from behind me.

Relief flooded my mind, but the part I had let take over still stood cold and calculating, holding the mind of the man with his gun pointing at 'Waller's' head.

Waller shrugged. "Technically, I did not do anything. The doctor did."

"Waller," I said, and my voice was unrecognizable to my ears. It was just as cold as Waller's had been, and I heard Blake gasp behind me. "What is your business with Lucy? Because you know I will never let you take her or me."

What the hell was going on? Coldness began to seep through my veins. My voice had not even sounded like my own when I had spoken so coldly. Was this force that had taken over me, the one that lived in the darkest recesses of my mind, another entity entirely?

I remembered dreaming that I had lost Lily, that she had been someone special to me, and they had taken her. Did Waller think I was this Lily person?

Waller seemed surprised by me and tilted his head at me questioningly. "Well, it would seem that Lily remembers, even if Lucy does not. I am still going to take you, though, little girl."

An evil chuckle escaped my lips as I replied, "I am not your little girl anymore, Waller. I suggest that you cut your losses and leave. You have lost this battle."

I felt Blake at my back as he drew up closer to me. He put a hand on my shoulder, and I flinched in my mind, but the part of me that held me in its grasp stayed steady and firm.

The same desire that I always felt at Blake's touch curled through me and affected the presence inside me just as much as it affected me. That did not surprise me. Blake's voice and touch had pulled me out of its hold before.

It did, however, make me jealous.

"I am not going anywhere without Lucy," Waller said, taking a small slow step forward.

I pushed the man holding the gun forward, had him cock it, and hold it steadily at Waller's head. My voice was firm as I replied, "Well, tell your boss you failed. I will not let you take her."

"You seem awfully brave hiding away inside of Lucy as you always have," Waller said, but he did not step forward again.

"Where else would I be?" was my enigmatic reply, and suddenly I was alone in my own head again.

Fear gripped my heart as I thought about my hold over the man, but he still stood with his gun trained on Waller's head. The tingling sensation had left me, causing me to wobble weakly on my unsteady legs.

Blake caught me in his arms and hauled me up against his chest, holding me tightly from behind. I heard a strangled gasp leave his throat, and his voice was barely a whisper in my ear.

"Lily..."

The familiar name swirled around in my mind for a moment. Lily...Lily...I knew that name. The memory ran through my mind but did not hit me forcefully as the other memories had. This time, it flowed through my brain softly, warmly, almost comfortingly.

It had been Lily's doll that Dianna had tried to steal from me that day, and I had made her give it back. I made her, just as I had made Dianna walk toward the window and made the man point a gun at his boss's head.

"No, sister," a voice said inside my mind. *"Making Dianna walk toward that window and the man in front of us holding the gun was all me."*

I jerked my head around to see a woman standing beside me. Her voice sounded just as mine had when she had taken control of my mind, and she was still talking to me inside my head even though I could physically see her now.

She turned to face me with that malicious smile, and the likeness between her and me caused icy chills to shoot up and down my spine.

She looked just like me, except she had blond hair instead of black, and her blue eyes were more of an icy blue than a sapphire blue like mine. Her face was sharper somehow, with a more pointed chin, and her skin was just a bit darker, as if she had a slight tan.

"Sister?" I squeaked in disbelief.

Lily's smile turned gentle and sweet as she said, "Yes, sister. Twin sister. But you no longer remember that because of this asshole."

Her voice had gone sinister as she said the last part, and she gestured angrily toward Waller. Her tone became sweet once more, and her smile was even sweeter as she turned her icy blue gaze to Blake.

"Hiya, Blake," she said. "It's been a long time."

Blake did not seem to acknowledge her presence at my side, but he did flinch as Lily's words flowed out of my mouth. She had spoken to me inside my head and now talked to Blake through me.

Could she not speak for herself?

Lily turned her attention to Waller again, and her face turned vindictive and cold. The rapid changes in her expression were dizzying, and I leaned back into Blake's arms as the pain in my shoulder and leg began to throb.

"Lily, Lucy has been shot. Twice," Blake said, and I heard his voice crack with worry. "I have to get you two someplace safe. She cannot handle this much exertion to her system right now, which means you are not safe either."

What had Blake meant by that?

My head swam with dizziness and confusion. The blackness began to take hold once more, drifting into the corners of my vision and threatening to take over. I was holding on to a thread of consciousness with the overbearing pain wreaking havoc on my body.

"I got this, Blake. Get us out of here," Lily said through me, and then she raised her hand and closed it into a fist.

I struggled to see what was going on, but Blake turned me away from the scene, scooping me into his arms and running down the sidewalk. The blackness enveloped me as I heard a single gunshot reverberate down the street, and then I passed out in Blake's arms.

CHAPTER 10: Restoration

My eyelids fluttered open slowly, and water filled my eyes at the sudden brightness. The lights overhead were unbearably bright, so I turned my head away and attempted to open my eyes once more.

My vision cleared slowly as my eyes adjusted to the light, and I could barely make out Blake slumped in a chair beside me. I was lying on a soft bed in a strange room, and I could hear the beeping of hospital monitors above my head.

The room did not look like a hospital room, though. I glanced around at the simple table under the window, minus one of the chairs. I assumed that was the chair that Blake sat in now.

The heavy, green drapes were closed over the window, but the lights above my head were bright enough anyway. There was a small bedside table beside me where Blake sat in his chair. The walls were soft tan, accentuating the green curtains, and the floors were polished wood.

I had never known of a hospital with wooden floors, nor did hospital rooms usually have any color. I turned to the opposite side to find a dresser against the wall next to a door. The door was closed, but another door was open on the side wall. Judging from the light streaming from the open door and the bit of white and black tile I could see on the wall inside; I guessed that this was a bathroom.

"Lucy?" I turned back to Blake to find his eyes open. He was watching me with a searching look on his face.

I smiled, and his face looked relieved as he sat straight in the seat and reached for a glass sitting on the bedside table. I opened my mouth to speak, but Blake placed a finger to his lips and shook his head.

"Shhh, do not try to speak. You need to drink some cool water first." He put a hand behind my head and gently raised it, placing the straw that was in the glass to my lips.

Pain rocketed through my arm when he raised my head. I gasped at the sharp agony, and Blake winced and stopped moving my head. He sat the glass back on the table with a pained look.

"Lucy, I am so sorry. Here, let me try raising the bed instead." Blake's voice was full of emotion.

He lowered my head back to the bed ever so tenderly, and the pain subsided somewhat. Then, he pushed a button on the side of the bed, and my entire upper body began to rise. Pain sliced through me once more, but it was bearable.

Once I was halfway up, the pain receded, and I could shift into a comfortable position and raise my head from the pillow. Blake brought the straw to my lips again, and this time I took a sip of the cool water.

It burned going down at first, but the second drink felt better. The water was good and soothed my tumultuous stomach. I sighed in relief and lay my head back on my pillow.

"Where am I?" I asked. My voice was not as scratchy as I had expected, and it did not hurt when I talked. The water had helped immensely.

"We are in the home of a friend. We are safe." Blake smiled comfortingly and sat back in the chair. "I suppose you have questions."

I scoffed sardonically. "Where do I start?"

"You could ask me a bunch of questions, and it could take forever, or you could meet my friend, and she may have another solution for you." Blake looked at me expectantly.

I frowned. "What do you mean another solution?"

"Why don't you meet her, and she can explain," Blake said.

I looked at Blake sitting in the chair. He seemed calm and collected and not nervous or scared at all. I trusted his judgment and always had. If he was not worried about this other solution, it had to be safe.

I swallowed hard and said, "Blake, my life has been a big ball of confusion ever since we left for the mountains. I have had crazy dreams that are beginning to seem more and more like memories. People are chasing us, trying to take me who knows where. I have been possessed by someone who says she is my sister even though I am an only child. I tried to kill my best friend. I ran off my boyfriend. The list goes on and on…."

I trailed off and took a deep breath to collect myself. I did not know how much more of this I could take. I felt as if my life was spinning out of control, and I was powerless to stop it. Was my life even my life anymore? I did not know, but I did know that if Blake had a solution to all of this madness, then I would take it.

"What I'm trying to say is," I said, feeling a bit calmer than I had before. "if you think this friend of yours can help me, then yes, I would like to meet her."

Blake smiled in relief. "Good. She will be here soon. She will be happy to see you."

I raised an eyebrow in surprise. "What do you mean by that? Does she know me?"

Blake shifted in his seat. "Yes, and you know her as well. She may be able to help you get your memories back."

I gazed at Blake in disbelief. "Get my memories back? The doctor says it will never come back."

Blake sighed. "Wait until our friend gets here and talk to her. Everything will make sense soon."

I nodded. "Alright. When is she supposed to be coming?"

"Right now," said a voice from the other side of the room where the door was. I had not even heard it open.

I turned my head to see shining jade green eyes, a pretty face, and wavy brown hair. She was just as slim and graceful as I remembered her despite the years that lined her happy face.

Happiness swelled inside me, and I ached to jump from my bed and wrap my arms around her neck as I used to when I was little. The pain in my shoulder when I tried to sit up reminded me that it would be a bad idea. However, I did not have to move. She came to me.

Miss Megan bent over me and very gently gathered me into her arms. I winced in pain, and a choked sound escaped my lips, but I did not know if it was from pain or happiness at seeing Miss Megan again.

Megan must have taken it for a painful sound because she eased me back to the bed with an apologetic smile. "Oh, my dear, I am sorry. I didn't mean to hurt you."

I shook my head, still smiling, and said, "The pain was worth it. I missed you so much."

Both of our voices were thick with emotion as we spoke.

"Is this your place?" I asked curiously.

Megan nodded. "Yes, it is. I have been here for a long time helping others like you."

"You mean other little girls with brain injuries?" I asked.

Megan shook her head, and her smile faded. "No, Lucy. You never had a brain injury. Your memories were not taken away by an accident."

My breathing and heart rate sped up with anxiety. My body tensed with anxiety, and I knew I did not want to hear what Megan would say next. Whatever it was, I knew it was going to tear my world apart.

I gathered myself, preparing for the worst, and stared into Megan's jade eyes as I asked, "What happened to me?"

"You were decommissioned, Lucy. Your memories were stolen from you, and so were your abilities." Megan remained calm as she returned my stare.

I was far from calm. I was breathing too fast, and the monitors above my head were beeping faster than they should have. I tried to slow down my breathing and calm my rapidly beating heart, but that dreaded word kept running around and around in my mind.

Decommissioned…decommissioned…decommissioned.

Then, a memory slid into my mind, one I had almost forgotten, and thought was a dream. It had been Megan scolding me for using my power over Dianna and telling me…

"You know you are not supposed to use your powers. Do you want to be decommissioned?"

I remembered being frightened of that word.

Another memory worked its way into my mind. Blake and I were strapped to hospital beds with a doctor and Waller in the room. I remembered talking to Blake with my mind…

"Blake, listen to me. Let the doctor decommission me, and you get away. You can protect the others and get me back somehow. I know you can. I trust you."

I turned my gaze to Blake, who stared back at me with a tortured expression. "I told you to let them decommission me," I said, but it was more of a statement than a question.

Blake's eyes widened in surprise. "You remember that? How?"

"I dreamed about it," I said in a whispered voice.

"This is good," Megan said. "If you are gaining your memories back in your dreams, then the procedure is bound to work."

I frowned and turned back to Megan. "Procedure? What procedure?"

Megan shifted on the bed beside me into a more comfortable position. She placed her hand on my uninjured leg and patted it comfortingly as she spoke.

"We have been working on a procedure to give decommissioned children back their memories. It is not invasive, but it is not without risks. There is a slight chance that it will not work completely, but we have recently had a high success rate. I feel confident it will work on you, Lucy, since you are already gaining memories."

"She has not had her meds in two months," Blake said. He leaned up in his chair and rested his elbows on his knees. "Heather used to put them in her doughnuts, but she has grown a dislike for them since we have been back."

Megan's eyes narrowed as if she were angry. "Would this have anything to do with a certain sister?"

Blake nodded. "Uh-huh. She made an appearance already, and her memory is intact, but I can't complain since she was the reason we got away and were able to get here."

"We will still need to sever the hold. It is too dangerous," Megan said.

Blake sighed, nodding his head in confirmation before leaning back into the chair.

I looked back and forth between the two, confusion causing my head to swim. "What are you two talking about?" I asked in irritation.

Megan's gaze softened, and she turned her attention back to me. "Do not worry about it now, dear. It will all be clear after the procedure."

I took a deep breath and said, "Alright, let's do it."

Megan smiled as she brought her hand to my arm and ran her finger along the charm bracelet, still dangling from my wrist. "I see you got a longer chain and more charms too."

I returned her smile as I held up my arm to allow the charms to dangle in the air. "Yes, they represent…."

I stopped suddenly and turned my alarmed gaze to Blake. "Where…"

He cut me off quickly, making a calming gesture with his hand. "They are here with us and safe. Everyone made it."

I let out a relieved breath of air as I nodded my head. "Okay, good." I turned my attention back to Megan to explain each charm to her. I stopped at the gold heart and turned to Blake once more.

Blake chuckled and said, "I gave it to her to represent the hope that one day she would return my love."

Megan shot me a disappointed look. "You two are not together?"

I frowned and shook my head. I did not want to explain this to Miss Megan.

She frowned as well, but hers was more of a disappointed frown than an angry one. "Well, I figured that memory or no memory, the way you and Blake were so inseparable when you were little…well…."

She trailed off and rose from the bed, still frowning as she added, "N…never mind. Get some rest. We will start the procedure as soon as you have healed from your injuries."

I nodded, and the frown relaxed from my features. I smiled reassuringly at her as I said, "I will. Thank you for taking care of me again."

Miss Megan chuckled and placed a gentle kiss on my cheek. She gave me a somber smile and then turned and left the room, leaving Blake and me alone. I watched her go, not wanting to face Blake. After Megan shut the door softly behind her I shifted my gaze to the bed.

I reached up tentatively and touched the sticky pads stuck to my forehead, hair, sides of my head, and all over my chest.

"What are these?" I asked softly.

"They are electrodes for the monitors. We monitored your brain and heart activities in case you had more dreams." Blake's voice was deep and sensual as he spoke, sending tiny shivers of longing up my spine. Did he have to talk in that tone?

"I did not dream this time," I said weakly, and I hated how my voice quivered.

"We know," he said.

From my periphery, I saw him rise from the seat and slowly walk over to me. He touched one of the electrodes gently, tracing his finger around the circular sticky pad and then tracing it along my skin at the edge of the pad. His finger was gentle and warm, sending shockwaves of desire through me.

The heart monitor began beeping rapidly as my heart rate picked up, and my breathing became ragged as the tendrils of longing played along the inside of my body.

Blake chuckled, low and seductive, and I swallowed the lump that had formed in my throat. He bent down low over me, his breath tickling the sensitive spot on my neck below my ear.

My breath hitched in my throat as he began to speak, spilling his warm breath all along my skin, and I clutched the bedsheets into my fists to keep from swooning back onto the bed.

"You cannot hide how your body responds to me when you are hooked up to these machines. Your body and the machines do not lie as your mouth does." His voice growled with seduction as he spoke, and he nipped my earlobe before moving away from me.

I gasped, and a shiver ran through my body. The monitors went wild.

Blake laughed triumphantly and said, "I think we should take these off of you before we bring the whole troop in here after us thinking that you are having a heart attack or something."

I shot him an angry glare that did not resonate with the intense need for his touch that sang through me as his hand gently removed the electrodes from my body. He took the ones from my forehead and hair first, using a special lotion to unlock the glue from my hair so that he would not pull it out with the sticky pad.

After he had removed them all from my head and hair, he began working on the ones on my chest. A few were very low, so he had to pull the hospital gown that someone had dressed me in so far down that my nipples were almost exposed.

I saw the heat swirl into his dark brown gaze as he reached for the furthest one down, and his wrist inadvertently brushed across my hardened nipple as he grasped the pad and pulled it off.

I gasped, but not from the sharp pain of the pad coming off my skin. The sensations running through me intensified when his wrist brushed across my nipple so sharply that my body began to tremble.

Blake's dark, captivating gaze bore into me while he gently lifted the electrodes from my skin. He placed his lips against my ear again when the last one was gone.

"Would you like me to help you take a shower?"

The suggestiveness in his tone made the trembling worse, and I thought my heart would burst from my chest. My breath was coming in short, ragged gasps, and I tried to take a deep, shaky breath to steady my breathing.

I swallowed hard and tried to make my voice sound as angry as possible. "No, I can manage it myself."

His hand touched my face, but his mouth did not move from my ear. "You will have to take the sling from your arm, and it will be hard for you to stand on that leg. Are you sure you can manage?"

His lips brushed across my face as his fingers stroked my cheek. A low, soft moan escaped my lips. I had not even meant to make that sound. I clamped my lips shut to prevent any other sounds from coming out.

I could not answer, so I nodded.

Blake chuckled low and enticingly in my ear, and I shivered again. "Alright, then. I will have Miss Megan come in and help you out of your sling and gown."

He pushed my cheek gently with his fingers, turning my head to face him. His dark, sensual gaze made my toes curl, and I knew he would kiss me. I gasped as his lips came ever so close to mine, and I wanted to pull away. I knew the fire that his lips would bring, and I was barely hanging on as it was.

I squeezed my eyes shut, waiting for the body-wracking sensations that would make me his prisoner, but his lips only brushed across mine so lightly that I thought I had imagined it. Then I felt the bed shift, and I opened my eyes to see him walk around the foot of the bed and head for the door.

He did not look back as he left the room, closing the door softly behind him. A heaviness settled in my chest as I looked at the closed door and felt the loss of Blake. All the emotions and sensations he had left unsatisfied and swirling inside me were too much to bear. They coalesced around my chest, needing release, and a soft sob escaped my lips, and then another and another until great wracking sobs shook my entire body.

I placed my head in my hands and cried.

PART THREE

ASCENDING

CHAPTER 11: Hidden

Miss Megan found me sobbing out my frustrations and eased me gently into her arms. She held me as close as she could without hurting me until the sobs ceased, and my body trembled with the release of emotion.

She did not say anything or ask any questions. Instead, she held me until I felt as if I were ready to collapse from exhaustion, and I could not cry anymore.

Slowly, she helped me out of the sling and my clothes, helped me wobble to the bathroom, and helped me take a shower and wash the sticky stuff from my hair and chest.

I felt better after my shower, and even my shoulder and leg felt better. The bullet had gone through my calf, damaging the muscle but missing any bones. The bullet that hit my shoulder had only grazed me, even though it felt like I had been hit by a truck. It had taken a good size chunk out of my shoulder, though.

I would heal, and I would be fine, at least physically. Mentally was another story.

Megan offered to help me brush my hair, and all the times she had brushed my hair when I had been in the hospital under her care came back into my mind. I accepted and was relaxed under her touch as I listened to her explain the procedure as she brushed my hair.

The serum would make me sleep as memories came back to me in dreams. It may take a couple of sessions, and hopefully, I would remember everything. I was optimistic that the procedure would work since I had already been gaining some memories through dreams, even though I did not know which were actually memories.

Miss Megan also told me more about my sister and that I needed to be wary of her when I finally did remember her. I wondered what she meant by that, but I did not ask. Instead, I bade Megan goodnight as she put everything away, tidied up my room a bit, and then left me alone.

I lay in bed and closed my eyes, thinking about my sister and that dark part of my mind that reminded me of her. That part of my brain held a dark abyss that tried to pull me in and trap me whenever Lily tried to take over my body and do bad things.

I thought about how Blake seemed afraid of her, and I wondered why. I also wondered why my sister seemed so mean and cruel. On the other hand, she had saved us before, so maybe she was not as malicious as everyone wanted me to think.

As if my thoughts had conjured her, I opened my eyes to find her standing by my bed, staring down at me with her icy blue gaze. I stifled a scream that lodged in my throat.

"You cannot get rid of me so easily, sister," she said in her menacing tone. "I will fight this, but I will never forgive you for it."

I swallowed the lump in my throat and tried to remain calm, even though my pulse threatened to jump out of my neck. What was she talking about?

"Lily, why are you angry with me?" I asked, and my voice was calmer than I felt.

"You want to get rid of me again," she said.

"What do you mean, 'get rid of you again'? I asked.

"If you have that procedure done, then you will lose me like you did when you had the other procedure when we were little," she answered sullenly, and all the fight had seemed to leak away from her all at once.

I frowned in confusion. Her face was sad and angry, and it hurt my heart. It was so unsettling to look upon her face that was so like mine. I turned away from that gaze, took a deep breath, and then let it out slowly.

"I do not remember when we were little," I said in a low voice. "That is why I want to have the procedure. Don't you want me to remember you?"

I turned my pleading gaze back toward Lily, begging her to understand, but she was gone. I frowned in confusion. I had not even heard her leave.

The door opened, and Blake strolled in, gazing at me with that heated gaze that made my blood pump faster through my veins.

"Do you feel better after your shower?" he asked in his deep, sultry tone.

I nodded. "Did you see Lily?" I asked curiously.

Blake frowned and shook his head. "No. Why would I have seen Lily?"

The expression on Blake's face sent icy shivers of warning up and down my spine. "She was just here. She had just left when you came in."

I saw Blake's throat work as he swallowed hard, and I thought I saw a flicker of fear in his brown eyes.

Why was he so afraid of her?

He gave me a direct stare and said sternly, "Lucy, you cannot trust anything she says. Do you understand me? You do not remember her, but I do. She is trouble."

The cryptic warning sent alarm bells going off inside my head just before I felt that dark abyss reaching out to the front part of my brain again. I tried to clamp it down and close it off, but the pull was sudden and intense, and before I could do anything to stop it, I was pulled into its cold darkness.

Then, I felt her. Lily was there, and she was taking over me again. I could feel her triumph and glee as she took the wheel and left me back in the deep abyss, alone and confused about what was happening.

I was still in my own body. I could feel and hear everything I said and did, but I was not in charge. I was not controlling anything. Lily had complete control over me, just like the day she had tried to make Dianna jump from the window.

How was she doing this to me, and why?

A malicious smile spread over my face as I rose from the bed. I walked steadily toward Blake and felt no pain from my hurt leg. My movements were graceful and predatory, and my smile widened when I saw the fear in Blake's eyes.

I stopped inches from him and said in a mockingly sweet tone, "Blake, why do you say such things about my sister?"

I saw Blake's eyes narrow in anger, but he quickly gained control of his features and said, "Lily, I know that is you. You cannot fool me when it comes to Lucy."

I laughed huskily. "I sure fooled you when we were kids."

"Bring Lucy back," Blake said, and I jerked in surprise at the anger in his tone.

The front part of my mind, which Lily controlled, did not react at all to Blake's anger. Instead, a deep, resonating laugh escaped my throat, and I threw my head back as the laughter filled the room.

"If Lucy wants out, she will have to fight her way out. I want to have some fun before I go away." My voice was calm, controlled, and contained so much malice that terror filled me inside the abyss. What if she tried to make Blake do something horrible, and I was powerless to stop it?

"Relax, sis, we are just going to have a bit of fun," Lily's voice rang in my head.

"What are you going to do?" Blake asked, mirroring the question I was thinking. I could hear the trepidation in his tone that matched what I was feeling just now.

I stepped closer to Blake, running a finger from his shoulder and down his chest and stomach. I placed my hand flat over the muscled plains and caressed his abs with the palm of my hand.

"Hmmm," I purred seductively. "I can think of a few things."

Desire mixed with fear filled me up as I fought to pull myself from the abyss in my mind. I struggled and fought, but the pull only became stronger. It was as if I was drowning in my own brain, and I struggled to breathe around the sensation.

The disgusted look on Blake's face sent a stab of pain through my heart as he grabbed my wrist and pushed my hand away from his body.

"Do not touch me," he growled furiously.

"Do not be so coy," I said, seemingly unaffected by Blake's rejection. Of course, the part of me that was me and not Lily was hurt, but I shook off the emotion.

Blake knew I was not myself. Had I been myself, Blake would have already had me lying on the bed with his body covering mine, kissing me senseless and running his hands over my body.

That thought sent a river of want and need running through my entire body, and I shivered from the effect. The front part of my mind was not unaffected either, but it only fueled Lily's maliciousness even more.

"You know you want this, Blake. You have wanted it for a very long time." I stepped closer, so close that my breasts brushed against Blake's lower chest.

A ripple of pleasure coursed through me from the contact.

"I want Lucy, not you," Blake said through gritted teeth.

"But this is Lucy," I said with a seductive giggle. "Well, at least it is her body."

"I don't want just her body," Blake said with resolve. He swallowed hard and then added, "I love her. All of her."

Warmth coursed through me at those words. I knew Blake loved me and had known it for a long time, but to hear him say it made my heart flutter.

I placed my hands on Blake's hips and pressed against him. I stood on tip-toe and brushed a kiss across the pulse in his neck, suckling slightly before pulling away.

A devious smile spread across my face as I said, "Your body says differently. I know you are turned on right now."

Blake only shook his head, and his jaw tensed as he fought to control himself. His back and palms were pressed against the wall, and his face was turned away from me.

"No? You do not want to play?" I said with a mock pout. "We will have to try harder."

I moved my kisses down to his chest, running my hands around to the front of his body. I suddenly fought harder, trying to pull my hands away from Blake. I did not want to go where Lily was trying to take me.

My hand brushed along the front of his pants, and I felt Blake's erection against my palm. I stiffened inside, but outside, my hand clasped around the outline of his erection on his jeans.

Blake growled low in his chest, grabbed me around my waist, and pulled me up to him, ripping my hand away from his groin. My hands went to his shoulders, and he turned me and placed my back against the wall. Then he pushed into me with his hands on my hips, pinning me against the wall with his body.

I smiled triumphantly as Blake's lips crashed into mine. His kiss was rough and invading, his tongue plunging into my mouth with such ferocity. He nipped at my bottom lip hard, and I tasted the copper taste of blood.

I gasped at his rough treatment and wanted to push at his chest, but Lily was in control, and she liked this. I just wanted to wither inside my mind and never come out, but my hands slid into Blake's hair and grabbed handfuls of the black locks.

Hurt and betrayal swelled inside me. Blake had said he did not want her, but his actions belied his words. It was my body, but he knew it was not me in control. He was taking advantage, taking what he wanted from me, and I was powerless to stop it.

The fear in my gut that was always there, the fear of losing him forever, welled up inside me and burst forth, mixed with anger, betrayal, and rage.

I fought to come up to the surface, fought against the force that held me deep inside my mind. Finally, I broke the abyss only barely, enough to feel that tickle of energy running up and down my arms.

I could feel the buzzing sensation filling my arms and driving deep into Blake's mind. I could feel Blake inside my head, screaming and fighting to stop what he was doing.

He was fighting, too.

Lily had us both under her control.

The betrayal that had been gnawing at my gut eased. However, the anger and rage grew. Why was Lily doing this? Did she think she was helping me, that this was what I wanted? Or was what Blake had said true? Was Lily dangerous? What could she hope to gain from this assault on Blake and me?

The momentary distraction of the questions running through my mind had given Lily an advantage. I was forced into the abyss again, and the tiny bit of control I had gained was gone.

Blake's tongue slid along my bottom lip, licking away the blood, and then he sucked my bottom lip into his mouth. He pushed himself into me harder, and I could feel his erection against me, pushing toward that secret place that had never yet been touched or explored.

The sensation ripped through me, and the sudden and complete urge to be filled by him forced a moan of pleasure from my lips. I heard an answering groan from Blake as he tore himself from my lips and rained kisses along my jaw, nipping my earlobe and then kissing down the sensitive spot on my neck.

"Oh, yes, Blake. Take me," I whispered wantonly as the carnal lust that had awoken inside me curled through me.

Blake placed his lips against my ear and whispered, "Lucy, fight this. I know you can."

His reassuring voice flowing into the deep recesses of my mind stirred the fight in me once more. I pushed against the invisible force that locked me in the abyss, pushing with everything I had.

Outwardly, I fisted my hands into Blake's hair harder and pulled his head from my ear. "No speaking to the prisoner," I said chidingly and then licked up the side of his neck.

I lifted my feet from the floor and wrapped my legs around his waist, pressing harder into his jean-clad erection. Blake pushed back, pushing so firmly that the material of my panties went against my sex, which was wide and open due to the positioning of my legs around Blake's waist.

I gasped in pleasure as oceans of wanton need flowed through my soul. It even reached the deep recesses of my mind, where I struggled to break free of Lily's hold.

It made me pause for a moment.

Focusing on the need and want washing into the abyss and over me strengthened me, and I broke through just a bit more. I could feel Lily's hold weaken, and I felt her panic as I clawed my way forward.

Blake's lips were on me again, rough and fierce, and his hands pressed tighter around my hips as he pushed into me, pinning me more firmly against the wall so that he could run his hands up my sides and to the base of my breasts.

He leaned back but kept his lower body pressing me tightly to the wall so he could rest his hands under my breasts. His thumb brushed over my breasts, grazing my hardened nipples as they caressed me.

I broke the kiss, threw my head back against the wall, and moaned in pleasure. "Take me, Blake. Do it." I whispered lustfully.

Blake's hands slid down to the waistline of my pants. As Blake pulled away enough to unbutton my pants and his jeans, my legs slid to the floor so I could stand alone. His tortured brown gaze bore into mine as he slid the zipper down on his jeans.

Inside the deep recesses of my brain, I was terrified. How far was Lily going to make us go? All the way?

No, I couldn't. I had kept Blake at arm's length for so long, even though I knew I wanted him with a force so large that it would consume me. I wanted to be consumed, but not like this.

Not like this.

The realization that I wanted Blake was not new to me, but I had been afraid of losing him. However, I knew now that I would never lose him, no matter what happened.

I knew now that he felt the same for me as I did for him.

He had said he loved me before, but I had doubted what that meant for Blake.

Now, I knew.

Now, I knew that he loved me, and it was not only lust. If it were only about sex, Lily would not have to force him.

The decision to finally let Blake in strengthened my resolve to claw free from Lily's hold, and I broke free just a bit more.

I wanted Blake, and I was not about to let Lily have the first taste.

Blake was pulling his jeans down his legs as I watched. The tortured expression on his face cut through my heart. He took off his jeans and leaned into me in only his boxers. He reached out to me slowly and grasped the waistline of my pants, pulling them down ever so slowly over my hips and legs.

I placed my hands on his shoulder for balance as I stepped out of my pants, and my hands remained on them as he came up and captured my face in both hands. Then, he bent down to me and kissed me softly.

The tenderness of his kiss left me reeling, and the fact that we were only in our underwear scared the hell out of me. It made me fight harder against the pull of the abyss.

Blake pressed against me again, pinning me to the wall and tracing kisses down my jawline. He pressed his lips to my ear as I clawed my way through the haze and freed myself a bit more.

His breath was hot against my face as he whispered, "God, Lucy, I want you so bad. But not like this. Please, God, not like this."

I swallowed hard.

"Blake," I whispered, the tortured emotion in his voice ripping into my very soul, and I was surprised to find that I was no longer being controlled.

"Lucy?" Blake whispered hopefully as his hands left my face to trail down my arms, caressing my skin on the way down.

I had broken free. I was in control again. I checked the buzzing sensation in my arms, the link between my power and Blake's mind, and found it empty.

We were free.

Tentatively, I checked the back recess of my brain and found the abyss swirling menacingly, but it was pushed back from the front of my mind and lying dormant once more.

Lily was gone.

I sighed in relief and wrapped my arms around Blake's neck, pulling him closer to me and placing a kiss on his neck. I buried my face inside the recess between his neck and shoulder, and a great sob escaped my throat.

I felt Blake's arms wrap around my waist, pulling me up to his chest and picking my feet up off the floor. He carried me over to the bed and lay me down gently.

My arm and leg began to throb with pain again, chasing away the lustful sensations that had been churning around inside me. Blake's worried face hovered over me, but he kept his body off me as he laid me down.

"Lucy, I am so sorry." His voice was so wrought with remorse and pain that it made me sob harder.

"It wasn't your fault," I croaked through tears.

Blake touched my face tenderly, wiping away my tears and brushing my hair from my face. Then, he sat gently beside me and bent down to place a chaste kiss on my forehead.

"I don't know what I would have done if…I mean, I want to, but…" he paused as he gave me a tortured look, and then his head fell into his hands.

His tortured whisper rang through my ears, "Oh, God, what have I done?"

The emotion in his tone tore at my heart. I sat up on the bed beside him and placed my hand on his leg. He raised his head from his hands and looked at me questioningly.

"Blake, please don't. It wasn't your fault." My voice was calm but still thick with tears.

Blake's face hardened as he stood and picked my pants up from the floor. "We have got to get her out of you," he said menacingly.

He gently helped me put my legs into my pants as I responded, "What do you mean by that? Is there a way to keep her from taking over my mind?"

He helped me stand, pulled my pants up, fastened them, and then turned to find his jeans.

"Lucy, she is inside your mind."

He picked up his jeans and began pulling them on as I struggled to stand up over the pain coursing through me from my leg and shoulder.

"Not anymore. I pushed her out," I said as I sat back down on the bed to alleviate the pain.

Blake fastened his jeans and sat on the bed beside me. He kept his hands in his lap as he turned to me with a solemn expression.

"I don't know how to explain this to you," he said quietly. He blew out a breath as he ran a hand through his tousled hair. "Lily is not here physically. She is inside your mind but separate from you simultaneously."

I frowned in confusion. "Blake, I saw her. She was standing there right beside us when Waller was trying to take me."

Blake sighed in frustration and shook his head. "Yes, I understand that you see her, but no one else does. We never did."

A chill spread up my spine as I listened to his words. Memories pricked at the back of my mind, begging to be set free, but I fearfully pushed them away.

My voice was shaky as I asked, "What do you mean, Blake?"

"She hides inside your mind where she had been hidden since you were born." Blake's tone was hushed and low as he spoke, sending chills up my spine and coursing through my body.

"She was your twin, but she died in the womb, and you absorbed her. It is more common than you think for normal pregnancies. It's called Vanishing Twin Syndrome. However, in your case, it caused Lily to become a separate entity because your DNA and mind are not normal. She is hidden inside your brain because she does not have her own body to live in.

You can see her sometimes in physical form, but it is only your brain trying to make sense of speaking to someone that is inside of you and yet separate from you. So she is not really there.

She takes control of your body and makes you do things you would not normally do when you are scared or threatened. She is dark and malicious, but even so, she has always protected you for her own selfish reasons. She just went too far this time."

Blake stopped suddenly, probably because of the horrified look on my face. I stared at him in fear and confusion as I tried to absorb everything he had just told me.

"I don't understand all of this," I said, and I could hear a slight tremor in my voice.

"I know you don't right now, but you will after you get your memories back," Blake said with a sad smile. "I only hope we will be able to do that before she makes you do something that you will regret."

The door burst open, and Miss Megan stormed into the room. Her gaze took in the two of us sitting on the bed with forlorn looks on our faces.

"Did Lucy use her magic?" she asked in a worried tone.

Blake stood slowly as he answered, "It was Lily. She is back to her old tricks."

"Well, then, I would say that we are in a spot of trouble." Megan's worried gaze took us in, and icy waves of fear coursed down my body.

"What has happened?" Blake asked anxiously.

"The trucks are coming," she whispered, the color draining from her face.

I could tell she was trying to stay calm but was beginning to fail. Her hands began to shake as she rubbed them up and down her pant legs and then clasped them together in front of her.

"Go round up the others," Blake said, and I could see the determination gather in his brown eyes. "We are leaving. Now."

"Where are we going to go?" I asked, dread causing my voice to tremble.

"We have to go to the institution," Blake said in defeat. "I have tried to avoid it, but we have no other choice now."

My head swirled with confusion, fear, and pain. That dark place in the back of my mind beckoned, but I fearfully pulled away from its reaching embrace. I did not want to be trapped there again, did not want Lily taking over me again.

"Come on, sister. I will help you remember," she said enticingly, her voice echoing inside my head.

"No!" I said, and I said it aloud.

Blake jerked his gaze to me and raised his eyebrows questioningly. "Lucy, it is the only place we can go at this point."

I started to explain that I had not been speaking to him, but a sudden pull in my mind made me cry out in alarm. Blake was at my side in an instant.

I gave him a pleading look and opened my mouth to speak, but no sound came out. I was being pulled away again, and I fought with everything in me not to be pulled down into that abyss.

"Megan, it's happening again," Blake said. He released me and backed away as if afraid to touch me.

My heart gave a painful thump at his rejection, but I could understand his hesitation to touch me just now.

"We have no time, Blake. We have to do it now," Megan said as she pulled a syringe from the bedside table drawer.

Blake's eyebrows rose, and he gave Megan a fearful look. "Megan, are you sure? We have to leave, and you said it would make her sleep."

"You can carry her," Megan said matter-of-factly.

Fear caused my heart to race. "What is that?" I asked as Megan came toward me with the syringe.

The abyss pulled me harder, but I scrambled to stay in control.

"It is the first round of serum," Megan said. "It will make you sleep and keep her from coming out. You can trust me, Lucy."

I did. I had always trusted Megan, but Lily did not.

She began to fight, clawing her way to the surface of my mind, but I stubbornly pushed her back.

I gritted my teeth. "Hurry. She doesn't want you to give me the shot."

Blake moved quickly, wrapping his arms around me tightly and pinning my arms to my sides. I seethed as my shoulder burned with pain at the abuse.

"I'm sorry," Blake whispered against my ear.

I did not respond. I stood still in his embrace, concentrating on keeping the abyss from swallowing me up long enough for Megan to administer the shot.

I felt her rub my shoulder with an alcohol pad and then the needle's prick as it entered my skin. A slow burn coursed down my arm as the medicine entered my system.

Blake picked me up into his arms. I could feel the medicine's trail as it flowed through me, and everywhere it touched paralyzed my muscles. I began to panic, but Blake's face loomed in my vision.

"It is normal, Lucy. Relax and let it take hold. I got you."

Blake's voice was calm and soothing, and I relaxed in his arms. I felt the medicine trail close to my heart, and I began to panic again. Would it stop my heart? Fear clawed its way inside me, but Blake's soothing voice penetrated my murky thoughts.

"I'm right here. Everything is going to be fine."

His voice calmed me, and I relaxed once more, letting the medicine pull me into the darkness of surrender.

My eyes fluttered closed, and I drifted off into oblivion.

CHAPTER 12: The Doctor

Bright, intense light cut through the darkness and fuzziness in my mind. I was lying in a cloud of softness with solid arms wrapped around me, holding me close to a hard body that was breathing deeply and steadily.

I felt safe and comfortable and did not want to leave the protective shell I found myself in upon awakening.

"Lucy, honey! Breakfast!" my mommy called out.

The smell of freshly cooked bacon hit me, and I stretched my arms up over my head, careful not to accidentally punch my daddy in the face.

My stirring must have awoken him because he chuckled humorously and said, "Good morning, beautiful."

I smiled up at my daddy sleepily. "Good morning, daddy."

His smile widened as he asked, "Do you know what today is?"

I nodded vigorously. "It is my birthday. I am three years old today."

Daddy chuckled and said, "You are such a smart girl, Lucy."

I smiled proudly at my daddy's praise.

"You're such a little daddy's girl. It makes me sick," the jealous voice of my sister resonated inside my mind.

"You are not going to ruin my special day," I hissed back at her, and then I clamped the door to the dark spot in my brain tightly shut.

Lily would be livid with anger when I let her back out to play, but I was not in the mood for her tricks today. I wanted to enjoy my birthday without her interference.

Guilt swatted at me, but I ignored it. Lily did not have a birthday. She had never been born. She lived inside of me and always had. I supposed she could share my birthday, but her jealousy and hatred of my life caused her to act too recklessly.

I had to keep a tight grip on her at all times.

Daddy shifted and rolled away from me as he said, "Come on, princess. We better get out of bed before mommy sends a search party for us."

I giggled at daddy's silly joke and rolled off the opposite side of the bed. My tiny feet hit the floor, and I took off for the kitchen before daddy could stop me.

The smell of pancakes and bacon assaulted my nose as soon as I stepped into the warm kitchen, and I took a long appreciative sniff of the delicious aroma. Of course, I had smelled the bacon when I awakened, but I had not smelled the pancakes until now.

I climbed onto one of the chairs, sat at the table of our eat-in kitchen, and smiled at mommy, who stood at the stove, flipping a pancake in the pan.

She turned to smile at me, and I could see the worry in her eyes.

"What is wrong, mommy?" I asked softly.

She turned without answering and slid the freshly cooked pancake onto a plate. Next, she pulled a couple of pieces of bacon from the pile of cooked bacon that sat on a paper towel-lined plate and placed them beside the pancake.

She carried the plate to the table, sat it in front of me, turned to a drawer, pulled out a fork, and sat it on the plate. She picked up the syrup bottle and turned it over my pancake, allowing a good amount of the syrup to cover it before turning the bottle back up and snapping the lid closed.

"Eat your breakfast," mommy said sternly, but her eyes were soft as she stared at me.

"Mommy?" I asked, wanting desperately to know what caused the sadness in her eyes.

I didn't like mommy to be sad.

She smiled, but it was not a happy smile, and turned back to the stove as daddy walked into the kitchen. He kissed mommy on the cheek and then turned to prepare his plate.

I shrugged and picked up my fork. If mommy did not want to talk about it, I would not force her. Besides, it was my birthday, and I wanted to enjoy it. So I would let the adults handle their own problems.

I started to eat when I heard the roar of engines from the window behind the table. Mommy stiffened and turned to daddy with a question in her eyes.

"Couldn't they have waited until she had her breakfast?" mommy asked.

Daddy sighed. "The sooner, the better, dear. It has to be done."

A tear trickled down mommy's cheek as she came over to me. I had a bite of pancake in my mouth, so I swallowed it quickly as mommy sat beside me.

She smiled and swiped the tear from her cheek with her hand. "Lucy, your daddy and I have something to tell you."

"You are going on a birthday trip," daddy said, interrupting what mommy was about to say.

I looked back and forth between them questioningly. "What do you mean?" I asked.

"Well, since you are so smart, you will go to a special school with other children your age who are also smart like you." Mommy's voice was chipper, but the look in her eyes was miserable.

I knew the answer before I asked the question due to the look in mommy's eyes, but I had to ask it anyway. "Are you and daddy coming?"

"No, princess," daddy answered. "We cannot come with you, but we will be able to visit you all the time."

"They are lying," Lily's voice sang out in my head. *"If you leave, then you will never see them again."*

Fear squeezed my heart tight, and I could not breathe correctly. I heard the front door of the house slam open, and my parents jumped in surprise. Daddy picked me up and turned to face the intruders as they swarmed into the kitchen.

There were too many of them. They surrounded us in their dark suits and intimidating presence, and I could feel my daddy tremble as he held me in his arms.

"It is time to say your goodbyes," said a growling, menacing voice.

A man stepped out of the ring of men that had us surrounded and stepped forth into the kitchen. His domineering presence sent my heart skittering into my throat, and I could feel Lily pushing me to let her out.

She did not like it when I was afraid.

"Can she at least finish her breakfast?" daddy asked sadly.

"We have a schedule. Hand us the girl, and then you can go about your day," the man answered harshly.

Daddy sighed in defeat and gently placed me on the ground. "Go with the men, Lucy. You will be safe. I will send your things later."

I looked at my daddy with wide, frightened eyes as a tear slid down my cheek. I saw his eyes tremble as he turned away from me. Then, I looked over at my mommy, and she was not looking at me either.

Were they really going to give me away?

"I told you they did not love you," Lily's voice taunted me.

I felt a surge of prickling energy tingling in my fingertips, and I shut my eyes in dread. Lily was taking over, and when I was this scared and distraught, I could not stop her.

I narrowed my eyes and turned to the giant bald man looming over me with his hand outstretched. I fell into the abyss with Lily in charge as his great hand extended to grab me.

"Do not touch me," Lily's voice seethed out of my mouth.

"Well, you have some fire inside of you, don't you," The big bald man said.

"Oh no," I heard my daddy say. He knew that Lily had come out to play.

I heard mommy sob brokenly. She knew as well.

They knew that when Lily came out, there was always trouble, but right now, Lily was angry at them as well. She was mad at them for giving us away.

The bald man grabbed my arm, and I latched onto his mind before he could react. His eyes widened in surprise as I ordered him to turn and grab one of the surrounding men's guns.

Deep in the recesses of my mind, I screamed out to Lily.

"NO. That is too cruel. Please, don't do that."

She did not listen to my pleas. I watched in utter horror as Lily forced the bald man to start shooting the men surrounding us. I heard my mommy's terrified screams and my daddy calling out to me in shocked disbelief.

I laughed sadistically as the bald man with the snake tattoo gunned down his men and then turned his gun toward my parents.

Anger blossomed inside me, deep and rage-filled, and I clawed my way back to the front of my mind and shut Lily down, casting her deep into that darkness and closing the door shut before she could do any more damage.

The bald man lowered the gun, breathing heavily and shooting me a hateful glare.

"You were going to make me shoot your own parents?" he asked in disbelief.

I lowered my gaze and answered somberly, "It wasn't me. It was Lily."

"Lily?" The bald man asked.

"This is what we were telling the doctor about," daddy said in a defeated tone. "We love Lucy, but we did not know how to handle Lily any longer, and now she has killed people."

The bald man nodded in understanding as he gave me a sympathetic look and said, "Well, we will fix that when we get you to school."

I raised a questioning glance at him, but his face remained stoic. He motioned for me to follow.

"Come this way, Lucy. I will not touch you again. We do not want to give Lily a reason to come back out."

I glanced back at my parents, but they looked away from me and did not say a word. My mommy was huddled into daddy's side, crying wordlessly as great sobs shook her body.

They would not even look at me.

"I will have this cleaned up," the bald man said, gesturing toward the bloody bodies on the floor before turning and walking away. "Come, Lucy."

Tears streamed down my face as I turned and followed the bald man out of the kitchen, out of my house, and away from my life.

*** APRIL 5, PRESENT DAY ***

I gasped, and a huge lungful of breath entered my oxygen-starved body. I had been holding my breath as the end of the memory played out in my head.

Tears were running down my cheeks, and the pain in my heart exploded throughout my entire body. Sobs wracked me as I awoke from the state of remembering and into the present, and I curled myself into a tight ball and cried out my frustrations.

My parents had given me up. They had promised to come and visit, but they never did. The school they had sent me to was not even a school. It had been a hospital-like facility that had done unspeakable things to me and others like me.

It had been more like a prison. A prison for mutated DNA patients like me.

I lay in the strange bed and cried until I could not weep any longer, and then I sat up in bed and stared at the wall.

I thought about the memory and how alone I had felt when I realized my parents were giving me away. I thought about Lily's anger and what she had done to the men.

Now I could see what Blake had been talking about when it came to Lily. She had been vicious and cruel, but at the same time, she had tried to protect me from the men.

I did not agree with her methods, nor did Blake. We both thought that Lily was too cruel.

As if my thinking of him had conjured him up, he came walking into my bedroom with a worried look on his features. He frowned slightly when he saw me sitting up in bed, staring at the wall in front of me.

"Lucy?" he asked tentatively.

I turned to look at him and smiled sadly. "Hi, Blake."

"How are you feeling?" he asked as he moved carefully into the room.

"Like I'm losing my mind," I answered jokingly, but I was not feeling very jovial.

I saw Blake visibly relax and let out a relieved sigh. I knew what he had been thinking. He had been wondering if Lily had taken back over or not.

But she had not. She was gone again. The abyss in the back of my mind lay empty.

"I think the procedure is working," I said with a hopeful note. "I had my first memory."

Blake sat down in the chair that was beside my bed. "Do you want to talk about it?"

I turned to hang my legs off the side of the bed. It was a comfortable bed, but it seemed so cold and unwelcoming. I gazed around at the clean white room with its hard, polished marble floors and different medical equipment placed strategically throughout.

"Where are we?" I asked, ignoring Blake's offer to talk. I was not ready to talk about it just yet. I was still processing.

"We are at the institution," Blake answered.

"Okay, and where is the institution?" I asked frustratingly.

"You shouldn't know that," Blake said enigmatically. "It is best that you remain unaware."

"Fine. Let me try a different question. What is the institution?" I asked.

"Now that I can answer," Blake said with a smile. "This institution was founded by Dianna's mother, whom I believe you know, and my father, whom you also know."

I frowned and gestured for Blake to continue.

"Keep in mind, Lucy, that we had to give you a whole new life after you were decommissioned. As a result, some people in your life are not who you think they are." Blake paused speculatively for a moment.

"I am already starting to understand that, Blake. Just get on with it already," I said, rolling my eyes in exasperation.

"Okay," Blake said, and then took a deep breath and blew it out slowly before continuing. "Dianna's mother is Megan."

Surprise shook me, and I widened my eyes and stared at Blake in disbelief. "Really?"

Blake nodded, but a twitch of a smile raised the corners of his mouth. "She thinks of you as her daughter as well, as if you and Dianna really were sisters."

My surprise turned to warmth and love, and a bright smile spread across my face. "I always thought of Megan as a mother figure. She was the closest thing to a mother I had while I was in the hospital after my…well…whatever happened to me up there on that mountain. I still don't have that memory back yet."

"You will soon enough," Blake said confidently.

"So, who is your father?" I asked.

"Doctor Sam Sheppard, your doctor," Blake said. "I am Blake Montgomery, though. I have my mother's last name. She never took my father's name after they were married for work purposes, and they both agreed to let me have her name. They thought it sounded better."

He sat nervously, waiting for my reaction, and I saw him visibly relax when I smiled and said, "Well, that is good. I did not want to have to get used to calling you something else whenever I need to scold you."

Blake laughed, a hearty, happy laugh that made me smile and chased more of the sadness away.

"So, the doc and Megan run this place?" I asked as I looked around the large room once more.

Blake nodded proudly. "Not only that but, as I said before, they built it. They built it to help other children like us and to bring down the organization."

"What organization?" I asked curiously, but Blake chuckled and shook his head.

"A few more bouts of the procedure, and you will know everything yourself." He said as he stood from the chair.

I hopped down from the bed, and pain shot up my leg. I had forgotten about my leg and shoulder. I winced but stood my ground as I reached out to Blake.

"You're leaving?" I asked in disappointment. "You just got here."

I hobbled toward him, but Blake took a step back. I froze. Pain and hurt lanced through my heart, and I did not try to hide it as I pierced him with my agonized glare.

Blake closed his eyes tightly and said, "Lucy, please don't look at me that way."

"Blake, what is wrong? Please, I need you to hold me right now."

I had finally admitted how much I needed him and hoped it was not too late. I felt vulnerable and naked, standing at the edge of a precipice and ready to fall in at any moment. Would Blake catch me, or would he let me fall to my death?

He opened his eyes slowly and gave me a tortured look as he took one more step back. "I don't know if it is safe, Lucy. I don't want to be forced to hurt you again."

Then, I understood his hesitation. I was afraid too, but we could not shy away from each other forever because of Lily.

I took a shaky step closer, reaching my hand out for him as I said, "She is gone for now, Blake. I need you. The memory I had was awful."

I saw his throat work as he swallowed, and his eyes grew even more tortured as he watched me walk closer to him. He stood his ground this time and did not move, nor did he move forward or reach out for me.

His voice was strained as he stuttered, "Lucy…I…."

I interrupted before he could say more, putting all the emotion I was feeling into my voice and face. I wanted him to see and hear how much I wanted his touch…needed his touch.

"Please, Blake. Don't let Lily's actions keep you away from me. I need you."

That was his undoing.

With a tortured moan, he closed the distance between us, scooped me into his arms, and carried me back to the bed. He laid me down gently, climbed onto the bed beside me, wrapped me up in his arms, and pulled me close.

We lay face-to-face as he laid gentle kisses all along my eyelids, cheeks, and forehead as he whispered my name repeatedly.

"Lucy…Lucy…my sweet Lucy."

I raised my face to him, inviting him to capture my mouth with his as he rained kisses all over my face. He placed his lips to mine softly, tenderly, and began to move his lips over mine. He kissed me slowly at first, and when I parted my lips under his, he gave a needful groan and deepened the kiss, sucking my bottom lip into his mouth and swiping it with his tongue.

Liquid desire shot through my veins, bringing forth a sound from my chest as I draped my leg over Blake's hip to drag him closer to my body, which was my hurt leg. My good arm was trapped under me, so I brought up my other arm to wrap my fingers into his hair as he kissed me.

Pain shot through my arm, and I pulled away from the kiss to gasp at the sudden agony of trying to use both of my hurt extremities simultaneously. Blake moved back away from me instantly.

"Dammit, Lucy. You are still hurt." His voice was chiding but gentle as he rolled off the bed and helped me gingerly sit up.

I let out a soft chuckle, which was mixed with a sob. "I forgot. I just needed you to hold me, Blake. I needed to know that you still wanted me. My mother and father did not want me anymore."

"Oh, Lucy," Blake said, and he knelt on the floor in front of me where I sat on the bed with my legs hanging off. He gazed up into my eyes, and the brown color of his irises shone in the overhead lights.

"Lucy, I will always want you. Never doubt that, okay?"

I nodded but was too choked up to reply. Blake wiped at a tear that fell down my face as he smiled up at me, and just like that, the doubt and sadness disappeared.

Blake's smile was my whole world.

There was a knock on the door, and Blake stood up suddenly.

"Who's there?" he asked loudly.

"It's your father," a deep voice called.

Blake smiled, and my heart jumped in my chest. I had not seen Doctor Sheppard since my last and final check-up when I was only twelve years old. However, I had always liked him and was excited to see him again.

Blake walked over to the door and opened it, smiling broadly at the tall man that strolled into the room. He was lean and lanky, just as I had remembered him, but his black hair was now streaked with white, and he wore spectacles over his faded blue eyes.

He had the same sharpness to his features and the same strong jawline, but now he had wrinkles along the corners of his full lips and almond-shaped eyes. Now that I knew Doc Sheppard was Blake's father, I could see the strong resemblance between him and his son.

Other than the color of his eyes and Doc's face being thinner, they could have passed for twins. It made me wonder if that had been the reason I had liked him so much.

Doc smiled brightly at me and said happily, "Lucy, how is my favorite patient today?"

'*Nope, that was not the only reason,*' I thought. Doc had a quality about him that made him likable.

I gave Doctor Sheppard an equally bright smile and said, "Doc! I have missed you."

Doc came over to the side of my bed and sat in Blake's recently vacated chair.

"I missed seeing you as well, Lucy, but Blake has kept me informed of your well-being," Doc said kindly. "How are your injuries today?"

"I am better, but my arm and leg still hurt," I answered.

The doc gave me a piercing gaze, then slid his gaze to Blake. He clucked and said, "Well, your arm and leg would heal faster if my boy could learn to keep his hands to himself."

Blake's pale skin darkened to a crimson red across his cheeks, the bridge of his nose, and his forehead. I stared in surprise. I had never seen Blake blush before.

Hell, I had never seen any grown man blush before. I placed my hand over my mouth to stifle my laughter as Blake darted an indignant look toward his father.

"Dad, do you always have to embarrass me?" he asked, huffing.

Doc shrugged and said, in a matter-of-fact tone, "It is one of my fatherly duties."

I could not hold back any longer. Laughter erupted from me, and I doubled over on the bed. Blake shot me an irritated look.

"Don't encourage him," he said frustratingly, making me laugh harder.

Blake huffed and sat down in the other seat next to the table, waiting for my bout of hysteria to wear off. Doctor Sheppard left his seat, went to the closet, and pulled out a folded wheelchair.

He unfolded it and rolled it over to me. With a smile, he said, "If my chivalrous son would not mind rolling you around, how about we take a tour of the hospital?"

I glanced at Blake, who was still sulking in the chair. "I would like that," I said.

Blake looked up at me with a hopeful glance. "I would love to escort you around, Lucy."

I smiled and held out my hand to him. "Help me into the chair?" I said.

I did not really need it, but I knew that he loved having any excuse to touch me, and right now, I just wanted to wipe that sullen look from his face.

It worked. He smiled brightly and took my hand, helping me stand, hobble over to the chair, and sit down in the wheelchair. He bent down over me and placed his mouth next to my ear.

"Are you ready for your carriage ride around the town, my lady?" he asked jokingly.

I laughed and said, "Take me away, sir knight."

Blake rolled me toward the door where Doc stood, holding it open for us. He shook his head at us, but he had a smile on his face.

He peered at me over his spectacles as I rolled past, and just that one look into my eyes told me everything I needed to know. He was happy to have me back.

And…

I was home.

CHAPTER 13: The Organization

The hospital, or the Mutated DNA Research Hospital as it was called, was not very large. The hospital housed a team of doctors and scientists that did various jobs that I did not understand. They had a vast laboratory where they all worked at their separate stations.

In addition to the massive lab room, the facility had rooms for the doctors and scientists to store their things in, examination rooms, and standard living rooms such as a sitting room, a kitchen, a sizeable cafeteria-style dining area, and a cozy library for down times.

There were other personal rooms that Doc did not show me because they were private living quarters for the doctors and scientists that lived on campus. Dianna and Chris had each been given a room to stay in, as had I.

I had many questions which Blake and Doctor Sheppard were happy to answer, but many of the answers were complicated and confusing. What I could understand was that some children were born with a mutated DNA strand. The mutated DNA gave these children particular abilities to manipulate and control things; this hospital helped those children and studied their condition.

Blake, Doctor Sheppard's own son, was a mutant. He had the ability to control the elements; earth, air, fire, and water. He had a 'physical' power, so he was considered a physical.

In my case, I could manipulate minds, which was considered to be one of the most powerful 'mental' abilities; I was a mental. However, my mind and abilities were different.

I had been born with another entity in my brain. My twin sister lived inside my mind because I had absorbed her into myself in the womb. This was common in normal pregnancies, but mine was different because of the mutated DNA strand.

Doctor Sheppard and Blake did not explain much about the other organization to me as we toured the hospital of MDRT, which was the short name for the organization of Mutated DNA Research Team, the organization that Doc and Megan had founded.

Blake said he would explain more about the other institution when I gained more memories back. That was fine with me. I did not want to know much more about them from what I already remembered. After all, they were trying to kill me.

After the tour, Doctor Sheppard left us at the door to my room and went off to catch up on his work. Blake silently rolled me into my room and helped me out of the chair and back onto my bed.

He folded the chair back up and placed it back into the closet. I watched him work, watched the muscles in his arms bulge as he lifted the chair into the closet. His tousled black hair was getting long and hung almost to his shoulders.

How long had it been since he had cut it?

He turned back to me and caught me watching him, and a sly smile stretched across his lips. I felt the heat crawl up my neck and cheeks, but I smiled shyly and held his gaze.

He stalked over to me, graceful and slow, and my heart leaped into my throat. He stopped before me and bent low to place a chaste kiss on my forehead. I raised my face to him, wanting him to kiss me again, but he drew back quickly with a mischievous gleam in his brown eyes.

"We will pick up where we left off after your shoulder and leg are healed," he said softly. He stroked my cheek gently with his hand before turning and walking toward the door.

He turned back to me before exiting and said with a soft smile, "get some sleep, Lucy. I will see you tomorrow."

He left, closing the door soundly behind him.

I sighed and got up to use the bathroom before showering and going to bed. It had been a long couple of days, and I felt I could finally sleep peacefully without the complication of nightmares.

Tomorrow, I would take another bought of memory serum, so I would not be getting any peaceful sleep then. I was hoping to get some undisturbed rest tonight.

My head felt clearer without the dark presence of my sister lurking around in its depths, thanks to one unexpected side-effect of the memory serum.

The injection Megan had given me just before we escaped her home awakened receptors in my brain, bringing my memories back during sleep. The unexpected part was that the awakened receptors had reactivated a chip that had been surgically implanted into my brain when I was a child.

I did not have my full memories of that event yet, so Blake and Megan explained; The chip was a device that kept that dark side of my mind dormant, which kept Lily out of my head. The way I understood it was that the chip kept Lily asleep. If the chip ever malfunctioned or was deactivated again, Lily would be able to awaken once more.

The chip had malfunctioned before because the organization had tried to recommission me. The recommissioning serum shut down reactors in my brain, which took away most mutant's memories during the recommissioning process. Unfortunately, the parts that were shut down were connected to the chip.

Lily awoke for a time and had complete control, and I was out of commission. I had been locked down in a sleep state, and Lily had caused some chaos during that time; her troublemaking had assisted in my escape from WAMB, so we could not be too angry with her.

When MDRT finally captured Lily, Doctor Sheppard deactivated the chip, bringing me back out and trapping Lily inside again. The scientists came up with a serum that would keep that part of my mind dormant without the aid of the chip, but I had to take weekly doses of it.

Hence, the jelly doughnuts that my 'mom' would bring me every week. Lily had begun to awaken when I failed to eat the doughnuts during my birthday trip.

I stared at myself in the mirror as I stood in the bathroom, waiting for the running water in the shower to heat up before stepping in.

I frowned at my reflection. I noticed that my hair had gotten lighter. It had been black for as long as I could remember, but now there were a few light blond wisps hidden throughout. I raised my eyebrows in surprise. I kind of liked it, but I wondered why it happened.

I turned my attention back to the shower and stepped inside, relishing the feel of the hot water sliding over my body. Every muscle relaxed, and I enjoyed the sensation of the water for a time before I began to wash my hair and body.

When I finally emerged clean and refreshed from my shower, the mirror was steamed over, and I could no longer see my reflection.

I rolled my arm around gingerly, testing my sore shoulder as I turned my head to see the wound. It was still an angry red gash, and I figured it would need another bandage, but I could not do it alone. My leg, too, would require another bandage, I realized as I looked down and saw pink rivulets of water running down my calf. It must have started to bleed again under the spray of the water.

I sighed and wrapped a towel around my body before leaving the hot, steamy bathroom and stepping out into the cool hospital room, which would be my bedroom for an undesignated amount of time.

Thankful that I had been able to keep up with my cell phone through everything that had happened, I picked it up from the bedside table and unlocked the screen. I already knew who I wanted to call. Blake picked up on the second ring.

"Hello?" I smiled at the deep tenor of his sleepy voice, but a pang of guilt wiped the smile from my face.

"Blake? Did I wake you?" I said softly into the phone.

"Lucy?" he said. "Why are you calling so late? Is everything alright?"

I sat down on the bed as my leg began to ache. "I just got out of the shower."

I heard Blake's mischievous chuckle over the line and knew that a snarky comment was coming before he even said anything.

"Well, please be my guest if you want to talk dirty over the phone." His voice had dropped to his low, seductive tone that made me shiver with pleasure.

I scoffed playfully. "Blake, be serious. I need your help."

"Oh, I think you can manage to talk dirty to me all on your own," he said seductively.

I swallowed hard. He was right; I sure could think of some dirty things that I wanted to do to him, but now was not the time.

Plus, I would only embarrass myself anyway.

I cleared my throat and rolled my eyes at his antics as I responded, "Seriously, Blake. I need help with my arm and leg. I need new bandages."

Blake chuckled. "Why didn't you call Megan?"

'*Because I want you to come over here and kiss me senseless again*,' I wanted to say, but instead, I said, "Because I knew you would not yell at me for waking you."

"No, but I can think of some other interesting ways to punish you," he said, and my heart fluttered in response.

Yes, please.

…Blake lightly slapping my naked ass while I lay on my stomach on the bed, right before he climbs over me and…

"Lucy, are you still there?" Blake's voice crashed through my thoughts.

I shook my head to clear it of the thoughts I had running through my mind as I answered, "Yes, I'm here. Are you going to come help me or not?"

My tone sounded more irritated than I had wanted, but how could I not be frustrated when he put those thoughts into my head?

Blake chuckled again, seemingly aware of what kind of thoughts he had put in my mind, and answered, "Yes, Lucy. I will be right over."

"Thank you," I said more softly. "I will see you soon."

"See you soon," he said and disconnected the call.

I took a breath and rushed to the bathroom to brush my wet, tangled hair, hoping that I would be able to get it brushed with one arm. I managed it somehow and had only just gotten all of the tangles out when there was a knock on my bedroom door.

I was thinking how fast Blake had gotten to my room when the familiar buzz of energy flew up my arms. I sucked in a breath, thinking that Lily was trying to wake up, but that was not it. I concentrated on the buzzing momentarily, and a feeling of dread ran through my entire body.

I did not want to open that door. I could feel that someone was on the other side of that door that meant me harm, which meant that it was not Blake. My heart sped up and threatened to beat out of my chest, and my breath became short and ragged.

Who was on the other side of that door?

"How the hell did you get in here?" I heard Blake's voice thunder down the hallway outside of the room.

I heard a maniacal laugh and sounds of a struggle, and then Blake let out a loud 'oomph!' sound.

Blake!

I rushed to open the door, gripping the towel around me like a lifeline.

"Blake!" I shouted as I stepped out into the hallway and ran into something rigid and unmoving.

"No, Lucy!" I heard Blake yell, and then a vice-like grip clamped around my uninjured arm.

I squeaked in protest and looked up at my captor to meet a pair of stormy gray eyes. "I got you now, girl, and you will come with me this time whether you want to or not!"

I struggled with all my strength to pull away from his grip, but he only tightened his hold and pulled me roughly against him, wrapping me in one of his bulging arms with my back to his front.

The towel had slipped in my struggles, exposing one of my breasts, but Waller's arm covered it as he held me to his chest. I kicked and screamed in his arm, but it was no use. He was much too strong.

The sound of a gunshot had my heart leaping into my throat, and I froze, not wanting to look down the hallway, not wanting to see if Blake had been shot.

I lifted my gaze with dread and breathed a sigh of relief when Blake's brown gaze met mine. One of the men in suits had him pinned to the ground with one knee. He was raising Blake's head off the ground by a handful of his hair with one hand and had a pistol in his other hand aimed at the back of Blake's head.

"No, please," I whispered, and my voice cracked with terror.

"You can come with me quietly, and lover boy can live to see another day," Waller said into my ear. "Keep fighting me, and you will see his brains splattered all over this nice, clean floor."

I instantly stopped fighting and went limp in his arms. Tears began to fill my eyes as I stared into Blake's tortured face. His eyes narrowed in fury, and I knew he was going to try something, but I begged and pleaded with my eyes as I shook my head slightly.

"Lucy…," his voice was strained from being held down, and my heart broke at the desperation in his tone.

"Please, Blake. I could not bear to see…." I trailed off, but I knew he had understood.

The suit let go of his hair, and he dropped his head to the floor. The suit stood, but Blake remained on the ground, and I thought I heard a tortured, muffled scream of rage as Waller turned me around and started walking, pushing me forward in front of him.

I tried to take one more look over my shoulder, but Waller shoved me forward and made me stumble. I caught myself and wrapped the towel securely around me again as I wobbled unsteadily down the hallway toward the exit door at the end of the hall.

I felt a tingle of something in the back of my mind, but I made no reaction. Instead, I walked more quickly, not wanting Waller to touch me, fearing that if he touched me, he would be able to tell that I was using my gift.

Apparently, he had not needed to touch me.

"I can feel that, Lucy. Do not try anything. I do not want to be forced to hurt you," Waller said in a threatening tone.

"I am not doing it on purpose," I said innocently. It was true.

"Fine, but Lily had better stay put, and I know she can hear me."

I smiled inside. Good, let him think it was Lily. That would give me time because I knew what this was. This was my own power filling me. I kept walking and concentrating on that spot inside my mind, reaching out to Blake because I knew that was who was trying to reach me

"Lucy," his worried voice echoed in my head. *"Lucy, stay calm, okay? Can you do that?"*

"I am calm," I answered silently, keeping my mind's voice steady. *"What do I do?"*

"Do whatever they say. Don't panic, and don't act irrationally. We will come for you." Blake's voice was direct and commanding, and I knew he would do what he could until I was safe.

I closed off the connection quickly as we came to the exit door, and the buzzing energy was gone when Waller grabbed my upper arm before opening the door.

"I cannot have you falling down the stairs now, can I?" he sneered as he opened the door and ushered me through. "You be a good girl for the nice man now."

He nodded to one of the suits, and the man picked me up quickly and hauled me over his shoulder. I gripped tightly to the towel, holding it on me as I was draped over the man's shoulder and carried down the stairs.

It was humiliating, and I only hoped that I was adequately covered. Tears began to fall from my eyes as I flopped helplessly over the stranger's shoulder as he carried me down three flights of stairs. We finally reached the bottom, and the man sat me down on my feet.

I gripped the towel around me, narrowing my eyes at Waller as he approached me with a smirk.

"You could at least have let me get dressed," I said, keeping my voice calm and steady.

"I have provided clothes where you are going," Waller said, and I shivered at the coldness in his tone. "I am not hip to the latest trends, but they will due."

Was this a joke?

If he was going to kill me, why didn't he get it over with? Why would he even offer me clothes, much less have some ready for me? I did not ask. I was not sure I even wanted to know the answer.

"I thought you were dead," I said calmly. I knew I was goading him, but I wanted to buy some time. I did not want to leave this place with him.

Waller's smirk widened. "I knocked the gun away before that brainwashed idiot could shoot. You should not have turned away before Lily could finish the job."

I snarled. "If I had known then what I know now, I would have done it myself," I seethed.

Waller scoffed and replied, "you are too soft for that, Lucy. That is what you have Lily for."

I narrowed my eyes at him, but he only pointed toward the exit door and said stonily, "Go, follow the soldiers, and do not lag. Do not make me force you again."

I swallowed the lump in my throat and turned to exit the door with the suits. I followed behind at a steady pace as I gritted my teeth against the pain in my leg.

We walked across a tiny parking lot, and I glanced longingly at the red sedan parked there. It was Blake's. Cold chills ran through me as I spotted the solid black SUV in the lot.

I needed to get away before we got to the SUV, but what could I do? If I ran, they would shoot me. The suits all wore those exasperating metal bands, so I could not use my power on them.

Suddenly, a memory reached the surface of my mind. It was not a lost memory but a recent one and one that I had just been discussing with Waller.

Lily had been in control of my mind as we had run from the suits back home. She had taken over one of the suits, even though he had worn his protective band.

I remember her thinking inside my head that she could not take Waller's mind, but the suits were easy. How had she done it? I concentrated hard, and the familiar tingling of energy came, starting at my fingertips and running up my arms.

I was careful to stay ahead of Waller so that he would not suspect anything. Discreetly, I pointed my palms out in front of me and sent the prickling rush into the suit I was following. Nothing happened at first, but then I felt the energy attempting to enter the man's mind.

I hit some barrier, and I knew it was the protective band preventing my entry into his mind. I huffed in frustration as I noticed the trucks getting closer, and I pushed harder against the invisible shield.

I pushed as hard as possible, but it was no use. How had Lily done it? Suddenly, the answer rushed into the front of my mind. The bands were defective. There was a weak spot in the shields; a hole in the tight shields was right under the ear.

How had I known that?

There was no time to question it now. I simply gathered all the energy I could and aimed it at the precise spot where I knew it would enter, and a rush ran through my body when my mind connected with the suit's.

I surged forward with a sudden burst of speed as I sent my silent commands to the suit. I glanced behind me to see Waller's surprised eyes follow my movements, which was just what I wanted to see.

While he was distracted, I commanded the suit to punch him in his smug face, which caused a series of chaotic commotions that gave me a chance to slip away and hide behind one of the other vehicles in the lot.

The suits were confused as the traitor, the suit under my command, continued to fight Waller and the other suits. He was getting his ass kicked, but it was still a distraction. I peeked around the side of the white car I had hidden behind and saw Waller peering around the parking lot as the suit was taken down and subdued.

I snapped my mind away from the suit and sent the energy away from me. I needed to concentrate on getting away and hiding, and I could not do that if Waller felt my power. Besides, I no longer needed the suit. I ducked back behind the vehicle as Waller's gaze came close, hoping he had not seen me.

I searched my surroundings, not having the time to look at them before, and had to stifle a gasp of surprise at the massive amount of trees surrounding the building. It was as if someone had built the hospital in the middle of a dense forest. A single road led out of the parking lot and down a tree-lined lane, but there were no other roads or paths around.

My heart leaped with hope. If I could make it into the trees, I could surely find a place to hide. There was probably a bush or underbrush thick enough to hide me, or I could climb up into a tree and hide in its branches. The possibilities were endless, but first, I had to make it to the trees. If I ran and they spotted me, they would shoot me. I would have to be stealthy.

As slowly and silently as possible, I peeked around the side of the vehicle once more. The edge of the parking lot and the beginning of the tree line were only a couple of feet from my hiding spot. If things went my way, they would search on the other side of the parking lot.

I breathed a sigh of relief when I spotted Waller and two of the suits scanning the area around Blake's car, and the other two suits were kneeling and peering under the SUVs.

This was it. It was now or never.

Crouching down as low as I could, I moved quickly and silently toward the line of trees. I held my breath, expecting at any moment to hear a shout of discovery or a gunshot, but none came. I crashed into the trees and breathed a sigh of relief, but my liberation was short-lived as I glanced at the area around me.

The floor of the forest was not going to be easy to traverse. Thick underbrush and weeds littered the forest floor. I moved forward carefully and realized that fallen branches and other things were hidden under the weeds and underbrush.

I would have to move carefully and slowly, but I did not have time for that. I was also barefoot, which hindered me even more. Oh, and how could I forget the stupid towel, which was the only cover I had against my nakedness?

Every step I took forward would snag the edges of my towel, causing me to grasp it harder against my chest. My leg ached, and my shoulder began to throb painfully. I turned to gauge how far I had traversed into the woods, and my heart sank as I realized I had only gone a couple of feet in.

I could still see the men searching the parking lot through the branches of the trees, and one of them began scanning the tree line around the parking lot.

I turned and began to push my way through the dense forest more quickly, ignoring the snagging branches and allowing the towel to fall to the forest floor. I could not afford to be modest if I was going to escape.

The branches and weeds scratched against my bare skin, and I winced in pain with every scrape, but I pushed on. I dared another glance over my shoulder and was relieved to find that I could no longer see the parking lot.

Good. That meant that they could not see me either.

I turned and pushed on and noticed that the darkness began to creep around me. The further into the woods I went, the darker it became. The tops of the trees hid the sunlight, and only strips of it could be seen fighting through the branches of the trees.

The land began to slope upward, and I found myself using my hands to climb up through the denseness of the forest, grabbing onto branches and using them to pull me up the inclined ground. Stabbing pains began to shoot through my arm and leg, but I ignored them and pushed on.

I came to the top of the steep hill that I had been climbing and crumpled to the ground in relief when I found clear, grassy ground at the top. I sank into the soft grass and sat for a moment, allowing the shooting pains to calm to a dull throb. I checked my arms and legs and found angry red welts and scratches all over them, and I could only imagine what my back and buttocks looked like.

A sound reached my ears, the snapping of twigs and the swishing of bodies moving through the underbrush. My heart began to race inside my chest as I scrambled to my feet and prepared to run down the other side of the hill. I glanced around quickly for somewhere to hide, thinking that maybe the person would pass me by and I would not have to run down the hill.

There were a few trees here, but all the lowest branches were broken or too high for me to reach. There was a large clump of underbrush and weeds that I could hide in, but in my naked state, I would probably do more damage to my body than was safe.

The sounds grew closer, and I turned to spring down the hill, but the sound of a voice stopped me dead in my tracks.

"She is in this area somewhere," Blake's worried voice said. "The towel was hers."

"She better be," another voice said, and chills ran up and down my spine at the sound. "If we do not find her by morning, you are dead."

Waller.

He had Blake, and he would use him to find me and take me away. I sighed in defeat. This would never end until he had me. I began to feel Dianna's words she had spoken back in our dorm room. I did not understand them at the time, but I understood them now.

"Fine, Blake. Take her and hide her away as you have done her entire life. You can't run forever, though. They will find you."

In an icy tone, she added, "And when they find her, you know what they will do."

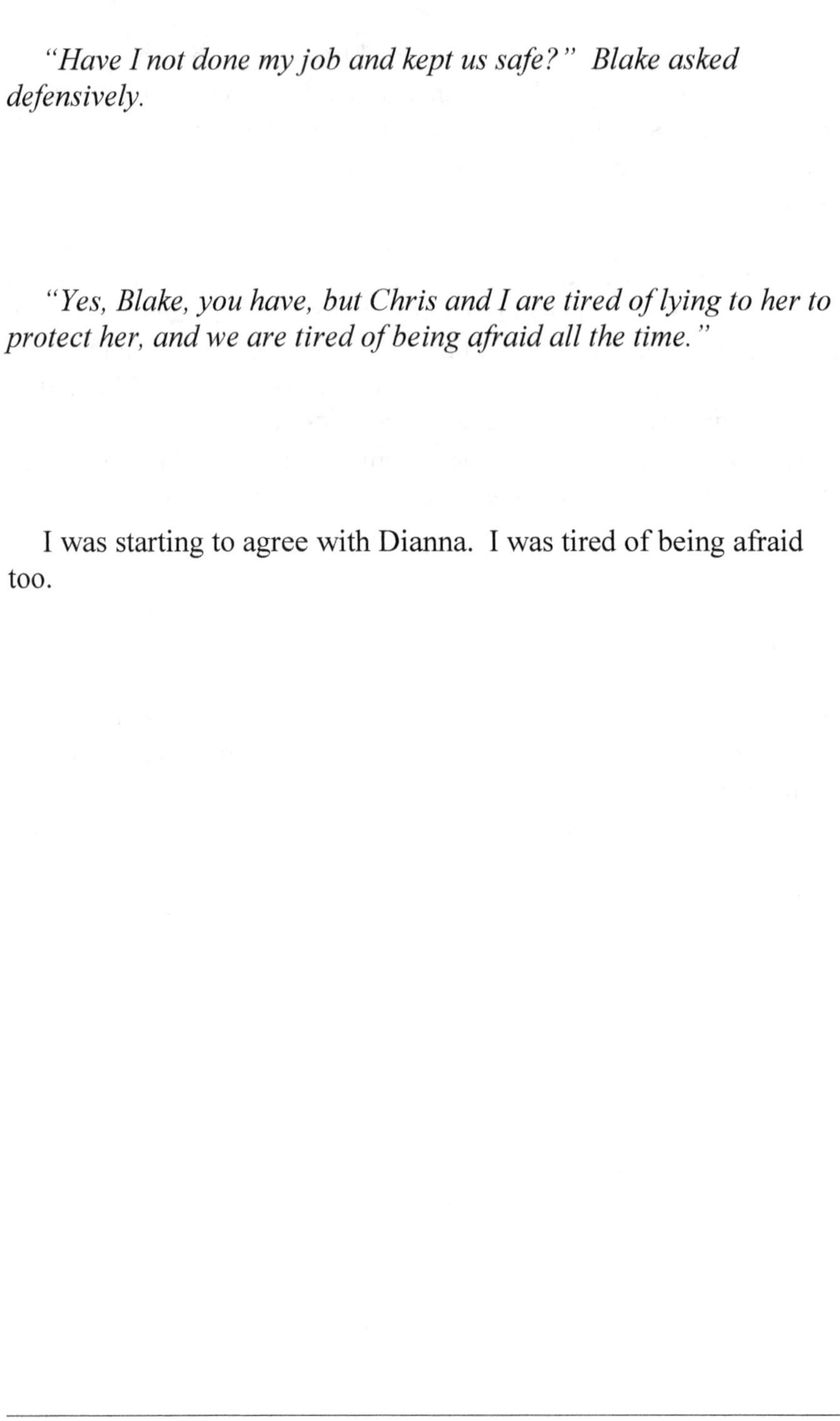

"Have I not done my job and kept us safe?" Blake asked
defensively.

*"Yes, Blake, you have, but Chris and I are tired of lying to her to
protect her, and we are tired of being afraid all the time."*

I was starting to agree with Dianna. I was tired of being afraid
too.

CHAPTER 14: The Great Escape

The voices were coming from below, so I lay on the ground and peeked over the steep hill's edge. They were moving around the bottom of the hill but made no move to begin climbing.

This was good.

If they stayed at the bottom of the hill, then I could track their movements and devise a plan to save Blake from Waller's clutches.

"She could not have gotten far without clothes," Blake said. "She has to be around here somewhere."

Blake continued to move around the bottom of the hill, and Waller followed close behind, pointing a rifle that he had balanced on his shoulder at Blake's back.

There were no suits, and I wondered where his men were.

I was about to follow the movements of Blake and Waller as they circled the hill when I heard a low, slow growl behind me. The hairs on the back of my neck stood on end at the sound, and I turned slowly around.

The biggest black cat I had ever seen crept silently out of the underbrush. The large, yellow eyes regarded me silently. Its sleek, black fur reflected the sunlight slanting in through the tree branches as it crouched and lowered to the ground as if to spring on its prey.

I must have been the prey.

My eyes went wide with fear, and I wanted to scream. I clamped a hand over my mouth to stifle the sound. If I screamed, I would alert Waller to my presence and put Blake in danger.

I bit back my scream and shrank back to the ground. I was about to be torn apart by this wild panther. I choked back a sob as it crept closer, moving slowly and low to the ground.

I noticed something dragging the ground under its mouth, and my eyes widened in surprise. It was clothes! This giant panther was bringing me clothes!

Dianna's face came to mind, and I pictured her sitting in a dark room with her fingers against her temples. Obviously, she could control all forms of wildlife, not just birds. She had probably called the cat to her window, dropped the clothes out, and ordered it to find me and give me the clothes.

I prayed with everything in me that this was the case.

The panther moved closer, and I could now see the bundle of clothes more clearly. I could see they were neatly bundled as if someone had arranged them that way. The cat made no move to harm me in any way.

I wanted to laugh out loud, but my hand was still clamped over my mouth. I watched the panther drop the clothes at my feet. Then, tentatively, I reached out and grabbed them, holding them up against my chest as I waited for the cat's next move.

It backed away silently, moving toward where it had appeared, then turned and fled silently back into the underbrush. I moved quickly, standing and pulling on the clothes it had brought me.

The clothes were rolled up and tied into a bundle, and I was delighted to find hiking boots tied up in them. I pulled on the sweat pants, long-sleeve t-shirt, and socks, then put on the hiking boots and laced them up.

I felt better now that I had some clothes. I wished she had sent underwear, but I could not complain. I had clothes.

I heard the growl again, but it was coming from below, close to where I had last seen Blake and Waller. Again, my heart fluttered in my chest.

The cat had finished its mission, so it was probably free from Dianna's control. Was it going after Waller and Blake? I crept to the edge of the hill where I thought Blake and Waller were and saw them standing very still and peering toward a thick pile of underbrush.

I could not see into it from up here on the top of the hill, but I could guess that the panther was under there, creeping up on them much as it had on me.

Waller had the gun pointed at it, but it did not seem to be slowing it down. Suddenly, Blake glanced up and caught my eye. I gasped. Did he know I was up here? I could have sworn I saw him wink before he turned his attention back to the advancing cat.

Waller took aim and pulled the trigger, but Blake shoved his entire body into Waller at the last second, and the shot went wide. The cat took its chance and sprang onto Waller, and Blake ran as fast as he could through the thick forest floor. He climbed up rapidly, heading straight for me as the panther battled his prey.

I could hear Waller's screams of pain and rage as the cat continued its assault, but I paid no attention to that battle. I only had eyes for Blake as he climbed to the top of the hill and came straight toward me.

I got to my feet and ran toward him, meeting him halfway and throwing myself into his arms. He caught me easily, wrapping his arms around my waist and pulling me up against him. I wrapped my arms around his shoulders and my legs around his hips, clinging to him tightly as I buried my face in the crook of his neck.

Pain shot through me, reminding me I was wounded, and I cringed in his arms. He loosened his hold, but I only tightened mine. It caused more pain, but I did not care.

"Lucy, we have to move," Blake said in a whispered voice. "The others are waiting. The panther chased off the suits, so it is only us and Waller now."

"I don't think Waller will get away from that cat," I whispered, not moving my head from Blake's shoulder. "I don't hear him screaming anymore."

"Don't underestimate him," Blake said darkly. "You are right. I don't hear him or the panther anymore, which means we have to move…now."

Blake grasped my legs and unwound them from his hips, and I reluctantly slid to the ground. He took my hand and whispered, "Try to keep up, okay?"

I nodded, and Blake pulled me down the other side of the hill along a path I had not even seen. The trail was so narrow that I had to follow behind, but Blake kept his hand behind him so I could clasp his hand in mine.

The path went downhill a little and then went on gently rolling land for what seemed like miles. Blake would stop here and there and look around. He seemed very intense, and I would stand and watch as his brown eyes darted all around his surroundings.

His handsome face was set in a stony glare, and tension sang up and down his muscular arms. He would stand like this for a long moment and then turn his gaze to me and give me a comforting smile before turning and moving along.

My shoulder and leg sang with agony, and a massive headache began at the base of my neck, working its way into my temples. The forest's darkness fell around us, and I could no longer see anything but the dark shape of Blake in front of me. I jumped at every sound and flinched each time my step or Blake's would snap a branch at our feet.

Finally, after what seemed like hours of hiking up and down hills, around giant puddles of water, and through tiny trickling streams, we came out of the tree line and into a clearing of long, gently swaying grass and a few trees.

The sky spread above us, no longer hidden under the copse of trees, and I gasped at the wonder of the twinkling lights above. I remembered the stunning sight back on the mountain weeks ago, but the view above me now was even more impressive.

I could see the Milky Way's dusting spread across the sky from one end to the other. We were surrounded by mountains in the distance, and the heavens stretched above us from one mountaintop to another.

I gasped in amazement. "We are in the mountains!" I exclaimed, and I could hear the wonder in my voice.

Blake smiled down at me. "Yes, we are," he said softly.

I smiled and lay my head against his arm. "Are we in Kentucky?"

Blake chuckled and answered, "Close. We are across the border in Virginia for now. My father opened this place not long after…well, after your experience on the mountain. He felt it better to keep you close until you were completely healed, and then he hid you in Florida. You will remember all of this later, hopefully."

"Where are we headed?" I asked curiously, gazing around the clearing. I could not see too far in front of me, but what I could see seemed huge.

"Well, we will sleep here for now," Blake answered.

I raised my eyebrows at him. "We are just gonna lie down and sleep on the ground?"

Blake laughed aloud and shook his head. "No. There will be supplies coming. You will see. Let's just sit, relax, and watch the stars."

"What if Waller finds us?" I asked worriedly. "There is no cover here."

"Waller is long gone from the forest by now. He would not have followed us this far, I am sure." Blake sounded confident, which eased my fears. "We will move to the smaller hidden facility tomorrow. It is hidden in the mountains as well."

I sighed and sank gratefully down to the ground, glad to be able to stop walking and rest my sore leg and arm. I rolled my shoulder around, trying to stretch it out and keep it from stiffening up.

It hurt, but I kept up the exercise. I did a few more stretches to ease the ache in my muscles and caught Blake watching me hungrily. I simply smiled and kept stretching.

When I was done, I scooted over close to him and lay back on the ground with my hands behind my head to look up at the amazing starry sky.

Blake lay back next to me in the same position. I saw him out of the corner of my eye looking over at me, so I turned my head and quirked an eyebrow at him.

"What?" I asked.

"We need to check your injuries," Blake said softly. "But that would require you to take your clothes back off."

There was no playfulness or joking in his tone. My heart instantly began to race. There was no way I could get naked in front of him without something happening, Something that would change our relationship forever.

I swallowed hard. "I don't think my injuries are serious. It's just some minor cuts and scrapes."

"They could get infected, though," Blake said. "If we don't clean them properly."

"Well, we don't have anything to clean them with right now anyway," I responded, jokingly adding, "I think you are just trying to get me naked."

That made him laugh, and it made me smile. I loved seeing Blake happy.

His laughter faded, and in a serious tone, he said, "Seriously, Lucy, we will need to clean those cuts and scrapes soon."

"What do you suggest?" I asked, curious how we would clean anything without water or soap.

"There is a small stream close by. We can clean you up there." Blake watched me warily as I thought about his suggestion.

"What about the supplies that you said were coming? Could we just wait for those?"

"We could, but there is blood seeping through your shirt already," Blake said as he reached over and ran a finger over a spot near my stomach.

There were no exotic sensations at his touch this time. Instead, a sharp pain followed his tracing fingertip, and I sucked in a breath and moved away from his touch.

"Ouch, that hurt," I said, leaning away from his finger.

"I imagine so," Blake said in an apologetic tone. "Let's get to the stream and clean those quickly, or at least find a way to stop the bleeding."

I rose from my position, sighing heavily, and nodded. I had just gotten comfortable and had not wanted to move. I looked down at the spot where Blake's fingers had been and saw the blood seeping through my shirt.

"This way," Blake said as he rose and reached for my hand. "It isn't far."

I took his hand and followed his dark form through the tall grass. Here in the clearing, the darkness was not as complete as it had been in the forest, but it was still dark. I could see a bit more as my eyes adjusted, but it was still too dark to make out any details.

It did not take long to reach the stream. The grass was not high here. Instead, it was bare muddy ground with a few rocks and a huge boulder that sat by the stream. The stream's banks were smooth and flat, with only a tiny indenture to allow the very shallow water to flow over the rocks.

Blake led me to the stream's edge and instructed me to sit down on the boulder. He took off his shirt, and I sucked in a breath at the sight of his bare chest and stomach.

It was a stunning sight. Even in the darkness, I could make out the ripples of toned muscles and the smoothness of perfect, pale skin. I watched his muscles work as he ripped his shirt into strips and dipped them in the cool water of the stream. He lay a few dry strips aside and brought the wet ones over to me.

Blake smiled down at me as I sat on the boulder, and a mischievous smile spread across his chiseled features.

"Now comes the part where I attempt to get you naked," he said jokingly.

I was not laughing. My heart was beating frantically, and my breathing was quick and ragged. I knew I was staring at Blake's naked chest like a love-sick schoolgirl, but I could not help it. Blake was absolutely exquisite.

Blake leaned down in front of me with a serious look after a few awkward moments of unresponsiveness from me. He caught my gaze, forcing me to give him eye contact, and gave me a comforting smile.

"Lucy, you do not have to do this if you are uncomfortable, but at least let me look at that one on your stomach. It is still bleeding, and that is not good."

Blake's voice was calm and soothing, which eased my torn and shattered nerves. Blake probably did not understand why I was so tense, and I was too embarrassed to explain it.

I had never been naked in an intimate situation with a man.

Greg and I had kissed and made out a few times, but I had always stopped it before it went too far. The closest anyone had ever come was Blake when Lily took us over. I did not count that time.

A twenty-one-year-old virgin was unheard of these days, but here I was. I had never talked to Blake about his sex life. How experienced was he? Would I be too inadequate for him?

I sighed angrily at myself. Now that I had broken through the fear of losing him and allowed myself the freedom to have him, I was frozen with anxiety.

'*Just get a grip, already. You are a grown woman…act like it!*' I chided myself.

I took a deep calming breath, grasped the hem of my shirt, and yanked it up to under my breasts. Squeezing my eyes shut, I lay back on the boulder and balanced on my elbows to give Blake better access to my stomach.

The first touch of the cool cloth on my skin stung, and I flinched violently. A small yelp of pain escaped my mouth.

I heard Blake suck in a quick breath and mumble, "Sorry."

I was better prepared the next time I felt the cold wetness caress my skin, and after the initial sting and burn, it helped soothe the scrapes and cuts. The one still bleeding hurt badly, and no amount of the cooling cloth's touch eased it.

The touches left my skin, and I opened my eyes to find Blake walking back toward the stream with a handful of blood-soaked cloth. I frowned. It must be bleeding a lot.

I looked down at my stomach and saw the angry red gash still oozing a bit of blood. It was long, from the top of one side of my stomach and running diagonally to the bottom of the other side of my stomach. It looked deep but not deep enough to need stitches.

Other minor cuts and scrapes surrounded and cut across it in angry red lines, but these were surface scratches and no longer bleeding. I wondered how bad my back was. Judging from my stomach, I had better suck it up and let Blake look at it.

I glanced up, and my eyes caught his as he returned to me with the freshly washed cloth strips. He held my gaze as he knelt before me and placed the cool strips on the boulder beside me. The heat in his eyes was drowning, and I stared, lost in those chocolate depths for a moment before mentally shaking myself and coming up for air.

He broke the gaze and took up one of the cloth strips. He hesitated over the large cut, took a deep breath, and gently pressed it against it. It stung, but not as bad as before, and I sucked in a quick breath through my clenched teeth.

It made a sharp hissing sound, and Blake flinched, glancing at me apologetically before pulling the cloth away. He gently cleaned the blood away before taking up one of the dry cloths he had put aside and pressed it firmly to the wound.

That hurt.

I let out a yelp of pain, but Blake held the cloth firmly in place even as I wriggled to get away. He raised his other hand and grasped my hip, holding me in place as he brought his eyes up to meet mine.

They held a tortured expression which relayed in his voice as he said, "I am sorry, Lucy. I hate causing you pain, but I must stop the bleeding."

I nodded and forced my wriggling body to hold still under his touch. He held me there a bit before lifting the cloth slightly and bending his head to peek underneath. Seemingly satisfied, he lifted the fabric away and nodded.

"The bleeding has stopped now. It should be alright until we can get some bandages and medical tape. There should be a first-aid kit in the supplies." His voice was low, as if he was talking to himself, and I had to strain to hear.

He lifted his gaze to meet mine as he pulled the hem of my shirt back down. "I think you will live," he said with a wink.

I smirked and said, "Thanks, doc."

His features turned into one of carnal lust as he replied, "No, that is my father, but if you want to play doctor with me, then I will happily comply."

My mouth dropped open as heat instantly washed over me in a sudden inferno that melted my veins and colored my neck and cheeks red. My heart immediately sped up as his hand reached out to help me into a sitting position.

Blake chuckled lightly. "Relax, Lucy. I am teasing you. You are safe from my carnal assaults."

Blake's touch left me as I got into a sitting position, leaving me cold and empty. I held his gaze and gathered my courage. I needed to be bold. I needed to let him know that I had given in, that he was free to touch me and…well…

"I don't want to be safe from you anymore," I blurted out before losing my nerve.

Blake's eyebrows rose, and his eyes widened in astonishment. The lustful look was gone.

He stared at me for a moment with that surprised look before asking, "What did you just say?"

I swallowed hard. "I said I don't want to be safe from you anymore. I want you, Blake. Now."

And then the lustful look was back, only this time it was different. There was a knowing in his gaze now. The heated look in his eyes was free from uncertainty and careful regard. Now his eyes held the knowledge that he was free to have me, which made the look even more seductive than ever before.

It made me gasp, and I was suddenly afraid of the intensity of his gaze. I shivered as he grabbed me around the waist and pulled me up into his arms. My arms immediately went around his shoulders as his mouth crashed into mine.

He brought one hand up to weave into my hair, holding my head in place as he ravished my mouth with his. I grabbed a handful of his hair and held on tight, riding the waves of passion that collided into me with his kiss.

This was different than ever it had been. It was no longer tentative, uncertain, or unknowing. This was a carnal knowledge that no longer had to hold back or be careful. This was a real kiss.

I sighed happily and relaxed into him, relaxed into the kiss. He nipped at my bottom lip lightly, then sucked it into his mouth and ran his tongue over it. It brought a sound of pleasure from my throat and an answering growl of pleasure from Blake.

He sank to his knees, taking me with him and never breaking the kiss. He leaned forward slightly, and I slid my legs around so he could take me down to my back. My legs wrapped around his hips as he laid me gently onto the ground and covered me with his body.

He broke the kiss to trail kisses across my jaw and neck, suckling lightly on the sensitive spot right below my ear. I moaned in pleasure and arched my back, pressing my body into his hardness as his hands slid up under my shirt and caressed the bare skin of my stomach, being oh-so careful of the large cut there.

I was drowning in pleasure, lost in Blake's kisses and touch. Torrents of desire flooded my body to my toes, and pulses of electric yearning coursed through me from my core, from the secret place that longed to be filled by his hardness.

The new sensation was overwhelming and a little scary, but the desire overrode the fear in a stunning crescendo of fiery waves that touched every sensitive nerve ending in my body.

I was lost in Blake, so lost in the sensations that I was confused when he broke away from me suddenly, leaving me a panting, melting puddle on the hard ground. A squeak of protest left my chest, and I reached for him, not wanting him to stop.

"Shhh!" he said urgently, grabbing my hands and hauling me back into a sitting position. "Someone is coming."

He shifted to my back and wrapped his strong arms around me. I could feel his rapid heart beating furiously against my back, and his ragged breath sent heat rushing over my neck. It made me shiver with desire, the fleeting sensations of pleasure still coiling inside me.

"Do not panic," he whispered in my ear. "Stay calm and stay silent. They won't be able to see well in the dark."

The pleasurable sensations left me in a rush, leaving me shivering and cold. Even the heat from Blake wrapped around my back could not drive away the chilling feeling. My senses went on alert, and I could now hear the swishing of the tall grass as someone closed in on our location.

As I listened closer, I realized that more than one person was traversing the tall grass and coming closer to the clearing around the stream. We were exposed. We had no cover other than the giant boulder, but we were stuck here on the ground, and the boulder was a few feet away behind us.

Fear caused my stomach to flutter nervously, and goosebumps broke out along my skin. My heart still beat rapidly from the sensations that Blake had elicited from me, but now it beat with terror. I tried to calm my breathing. I knew I was breathing too loudly, and whoever was coming toward us could hear it as they drew closer.

I clamped a hand over my mouth to stifle the sound as I felt Blake's arms tense around me. His entire body stiffened at my back as the swishing sounds of the grass grew closer, and I stifled a scream when two dark figures emerged from the grass into the clear ground around the stream.

"You two are going to catch a cold if you continue rolling around in the mud," came Chris's joking voice, and I breathed a deep sigh of relief.

Blake's body relaxed at my back, and he also released a relieved sigh. The sudden release of tension and nerves elated me, and a giggle escaped my still-stifled mouth. I dropped my hand from my mouth and laughed aloud with relief.

I heard Blake chuckling behind me as he rose to a standing position. "You scared the life out of us," he said between laughs.

I placed my hand on my chest over my rapidly beating heart as the laughter subsided. I felt a hand wrap around my uninjured shoulder, and I let Blake haul me to my feet.

"What were you two doing on the muddy ground?" Dianna asked as she came into view.

"Do you really have to ask?" Chris said humorously, quirking an eyebrow at Dianna as she shot him a playfully sour look.

Suddenly, Dianna's eyes lit with knowledge, and she turned to me with a surprised expression. "Oh! Were you…are you two finally…well damn."

A smile spread across her face as she continued babbling, "Oh my God…I am so sorry we interrupted…here…here are the supplies…we will leave and…."

She dropped a duffle bag she had been holding at my feet and began to back away. Chris stopped her with a hand on her back.

"Chill, Dianna. I am sure if they want to continue, they can after we get the tents set up. It will be better than rolling around on the ground."

"Oh, yes, right," she said and picked up the duffle bag.

I laughed and shook my head at her. "It's fine, Dianna. We do need to set up camp, and please tell me you brought food. I'm starving."

Blake wrapped his hand around my waist from behind and drew me to him. He placed his mouth next to my ear and whispered, "I'm starving too, but not for food."

I shivered with pleasure, and a smile broke out on my face as I leaned my head back into him. He kissed my temple before releasing me to step around me and help Dianna and Chris with the supplies.

I stood there and watched Blake rummaging around the duffle bag for a moment, then he pulled out a first-aid kit. He raised it triumphantly and smirked at me.

"You want to play doctor," he asked mischievously.

I placed a seductive look upon my face and bore into his gaze, nodding coyly as I watched his eyes heat up with desire.

Why, yes.

Yes, I did.

CHAPTER 15: Taken

I could barely contain myself as we set up camp a little way from the stream in the tall grass on the flattest spot we could find. We cleared some of the grass away to build a small fire for cooking.

The knowledge that I would finally have Blake later was tearing at me and I could not concentrate on anything else. Had Dianna and Chris not interrupted us, I would have already had him back at the stream.

The memory of the sensations that had run through me filled my mind and made it hard for me to contain the urge to walk up to Blake, tear off our clothes, and beg him to ravish me then and there.

Somehow, I was able to control myself long enough for the men to get the tents set up and build a fire. I enjoyed watching Blake work while Dianna and I cooked, especially since he had never put a shirt back on, and I got to watch his muscled form as we worked.

I savored the skewered shrimp and baked potatoes. They were delicious, and not only because I was starving. The fresh fruit that Dianna had brought made the perfect dessert. Finally, we were done eating, and Blake took me into our tent so he could tend to my wounds.

I was suddenly nervous as I sat next to my sleeping bag inside the tent. Blake sat in front of me, rummaging through the first-aid kit. He placed some bandages, medical tape, antibiotic cream, and alcohol next to the kit and then motioned me to come closer.

I scooted forward as my pulse sped up, and my breathing became quick and shallow. I tried to hide my nervousness, but I felt I was doing a poor job of it.

"Lie down on your stomach so I can look at your back," Blake said in a soothing tone.

I was sure he had seen how nervous I was and was trying to calm me with that voice.

It was working.

His voice calmed my racing heart, and I lay down on my stomach as instructed. I flinched slightly when I felt Blake grasp the hem of my shirt and lift it to my shoulders.

"Relax, Lucy. I will try my best not to hurt you," Blake said as he sat on his knees beside me.

Cool wetness touched the skin of my back, and I flinched again. I tried to relax, but the sharp stinging sensations that ran through me as Blake ran a cold, wet cloth along my back made it difficult. He had to keep pushing the hem of my shirt up because it refused to stay in place.

I heard him grunt in frustration, and then he asked, "I don't suppose you would be comfortable taking the shirt off?"

I stiffened, but I knew he was right. The shirt was posing a problem and preventing him from washing the scrapes properly. I raised to my knees and started to pull the shirt over my head, but Blake's hands on mine stopped me.

He looked into my eyes with a heated gaze as he moved my hands away from my shirt.

"Let me do it, please," he said, and I shivered at the desire in his tone.

I was frozen, too afraid to speak, fearful my voice would come out too shaky. I nodded and dropped my hands to my side, watching his brown eyes as he grasped the hem of my shirt.

He lifted it from the back and pulled it up over my head, leaving the arms intact and the front pulled low. He pulled the front up under my breasts, and his knuckles brushed my naked skin along the way.

It made me shiver, and a seductive smile spread across his face. "Leave it like that until I am done cleaning your cuts," he said.

His gaze grew more heated as he added, "Then, we will see about taking it all off."

I swallowed hard and lay back down on my stomach. The desire in his tone and the seduction in his eyes helped me not think about the tiny shivers of pain that ran through me as he cleaned the cuts on my back.

After he was finished, he instructed me to turn over so he could re-clean the large cut on my stomach, spread the ointment over it, and bandage it. I held onto my shirt over my bare breasts as I watched him care for the cut on my stomach.

The sensation of his hands on my bare skin had me practically squirming until I felt as if I could bear it no longer. Finally, he was finished, and I sat up as he began to clean up the mess.

He packed the first-aid kit away and stuffed the dirty rags into a plastic bag that he had pulled from the duffle bag. He put the bag aside and then turned to me.

"Are you ready to lie down?" he asked, and the unasked question lingered in his gaze as his eyes traveled up and down my body.

I did not answer. I scooted over to my sleeping bag and lay back, never taking my eyes off Blake's intense gaze. He moved toward me on his hands and knees, and his graceful movements reminded me of the panther. My heart pattered frantically in my chest as I thought of myself being the prey.

He moved over me, covering my body with his and being careful of the bandage on my stomach. He placed both hands on either side of my head and balanced himself over me. Slowly, he leaned into me and placed his lips gently over mine, kissing me tenderly with lips and tongue.

I grasped his head between my hands, moaning in ecstasy at the gentleness of his kiss and the feel of his body over mine. I arched my back, pressing myself into him as pleasure coursed through me.

Blake gently lowered himself onto me and ran one hand down my side, keeping his other hand against the ground for support. He slid his hand under my shirt, which I still held against my breasts.

He cupped my breast in his hand, and desire shot through me so intensely that I thought I would pass out from the pleasure. I cried out against his mouth as an answering growl of ecstasy vibrated through his chest.

It was the first time he had touched me so intimately without Lily's influence, and the sensation was divine.

My hands played along his back and down to his solid buttocks, pressing him down to me as I arched up into him. The shock of feeling his hardness against me sent another cry of pleasure from my mouth. Blake pressed down harder, grinding his erection against me, and fiery coils of sensation spread through me.

Blake rolled my hardened nipple between his thumb and forefinger, sending rivulets of want spiraling down to my core. He broke the kiss and rose off me, and I whimpered in protest. But then I gasped in pleasure at seeing his muscled chest and stomach. I had forgotten for a moment that he was shirtless.

He caught my eyes with his intense gaze as he reached for the shirt. The heat in his chocolate depths mesmerized me as I raised my arms so he could take my shirt the rest of the way off. He tossed the shirt away, and I averted my gaze as he stared down at my bare breasts.

"Look at me, Lucy," Blake said in a strained whisper, and the intense desire in his tone made me shudder with longing. I slowly turned my eyes back to his and saw his throat work as he swallowed hard.

"You are beautiful," he whispered as his eyes roamed over my face and down my naked torso, lingering slightly on my bare breasts.

He lowered himself back onto me, and the electric contact of his bare chest against my naked breasts sent shockwaves of hunger through my entire body. I sighed in pleasure as Blake planted kisses on my neck, down to my chest, on the skin between my breasts, and finally, he captured one hardened nipple with his lips, suckling it into his mouth and flicking it with his tongue.

I cried out, grasping a handful of his hair in one hand and running the other hand down his back, relishing in the feel of his hardened muscles under my palm.

Blake ran his hands down my side as he suckled my breast and then moved to the other breast as his hands caressed my hips. He slid his fingers of one hand into the waistband of my sweatpants, playing along the bare skin of my hip.

The pleasurable sensations running through me intensified as his mouth worked at my breasts, switching from one and then to the other as his hand continued to play inside my sweats.

He rolled to the side so he could run his hand to my stomach, and fire shot through my veins when his hand dipped into my sweats to play with the fine hairs of my mound.

I arched into his touch, begging him to go lower and fill the need that burned within me. I tugged at his hair, pulling his head up from my breast to bring his mouth to mine again. I wanted his mouth on me. I needed him to kiss me as he touched the secret place that had never been touched by a man.

He kissed me deeply as he played with the hairs on my mound, and then he broke the kiss to gaze into my eyes. The longing in his eyes as he pierced me with his gaze made me gasp, and shivers of electric desire shot through me when his hand dipped lower and cupped my sex in his palm. I cried out, arching my spine and throwing my head back as I shut my eyes.

"Lucy," Blake whispered roughly. His voice was thick with hunger as he said, "I want to see your eyes."

I lowered my head and slowly opened my eyes. My eyelids fluttered as sensations shot through me, and I tried to keep them open as I felt one of the fingers of his hand slip into my folds.

It came near my entrance but moved up and began to move slowly in circles, caressing the sensitive spot above my opening. Intense sensations of ecstasy that I had never felt before washed over me, and my insides throbbed with the need to be filled.

I moaned low in my throat as I tried to keep my gaze fixed on Blake's eyes. "Please," I whispered, and my voice was rough with desire.

He bent down so close that I could feel his hot breath on my lips. His breathing was ragged, as was mine, and his voice was taught as he asked, "Please, what?"

His finger continued to caress me, and my hips began to move in time with him. A sensation of pressure began to build between my legs, threatening to spill out into me and wash me away in pleasure. The throbbing of my inner walls became stronger until I thought I would die from the need for him to be inside of me.

Blake bent down and nipped at my ear, eliciting another cry of ecstasy from me. "Please, what?" he repeated into my ear.

I could not think, could not speak. I was awash in the sensations that he had ignited inside of me. I held him tightly, one hand in his hair and the other with a death grip on his bicep.

His finger stilled, and he pulled it away from me. I whimpered in protest, but he quieted my pleas with his lips, delving his tongue into my mouth and swirling it across my bottom lip.

He broke away and moved back to my ear, whispering more softly this time, "Please what, love?"

I found my voice, and my tone was desperate as I whispered back, "Please, take me, touch me, please, Blake, please."

A deep growl of desire issued from his chest, vibrating against the skin of my neck as it escaped his mouth. He nipped at my neck, sending a sharp rivulet of desire coursing to my core.

He sat up on his knees and moved down, grasping the waistband of my sweats and pulling them slowly down my hips. He stopped with the waistband just below my thighs, rolling his hungry gaze down my body. He bent and planted kisses on my bare stomach as he eased my sweats down lower, almost to my knees, and then stopped again.

He planted kisses along my hips and across to my mound, then kissed atop the light sprinkling of hair covering my sex.

The sensation was divine.

Pleasure coursed through me, and the building pressure in my core throbbed uncontrollably. The fire roaring through me threatened to melt me into a puddle on the tent's floor.

His mouth continued its assault on my lower stomach and hips, and then he moved his kisses back up to my breasts as his hand replaced his mouth on my stomach.

His hand dipped lower and cupped my mound, and then he pushed his fingers inside my folds again. I wanted to spread my legs, give him more and let him take all of me, but my sweats were still at my knees, pinning my legs together.

His fingers played along the inside of my folds, coming desperately close to my opening. My hips began to buck uncontrollably as the desperate need to have him drive a finger into me overtook me.

I felt I would die with need if he did not take me. "Please, Blake, please," I begged in a whispered, broken voice.

Finally, when I felt as if I could take no more, he slipped a finger inside my entrance, and the sensation of it crashed into me so intensely that my whole body shuddered with ecstasy.

I cried out once, twice, three times as his finger slipped in and out of me, and my wall's throbbing intensified as the pressure spilled over and spread through my very soul.

My body reacted automatically. My hips thrust upward, my back arched, and I threw my head back as I rode the pulsing sensation that took me away on a tide of exotic bliss. A long cry of gratification tore from my throat as I rode the waves crashing through me, and then I was coming back down from my first-ever orgasm.

My entire body trembled with the release, and my heart beat furiously in my chest. I struggled to catch my breath as Blake pulled my sweats the rest of the way down and tossed them aside. He took off his pants and stood over me on his knees as my eyes took in his sensational nakedness.

I swallowed hard as my gaze roamed his body, and my eyes widened as they took in his toned chest, washboard abs, and the trail of dark hair on his stomach that started under his belly button and led down to the thicket that housed his massive erection.

Blake lowered himself slowly onto me, spreading my legs with his knees as he positioned himself against my opening. He balanced with his elbows on either side of my head as he leaned his forehead against mine.

He held my gaze and whispered raggedly, "I love you, Lucy."

And then he was slowly and gently easing his hardness into my entrance. He filled me, stretched me, and the pressure that had been released began to build again as my walls throbbed around him.

Suddenly, there was a sharp pain that drove through me and up into my stomach. I cried out in pain, and Blake froze inside me. He kissed me gently and eased out of me just a fraction as his lips moved over mine.

"It only hurts for a moment," he whispered against my lips. "Tell me when it stops."

He continued to kiss me, and after a brief second or two, the pain stopped just as he said it would. I continued to savor his kiss, relishing the feel of him inside me even just a bit.

We were both breathing raggedly, and I could feel Blake's heart beating rapidly against me, just as rapidly as mine beat against him. I moved my hips up, taking him a bit deeper inside me, and there was no pain this time.

"The pain is gone. Take me, Blake. Please, take me," I whispered against his lips.

A moan of pleasure slithered from his mouth, and he pushed further into me. My body shuddered as the pressure began to build again, and I pushed my hips up further, begging for more of him to be inside me.

He lowered himself fully into me slowly, and when he was buried all of the way inside me, he began to pull out again. He pulled almost out before pushing into me again, and the pressure built as my walls pulsed around his hardened shaft.

This time, when he was buried deep inside me once more, he ground himself into me, rubbing himself against the sensitive spot his fingers had played on.

The sensation was incredible, and a cry of ecstasy escaped me. Blake pulled himself almost out again, then buried himself inside and ground against me again.

Thrills of blissful sensation filled me as the throbbing of my walls caressed his hardness, and again he pulled out, pushed in, and ground against me. The pressure inside threatened to spill over as he found his rhythm, pulling, pushing, and grinding until I shuddered with the need to release the pressure.

Finally, after one last push and grind, the pressure spilled over once more, this time more intense. My walls throbbed around him, and I felt an answering throb from his shaft as his hot liquid poured into me.

My cries of ecstasy mingled with Blake's as we rode our pleasure together. He stayed buried deep inside me as the waves of release rolled over us, and then he pulled out of me and collapsed beside me, satisfied and spent.

He rolled to his side and gathered me in his arms, holding me tightly as we relearned how to breathe. My head rested against his chest, and I concentrated on the feel of his slowing heart against my cheek as my own heartbeat slowed to a steady pace.

He kissed my head and sighed happily, causing a smile to spread over my face. His arms tightened around me, and I cuddled into him.

My voice was hoarse from screaming out my pleasure as I whispered, "I love you, Blake."

Blake's voice was torn with emotion as he answered, "Lucy, my sweet Lucy. You already know I love you."

I sighed with contentment as my eyelids fluttered closed, and it did not take long for me to fall fast asleep, wrapped in Blake's arms.

PART FOUR

AWAKE

CHAPTER 16: Memories

*** MARCH 27, EIGHTEEN YEARS AGO ***

I was sad. I could not believe my parents had given me away to people I did not know.

We drove for a long time, and then the bald man took me into a big metal building and took me to a doctor. The doctor took me into a room and made me lie on a big metal table.

I began to cry when they put the straps on my arms and legs.

"Hush, now," the doctor told me. "This will not hurt."

He lied.

He gave me a shot in my arm, and pain lanced through my head. I cried out in agony over and over, but no one came to comfort me. My head became cloudy, and my eyelids grew heavy as the pain lessened.

Finally, it was over. My eyes closed, and I could not open them as darkness overtook me, and I fell asleep.

When I woke up, I was in another room on a regular bed. My eyes were puffy and swollen, and my head still hurt. I reached up to rub my head and found bandages all around it. What had happened to my head?

Curiously, I looked around the pink and white bedroom and was pleasantly surprised to find all my things around the room. The baby doll that Lily loved to play with when she was controlling me sat on the bed beside me, and I cuddled it up.

Lily would love this room. She liked pink. Maybe she knew what had happened to my head. I cuddled the doll harder and reached for her in my mind to ask her.

She was not there.

Frantically, I shut my eyes and reached deep into the big black spot in the back of my brain, but there was nothing there.

I began to cry and sob uncontrollably. I was alone in my head for the first time in my life.

Lily was gone.

*** APRIL 2, SEVENTEEN YEARS AGO ***

I did not want to do this again. I had done this thousands of times over the past year. I was four years old and too old for this game. I had already learned all of my ABCs, could read from the storybook they had given me and could write my name and other words I knew.

My brain was fine now, other than the fact that Lily was no longer there. The bandages were gone, and the small incision on the back of my head had healed with barely even a scar. So, why did I have to keep telling them what stupid shapes I could see in those crazy pictures?

I sat with my arms crossed over my chest while the lady held the shapes up for me. "Come on, Lucy. Don't be like that. If you do this one more time, they may let you go to my school. Wouldn't you like that? There will be kids your age there."

Miss Megan continued to coax me until I finally blew out a breath of frustration and said, "Fine. But there better be kids I like there."

"There will be. I promise," she said with a smile and held up the first picture.

"Now, tell me what you see."

"A bunny rabbit," I said automatically. I already knew all the pictures by heart.

"Look more closely," Miss Megan said. "See if you can see anything different this time."

I huffed impatiently but did as she said. I stared at the swirling black-and-white lines of the picture, trying to see if I could see any other shapes in the nonsensical image.

Frowning, I realized that there were other things in the shapes if I concentrated hard enough. I smiled widely when I saw the butterfly.

"A butterfly!" I called out triumphantly.

"Very good! Let's see if you can find more in the rest of the pictures."

I was no longer bored now. I was excited to see if I could find anything else in the other images.

And I was excited to finally go to school.

*** JUNE 23, SEVENTEEN YEARS AGO ***

I stared at all the strange faces staring back at me as I stood in front of the class.

The boy with black hair sitting in the front smiled brightly at me as Miss Megan introduced me to the class, and he watched me as I walked to my desk behind him.

He leaned over as I passed and whispered, "Hi, Lucy. My name is Blake."

I smiled at him as I passed. I liked him. I hoped we would be friends. I turned my attention to the front of the class as Miss Megan began to speak.

"Now, class, I know that you know the rules, but I will review them again so that our new student, Lucy, knows them as well."

Miss Megan walked to the chalkboard and began to write each one as she said them.

"Rule number one is to stay in the classroom at all times during school. Rule number two is always participate in class. Rule three is never use your abilities unless otherwise directed by an adult."

She turned after writing the rules and asked, "Is everyone clear on the rules?"

"Yes, Miss Megan," we all answered together.

"Good, then let's get started."

*** MARCH 26, SIXTEEN YEARS AGO ***

"Happy birthday, Lucy," Blake said as he held out the teddy bear he had brought me.

I smiled happily as I took the soft bear and snuggled it against my cheek. "Thank you. How did you get this?"

"My dad got it so I could give you a birthday present," he said, shrugging.

"Tell him I said thank you," I said as I gave Blake a bright smile.

"You can tell him yourself," Blake said, and I thought I heard sadness in his voice.

"What's wrong, Blake?" I asked nervously.

"Miss Megan said you would miss class today because you have an appointment with my dad."

I raised my eyebrows. "Oh, yeah. I forgot about that."

"You are five today, so they must give you the big test."

"The big test?" I asked, and I could tell that Blake was nervous about it.

"It is the test where they make you use your power and see what it can do," Blake said. "I had mine done last month. They will place us in certain classes next year depending on how strong your power is and what type it is."

My heart fluttered with fear. "But, Blake, that means we may be separated next year. I am a mental, and you're a physical."

Blake nodded. "I know."

"No, I don't want to be separated from you," I said, and my voice sounded whiny like a baby's. I didn't care.

"I don't want you to go to another class either, but what can we do?" Blake's eyes were sad as he stared at me.

I clutched my bear to my chest and said, "We won't be able to see each other if I go to another class. When we aren't in class, we have to stay in our rooms or go with the men when we have to do those dumb tests."

"I'll find a way, Lucy. Don't worry," Blake said and gave me an encouraging smile.

I shook my head. "No, Blake, please don't get into trouble. I don't want you to get decommissioned."

"I'll be careful, Lucy. I would do anything for you."

*** FEBRUARY 20, FIFTEEN YEARS AGO ***

I was angry. It was just the first day of school in my new classes, and the little girl had taken away the doll.

It was Lily's doll.

"I do not share her," I seethed. "Everyone else knows that. It is time you learn that."

The tingling sensation started in my fingertips and spread down my arms. I held out my hand, palm facing her, willing the tingling to flow out of my hand toward her.

I saw recognition in her eyes as I took control of her mind, willing her muscles to hand over the doll to me. Her jade-green eyes filled with confusion and widened in fear when she looked at my face, and she shakily handed me the doll as her muscles obeyed my commands.

"Lucy!" the teacher's angry voice shouted. "How many times do I have to tell you that you are not allowed to use your gifts? Do you want to be decommissioned?"

"Why did you do that, Lucy?" Miss Megan asked in a calmer tone.

I began to cry. The sadness that came whenever I had to explain the doll to anyone wracked my tiny body, and my voice was thick with tears as I answered, "she had my baby doll, the one that belonged to Lily."

"Honey, I know that you miss her. What happened to Lily was awful, but you cannot keep this up. I do not want the same to happen to you."

I took a deep, shaky breath and nodded my understanding. Then, I turned to the little girl still huddled on the floor, crying. Guilt shot through me as I handed the precious doll to her with a smile.

"Here, take her. I am sorry," I said to the crying girl.

She reached up tentatively and gingerly took the doll from my hands. She cradled it as if it were precious, and it was. "Thank you," she said in a whispered voice. "I'm Dianna."

The door to the classroom opened with a bang, causing Miss Megan and me to flinch in surprise. The huge, bald man with the snake tattoo curled around his neck came into the room. Miss Megan reached out slowly and grabbed my arm. She pulled me to her and wrapped me in her protective embrace.

It was Waller, the man who had taken me away from my parents, the man who made me run those crazy drills once a week, and the man who would always comfort me when I was sad.

I was not supposed to tell anyone about it, though. He had made me promise.

"Lucy Spears!" Waller called out.

"What do you want with Lucy?" asked a tiny yet intensely angry voice.

"Don't worry about it, boy. This does not concern you," the scary bald man said with a sneer. His tattoo bulged out on his neck as he stepped further into the room.

The man was trying to be scary, but I knew he was not always this way. He only acted this way when coming to collect someone to be decommissioned. The thought made me whimper.

Was he really going to let them decommission me?

Blake stepped forward with his arms crossed over his chest like a grown-up. He had feared that we would be separated, so he had pulled some strings with his dad so that he could be in the class with the kids with mental abilities, even though his was a physical one.

I was glad.

"Lucy, when I do this, you must run, okay?" he whispered, too low for anyone else to hear except for Miss Megan, who gave an imperceptible nod of her head and loosened her grip on me.

"Try not to hit Waller," I whispered. "He is not as bad as everyone thinks he is."

Blake looked at me as if I were crazy, but he nodded his consent anyway.

The men that came with Waller into the room wore protective metal bands, but Blake was not a mental. He was a physical, and the bands did not protect against that.

I nodded and prepared myself. I knew what I had to do. I felt the tingling in my hands and pulled myself from Miss Megan's arms. I looked at Blake and nodded, and Blake thrust his hands out suddenly, unclenching his fists and releasing a spray of fire that shot out toward the men, far enough away from Waller to allow him to dodge out of the way.

"You're not immune to fire, you bastards!" Blake shouted, surprising me with his use of the b-word. He must have been livid to curse that way. Then again, he usually was when I was being threatened.

He shot another spray of fire, which caught one of the bookcases and sent it into a raging inferno. Kids began to scream.

I concentrated on the tingling in my arm and sucked in a huge breath. Then, I shot my gift out with all my might, aiming it at every mind in the room.

'*Calm down and get out,*' I said in my mind, willing all the other brains to follow my commands.

It was too hard. There was too much fear, and I could not get them to listen.

"I can help," said a small voice beside me. It was the red-headed little girl, still cradling the doll in her arms.

Dianna, was it?

"How can you help?" I asked her, raising my eyebrows.

She smirked and said, "watch this."

She raised her free hand to her head and squeezed her eyes shut. She looked as if she had a headache. Then, a few seconds later, a flock of birds flew in through the open window and began flying around the room, going toward the men and pecking at their eyes and heads.

They threw their arms up in defense and began shouting at the birds, and Dianna giggled at the commotion. The fear in all the brains that I still had my mental clutches in turned to humor, and I was able to gain control of them all.

I urged all of the minds under my control to run, and Dianna, Chris, and Miss Megan followed.

Blake turned to look at me, and his eyes glowed a burnished gold, lighting up his face with his power. "Go, Lucy," he said sternly.

"I'm not going without you," I said. There was no way I was going to leave him here.

I could no longer see the man and could no longer see Blake. Panic gripped me as the smoke went up my nose, filling my lungs and causing me to choke.

I fell to the floor, remembering our fire drills and what we were supposed to do in a fire. Stay close to the floor, crawl under the smoke, and stay calm. So I did.

The smoke was thinner on the floor, but it was still seeping into my nose, and I could not breathe. I tried to stay calm, but my heart skittered with fear causing me to breathe in short, quick gasps that filled my lungs with smoke.

I started coughing, deep wracking coughs that weakened my body and brought tears to my already stinging eyes. I could feel heat from the fire lapping at my back as I crawled on the floor, fumbling around with my hands for any sign of Blake.

"Blake, where are you?" I choked out, coughing up smoke and inhaling more with each breath I took.

He did not answer me. Strong hands lifted me, covering my mouth with a cool cloth. I screamed and struggled, but it was no use. The hands that held me were too strong. I was captured.

*** FEBRUARY 21, FIFTEEN YEARS AGO ***

"Stop fighting, kid, and hold still. It won't hurt if you don't fight," Waller said.

I was buckled down to a bed with Blake buckled down on another bed beside me. I turned my head to look over at him squirming and fighting to break free from the restraints.

A man in a doctor's outfit was trying to hold down his arms with one hand, and he had a syringe full of a milky white liquid in his other hand.

"Leave him alone!" I shouted and was surprised at the strength of my tiny girl's voice.

The doctor began to argue with Waller, who was in the room with me. They were arguing about who to decommission first.

"Lucy, can you hear me?" Blake asked, but he did not speak out loud. Instead, I heard his voice in my mind, and the power in my body instantly latched onto it.

"Yes, I hear you," I said silently.

"Get away if you can. I will distract them, but you have to run."

"I told you before that I am not leaving you," I answered stubbornly.

"Lucy, you have to get away. I can't stand to see you get hurt." Blake's tiny voice was sad and pleading, and I turned my head and gave him a steady look.

"Blake, listen to me. Let the doctor decommission me, and you get away."

"What?" his voice was incredulous, and he started shaking his head rapidly.

"Blake, listen to me! There is not much time. My abilities cannot touch them with their protection bands on, but yours is a

physical ability, and you can get around their shields. You can get away. You can protect the others and get me back somehow. I know you can. I trust you."

Blake's breathing was coming in fast, rapid gasps as he listened to my voice in his head, and his wide, scared eyes were focused on my face. Then, slowly, I watched the understanding resolve fill his eyes, and they began to glow a molten gold color as his power filled him.

"I will bring you back, I promise. I will find a way."

"I know," I said as I gave him a sad look. *"Find me. Save me. I love you."*

"I love you too," I heard him say as his features set into a determined look.

The doctor came over to me with the syringe held up in one hand. I began to whimper as he grasped my arm and held it down. He rubbed my arm with an alcohol swab to ready the spot, then shot the needle into my upper arm right below my shoulder.

I let out a tiny whimper of pain as I felt the liquid enter my body.

It burned.

When the doctor began to lean away from me, I heard a scream of pain from across the room. The doctor jumped violently and turned toward the source of the sound.

I turned my head to see Blake's hands free, his wrists and hands covered with blood. He had bloodied himself by pulling his hands free from the restraints while the man and doctor had been distracted.

I watched as Blake used his ability to knock down the doctor and Waller and escape. I could have sworn for a moment that I saw Waller smile as he pulled himself up from the floor, but then his eyes found mine with a tortured look as sudden pain shot through my head, and I screamed. I had never felt pain like that in my life. It raged through my head so forcefully that I could only close my eyes and scream.

Waller came to my side, picked up my arm, and held my hand as I writhed in pain. I felt him patting my hand comfortingly, and some of the pain eased away with his touch.

Darkness swirled around me, thick and heavy, and stars floated around the inside of my eyelids. Thoughts and emotions were ripped from my mind as the decommissioning serum took hold and tore me away from myself.

A welcoming void stretched before me, beckoning me into its blissful, painless embrace. I reached for it with a smile, welcoming the darkness, welcoming the abyss, and the release from this pain.

I drifted away with Waller holding my hand and knew no more.

*** FEBRUARY 23, FIFTEEN YEARS AGO ***

Lily was back! I woke up still strapped to the table, and I could feel Lily again. I reached into that space to welcome her back and froze.

Something wasn't right.

I was trapped in the space, not her. Lily was here, but she was in control, and I was trapped in the void in the back of my mind. Usually, when Lily took over, I would drift around in my head with her. I never went into the abyss because I was afraid of it. I was afraid I could never get out.

How had I gotten here? Had Lily put me here while I was unconscious?

"No, sister," I heard Lily say to me. "The decommissioning serum brought me out to play. That little chip they put in our head that took me away reacted to the serum they gave us and did a little reverse trick on us. You are stuck now, and I am free. It is my turn to live."

Her voice was cold and calculating. I had never heard Lily speak like that before. She would get angry and cause trouble sometimes, but I had never heard cruelty in her tone. She was usually just mischievous.

What kind of trouble would she cause if I could not shut her down and control her?

"No!" I called out, but it was no use.

Lily laughed an evil laugh that sent terror coursing through the abyss. The door of the dark space where Lily had always dwelled slammed shut with me inside. I was stuck, stuck in the abyss with no way out.

I had no idea how long I floated in nothingness, unable to tell what was going on outside. After a time, I forgot where I was, forgot who I was. I was nothing; I was nowhere.

My old life fell away as the serum took hold, but there was one thing that I hung onto that I would never let go of. I refused to let go of the memories of my friends, especially Blake. I fought against the forgetful void pushing into the corners of my mind, and held onto the moments that were special to me of my friends and Blake.

I refused to let them go.

My old life fell away as the blackness gathered around me, and I drifted into the darkness and waited for Blake to save me.

CHAPTER 17: Lily

It was good to be free. I had lived my entire existence stuck in an abyss in my twin sister's head, and now it was my turn to live and be free.

I shut the door on the abyss as the decommissioning serum took hold of her mind so the serum could not reach me. It had messed with that chip that had kept me asleep all this time. It had awakened me, pulled me out of the abyss, and trapped Lucy inside; now, she had no knowledge of who or where she was.

Lucy could stay back there, an empty shell of herself, and I could live her life. I would finally have what I had always wanted, and I would not have to answer to anybody. I would show those stupid adults what my powers could really do now that the power and this body were mine.

I was still strapped to the stupid bed, but that was okay. I would get free as soon as some unsuspecting adult came into the room to take me to my 'new life.'

The door to the room slammed open so hard that it bounced off the wall. I turned my head as far as possible to see two men enter the room. They both wore long white lab coats and seemed to be arguing.

"Where is my son?" the black-haired one asked in alarm.

"He got out of the restraints and ran off before we could give him the serum," the blond one answered.

"Good. I did not give permission for him to be decommissioned."

"No one asked for permission," another voice said from my bedside. It was that bald man that had taken Lucy and me from our home. He was standing by my bed, and I had not even noticed him.

Anger flared through me, and the tingling sensation came to me easily. It ran up and down my arms, and I welcomed it with a smile. I turned my hands up and sent it out toward the bald man, and it hit a wall.

Solid and impenetrable, the wall stopped my power and refused to let me take his mind! I had never experienced anything like that before. The man looked down at me and pierced me with a knowing gaze.

He smirked triumphantly and raised his arm, pointing to a metal band that he wore on his wrist. "Lucy, you know you can't get to us when we wear our bands. Why are you even trying?"

The dark-haired doctor whipped around and stared disbelieving at me. "Lucy?"

I pretended to cry, closing my eyes tightly and squeezing fake tears from my eyes. The man had sounded almost relieved when he had said Lucy's name as if he cared for her. Maybe I could use that to my advantage if he thought I was Lucy. Perhaps, he could get me out of here.

"I thought you decommissioned her," the dark doctor said to the blond one.

"We did. We gave her the serum, and she fell asleep for a time," the blond doctor said defensively.

"Doctor Sheppard, I saw Doctor Stan here give her the shot myself," the bald man said. "I have been standing by her bedside and watching while she slept. She only just awakened right before you came into the room."

Well, at least he had been good for something. I now knew the names of the doctors. I prepared to use my best whiny voice as I pretended to hiccup tears.

"Doctor Sheppard, help me, please. It hurts. My head hurts."

Doctor Sheppard turned his attention back to me, walking over to the bed and patting my arm. That was all I needed. I tried for his mind even though he had on one of those silver bands.

It did not work.

"Release Lucy at once," Doctor Sheppard said in a commanding tone.

I smiled deviously. He was going to help me anyway.

"You are not in charge here, Doc," the bald man said. "That was what I was trying to tell you when you came barging here demanding us to release your son. The kids messed up. The boss man wants them decommissioned."

"Apparently," Doctor Stan began. "the serum did not work on Lucy. What does the boss man want us to do about that?"

The bald man chuckled. "Oh, it worked all right. Look at her eyes. Lucy is no longer with us."

Stan's eyes widened as he turned slowly toward me as if he were in a horror movie, and he knew the killer was right behind him.

This would not do. How did they know about me? I did not know any of them. How long had Lucy been here without me?

Stan's eyes were still wide and filled with horror, which was reflected in his tone when he said, "Waller's right, Doctor Sheppard. Look at her eyes."

Doctor Sheppard jerked away from me and stepped back, gazing at me with fear-filled eyes that held a tinge of sadness. "Lily. How did you get out?"

"How did you know, Waller?" Doctor Stan asked.

The bald man shrugged. "I spent much time with Lucy when she ran the obstacle courses for us. I know her pretty well. Let's just say that we have a love/hate relationship, and if that were Lucy, her eyes would be kinder. Lucy is a sweet girl."

"How the fuck did this happen?" Doctor Sheppard asked, and I could tell he was angry now.

I rolled my eyes. I guess it was up to me to explain it to these stupid adults.

"That stupid serum you jerks gave Lucy shut down the reactors that run the chip that you idiots put in our brain, and it woke me up and pulled Lucy down where I used to be. Your precious Lucy is gone, so you may as well let me go." My voice was cold and mean, but it was a child's voice. I hated sounding like a toddler. I wanted an adult, scary voice.

"There is no way you will be going anywhere," the bald man said, and he raised his arms and snapped his fingers.

Men in black suits began to file into the room. Eight of them, I counted as they came in and surrounded my bed, pushing Doctor Sheppard and Doctor Stan out of the way.

"This is the last straw. I want out. I never signed up to treat these kids this way, especially my own son. I thought we would be researching how to help these children, not treating them like science experiments." Doctor Sheppard stalked toward the door when he finished speaking.

"You know the boss will not let you go that easy," Waller said. "You are one of his best doctors."

"We will see about that," Doctor Sheppard said as he stalked out the door.

I snickered and looked up at the bald man. "Guess he told you," I taunted.

"Shut up, girl," he snarled down at me.

"Make me," I said with a malicious smile.

The bald man shook his head. "I will never touch you again, Lily. I already told you that once."

I giggled at the memory of what I had made him do the last time he had touched me. The sight of the men being gunned down had excited me, and seeing them lay on the floor with blood spreading out around them had fascinated me.

I wished I could take him over again. He would be such a fun toy.

My hands were tied to the bed, so there was no way I could reach out and touch anyone. I pulled my power into my hands and flung it out into the room, searching all the suits for one I could control.

They all had shields.

"Take her to the infirmary until the boss man decides what to do with her," the man said.

"Yes, Commander Waller," one of the suits said as he saluted him.

I almost broke concentration when the suits started surrounding me, but I held on. I was pretty sure I was onto something. A weak spot in the suit's shields.

I glanced around at all the pretty bracelets that they were all wearing. They were pretty much at eye level since I was lying on a bed, and they were surrounding me with their hands at their sides as if they were standing at attention.

Their bracelets were different from Waller's. Waller's was thicker and sturdier, whereas their bands were thin, and I had found the weak spot. One tiny little hole right under the ear where they wore their speakers for their communication devices.

The devices interfered with the electrical signal that created the shields, and if I could direct my power just right and slide in…

There!

Gunshots and screams echoed down the empty hallway. I took another one and had him unbuckle my straps before I made the first one gun him down too.

I jumped off the bed and gingerly stepped over the bloody bodies on the floor, dodging the blood as best as I could with my bare feet. I could not avoid one large puddle, and my feet sank into the thick, warm liquid.

It felt good on my feet. I stepped around and splashed a bit as if I were playing in a puddle. Splashes of red coated the bottom of my white gown, the bottoms of my legs, and my feet.

I liked it. It was pretty.

"Stop right there, girl," a deep, commanding voice said. I lifted my head from the blood to see Waller stepping out from around the partial wall in the room where he had hidden.

I called my puppet over to me with his gun raised. "I'm leaving now," I said simply.

Waller narrowed his eyes at me as he said, "you may as well kill me too. I will never stop hunting you."

I shrugged my shoulders. "Okay," I said simply, making my puppet pull the trigger.

I watched as Waller's body jerked with every shot of the gun, but strangely there was no blood. Waller fell to the ground, lifeless and staring up at the ceiling.

I giggled and skipped from the room, then slowed down when I almost slipped on the tiled floors because my feet were covered in blood.

I would have to find a place to clean up. The adults would freak out if they saw a five-year-old running around with blood all over her.

I made my way down the building hall with my puppet behind me. I motioned him to my side and ordered him to take me out of this place and drive me somewhere. I did not care where.

My puppet did as he was told.

We were at least a mile away from the organization's compound when I heard something rustling in the back seat. I whipped my head around to see a boy sitting up from under a blanket where he had been hidden the entire time.

"Hey, Lucy," he said with a triumphant smile.

He had black hair like Doctor Sheppard and dark brown, almond-shaped eyes. I stared at him, not knowing what to say. I did not know him. He must be some kid that Lucy had befriended in this place while I had been asleep.

His smile faded as he took in my blank expression. "They did it, didn't they?"

I did not answer.

The boy released a sad sigh, and I thought I saw tears well up in his dark eyes. I resisted the urge to sigh impatiently. Of course, Lucy would befriend this stupid, bleeding-heart little boy.

"Well, I guess you do not know who I am anymore," he sniffed. "I wonder how you used your power to take over the man here."

Uh-oh…

Thinking quickly, I sent a silent command out to the suit as he maneuvered the car down the empty two-lane road and prayed to God that I was right judging by the facial structure and the hair.

He looked an awful lot like Doctor Sheppard.

"Your father hired me to save Lucy," I made the suit say.

"Oh," the boy said, and I breathed a sigh of relief. "Well, it is a good thing I decided to tag along when I saw you taking Lucy to the car. Where did all the blood come from?"

Thinking quickly, I made the man answer, "Waller was shooting at our men, and Lucy had to walk through the blood to get away."

The boy shivered and gave me an apologetic stare. "I'm sorry you had to go through that."

I shrugged and put sadness into my tone as I said, "It wasn't your fault. I am okay."

I almost puked at the sick sweetness of my tone, but it was how Lucy would speak, and I was trying to play a part.

"I guess I should introduce myself since you do not remember me anymore," the boy said.

His voice and features were still sad, but the tears disappeared. I was glad for that because I did not know how much more crying I could take from this kid.

"My name is Blake, and we used to be really good friends," the boy said.

I smiled my sweetest smile and said, "Hi, Blake."

"So, where are we going?" Blake asked, looking toward my minion.

I made him answer, "the first motel or hotel we can find, and then I call your father and tell him where we are."

This seemed to satisfy the boy, who sat back in the back seat with a nod. I smiled widely.

This was going great so far. Soon, I would be away from this place and these people.

Soon, I would be free.

But first, I had to get away from Blake, and I knew the perfect place.

CHAPTER 18: The Mountain

*** MARCH 24, FIFTEEN YEARS AGO ***
*** LILY'S POV ***

"Maybe this is where dad will catch up to us," Blake said as we entered yet another hotel room with the suit.

Three weeks. It had been three long weeks of traveling, shopping, staying in hotels and motels, and keeping up the ruse of me being Lucy and the suit being our caretaker.

It had not been as difficult as it sounds. The suit obviously had some great credit cards or had been charging everything to the organization, which I had learned much about from Blake with the right questions.

The World Against Mutants Bureau, or WAMB for short, was created to rid the world of kids such as us. Oddly, they use some of us to complete their mission, like Commander Waller.

He could sense and find others like us. When we use our ability, he could feel us no matter how far away we are. He could also sense when one of us is born and will take them out immediately or come get us later.

He dealt with the parents by telling them their baby did not make it or (in my and Lucy's case) by playing on their fears of having a child with strange abilities. He would tell them that we would be going to a special school where we would be taught to use our abilities constructively, but this is a lie.

It is not a school. It is a lab where we are tested and experimented on. They are trying to find a way to annihilate us, not save us.

Of course, since I had killed Waller, they would not be finding new mutants now.

Some diseases had been made by this organization to attempt to keep the mutated DNA strands at bay but had only spread through the human population. Instead of killing the DNA, they created sickness and death in normal humans.

That did not stop them from creating more in an attempt to perfect their efforts. Nothing they had done so far had worked, so they continued working with and experimenting on us.

Several children and adults had taken a great liking to Lucy. The more they tested and experimented on Lucy, the angrier they became at the organization they worked for.

Lucy was different from the others because of me. No other children in the organization had another being living inside of them. Lucy had become the focus of many tests and experiments, which angered the adults that loved Lucy, including Blake's father. They had begun making plans to leave the organization, expose them, and take them down.

It had all been because of Lucy. They had fallen for Lucy's kind nature and gentleness, and they all wanted to protect her and keep her safe.

It made me sick.

On the other hand, however, it also made the organization more determined to keep Lucy, so I assumed that we were still being chased by WAMB. The soldiers had probably been ordered to bring us back so they could have their precious Lucy back, and I could not have that.

"Can you call my dad and check on him?" Blake was asking the suit that I still had under my control.

I turned my attention back to the task at hand. This was getting tiring. I would have to get rid of Blake soon. The only reason I had waited this long was that I was not ready to be alone, but Blake and my stupid puppet were fast becoming tiring and boring.

"I will call him as soon as we get settled," I made the suit say.

Of course, he would not call Blake's father. I could make it seem like he was calling him, but he would be talking to an empty line. I had always invented some excuse for the suit to hang up whenever Blake would begin asking to speak to his dad, and so far, it had worked.

I could tell Blake was getting frustrated with this, but I would get rid of Blake soon. I would make it look like an accident. I had a plan, but we had to get to the mountaintop. There would be fewer witnesses there.

I could do away with these two idiots and then make a clean getaway myself without anyone ever knowing what happened. The fall down the mountain was very far, and no one would ever find them.

"I want to talk to him this time," Blake said.

"I will try to let you speak with him," the suit/I answered.

Blake nodded and went to check out our rooms. We had a suite this time with separate bedrooms, a sitting room, and an eat-in mini kitchen. I liked the suites the best.

This would be the last one before we reached the mountain. Tomorrow I would take us to the mountaintop, where I planned to get rid of Blake and the suit.

"The rooms are big. You'll like them," Blake said as he returned to the sitting room.

I smiled sweetly and answered, "I am sure I will."

"Your hair is getting lighter," he said.

My hair had begun to get lighter and lighter ever since I had taken over. I figured it would go all the way to blond in time since blond was the color of my hair when our brain gave me a physical form, and this was my physical form now.

Lucy was gone.

"I like my hair lighter," I said, shrugging.

"Me too," Blake said with a smile. "If you like it, then I like it."

I resisted the temptation to roll my eyes and gag. Instead, I kept the sweet smile plastered on my face. Blake held out his hand to me.

"Come on, I'll show you the rooms," he said.

I took Blake's hand and let him lead me to the bedrooms.

After enduring Blake's raving about the bedrooms and the huge master bathroom, we started down the hallway toward the sitting room. I froze when I heard the voices, but Blake pulled me along faster.

"I think I hear my dad," he said excitedly.

This was not good.

I stopped, causing Blake to stop and turn to me questioningly. "What's wrong, Lucy?"

"I'm scared," I lied, putting as much fake fear into my features as possible. "What if they want to take me back?"

"My dad won't take us back," Blake said. "He would not want me decommissioned."

"Blake, is that you I hear?" a voice called out down the hallway.

"Dad?" Blake answered.

I pulled my hand out of Blake's and ran into the closest bedroom, locking the door behind me. What was I going to do now?

"Blake!" an excited little boy's voice called out.

"We found you!" a little girl's voice said.

"Is Lucy with you?" asked a woman's voice.

Curiously, I stuck my ear to the door to listen to the conversation.

"Chris, Dianna, Miss Megan!" Blake called out. "Yes, Lucy is here. She has been decommissioned, though. She won't remember any of you. She got scared and locked herself in that bedroom."

"We will be able to fix her," the woman said. "Your father and I have set up a secret lab. It isn't very big right now, but we have done what we could with what little time and resources we have."

Fix me? There was nothing wrong with me.

"Dad!" Blake called out excitedly.

"Blake, I am so glad we found you," a man's voice said. I recognized the voice. It was the black-haired doctor, Doctor Sheppard.

"The man you hired has taken good care of us," Blake said.

"We did not hire that man," the doctor answered. His voice was low, as if he were whispering, and I had to strain to hear.

"We have been following a paper trail," the woman said. "The man with you has been using the organization's credit cards. It was not hard."

"Yes," Sheppard added. "But Waller is also after you, so I am relieved that we could get to you first."

This was definitely not good. Waller was supposed to be dead. How had he survived getting shot up like that? I remembered there was no blood, but how was that possible?

Then, I remembered the television shows I had watched with Blake. We thought it was neat that the suit…a.k.a. me… let us watch adult shows, and we would watch the shoot-em-up cop shows where the cops wore bulletproof vests.

They never bled when they got shot.

That must have been it. Waller was wearing one of those when I had made the suit shoot him.

I had to get out of here. I had to get away from these people. They could deal with the organization and Waller. I was going to start a new life far away from here, where no one knew me. I could find an unwitting set of parents to control, insert myself into their lives, and voila!

Blake's voice caught my attention again as I looked around the room.

"But, the man said…," Blake's voice was cut off by the doctor.

"Blake, listen to me. Lucy is not herself. Do you remember when she first came to us and told us about her twin, but everyone thought she was crazy?"

I was looking for a way out of here, wondering if I could climb down five stories from the window, when the doctor's words came to me. I pressed my ear back to the door curiously.

"Yes," Blake answered uncertainly. "Her twin sister, Lily. She always said that she lived in her head, but the doctors had taken her away."

"Exactly," Doctor Sheppard answered. "What you did not know, however, was that Lucy was telling the truth. She was a part of Lucy, living inside her brain. The organization put a chip inside of Lucy's brain that put her twin to sleep so that Lucy could live without being controlled by her sister."

"I don't understand," Blake said, confusion coloring his tone.

"Lily was awakened by the serum," the woman said. "The serum caused the chip to malfunction. It woke Lily up and put Lucy to sleep. We have to deactivate the chip to bring Lucy back."

"So, Lucy is not Lucy?" Blake asked, sounding even more confused.

"Right," the doctor said. "We have to take her to the lab. We will get Lucy back; hopefully, she will still have her memories."

Nope.

They were not going to do that to me.

I turned and walked toward the large window and peered out. There was a balcony, so the window was actually a door out to the balcony. I opened the glass doors and stepped out onto the balcony.

I heard pounding on the bedroom door.

"Lucy, come out," came Blake's voice through the door. "My father is here. He wants to see you. No one is going to hurt you."

I shook my head and turned back to the balcony. I was not going to let them take me and put me back to sleep, and I was definitely not going to let them bring Lucy back.

The pounding and coaxing voices continued, but I ignored them.

I climbed up onto the railing of the balcony and looked down. The ground loomed so far away, and my heart pounded with nervousness. I looked around at my surroundings, and my heart leaped with hope at seeing a fire escape only a few feet away from the balcony.

The ledge looked large enough to inch my way across to the fire escape as long as I kept my back to the wall. My heart lodged in my throat as I climbed over and balanced myself on the ledge, pressing my back onto the wall. I held onto the railing for balance but had to let it go when I started inching toward the fire escape.

I heard a loud crash and knew they had busted down the bedroom door. Any second, they would come out on the balcony and see me skirting my way across the ledge toward the fire escape.

I began to go faster, pressing myself even flatter against the wall. My heart pounded in my chest, and sweat began to drip into my eyes. I took a deep breath as the fire escape railing loomed closer, and then I heard voices yelling from the balcony.

"Lucy, you are going to fall," Blake shouted alarmingly.

Only a few more inches and I would be able to reach the fire escape.

"Lily," Doc's voice said sternly.

I stopped and turned my head to look back at the balcony.

"Lily, come back and let us help you," he said more softly.

I smirked. "Help me? You don't want to help me. You want to get rid of me."

"We can find a way for you and Lucy to co-exist," Doc said. "Just come back, please."

I shook my head and turned back to the fire escape. I scooted the inches I needed, grasped the railing, hauled myself over, and ran down the fire escape to the street below.

I ran until I could no longer hear the voices shouting and calling my name.

*** MARCH 26, FIFTEEN YEARS AGO ***
*** Lily's POV ***

The first-grade class of Daisville, Kentucky Independent Schools filed out of the yellow school bus and lined up along the side in a neat row. Two teachers and three chaperones stood and waited for the children to quiet as they each did a headcount of the students.

It was easy to take control of these minds and give them a false memory of the little girl that belonged in their class.

Little Lucy Montgomery. The quiet one, the one no one knew, and the one that was different and smarter than everyone else. It was easy to insert this memory into the students' and teachers' minds.

Twenty students in all calmed at the stern faces of the teachers and stood at attention, waiting for their instructions and eager to see a new piece of the world. The children were learning geography, and here in Pikesburg, Kentucky, the mountains loomed like giants over the city. The teachers had taken the students to one of the many lookouts so that they could see the majesty of the mountains.

I continued to pull information from the children, teachers, and chaperones just as I continued to insert little bits of memory into their minds, expanding my story even more.

Six-year-old Lucy stood at the end of the line. She had just turned six years old that very day, so this field trip was a birthday treat for her.

She was the youngest and most intelligent in the first-grade class, but being the smartest did not make her the most popular. On the contrary, it made her a loner in class. The games and shenanigans that the other children participated in held no interest for Lucy, and the other students did not understand Lucy when she wanted to discuss the meanings of life instead of playing with dolls and running away from the disgusting boys.

I smiled a wicked smile as these facts sank into all of the minds under my control. They all accepted me without question as I stood in line and waited for my name to be called.

"Lucy Montgomery," The teacher called the fake name, the name I had stolen from Blake and had planted into their brains, and I snapped to attention. "You will be in group three with Mr. Halcomb."

'*Great*,' I thought to myself as I walked to the group. '*My least favorite teacher…curse my luck. Why couldn't they have put me with one of the chaperones?*'

Mr. Halcomb's mind had been the hardest to crack, so I had to be careful in this group. I held back toward the back of the group as far as I could without calling attention to myself.

I trailed behind as my group made its way toward the fenced-off, concrete structure that looked out over the mountains of Pikesburg, Kentucky.

The large, concreted lookout was enclosed in a tight, chain-link fence to prevent anyone from falling, and the students up and linked their fingers into the holes of the fence as they stared out over the side of the mountain in wonder.

Whispered "oohs" and "ahhs" filled the air around my group, and I sucked in an awed breath as I caught my first glimpse of the land beyond the fence. The pictures I had seen of mountains on the computer did little to capture the wonder and fascination that came with the actual live viewing.

The land sprawled far below her, so far below that even the trees looked tiny and insignificant. I could see tiny dots resembling houses surrounded by minuscule trees and miniature lines along the land that had to be roads weaving through them.

I looked straight in front of me and was surprised to find clouds that looked so close that I thought I could reach out and touch them. The sky, which seemed to loom closely above my head, was dotted with cottony white billows all around me.

I stood at the very end of the line of students, a little ways apart from them but still within shouting distance so that I felt as if I were in my own little world surrounded by sky and clouds with the world below so far away.

I was awestruck at the sight, so much so that I failed to register that little prick of anxiety that shivered its way up my spine, so I was unaware when the dark figure snuck up behind me, so quiet in his treading that no one, not even the teachers, noticed its presence.

I was caught unaware as the figure grabbed me, wrapping me up tightly into strong arms with a hand over my mouth so I could not scream. I had a fleeting sense of danger as an acrid smell filled my nostrils. My vision went fuzzy for a second, and then the hand was torn away from my mouth.

I turned suddenly to see chaos.

The children were running and screaming in alarm as two large figures wrestled on the ground. It was Waller and the black-haired doctor.

The teachers were all trying to gather the running, screaming students while Waller and the doctor wrestled, rolling around on the ground as each attempted to gain the advantage.

I closed my eyes and concentrated, shoving a new memory into their minds…

There was no sense of movement, no indication whatsoever that little Lucy was gone. One second she was there, staring over the lookout with the rest of the class, and the next second she was just gone. It was as if she had vanished into thin air, leaving the space where she had been empty and void of her presence.

When it was finally discovered that Lucy was gone, it was too late. Lucy had been taken, and by the time the police organized a search and rescue, Lucy was far away from the mountains of Kentucky. There was nothing left to be done except return to school and call off the rest of the field trip.

The teachers and students began to file methodically onto the bus like good little soldiers, and I smirked as I watched them go. The bus doors closed, and the bus drove away. There would be no witnesses to what I was about to do.

I turned my attention back to the fight at hand.

Waller was on top with his hands wrapped around Doctor Sheppard's neck.

"Did you really think I would let you take her away from me?" Waller sneered into Doc's face.

Doctor Sheppard was grasping Waller's arms, trying to pull them away from his neck. His voice was raspy with strain as he tried to speak around the hands wrapped around his throat.

"She means nothing to you. Let the child have a life."

"I care nothing for the other children," Waller sneered as he tightened his hold. "I only care about taking Lucy home."

Suddenly, a bout of fire flew over Waller's head. Waller screamed and rolled out of the way as the fire came so close that it singed the top of his bald head.

"Blake, get back out of the way!" Doctor Sheppard yelled in a raspy tone and then started coughing spasmodically when Waller's hands left his throat.

I was so engrossed in the fight that I failed to register the woman that came up behind me and grabbed me up in her arms.

Dammit, I was going to have to stop letting myself get so distracted.

I pulled my power in quickly to begin taking over their minds, but I got distracted once more when I saw two other children come up onto the concrete platform and gather beside Blake. I had heard Blake call out names in the hallway back at the suite, and I wondered if these children were 'Dianna' and 'Chris.'

I saw…Chris?…hold out his hand and yell, "Herd him toward the fence, Blake!"

Blake directed his flame toward where Chris…this had to be Chris…was gesturing. The woman still holding me in her arms gasped, and I turned my head to look. A big hole melted into the fence, and Blake was leading Waller toward it.

"No!" shouted the woman that held me. "Please, Blake, do not do this. You cannot kill."

"He will kill us if we don't," Blake said as he shot another line of flames. "He will never leave us alone!"

"Son," Doctor Sheppard called out, but his voice was calm and gentle. "Son, I did not raise you to be a murderer. We will figure out another way."

Blake's face twisted as he fought with himself. This was my chance. I concentrated with all my might, connecting with Blake's mind and taking it.

"Do it. Kill the bad man," I commanded silently.

I pushed the urge into Blake, but Blake continued to fight.

"No," Blake said aloud. "Lucy would agree with my dad."

"Who are you talking to, son?" Doctor Sheppard asked in confusion.

Waller stood up, shaking his head, and began to advance toward Blake, but Blake shot another flame from his hands and drove him closer to the fence, closer to the hole.

I smiled triumphantly.

"Lucy was talking in my head, telling me to kill Waller. She would never do that." Blake's tortured eyes looked toward me, and I smiled back.

"Maybe you don't know me as well as you think you do," I said menacingly. "And you are not supposed to talk while I control you."

Blake's eyes narrowed as he fought my control. I had to admit he was good. No one else could fight me like that. It made me a bit curious about this dark-haired cutie.

"I know Lucy better than anyone. You are not Lucy. You just have her body," he choked out through gritted teeth.

I cackled as I drove my power into him and ordered him to stop talking to me and kill the man. Blake's eyes changed, and he turned back to Waller, raising his hand and stalking closer.

"No…Megan hurry…she has Blake. He cannot fight anymore," Doctor Sheppard said urgently.

That did not sound good. I assumed Megan was the woman holding me in place. What was she planning to do?

Hurriedly, I sent out a command to every mind on the platform. They could all go jump through that hole for all I cared. After they were all gone, I would escape once more.

There were no witnesses this time. I had waited long enough.

"Jump through the hole," I commanded silently.

I felt my power go out, felt it almost reach every mind on the platform, and then I felt a sharp pain in my head. I cried out in pain, and my concentration slipped.

The command fell away from the minds, and my control of Blake was released. Blake stopped shooting flames at Waller, and Waller sank to the ground in relief. Megan tried to stand up with me in her arms, but I struggled suddenly, and she lost her grip on me.

"What have you done to me?" I asked hatefully, turning around to look at Megan face-to-face.

"Lucy!" I heard Blake shout in alarm, but I ignored him.

My legs were wobbly, and my head started to get all fuzzy. I was dizzy and could not stand up straight. I staggered backward, waving my arms around as I tried to regain my balance.

Darkness began to take over my vision as I grabbed the air for something to hold onto and keep me upright. I saw the horror fill the woman's green eyes as she grabbed for me frantically, but she missed.

I fell backward.

"Lucy, No!" Blake screamed.

I waited for the ground to slam into my back as I fell, but there was no ground. The edges of the hole in the fence scraped my arms as I fell through it into the open air over the mountain.

Blackness consumed me as I fell.

And fell…I was falling…falling long and far, and I could not stop it. My stomach lurched, and my body filled with horror. I opened my eyes, and all I could see were the tops of tiny trees and the blue sky spinning in my vision as I flipped head over heels in a free-fall. My arms flailed wildly, my legs kicked uncontrollably, and I opened my mouth to scream.

I heard Blake screaming Lucy's name, and then I felt a strong wind surround me. The wind was so strong that it stopped my flipping, and I stopped falling. I was floating in the air like a feather drifting on the wind, and the wind was lifting me back up. I tried to open my eyes and see what was happening, but my eyes would not open.

I felt Lucy stirring in the back of my head, and I growled in frustration and anger.

No! I could not let her wake up!

I tried to tamp her energy back down and close the door of the abyss, but my mind would not respond. Nothing was responding, not my body or mind, and my eyes refused to open.

I was about to scream in frustration when someone grabbed my arm and pulled me into solid arms that cradled me as if I were a baby.

"She exhausted her powers," I heard Megan say. "She passed out from overuse of her energy."

"Oh," I thought. *"So, that is what happened."*

I felt the sting of a needle in my hip and the burn of medicine entering my system.

It only took a second for the medicine to send me into oblivion, and I was sucked back into the void of the abyss, screaming.

CHAPTER 19: Awake

I woke up screaming, still wrapped in the sleeping bag with Blake beside me. Blake grabbed me, wrapping me into his arms as he looked around for the threat. My screaming stopped abruptly, and I slumped into Blake's arms.

Sweat was pouring down my face, and my shoulder and leg ached with a dull throb that brought a groan of pain from my scratchy throat.

How long had I been screaming?

"Lucy, I'm here," Blake said softly. "Did you have another dream?"

I nodded and was about to explain my dreams and ask which had been actual memories when the zipper to our tent door ripped open, and Dianna and Chris tumbled in.

Chris fell into Blake's side, knocking him sideways and jarring me since I was still lying in his arms. Dianna fell into the other side of the tent and rolled to a kneeling position with her hands up as if she were about to punch someone.

Blake groaned as he pushed Chris away from him with one hand while still holding me with the other.

"You two would have done a wonderful job saving us," Blake said sardonically as he sat back up and pulled me with him.

"I told you to roll into your stance," Dianna said as she rolled her eyes.

"I did roll, but I rolled into Blake," Chris said as he reached his knees.

"We need bigger tents," Dianna said. "We can't even stand up in here.

"They were not made to stand up in," Blake said as he tucked the sleeping bag more firmly around me. "Lucy just had a nightmare, that's all. Now, give us some privacy so we can get dressed."

I was glad Blake had tucked the sleeping bag around me since I was still naked, and suddenly the memory of our lovemaking ran through my head. I blushed and buried my face into Blake's bare chest. My sleeping bag-covered body on Blake's lap was the only thing covering his nakedness.

I heard Dianna suck in a surprised breath, and I lifted my head to look at her face. Her eyes were wide, and her mouth hung open. Her eyes darted from me to Blake and then back to me again.

"Oh…my…God!" she exclaimed, enunciating each word. "You two did it! You finally did it!"

I squeezed my eyes shut and buried my face into Blake's chest again as I felt the blush heat even more. I felt the rumble of Blake's chest as he chuckled humorously.

"If by 'it' you mean made love, then yes, we did," Blake said.

"It's about time," Chris said.

"Finally!" Dianna exclaimed.

I just groaned and snuggled deeper into Blake's arms. Blake chuckled again.

"You always were so easily embarrassed," Dianna said, and I turned my head just in time to see her roll her eyes at me.

"Just get out," I said in exasperation.

"Come on," Chris said, grabbing Dianna's arm. "We are not wanted here."

"Well, don't take all day," Dianna said as she climbed out of the tent. "We have granola bars and water for breakfast."

"Yummy," I said sarcastically and rolled my eyes.

"Don't be ungrateful," Blake scolded playfully. "As soon as we get out of the woods, I will take you somewhere and get you a proper breakfast."

I waited until Dianna and Chris had exited the tent before leaning my face close to Blake's and whispering in his ear.

"I know what I want for breakfast, and it is not food."

I smiled when I heard his quick intake of breath, and then he was rolling over and taking me down with him. He covered me with his body as a lustful growl rumbled through his chest, and then he kissed me hard and needful, his tongue dancing with mine as I moaned with pleasure.

An hour later, we were getting dressed in the clothes that Dianna had brought us in the supply bag. It was only scrubs, but it felt good to have clean clothes.

Blake changed the bandage on my stomach that had been rumpled and damaged during our lovemaking sessions, and he cleaned the scrapes and cuts on my back and stomach again.

There were a few cuts on my buttocks that I had been embarrassed to let him clean the night before, but he cleaned them this morning.

When we had dressed, and Blake began to climb out of the tent, I grabbed his arm and pulled him back.

"I wanted to tell you about my dreams," I said. "I think they were memories; if they were, that means I remembered everything without the serum."

Blake raised his eyebrows in surprise. "Really? Everything?"

"Well…," I began. "I still have a few questions."

"Alright. Tell me about your dreams."

He sat back down and looked at me expectantly, and I told him everything about my dreams. His expression changed throughout the story. Sometimes he held a faraway look in his eyes as if he remembered something fondly. Other times, his gaze held anger, and then his gaze became tortured with guilt when I told him about his escape from the organization's facility.

When he had to leave me behind.

When I was done, I sat silently for a moment and waited for his reaction or response. He said nothing for a long moment, and I wondered if he would respond. Finally, he raised his gaze to mine with a serious expression.

"Everything you told me happened. They were memories. Lucy, I am so sorry I left you…," he began, but I cut him off.

"No, Blake. Don't you dare apologize. I told you to leave me, I told you I trusted you to get me back, and you did."

"I left you alone, and they woke Lily," Blake said, his tone rising in anger.

"Yes, and then you and your dad got me back. That was you that saved me from falling, wasn't it?"

Blake nodded. "That was the scariest moment of my life. I thought I had lost you."

Tears glistened in his eyes, and I scooted closer. I cupped his face between my hands and gazed into his eyes.

"But you didn't. You saved me, and then your dad put Lily back to sleep. You have nothing to feel guilty about." I kissed the tip of his nose and then his cheeks.

Blake closed his eyes, took a deep breath, and then let it out slowly. He grasped my hands in his and lowered them away from his face. He held my hands as he began to speak.

"By the time we had gotten you back to the temporary lab, you were waking up again. They had to give you a lot of medicine to get you to stay asleep, so they finally put you into a medically induced coma to ensure you stayed asleep. That is when dad opened the facility here to take care of you.

It only took a month to build and supply, thanks to dad's contacts and donations from people who support dad's cause. He kept you in the temporary lab until the building was done. During that time, they continued to work on a solution.

It took two weeks to develop the serum that would keep Lily asleep with the chip deactivated. By that time, however, your memories were gone, and they did not know how to bring them back. When my dad brought you out of the medically induced coma, you had no idea where you were or who you were.

After a week of being awake, Lily started to stir again, and they had to give you more serum. They still could not figure out how to bring back your memories without waking her up. My dad and Megan devised a plan to keep Lily asleep while we tried to figure out how to get your memories back, but they did not want to keep you in a coma the entire time.

They came up with the story of an accident since it was partly true. You did fall over the mountain. They continued to give you the medicine while you were in the facility for that year to keep Lily asleep. That gave them time to come up with a life for you.

They assigned you a mother and father and instructed your mother to give you the jelly doughnuts filled with the serum that kept Lily at bay. Dianna, Chris, and I refused to leave you, so my dad bought that entire apartment complex in Florida so we could all be together.

We all had assigned parents to watch over us while dad and Megan worked on a serum that would bring back your memories. They tested it on other children that had been decommissioned, and some of them had bad results.

I was angry at them for a long time because they had not been able to bring you back and were doing the same thing they had left the organization for. They were experimenting on kids.

I knew it was for a good cause, unlike the organization that was doing it to create a weapon to kill off our kind, but still, it was not right. They kept trying, though. After a long time, Dianna started begging me to take you back to her mother, but I no longer trusted them with you after seeing the other kids they had experimented on.

So…we kept living our lives, our false lives, all while keeping an eye on you and hiding from the organization. None of us dared to use our powers, and you did not even know you had powers. Then, we went on that damn trip, and you went without your serum and…well, you know the rest."

Blake finished speaking, and I took a deep breath to calm my heart, which had begun racing as I listened to him speak. They had all lied to me my entire life. While I knew it was to protect me, I still felt the sting of betrayal.

"Why did you wait so long to take me to Megan? Why did you have to wait until you had no other choice?" I asked as a lump formed in my throat.

Blake looked at me with a tortured expression. "I no longer trusted her, Lucy. Dianna tried talking me into taking you sooner, but I refused. I did not want you to end up like the others she had experimented on."

I raised my eyebrows. "What happened to the others?"

"They are walking shells. They have lost all memory of everything. It is as if they are comatose, just walking around in a daze, sleeping, and eating when forced…." Blake stopped talking and shuddered before continuing.

"I could not watch you turn out that way. I needed to be sure it would work, but then we ran out of time, and there was no choice."

"Well, I'm still here. It worked," I said sullenly.

"Yes, and I am so glad. Lucy, you have to know that I would have done it sooner had I been sure." Blake's tone held a bit of anguish as he looked at me apologetically.

I shook off the hurt feelings. Of course, I knew Blake would have brought me back sooner if he could. I could not hold hard feelings toward him for trying to protect me.

I sighed and patted his hand comfortingly. He smiled at me softly, and I returned his smile.

I pulled my knees up and rested my chin on them as I thought about everything that had happened and everything I remembered, and then icy fingers drew chills down my spine.

"Blake," I said in a haunted tone as I lifted my head from my knees and straightened my legs. "I saw Waller at the airport when we got to Kentucky. He knew where we were before Lily took me over and used her powers when we got home."

Blake frowned. "I remember you said that you had seen a man that scared you," he said as he ran a hand through his dark hair.

I nodded. "Yes, that was Waller. I know that now; he knew who I was when he saw me. I could tell by how he looked at me, but he did not approach me. Has he been watching me all along?"

Blake shuddered as he replied, "It would not surprise me."

"He is one of us," I whispered. "Why is he doing this?"

Blake only shook his head with a sad look in his deep, brown eyes. "I have asked myself that question for a long time."

CHAPTER 20: Safe

The trek through the woods only lasted half a day before we came out into a small town nestled in a valley. We found a motel and got two rooms for the night.

Doctor Sheppard and Megan picked us up the following day and drove us to a remote location deep in the mountains of Virginia. No one but Doctor Sheppard, Megan, and a couple of nurses knew the location of this smaller facility.

"WAMB raided the facility in Pikesburg," Doc said as we sat in a sterile cafeteria eating breakfast on the morning of our arrival. "We will have to operate out of this smaller one for a time."

"As long as this one has what we need to keep Lucy's chip functioning, we should be good," Blake said, giving me a wink. "We must all refrain from using our abilities to keep Waller from tracking us."

"Lucy no longer needs the serum since the chip is functioning again. And since she got her memories back on her own, she no longer needs the memory serum. I would say that Lucy can function without any extra care now." Doctor Sheppard smiled at me, and I returned his smile.

Blake, however, still looked nervous. "What if Lily finds another way out? Isn't there a way to extract her from Lucy permanently? If Lily wakes up again, she will ruin everything."

Doctor Sheppard looked fearful as he answered, "I have been researching that."

Blake's eyes darkened as he responded, "Please, father, tell me you are not experimenting on kids again."

"Not exactly," said Doc.

Blake frowned.

Doctor Sheppard cleared his throat before continuing, "We have been experimenting on embryos."

Blake shot up from his seat and pounded the table with his fist as he seethed, "You what?"

Doc held up his hands in a defensive stance. "Calm down, Blake. The embryos are grown, not taken from humans. We have not had the resources to grow embryos until recently, but we are learning a lot from them."

I cleared my throat nervously before entering the conversation. Swirling my fork around my pancake, I said, "Doc, I appreciate everything you are doing; I do. However, I am not comfortable with these experiments. I am uncomfortable with anything that takes or tortures any type of life, even if grown in a lab."

Blake smirked at his father and gave me an admiring, proud look. He sat back down, crossing his arms over his chest and giving his father a triumphant glare before picking up his fork and continuing to eat.

Doc took a deep breath and swallowed the bite he had been chewing. Shaking his head, he said, "These embryos are not alive. They are what an egg becomes when the sperm fertilizes the egg. In our case, the embryos are made artificially and are injected with strands of the mutated DNA that we can study. The embryos would never be able to become a fetus. They are grown from cells for experimentation purposes only."

I swallowed my bite of pancake, but before I could respond, Doc continued to speak. "Think about it, Lucy. If I could recreate the VTS the moment it happens, I could figure out how to extract the genes of the absorbed embryo from the viable one. If I can do that, then maybe I can extract them from you and take Lily out permanently."

I thought about it for a moment before answering, but the feeling of wrongness engulfed me. It did not matter if it could work; it was just wrong.

I took a breath and answered, "It just seems wrong, as if you were messing with nature. We were made the way we were for a reason, so who are you to try to find out what that reason is?" my voice was calm even though my insides were churning with irritation.

"I am a scientist, Lucy. That is what we do. What other way is there to study and find a way to help you and help others in the process?" Doc asked matter-of-factly and took a sip of his coffee.

"By helping us learn how to deal with life," I answered, throwing my hands up in frustration.

"It would be nice to find a cure for Lily, but not at that price. I am sure that others would not want that either. Maybe we just want a chance to live our lives while dealing with our differences constructively. Help us learn how to do that." I sucked in a breath, not realizing that I had stopped breathing while ranting.

Doctor Sheppard frowned at me in confusion for a long moment before responding, "I am a doctor first and foremost, so it is my job to find a cure for your condition. The scientist in me wants to learn the why and the how."

I closed my eyes and took a deep breath, trying to stay calm as I said, "Doctor, what I am trying to say is that we don't have a 'condition.' We are different, but that does not mean we are sick. If you want to know why we are different, do it, but do not use us as your lab rats. That makes you no different than WAMB."

Doctor Sheppard stayed silent for a moment as he sipped his coffee. His visage became thoughtful, and he took one more sip before answering, "I think you misunderstood me, Lucy. I know you are not sick. I know you do not need a cure for the DNA that makes you different. I am trying to help you control Lily, but I have to study the DNA structure that caused you to be stuck with an absorbed embryo."

He paused and took another sip, then continued with a shrug, "Also, I want to know the how and why because I am curious, not because I want to prevent the DNA from developing. I want to learn what makes you all tick."

I shrugged, "So do it, but do it without growing embryos that will just be thrown away like trash. Maybe, if you try asking permission, you will get plenty of help from us without forcing us."

The Doc's frown became more prominent as he put his cup down and stared at me in confusion. "What do you mean, Lucy?"

"Well, take me, for instance. I'll give you bodily fluids, that's easy, but I will not be subject to being injected with things that will do God knows what, running stupid marathons, or being put through stupid Rorschach tests and other mental exercises."

"I like the Rorschach tests," Blake said. His proud smile radiated my way as he continued, "and the 'stupid' marathons."

He used air quotes when he said stupid, and I shrugged with a smile.

"I like the marathons as well," Chris said as he entered the conversation with a wink toward me. "They keep me strong."

He flexed his arms and raised his eyebrows up and down, causing Dianna to fan herself dramatically.

I rolled my eyes and laughed, gesturing toward them as I said, "You see, you have plenty of us willing to help."

Doctor Sheppard glanced around the table at us with a serious expression, but the corners of his mouth lifted when they landed on Chris.

He cleared his throat and looked at me as he said, "Again, you misunderstand my intentions. I would never force you to do anything you do not want to do. You are right, Lucy. That would make me no better than WAMB. The embryos help my research, but if it makes you uncomfortable, Lucy, then I will stop."

I took in a deep sigh and ran a hand through my hair. My plate with the half-eaten pancake and remaining piece of bacon sat on the table, forgotten. My stomach churned, and I did not feel like eating more, so I pushed my plate away and picked up my cup of milk.

I drank the rest in one gulp before giving Doc a defeated look and saying, "I guess if you need these embryos, then I will find a way to deal. I trust your judgment, Doc. I always have trusted you and Megan, so do what you need to do. It would be nice to be in my own head alone."

Doc sighed in relief and nodded. "Thank you, Lucy, for your vote of confidence. I promise to do everything I can to help with Lily."

"How can we help?" Dianna asked.

"You are all adults now," Doc answered. "The best thing you can do right now is to ensure that other children are safe from WAMB and do not have to go through what you all went through."

Blake's visage grew dark with anger, and his tone held a fury that made me shudder as he said, "To do that, we need to take down WAMB."

"It will not be easy to take down WAMB," Doctor Sheppard said. "It is a big organization with big-time backing. You will have to come up with a seriously good plan."

"We will," Blake said. "But in the meantime, if we are going to stay here for any length of time, then we need supplies. There is a tiny town not far from here. I will take the truck and get what we need if you give me a list and the card."

Doctor Sheppard nodded. "Alright. Take Lucy with you so she can become familiar with her surroundings." Then, with a smile, he added, "Maybe she can see a mountain or two in the meantime."

Excitement fluttered in my chest, and I smiled widely. "That sounds great. I need to get out and get some air."

"Well, you can't go without us," Dianna piped in. "How is Lucy going to go shopping without me?"

Everyone laughed as we all got up from the table to prepare for our shopping trip. Blake took my hand as I got up from the table and led me down one of the many hallways that led out of the cafeteria.

"Follow me, and I will show you to your room," he said as we walked down the long white hallway.

Our footsteps echoed off of the empty walls as we passed several doors on both sides. We came to a set of double doors, and Blake led me through them and into a reception area.

There was no receptionist at the desk, and I stared at it in confusion. Blake chuckled at my confused stare.

"This used to be a medical center for cancer patients. My father still has a lot of renovations to do to this facility. He just bought this one recently," Blake explained as we passed the empty desk.

Another hallway parted from the one we were in after passing the desk, but Blake continued to the last door on the left of the main hallway.

There was another door on the other side of the hallway, and Blake pointed to that door. "I will be right in here if you need me. Dad made sure I was close to you."

He pointed back down the hallway toward the reception desk. "If you take the other hallway at the desk, you will come to Chris and Dianna's rooms at the end of that hall."

He pointed back down the way we had come. "And, of course, you can go back to the cafeteria. If you go back to the other end of the cafeteria, there is another hall. The doors down that hall are labs, examination rooms, and stuff like that."

I listened intently, wanting to know my way around since we would be here for a while. "What about the other hallways leading off the cafeteria?"

Blake answered, "Those are Dad's rooms, Megan's rooms, and a communal living area with televisions and sofas. Oh, and the kitchen. Each bedroom has its own bathrooms, and communal bathrooms are throughout the facility."

"You will have to take me on another tour, but this time I will walk beside you instead of being wheeled around," I said jokingly.

Blake laughed and nodded. "Alright. I will take you on a tour when we return from our shopping trip. For now, though, let's check out your bedroom."

"Deal," I said and smiled up at him before turning and opening the door.

My eyes rose in surprise. I had been expecting a sterile hospital room with one of those uncomfortable hospital beds, maybe a chair, and a television mounted on the wall. Instead, the room had been transformed into a beautiful homey bedroom.

The room was bigger than any hospital room I had ever seen, but I quickly saw why. There was another door leading out to the hall, a bit down from the one I had entered, and I could see marks down the wall and on the ceiling that signified a wall had been there at one time.

"Did they tear out the wall and make two rooms into one?" I asked Blake curiously.

"Yes, they did that with some of the bedrooms to make them bigger. They have not removed the extra doors yet," Blake answered.

I took in the rest of the room as I walked further into it. A fluffy beige carpet had been installed over the cold, hard hospital floor. A comfortable-looking double bed sat catty-cornered on the far left with two bedside tables on either side.

A door stood open on the left wall that, looking in curiously, I discovered was the bathroom. A large wardrobe closet sat catty-cornered on the far right, and a matching dresser with a large mirror sat along the right wall.

The room was in beige, blue, and light pink, with light blue Venetian blinds covering the two large windows. A beige sofa with blue swirls sat against the wall and blocked off the extra door, and a small entertainment center sat in the middle of the floor facing the sofa.

It was a lovely room, and I smiled happily as I skipped over to the bed and threw myself onto the soft mattress. The comforter felt silky against my hands, and the lavishly soft pillow cushioned my head wonderfully as I lay my head on it.

Blake laughed as he followed me over to the bed. "If you do not want me to trap you in that bed all day, you better get up and check out your wardrobe."

I sat up and raised my eyebrows at him. "Why? What is in the wardrobe?"

"Go check it out," Blake said mysteriously with a mischievous glint in his chocolate eyes.

I quirked an eyebrow in curiosity as I got off the bed and walked over to the wardrobe. I opened it slowly and glimpsed inside. I gasped in surprised happiness and opened the doors wider to reveal the clothes hanging in the wardrobe.

Shirts of many styles and colors hung on one side, and jeans and dress pants hung on the other. There were even a couple of dresses hanging between the shirts and pants in the middle.

Yanking open each drawer, I found panties, bras, socks, and hoses in various styles and colors. The bottom drawer held sneakers, ballet flats, hiking boots, and a pair of pumps with low heels.

I ran over to the dresser and began opening the drawers. They were filled with t-shirts, shorts, and pajamas. I smiled up at Blake in appreciation.

"How did they know my sizes?" I asked, my voice laced with emotion.

Blake smiled proudly and answered, "I told them, of course. I pay attention."

His answer made me suddenly want to cry. I knew he had paid attention to me, but the implications of just how much hit me at that moment. He had known me more intimately than anyone, even before I gave in to him. I flung myself into his embrace, wrapping my arms around his neck and pulling up on tip-toe to place a solid kiss against his full lips.

"I don't know how I can thank you for all of this," I said as I pulled back from him.

He pulled me in closer and buried his face in my hair next to my ear. "I can think of a few ways," he whispered, and I shivered with delight as all of those ways ran through my mind.

"I have something else for you, too," he said as he released me and stepped back.

I raised my eyebrows in curiosity as he reached into the pocket of his jeans and pulled something out, balling up his hand and hiding it in his palm.

"What is that?" I asked.

He raised his hand, gesturing for me to place my hand under his. His smile widened as I opened my hand under his closed one, and he opened his hand.

Something cold dropped into my palm, and I pulled my hand back and stared in wonder at the silver chain with the charms lying in my hand. My eyes widened, and unshed tears pricked the backs of my eyes.

"My bracelet," I choked out. "How?"

Blake took the bracelet from my hand reverently and gently hooked it around my wrist as he smiled into my eyes.

"I took it off you when we brought you to the organization after Waller's men chased us from Megan's house. I put it in my pocket, and it's been there since. I figured I would give it back to you later, but then Waller showed up and took you and…well, you know the rest."

"So, you had it with you the whole time?" I asked.

"Yep. I forgot about it in all the excitement, and then the night we…umm…."

"Made love," I supplied at his hesitation.

Blake smiled and nodded. "I was putting my pants on the next morning, and it fell out of my pocket. Thank goodness I saw it and put it back in my pocket. I told myself I would give it to you when we settled here."

I stroked the precious bracelet with my finger, touching each charm as I smiled happily.

I touched the gold heart, looking happily into Blake's eyes as I said, "I am so glad you found this. I would have been devastated once I realized I had lost it."

Blake pulled me to him as I gazed into the chocolate depths of his almond eyes. "I will always do everything I can to make you happy and keep you safe."

His voice was deep and husky, causing me to shiver with longing. My heart fluttered with happiness, and I took in a breath as he bent to kiss me. The soft touch of his lips sent coils of pleasure through me, and I curled my fingers through his hair to pull him closer.

He deepened the kiss, running his tongue across my bottom lip before delving into my mouth. His taste ignited a yearning deep in my core as my tongue danced with his inside my mouth. A moan of ecstasy escaped me, vibrating against our joined lips and eliciting a growl of lust from Blake's chest.

"Ahem."

Someone cleared their throat loudly, causing Blake and me to draw apart quickly. I turned toward the door to see Doctor Sheppard standing in the open doorway.

My face flamed with embarrassment as Doc walked into the room with a humorous glint shining in his faded blue eyes behind his wire-framed glasses. He was dressed in a white lab coat, jeans, and sneakers. He held one hand in the pocket of his lab coat and pushed his glasses up his nose with the other hand.

His tall, thin frame moved gracefully as he came fully into the room, and I suddenly realized where Blake had inherited his gracefulness from. Doc pulled a piece of paper from his pocket and held it to Blake.

"I got the list of supplies we need ready," he said as he handed Blake the paper. "You should learn how to close the door behind you."

Doc looked over to me and winked as my face heated. I averted my gaze as Blake took the list from Doc's hand.

"Thanks, dad. I'll try to remember that," Blake said sarcastically.

"You two be safe out there," Doc said, and I heard the humor in his voice.

I listened to Doc's footsteps leave the room before turning my gaze back around. "That was so embarrassing," I said.

Blake chuckled and took my hand in his. "Lucy, there is no reason for you to feel ashamed. Dad loves you as if you were his own. Trust me, he is thrilled that we are together."

I smiled as I took my hand back and began shooing Blake out the door. "He will not like it for long if we do not hurry and get ready. We need those supplies."

Blake huffed playfully. "Fine, I'm going. You are getting bossy already."

"I have always been bossy, and you know it," I teased as I pushed him further toward the door.

"See you in a bit," Blake said, and then he turned suddenly and gave me a quick kiss on the cheek before heading out the door.

I watched him walk across the hall to the other room, turning and winking at me before opening the door and going inside. I smiled, shut my door, and then walked to the wardrobe to decide what I wanted to wear for the day.

There were so many options to choose from.

I finally settled on a pink chiffon top with a white tank underneath and faded jeans with the pink ballet slippers that matched the top.

I went into the black and white tiled bathroom to find a wholly stocked cabinet next to the black pedestal sink with silver handles. A large tub that matched the sink sat in the far corner, and a partial wall hid the black toilet from the rest of the room.

It was a nice bathroom.

A full-length mirror hung on the wall between the sink and the cabinet. I found a brush and brushed my long hair, noticing that it was significantly longer than it had been before we had gone on our trip.

It was also significantly lighter.

My raven hair was now considerably streaked with blonde, and I frowned worriedly. What could be causing my hair to lighten this way? I decided I would ask Doc about it after we returned from our shopping trip, even though he had seen me and had not mentioned it.

I frowned even more as I realized Blake had not said anything about it, either. Had they not noticed? Shrugging, I continued to brush my hair and left it down instead of putting it up into its usual high ponytail.

I was delighted to find some makeup as well, and I brushed a bit of pink over my eyelids. I smiled at the effect. The color made my blue eyes brighter, and they practically glowed. I looked happy, and I knew the effect Blake's lovemaking had on me gave me that ethereal glow.

Satisfied with how I looked, I turned and left the bathroom. As I walked to the door of my new bedroom, I paused to turn and take a final look at the beautiful room.

The smile across my face widened, and I hoped it would never leave. I knew that was a child's wish, however.

I knew there would be a long and challenging road ahead before I could truly be happy, but I could not be sad either.

As long as I had Blake by my side, I would always have a little piece of happiness with me.

PART FIVE

242

SHATTERED

CHAPTER 21: Greg's return

I had not paid much attention to our surroundings when we arrived at MDRT's new facility. I had been tired, hungry, and more focused on getting a shower and clean clothes than I had been on my surroundings.

As we exited the facility, I looked around curiously at the landscape around the building. Mountains surrounded us. We were nestled in a valley with no other buildings or houses in sight. The parking lot was more significant than the one at the other facility, but like the other facility, only one road left the lot.

There were several cars in the lot. A black SUV that looked almost like WAMB's black rides, two 4x4 off-road pickup trucks, two sedans, and a little red sports car that was the same color as Blake's sedan. I wondered what had happened to his little car.

This road was paved, unlike the other one, and the land around the facility was not as dense. The gently rolling land was covered in kept grass that stretched far out on all sides that I could see before hitting the tree line of the forested mountains.

I could see a large flower garden with a bird bath, benches, and paths winding through it on one side and a wooden playground on the other side. It brought back memories of Megan taking me out to play on a playground when I had been living at the hospital after my 'accident.'

I wondered what was in the back of the building.

"What's in the back of the building?" I asked aloud as I climbed into the passenger seat of the black SUV that Blake had led us to.

"The cafeteria courtyard and more grass," Blake answered as he climbed into the driver's seat.

"A courtyard, huh? Can we eat out there when we come back?" I looked over at Blake pleadingly.

He smiled and nodded as he answered, "Yes, of course. It's peaceful out there if you can put up with the bees, flies, and ants."

"Eww," Dianna said as she climbed into the backseat. "I can't use my magic to chase them off, so count me out."

"You are such a sissy," Chris said, climbing in beside Dianna.

"Well, I am a girl, you know," she shot back. "Speaking of, do you boys see anything missing from this picture?"

Blake turned in his seat as he started the engine. "Boys? I don't see any boys in this vehicle."

He turned back around with a snicker as Dianna rolled her eyes.

"Details," she said. "That is not the point right now."

"Well, what is the point, drama queen?" Chris asked.

Dianna rolled her eyes again before continuing. "The point is that Lucy and I have lost all of our stuff, including our IDs, wallets, and purses. A girl has got to have a purse most of all."

"Dad is working on getting us all new IDs," Blake said as he pulled out of the parking spot and maneuvered through the lot.

"Exactly, and Lucy and I will need wallets and purses to carry them in."

"Are you trying to con us 'boys,'" Chris made quotes in the air with his fingers before continuing, "into letting you two go shopping on MDRT's card?"

"Why not?" Dianna said, shrugging. "My mom is a partner, and I am sure that Blake's dad will not say anything about buying his princess a few gifts."

I turned in the seat and glared playfully at Dianna. "I am not Doctor Sheppard's princess."

Blake chuckled and said, "He is rather fond of you, Lucy. I think he likes you better than me sometimes."

"So, will you take us then?" Dianna asked hopefully.

Blake pulled out onto the paved road and said, "I will call dad, and if he says it is alright, then sure, I will take you two ladies shopping."

Dianna made a happy little squeal and settled back into her seat. I chuckled and shook my head as I turned my attention to the front window.

The tiny one-lane road wound through a mountain pass, and some of the curves made me hit the invisible brake in my floor and grasp onto the dash for dear life.

Every time I would gasp and grab the dash, Blake would snicker and give me a comforting smile as he patted my leg, holding the steering wheel with only one hand.

That only made my nervousness worse. The road ran on for an eternity, winding around steep curves, climbing up, and then going down. I felt like I was on a roller coaster in a theme park.

My stomach became queasy as we careened down yet another incline in the road that ended in a sharp turn, and finally, we came to a stop sign. The road in front of us was a two-lane road that ran straight both ways and was flat. I breathed a sigh of relief and thought about how much I would dread the drive back.

Blake turned to the left, and I checked out the scenery on either side of the road. The large cliffs loomed way up into the air, topped with evergreens and other trees with shiny green leaves. Tall grass grew on either side of the road leading up to the base of the cliffs, and wildflowers dotted the grass in beautiful, colorful patches.

We came upon a bridge at one point, and I curiously peered out of my side window to see a large stream stretching through the cliffs and winding away into the distance. The water was a beautiful blue color that flowed across the land. It looked deeper than most streams.

"That's a stream that runs off of a bigger lake further up the mountain," Blake said as we drove over the bridge.

A small, quaint little town sat on the other side of the bridge with tiny two-story buildings on either side of the street. There were only two traffic lights on the short town road. We passed a few boutiques, a small gas station with only a few cars at the pumps, a town library, and what looked to be an old-time general store.

Blake turned the SUV left at the next light and turned onto a more extensive street with parking spaces on either side. The buildings on this side street were sparse, but after a couple of miles, we merged into a four-lane road.

Despite the bigger road, the traffic was still sparse compared to what I was used to. However, the stores we came upon were the bigger chain stores, and I recognized a few of them.

We pulled into a large strip mall that featured an office supply store, a convenience store, and a building supply store. There were also clothing stores, a furniture store, and a few restaurants.

Dianna tugged on my shoulder and pointed happily as she spotted her favorite brands hanging in one of the clothing store windows we passed, and I laughed at her enthusiasm as she urged Blake to hurry up and find a parking spot.

Blake found a spot close to the convenience store, and we all piled out of the SUV. Dianna came around and hooked my arm into hers, and we walked arm-in-arm toward the store's entrance.

"Blake did an awesome job picking out clothes for you," she said. "You look good in pink."

"You look nice, too," I said, smiling.

Dianna was wearing a flowing forest green blouse with open-shoulder sleeves and a sweetheart neckline that looked radiant with her red hair and pale skin. The tan capris and strappy sandals complemented the color of her top and showed off her shapely calves.

"Men know nothing of accessorizing, though. You need a cute scarf and a rope belt with that outfit," Dianna said as I took in her appearance.

I laughed as I nodded my head in agreement.

"Plus, some jewelry would be nice, too," she added.

I shrugged. "I don't need much. I have my bracelet, and that is fine with me."

Dianna suddenly stopped and grabbed my right arm, the arm I usually wore my bracelet on. She pulled it up and gasped at seeing the charm bracelet on my wrist.

"I thought you lost that back at the other lab," she said.

"I did too. Blake took it off me and stuck it in his pocket. He kept it for me until he could give it back to me."

"Okay, I take it back. Blake does know how to accessorize for you. That was the sweetest thing he could have done," Dianna said with a dreamy tone.

"I completely agree," I told her as we entered the store.

I felt warmth on my back and shivered at Blake's voice behind me. "I would do anything for Lucy," he said.

Dianna turned suddenly and smacked Chris on the shoulder as he came up beside her.

"Why aren't you ever that sweet to me?" she asked in mock anger.

"Owww," Chris said, dramatically rubbing his shoulder. "Abuse victims are not sweet."

"Whatever," Dianna said sarcastically. "You are so abused. Poor baby."

"Your eyes are going to get stuck in the back of your head if you don't stop rolling them," Chris said as he walked beside Dianna.

I laughed, and Dianna shot me a playfully angry glare. "Don't encourage him," she said.

It only made me laugh harder.

"Let's split up. We can get more shopping done faster that way," Blake said.

He tore the list in half and handed half to Dianna. "You and Lucy shop for the food, and Chris and I will shop for the other supplies. Meet us back here in an hour."

"Sounds like a plan," Dianna said as she took the list from Blake. "Come on, Lucy."

I followed Dianna, looking back longingly at Blake. He looked delectable today in a gray polo shirt, casual-fitting jeans, and his favorite sneakers. His black hair was tousled and hung toward his heavily lashed, sapphire eyes. I watched as he walked away, and my heart skipped a beat at the sight of his perfect butt.

"Stop staring at your boyfriend's ass and come with me," Dianna said, tugging my arm.

I turned and started to follow her, but I froze as her words sank into my mind.

She had called Blake my boyfriend.

I supposed he could be considered my boyfriend after our night of passion, but the word still seemed so foreign when I related it to him. He had been my best friend for so long that calling him my boyfriend seemed weird.

I looked up to see Dianna walking toward the back of the store, and I hurried to catch up to her.

"Where are we going?" I asked as we passed the food aisles and kept walking.

"I need to pee," she said, and then I realized that she was walking toward the bathrooms that sat at the back of the store.

I was still reeling from hearing Blake being called my boyfriend, so I was silent as we entered the empty bathroom. I glanced beside me at the mirrors and saw the lost and confused look on my face.

Dianna turned back to me, and I could see her eyes looking at me through the bathroom mirror. She saw my look and frowned in confusion.

"What is wrong?" she asked in concern.

I frowned and answered, "I was just thinking how weird it sounds to call Blake my boyfriend now."

"So, Blake is your boyfriend now?" a familiar voice asked behind me.

I saw Dianna's eyes go wide in surprise as she looked over my shoulder, and dread seized my heart as I turned to face Greg. We had not even heard the door open.

His hazel eyes pierced me with a saddened look that shot a pang of guilt through my chest. His sandy blond hair was pulled back on top and fastened into a small knot on the back of his head. The rest of his blond locks hung loose in the back and had grown to the collar of his black button-up shirt.

He had grown a small mustache and a goatee since I had last seen him. It softened the sharp planes of his face and emphasized the fullness of his lips. I had to admit that he was even more handsome than before.

I swallowed hard as he moved closer to me with that tortured expression on his face. He ran a hand over his goatee and took a deep breath.

"What are you doing in the girl's bathroom?" I asked, and I hated how shaky my voice sounded.

"I missed you, Lucy. I came all this way to find you. I followed you in here to talk to you, only to find out that you are with him now." He shook his head as he continued. "I mean, I knew that you had feelings for him, but I never thought you to be the type of person that would string me along like that."

My heart beat hard inside my chest as guilt consumed me. My voice was barely a whisper as I responded, "I…I…I did not mean to. I am sorry."

"Just tell me why," Greg said in an anguished tone.

"It was never my intention to hurt you," I said. "I never meant to be with Blake. I admit I had feelings for him…have feelings for him…but I fought them for a reason."

"Why did you finally give in?" Greg asked as he pierced me with his agonized glare.

"It just…it just happened," I said. I had no explanation.

I did not know what to say. I hated that I had hurt Greg, but I would never feel as strongly for him as I did for Blake. It would not have been fair to continue our relationship, and I probably would have broken it off with him in the long run, even if things had not gone as they had.

"Wait, wait, wait," Dianna cut in, stepping between Greg and me and facing me. "Are we going to ignore the fact that he even found us in the first place?"

Stepping back, I thought about what Dianna had said, and a cold, icy fear shivered through my body. I looked up to find Greg's eyes narrow into a glare, and then he smirked. He raised his hand toward Dianna, and his hazel eyes began to glow a hot-molten gold.

I opened my mouth to warn Dianna, but it was too late. I watched, as if in slow motion, as Greg's hand came up and grabbed Dianna's shoulder. Her eyes widened in fear and confusion, and then her entire body jerked with violent spasms before she collapsed to the floor.

"What did you do to her?" I cried in anger and worry.

"It was just a little shock," he said, shrugging as if it had not mattered that he had just hurt someone.

I looked down at Dianna's prone form and cried out in anguish as I saw her body still jerking as she lay on the cold tile floor. I collapsed to my knees to check on her, but Greg grabbed my arm and hauled me up.

"Don't touch her, you idiot. She still has electricity running through her."

I struggled against Greg's hold, but he was too strong. He wrapped his arm around me, pinning my arms to my sides.

"Help her!" I said pleadingly.

"It's too late," Greg said with a sneer. "She may survive if someone finds her fast enough."

I started to cry out for help, but Greg covered my mouth with the hand of his free arm. He backed me up to the wall opposite the sinks and held me against it.

"No screaming," he ordered as he pressed his body tightly to mine, pinning me against the wall.

I struggled with everything I had, wriggling my body and shaking my head from side to side to fight off his hand. I could tell by the tension in his muscles that he was having difficulty holding onto me, which made me struggle even harder.

I opened my mouth to bite his hand, but he only pressed his hand tighter to my mouth. My lips pressed into my teeth, and I felt a sting and the copper taste of blood. Part of his hand pressed tight against my nose, and I found it hard to breathe.

I was breathing hard from struggling, and my lungs became oxygen starved as I fought to breathe against Greg's hand over my mouth and blocking my nose. If he did not loosen his hold I was going to suffocate.

Blackness began to pool in the corners of my vision, and I fought to stay conscious. I went limp in his hold, hoping he would loosen his hand on my mouth if I stopped fighting.

Tears fell from the corners of my eyes and trickled down my cheek, and Greg finally loosened his hold on my mouth. I sucked in air through my nose, but it was not enough.

"I will let go of your mouth if you promise not to scream," he said.

I nodded, and he slowly lowered his hand away from my mouth. I sucked in a lungful of air and breathed heavily for a moment as my body caught up on oxygen intake. My vision cleared as I breathed deeper, and my heart slowed a bit.

It still beat hard against my chest in fear and dread. I glanced down at Dianna's still form lying on the floor, and a sob broke from my chest. Was she dead? God, please don't let her be dead.

"Why are you doing this?" I croaked out around the massive lump in my throat.

Greg still held me up against the wall, pressing his body into mine as he held my arms pinned to my sides. He leaned in so close that I could see the green and brown flecks still glowing in his irises.

Greg's voice was cold and cruel as he spoke, causing me to flinch with each harshly spoken word. "Does it matter? I am taking you whether you like it or not."

My heart pounded furiously inside my chest as I watched his eyes go cold and hard. My body began to tremble with fear and anxiety as tears fell from my eyes. Tiny, whimpering sobs escaped my quivering lips as I fought the urge to struggle against Greg's hold.

If I upset him, I might end up on the floor with Dianna, and then I would not be able to help her or myself. I had to stay focused on a possible escape. I fought past the terror squeezing my chest and clouding my mind as I closed my eyes in concentration.

"Come quietly with me now," Greg said in a softer tone. "If you come quietly, I will send someone here to help Dianna. I promise."

I opened my eyes and looked at Greg. His features had softened, but his eyes still held that hardness of before. I nodded, and he slowly pulled me away from the wall and unwound his arms from me. His hands stayed on me, gripping my upper arms in a vice-like grip that communicated his intent on keeping me near him.

"Where are we going?" I asked in a trembling voice.

"Just walk with me and act normal. I will keep you safe," he answered enigmatically.

I took one last glance at Dianna lying motionless as Greg led me out of the bathroom and back into the store. I looked around automatically for Blake, Chris, or anyone who could help me.

I did not know how Greg would react if I cried for help, and I did not intend to find out. I had to focus on staying calm and getting Dianna some help.

"You said you were going to help Dianna," I whispered as we walked up the central aisle.

I kept my movements casual, as if we were just two ordinary people shopping for groceries.

"I will let an associate know that someone is passed out in the girl's bathroom as soon as we see one," Greg said casually.

I looked around for someone wearing the familiar blue vests that signified they worked there. I spotted a man with the vest standing at a rack of nightgowns. He sorted through a cart full of more nightgowns, picked one up and inspected it, and then hung it onto the rack.

I pointed in his direction. "There is one."

Greg's hold on my arm tightened as he leaned toward me, placing his mouth against my ear. "Just act casual, follow my lead, and your friend will get help."

I swallowed and nodded as we moved closer to the unsuspecting worker. He glanced up as he noticed us drawing toward him, and a welcoming smile spread across his face.

"How can I help you this afternoon?" he asked in a friendly manner.

"My girlfriend here," Greg began, nodding his head toward me. "told me that she saw a woman passed out on the floor of the lady's restroom at the back of the store."

The brown-haired man darted his green gaze toward me and raised his eyebrows. "Is that so, miss?"

I frowned with worry, hoping it looked genuine, and answered, "Yes. I came straight out of the bathroom and told my…er…boyfriend, and then we came to find an associate. We do not have cell phones, so we can't call emergency services."

The man nodded and reached for a device that hung on his belt. He pushed the button and spoke into the device, telling someone to call 911 and explaining the situation.

He turned his attention back to us. "I will go that way immediately. Luckily, you found me first. I am a first responder."

With that, he pushed past us and hurried toward the bathrooms, and I breathed a sigh of relief. Dianna would get help.

I just hoped it was not too late.

CHAPTER 22: Kidnapped

"There, now will you come with me'?" Greg asked in a pleading tone. His eyes looked sad and hopeful, but I was not fooled.

I narrowed my eyes at him. "How did you find me?"

Greg's visage fell back into that cruel look as he replied, "You can ask questions in the car, and I may or may not answer. For now, we have to get out of here."

I knew he was in a hurry because he probably suspected that Blake and Chris were in the vicinity somewhere, and he was right. I looked around the clothing racks, and up and down the aisle we were standing in before turning back to Greg.

"Where are you taking me?" I asked again.

He pulled me up roughly with the hand still gripping my forearm. "You will find out when we get there," he answered harshly. "Now, move."

He pushed me away from his body and turned me, still retaining his hold on my arm. He began walking toward the exit, pulling me with him as I struggled to keep up with his long, hurrying stride.

I watched helplessly as the exit doors loomed ever closer, and my mind whirled with scenarios of what Greg intended to do with me. I pushed the thoughts away and tried to concentrate on a plan to get away from him when I suddenly felt a tingle at the tips of my fingers.

I felt my power begging to release and wondered if it would be wise to use my ability on Greg. Using my ability would alert Waller to my presence if he was still looking for me. Was I willing to risk it?

We were not at the facility, so even if Waller did come here, he would still not know the location of the new building. However, it would put him close to the site. I tried calculating how far away we were from the new MDRT headquarters, and judging from the hour's drive it had taken us to get here, I figured the building was hidden around fifty miles away in the mountains.

The mountains here were vast, and who knows how many tiny little roads led to other places hidden in its peaks, so it could be plausible that Waller would not be able to find the headquarters even if he did come here.

The exit drew ever nearer. I had to do something fast.

Closing my eyes so no one would see their glow and letting Greg's hand on my arm guide my steps, I concentrated on that tingling in my fingers, letting it spread up my arms and into my body. I pushed the energy out and into Greg's hand on my arm, willing it to enter his mind.

Greg stopped suddenly, only a few feet from the exit, and spun me around to face him. I opened my eyes to find his eyes narrowed in fury as he glared at me with those blazing hazel eyes.

"I can feel that, Lucy. I suggest you do not try anything, else the consequences could be disastrous. Do you really want these innocent people to get hurt or worse?" His tone was low and harsh as he spat his words at me.

I glanced around at the few patrons who were innocently shopping for their wares and pushed my power harder into him. If I could get his mind before he tried anything, then it would not matter. I could have him follow me out of the store to a more remote location before Waller could find us, and then I would deal with Waller.

The tendrils of power flowed into Greg's head and began to meld with his mind, but then a strong force pushed back and sent a spasm of pain through my head.

I gasped in pain, and my eyes widened as I stared into Greg's glowing gold depths. His eyes drew me in as if hypnotizing me, and I struggled to pull away from him. The tendrils of my power were shoved back into me so violently that it made me flinch, and then I felt something push back.

"I warned you," Greg said between gritted teeth.

Before I could do or say anything, a sudden burst of sensation flowed into me from Greg's hand. It was as if thousands of live wires had touched my flesh, and bites of pain pierced me like thousands of tiny needles pricking along my skin. My muscles were frozen for an instant, and then wracking spasms hit me.

The only thing keeping me on my feet was Greg's harsh grip on my forearm as my entire body convulsed with painful writhes and tremors that had me gasping for air even as my body refused to let me breathe.

I could not call out in pain or breathe, and my heart had ceased to beat. All I could do was ride the seizures as they flowed hard and unrelenting through my body. My teeth ground together hard as intense pain coursed through me with every spasm, and darkness began to enter the corners of my vision.

White spots danced before my eyes as the pain overtook me in its cruel grasp, and all I could think about was pain. It felt like an eternity had passed before the pain released me, and my entire body fell limp against Greg's chest.

My body shuddered with aftershocks as I leaned against his chest and tried to breathe. My heart restarted with a painful lurch, and it stuttered erratically before taking up its normal pounding rhythm. I tried to push away from Greg, but my body refused to comply with my commands, and a soft sob escaped my lips as I was held helpless in his grasp.

Greg pulled me up against him tighter and placed his head beside mine. "I told you, Lucy. Do not try me again," he said in a harsh whisper. "That was only a small shock. Do not make me electrocute you into unconsciousness."

He held me there for a moment as my muscles quivered, and finally, he asked, "Can you walk now?"

I took in a deep breath and stiffened. Something stirred in the back of my mind, something dark and angry. I felt the tiniest spark flicker inside my brain, and pain burst through my head.

I cried out as I brought both hands up to grip the sides of my head, and I crumpled out of Greg's grasp and to the ground, balling up into a fetal position as the pain in my head rode through my body.

"Lucy!" I heard Blake's voice call out to me. It sounded echoing and distant, and I tried to open my eyes to find him.

Pain shot through my head again, and I squeezed my eyes back shut to block out the harsh lights of the store. The darkness diminished the pain to a dull throb, so I closed my eyes tightly.

"Fuck," I heard Greg exclaim as he stood above me.

His rough hands grabbed me and pulled me up, eliciting a groan of pain from my lips. I was pulled up and cradled like a baby against his muscled chest, and then I felt us move quickly. I kept my eyes tightly shut against the pain as darkness swirled around in my mind.

I was jostled roughly against Greg's hard body, and my mind refused to focus on what was happening as the throbbing pain took all of my attention. The blackness in the back of my mind grew to overtake my thoughts as I felt Greg drop me onto something hard and firm. I tried to pick myself up and open my eyes, trying to determine where I was and what was happening, but my body refused to comply.

The darkness became massive, and I fought against its hold, even as I desired the release of my pain and fear. Trapped between the two warring forces inside me, I tried to pull myself away and concentrate on the sensations of my body.

I was curled up again, lying on something hard and small. It was narrow, and there was not enough room for my body, so my legs draped over the side. My arms were curled up to my chest, and my head was pushed against something firm.

I concentrated on the pounding of my heart as it beat furiously inside my chest and tried to slow my fast and ragged breathing. I took deep breaths to calm the panic that threatened to take me over, pushing back the darkness in my mind once again so I could try to open my eyes.

My eyelids fluttered with the effort to open them, and finally, I could open my eyes to tiny slits. My vision was cloudy, but I could just make out the back of a car seat looming in front of me. I realized suddenly that I was in the back of a car, and the awareness kicked in my other senses, chasing the darkness in my mind away and packing it firmly into the recesses of my brain.

The sound of the engine, the rich leathery smell of the interior, and the sensation of movement flooded me. I struggled to open my eyes and tried to move my body into a more comfortable position.

The pain in my head had receded, and my muscles felt stiff and unyielding as I tried to move. My eyes finally opened as I uncurled my hands away from my body. I pushed myself stiffly into a sitting position, using the back of the seat in front of me as leverage.

I sat up and glanced around. I was in the backseat of a moving vehicle and could see the back of Greg's head. Icy fear coursed through my veins as I spotted the sandy blond topknot and trailing loose hair. I glanced into the rearview mirror and caught his gaze as a broad, malevolent smile spread across his lips.

"Well, well, well. Look who's awake," he said in his deep, malicious tone.

My body trembled with terror even as I tried to keep a clear head and stay calm. Panic threatened to overtake me, but I tamped it down and returned Greg's stare with one of my own.

"Where are you taking me?" I asked with a furiousness that I most certainly did not feel.

"As I said before, you will find out when we get there," was his smirking answer.

"How did you find me?" I asked angrily.

"I can always find you with this."

He held up a small, square-shaped device with a tiny red light blinking on the screen. I frowned in confusion.

"What is that?" I asked.

Greg shrugged nonchalantly as if he had not just kidnapped me and we were having a normal conversation. "It's a tracking device. I have always been able to find you with this. It was not hard to place a tracking chip on you while we were dating."

"Why?" I asked.

"Because I was protecting you," Greg answered.

"From who?" I asked, getting frustrated with his short, enigmatic answers.

"My father will explain everything when he finds us."

Greg glanced at me in the rearview mirror, and I tensed as we made a sharp turn. His gaze darted back to the road as he maneuvered the turn and then shot back to me. I released the breath I had been holding as I glared back at him in the mirror.

"Can you keep your attention on the road, please?" I asked, trying to keep my voice calm.

Greg did not respond, but he kept his eyes on the road. He drove around a few more curves in silence and then pulled onto a dirt road that cut through the mountain.

The cliffs of the mountain loomed over us on both sides of the narrow road for a short distance, and then they fell away to reveal a large, open tract of land with tall trees and gently rolling hills.

The mountainside spread out to surround the land, and nestled in the center was a quaint little farmhouse with white siding and a black shingled room. Black shudders framed the windows of the two-story home, and a wooden porch extended across the entire front of the house.

The road led to a small, graveled parking area off the side of the house, and stepping stones lined the ground up to the steps leading up onto the porch. It would have been a beautiful home had it not been for the state of ill repair and neglect.

The white siding was old and discolored, with a few missing pieces here and there. The windows were boarded up, and one was completely broken out. A few black shudders were hung askew, and one was completely missing. The porch looked worn and weathered, and the steps looked rickety and unsafe. The stepping stones and parking area were overgrown with grass and weeds, and the gravel was barely visible under all the growth.

Greg parked the vehicle in the overgrown gravel and exited the car. He came to the back and opened the door, reaching in for me as I cringed back against the opposite side door.

A look of anger clouded his features, and he reached further in and grabbed my ankle, pulling me toward him roughly. I kicked at him with my other leg and scrambled to stay in the vehicle. He gave an angry growl and grabbed my other leg.

His voice was seething with fury as he said, "Don't fight me, Lucy. What I gave you back at the store was a playful slap compared to what I can do."

A sob escaped my throat as I stopped struggling and allowed him to pull me out of the vehicle, which I discovered was a large black SUV with blacked-out windows that looked like one of WAMB's vehicles. He held my arm tightly as he led me across the stepping stones toward the front porch.

"This isn't really our house. We found it abandoned and decided to squat." Greg's voice was calmer as he spoke, and I swallowed the compulsion to scream in rage at his casual tone.

He pulled me up onto the porch and led me to the door, which stood open and hanging askew on its hinges. He pulled me into the house's dusty, dark interior, and the moldy air's smell threatened to suffocate me in its embrace.

"I know it isn't much, but we will find a more suitable place after we are sure you are safe." Greg's tone was still mildly casual, and I glanced up at his face.

He looked pleased as he led me through the empty first room of the house and back through a small hallway. He opened the door at the end of the hallway, and I sucked in a surprised gasp.

"We fixed it up, especially for you," Greg said proudly as he made a grand sweeping gesture with his arm.

The back room looked clean and new. The window was open to allow the old smell to escape, and it revealed a beautiful view of the distant mountains and a sprawling land of tall grass, wildflowers, and trees.

The walls had been scrubbed, and the wooden floor cleaned. A sofa and a large bed, each set up against opposite walls, looked new. The bed had clean blankets and pillows, and a new-looking throw rug was on the floor beside it. There were no other furnishings in the room, but it was clean.

I took in the surroundings, and cold dread settled into my stomach as Greg led me to the bed. He turned at my hesitation, and a sly smile grew across his face.

"Don't worry, Lucy. Force is not my thing. When I have you, you will want it." His tone was low and seductive, but it did nothing except run shivers of disgust through my veins.

"Not likely," I said, wrinkling my nose.

Greg chuckled and responded, "we shall see, won't we? You liked me once."

"Are you going to explain what the hell is going on?" I asked, ignoring his comment as he sat down on the bed. I tried to keep my voice even as I spoke.

He patted the spot beside him, and I perched on the bed, muscles tensed and ready to leap away at any second. Greg only shook his head and chuckled as if it were amusing that I was scared of him.

"I was assigned to watch you by my father. He had been watching you for a long time but had decided to let you live out your fake life as long as he could, but now…."

Greg stopped speaking abruptly and shot me an angry look when I interrupted him, but I ignored it and went on anyway.

"Who is your father, and why was he watching me?" I asked.

The angry look vanished as Greg took a deep breath and then let it out slowly.

"I forget you did not know of any of this. You never knew me." He paused for a moment before continuing. "My father is Commander Gene Waller of WAMB."

My heart lurched with terror and disbelief, and a gasp of astonishment rang out in the empty room. I stared at Greg with wide, alarmed eyes as the implications of his statement froze my breath with horror.

Waller had been watching me for my entire life? What did that mean? Why had he waited until now to make his move? I knew that WAMB wanted me, so why had he not taken me until now?

I had so many questions swirling inside my mind, but I bit them back as Greg opened his mouth to speak. I would wait until he finished before asking any questions.

"WAMB ordered my father to find you and bring you back after your escape, but he never did. He had some sort of strange attachment to you during your stay at WAMB, so he decided to keep your location hidden from them. He lied to them for all those years just to keep you safe.

He assigned me to watch over you, but I did it from afar for so long. You never knew I was watching and who I was until you noticed me last year and began talking to me.

In the beginning, I played my part. I knew Blake had always been by your side, but you had always pushed him away for some reason. I felt it would be safe to pretend to have a relationship with you since I knew you would eventually give in to Blake, but you have to understand that he is dangerous.

I had no idea that being back on that mountain would trigger your memories, or I would never have let Blake take you up there. My father thought your memories were truly gone, but he was wrong."

Greg stopped speaking and caught my gaze. His features were twisted into a worried, tortured look that made my skin crawl. I soaked in all that he had said, and the dread and horror wound through my body.

Greg leaned closer, and I instinctually flinched away from his touch. He grasped my hand anyway and pulled me to him, wrapping his arm around my back and holding me in place.

He put his forehead against mine with that tortured frown plastered to his features as he whispered in a strained tone, "I won't let them hurt you. I will keep you safe."

I pushed away from him and jumped from the bed. My hands balled up into angry fists at my sides as I glared at Greg in a fury.

My voice quivered with rage as I spat my words into the empty room. "You are cruel and a liar. Blake would never hurt me, and I will never believe your stories, so you may as well let me go."

"Lucy, we are trying to save you," Greg said as he stood up and came closer to me.

I backed away and held my arm up to hold off his advancements. "Who is going to save me from you?" I spat.

The door banged open suddenly, and Greg and I both turned in surprise.

"I will," said a deep, commanding voice, and I shuddered with icy fear as I saw the black snake tattoo.

CHAPTER 23: Betrayed

Commander Gene Waller stood in the open door, his imposing presence taking up the entire doorway. His bald head glinted in the light from the window, and his stormy gray eyes took in my appearance.

I backed away automatically, noticing the scars that ran down one side of his face. They were red and angry lines as if someone had tried to claw his eye out of his head. I remembered the panther and shuddered. He had not survived that attack unscathed.

His eyes narrowed angrily as they shifted to Greg, and he stepped further into the room toward his son.

"What have you done, son?" he asked, and I shivered in response to the threat in his tone. "How did you get her to come with you? She does not look willing."

"Nothing that you would not have done," Greg shot back, seemingly unafraid of Waller's daunting tone.

"I told you to get her here willingly. I thought you would have some sway over her since you two are supposed to be dating, but I see the marks on her arm." Waller's eyes narrowed on me as he glanced at my upper arms.

Curiously, I looked down at them and gasped as I saw the angry red welts peeking from the bottom of my sleeves. I raised my sleeves and examined the welts to discover they were shaped like a handprint.

"I had to act out a break-up scene to get away from them to come get you when she started to break down. I was worried…."

Waller had stepped closer to me, examining my arms as Greg spoke. His fingers traced the red puffy skin, and I flinched away from him as a cold, furious glare filled his gray eyes.

He turned on Greg, interrupting him as he said in a booming voice, "You electrocuted her!"

Greg jumped slightly and said, "I did not give her that much, just enough to convince her to come with me. She didn't even pass out like her friend Dianna did."

Waller's voice bellowed, causing me to flinch as he yelled, "You electrocuted Dianna too?!"

Greg shrank back from his father's angry tone but recovered quickly. "I sent help to her. She was still alive when we left."

"You do not understand what you have done," Waller said in a lower tone. He pinched the bridge of his nose between his thumb and forefinger as he added, "I hope she is ok."

Waller's whispered, worried tone was almost too low for me to hear, but I had heard it nonetheless. Why was he worried about us all of a sudden?

"Father, you have done worse than that. Your goons shot her…twice," Greg shot back defensively.

Waller's voice sounded tired and defeated as he said, "first, that is why I sent you after her. I was tired of trying to force her to come with me, and I thought she would be more receptive toward you."

Waller's tone grew louder as he said, "Secondly, those were not my goons. They were actual WAMB agents. I tried to protect her from them, but her friends ran out into the street, and she followed."

I stepped up, crossing my arms over my chest and frowning in confusion. Waller turned back to me as I stepped closer to him. Waller's words made no sense, and the confusion overrode my fear as I interrupted the conversation.

"Hold on. What you are saying makes no sense. You were in the hallway. You tried to capture me, and then the trucks were waiting outside for us. How can you say that they were not with you?"

"I was trying to get you out of the building before they caught up to you," Waller said, and I thought I heard a hint of exasperation in his tone. "I do not want them to find you, and I do not want those simpletons at MDRT to have you, which is why I tried to take you from their facility."

I harrumphed in disbelief and replied, "I saw you with the soldiers, and what do you care what happens to me anyway?"

Waller huffed and moved further into the room. "I have a few trusted soldiers, but they follow my orders. They do not work for WAMB."

"If she would have come with me peacefully…."

Waller turned his gaze to Greg, interrupting again as he gestured toward the bed and yelled, "sit down and shut up."

Greg complied, and Waller turned his attention back to me. "I care what happens to you because I care about you, Lucy. I hated you at first…well, I hated Lily…but you were so innocent; as innocent as Lily was vicious, but you still loved her. That intrigued me."

He paused as he strode over to the sofa and sat down, leaning forward and resting his elbows on his knees with his hands clasped in front of him. His stern features had softened as he continued to speak, and his voice had grown deep with a hint of tiredness laced in.

"I can feel others that have the mutated strand; when a child is born with it and when someone uses their power. I can hone in on their location and find them."

Waller's gaze dropped to the floor as he spoke, and his tone became glazed as if he were remembering long-ago times and speaking them aloud.

"WAMB found me when I was very young. They realized what I could do and used me for their own purposes. I was never a kind boy, but at least I had morals. However, WAMB took my cruelty and made it worse. I was hardened by them and their lack of compassion. They did much to ensure that I would be hardened.

I lost my family to them. They took everything from me, but I still held onto my morals. I did what I could to ensure that, even though I was forced to do things that still make me cringe.

I was intrigued when they sent me to fetch you and told me of your abilities. I had never heard of a mental that had another being living inside of her due to Vanishing Twin Syndrome. I was horrified when I came face-to-face with you and saw it for myself.

You were so sweet and timid as Lucy, but then Lily took over and caused me to slaughter my men. I am usually immune to other mental's powers even without my bracelet, but Lily managed to get to me somehow, so I would not touch her again.

But you, Lucy, got to me. Every time you came to me for comfort, you made me fall in love with you a little more, like how a father falls in love with their child. I considered you mine and tried to protect you as if you were my own."

Waller paused and glanced at me with a thoughtful look in his stormy gaze. His gaze passed up and down my face and caused me to shiver. I kept my gaze steady, arms crossed over my chest, but my insides were quaking with anxiety.

"You got to me because of your endurance and capacity to love. You kept your kindness and innocence despite being run through multiple tests and procedures that would have broken others. You spoke of your sister often, and I wondered why you loved and missed her even though she was cruel."

He lifted his gaze to Greg, who sat silently listening to his father. He smiled softly, saying, "It reminded me of your mother. She loved me despite my cruelty before they took her from me and decommissioned her."

His eyes darkened at the memory, and my heart expanded in sympathy for this man. I frowned at that, but I could not help what I felt. He turned his gaze back to me, and the sad reminiscence in them compelled me to walk over to the sofa and sit down beside him.

I relaxed my arms, folding them into my lap as I met Waller's remorseful gaze with an understanding one of my own. He let out a soft chuckle and shook his head.

"That is what I am talking about. After everything I have put you through these past weeks, you are still willing to offer me comfort."

He shook his head as if to clear it before continuing his story. "I was intrigued by you so much that I combed over every file they had on you to learn more about you.

What I learned chilled me to the bone, and I knew I had to get you out of there somehow. It began to make sense to me why Doctor Sheppard insisted on putting you in every class with his son and why he had his hands in every decision regarding you."

He paused, and I saw his throat work as he swallowed, causing the snake tattoo to writhe around his neck as if it was alive. He pierced me with his stormy gray eyes as he rose to his feet and began to pace the room.

He refused to look at me as he continued to speak, and I felt an impending sense of doom. I knew that whatever he was about to say would tear my world apart worse than it already was. I stiffened in preparation as he began to speak again.

"WAMB wants to rid the world of us and use the ones they keep for their own purposes, but another organization out there wants something even worse than WAMB.

It wants to breed and create more of us and use us to take over the world, and its primary focus of this breeding is you. A traitor in our midst belongs to that other organization, a traitor that wants to steal you away and use you for their disgusting scheme."

His tone grew dark as his face scrunched up in rage. As he continued, I shook my head repeatedly, not wanting to hear the words I knew would crush my soul and send me over the edge. I had a sick feeling in my gut that I knew who the traitor was even as my mind screamed at me that I was wrong.

"Their plans for you were to simulate the VTS in embryos grown in a lab. When they learned to mimic the VTS, they would extract your eggs and repeat the process with each one, placing the mutated DNA in them before placing the viable embryo inside you after it had absorbed its twin.

Then the process would be repeated, creating an army of mentals that would follow orders peacefully, and then turn malicious and deadly when faced with war."

I thought about the conversation I had with Doctor Sheppard back at the new lab, about how he had been using embryos to recreate the VTS to help find out how to extract Lily from my brain.

He had lied to me.

He had not been trying to help me at all.

A vast void opened up inside my heart that was filled with the pain of betrayal and loss. I backed away from the flood of emotion that threatened to overtake me in its grasp. The void loomed ever closer, and I backed ever further away, but Waller continued to speak.

"When you escaped and were taken by the agency, they gave you a new life and left you alone, so I kept you safe from WAMB's notice as well. I knew their plans for you, knew that they were waiting for you to grow into breeding age to give them more time to complete their research, but I was content to let you live your new life and protect you from afar.

I wanted you to have some peace, at least.

I watched you for a long time, and then WAMB became suspicious, so I stayed away for a time. When my son became old enough, I stationed him with you so he could watch while I could not.

When Greg called me and told me Blake had arranged for you to take a birthday trip to the mountains, I knew the agency was about to make its move. I knew I had to do something to keep you safe."

Blake's face floated into my mind. I thought about all those years he had walked by my side, protecting me and keeping me safe.

It had all been a lie.

He had kept me safe for his father, assuring that I made it to breeding age so they could use me for their purposes. A sob broke from my chest as Waller's stormy gaze turned my way with a remorseful look. I shook my head over and over, covering my ears with my hands as if to ward off what he was about to say.

I could not hear this. It would shatter me. I would never be whole again. The void threatened to consume me, and I backed further away from it, coming ever closer to the abyss in the back of my mind.

"Lucy, Blake wants to take you back to his father. MDRT wants to use you to take over the world. Doctor Sheppard plans on building an army using you as his breeding horse."

The implications of what Waller was saying were too much. He was lying. He had to be. Blake would never allow anyone to hurt me, and Doctor Sheppard loved me as his own daughter, or at least that is what Blake had always told me.

Waller was trying to turn me against them, forcing me back to WAMB so that they could experiment on me. I could not even begin to comprehend betrayal that deep.

However, deep inside my mind, a tiny spark flickered to life. A small part of me that believed what Waller had said sent shards of pain shooting out into my chest as the void loomed over me.

Doc had been collecting embryos. Blake had been protecting me for my entire life. He had been the one to arrange my trip to the mountains, the very same mountains that housed the headquarters where his father waited to use me to build his army.

I crumpled to the floor, sliding off the couch as my heart felt like it would explode inside me. I struggled to take a breath around the pain as I curled into a ball and reached out for that blanket of the abyss to enfold me and take me from this cruel world of hurt and betrayal.

This could not be happening. Blake could not be using me to help his father with this ridiculous scheme. This could not be happening.

I repeated the mantra in my head over and over as an answering tendril reached out to me amid my pain. I pulled it toward me, welcoming the numbness that settled over me as the abyss opened and pulled me under, releasing the other that had been trapped there, waiting for her chance to come out and play.

I had escaped the void and ran into the protection of the abyss, and Lily had come forth and taken the pain for me. She could deal with the pain. She could keep it in the front of my mind as I lay hidden in the back, shielded by the darkness of the massive abyss.

My body uncurled, and my lips stretched into a malicious smile as I rose from the floor with Lily in charge. Waller's eyes widened, and Greg glanced confusedly between him and me.

I focused on Waller as I sashayed over to him, where he stood next to the bed. He moved protectively in front of Greg as I came closer, his eyes narrowing as I stopped a few feet from where he stood.

"Hello, Waller. Did you miss me?" I asked slyly.

His voice was strained as he said, "Lily."

Lily pouted her lips in mock remorse as she said, "You have shattered poor Lucy's heart, Waller. What did you think would happen when you finally told her?"

"Let her back out," Waller said through gritted teeth. "I followed your plans. I never told anyone that you were still active despite that damn chip, and I never told Lucy, either. I let you come out to play whenever Lucy needed you to take the pain. I let you come play when Lucy had to run drills with your promise that you would stay out of her head the rest of the time."

Back inside the recesses of my mind, I flinched in surprise. The entire time I had been in WAMB's institution, I had thought they had taken Lucy from me. How had she hidden from me?

"The chip simply hid that part of your brain from you, but I was still there," Lily answered, but the words had come aloud out of my mouth.

"Are you talking with Lucy?" Waller asked, and I heard a hopeful tone in his voice.

"Shut up!" Lily snapped angrily. "I held up my end of the deal. The only time I ever came out when we were in that horrid place was when Lucy could not handle it. I, however, like the pain."

Waller scoffed. "Do not pretend that you care for Lucy. You only wanted to get rid of her so you could have her body."

As the vast emptiness stretched toward my heart, I curled up in the abyss, but Lily soaked it up as if it were nothing. I could never do that. Blake had betrayed me, and I could not handle it, but Lily took the pain without flinching. Lily was right to have taken over.

"I do care for Lucy," Lily said, and softness entered her tone. "I was jealous of her for her life, for having a body, but that changed when I saw what she…what we…had to go through just because we were different. When I got away from that damn facility and thought I would finally be able to live and get rid of Lucy, I began to change my mind. Then, the others got us and made me sleep for a time."

Lily paused for a moment before continuing in a somber tone, "I had always protected her and shielded her from pain, even when I wanted her body, but I cannot protect her from this."

"What are you saying, Lily?" Waller asked.

Lily raised our eyes and stared into Waller's sad gaze. I saw the sadness and loss in Waller's stormy depths, and the compulsion to pull myself from the darkness and comfort him washed over me.

It was not strong enough to pull me up, however. I let the sensation blow away and dipped further into the abyss as Lily's hold on my body strengthened.

I knew that Lily had wanted to take over my body at one time. I knew that she had wanted a chance to live. I did not know that she had begun to change her mind. However, Lily would be happy to live knowing she was living to protect me from dying inside. I sank further into the abyss, glad to let her do that if that was what she wanted.

I did not even want to live after this. I would be content to sleep for the rest of our lives.

"Lucy may never recover from this," Lily said as my thoughts drifted to the front of my mind and washed over her.

Anger grew and radiated from Waller's gaze, and he turned suddenly to his son.

"This is your fault!" he boomed loudly. "They had finally repaired the chip to function and keep Lily at bay, and you just had to go and shock Lucy and wake Lily up!"

Greg flinched at Waller's loud tone and squeezed his eyes shut. "I never meant for that to happen," he said in a tortured voice. "I want Lucy to be safe too. How was I supposed to know that electricity would wake Lily up and take Lucy away?"

"It is an electronic chip, you dumbass. What did you think would happen when you shock an electronic chip with electricity?"

"I would have been torn from the abyss anyway after a revelation like that," Lily scoffed at Waller. "Lucy is not able to handle this on her own."

"Are you saying it is my fault?" Waller bellowed, causing me to flinch inside the darkness.

I sank further in, trying to escape the voices and emotions happening outside my body. It was too hard to face the void inside my heart and the promise of the crushing pain that would come with accepting that void.

"Yes, it is your fault, you idiot," Lily yelled indignantly. "You just told her that the boy she has been in love with for her entire life has never loved her and only used her to help carry out his evil father's schemes. What did you think was going to happen?" Lily threw his words back at him mockingly.

"Lily, you need to let Lucy learn to deal with life on her own, or she will never be able to handle anything stressful," Waller said. "I can help her deal. I used to do it when she was small, and I can do it now."

Lily shook her head and said, "No, not this time. It is too much. I do not think you realize the depth of love she had for Blake. He was her entire world, and no one will ever compare."

Greg flinched at that statement, and guilt tore through the void, causing me to sink further. This boy had probably genuinely cared for me, and I had thrown him aside for the boy who had betrayed me. Why had I been so blind?

Waller's voice was pleading, and my heart lurched painfully at the tone as he said, "I did not mean to hurt you, Lucy. Please, come back out. We can sing your song like we used to."

I knew Waller was suffering, just as I was suffering, but I did not care. I melted further into the darkness as Lily continued to drive our body. She could have it as far as I was concerned. If I could get myself to sink into oblivion and not face the vast emptiness of pain looming at the top of my mind, then I would.

Lily could take it. Lily could bat it away from her without a second thought. Lily could deal with the emptiness. Lily swallowed hard as she faced Waller, and a look of worry and concern flowed over her face.

"Waller, Lucy does not want to deal with this. Lucy does not want to come back out and probably never will."

Waller's eyes grew wide as Lily continued to speak, driving home the final nail in the coffin of the abyss.

"Lucy is lost to us…."

Waller shook his head in denial as Lily said with finality…

"Forever."

And I was.

I drifted into the blissful nothingness as I watched the world outside float away and give Lily full and complete control of our body. The vast hole of pain, loss, and betrayal grew further and further away as I watched myself drift into the abyss.

I welcomed the darkness, the cold, the paradise of numbness as I closed myself off from my body, Lily, and the outside world of agony.

I felt no pain, no sorrow, and no memories of anything. I was nothing; I was no more. I breathed one last breath and closed my eyes for what I hoped would be the last time. I felt the abyss close over me, trapping me in its embrace, and I sighed with relief.

The last thought that floated through the abyss and into the front of my mind where Lily walked was that I never wanted the abyss to open, ever again, but Lily did not close it. She tucked me safely inside like a mother tucking her child in for a long night's slumber, but she did not close it.

I wondered why, but I did not care. Whether she closed it or not, I was going to drift off to sleep and forget the outside world.

I never wanted to wake up.

CHAPTER 24: Lily's Reign

*** THE FARMHOUSE, Lily's POV ***

Waller ran his hand back and forth over his bald head as he paced around the room. Greg jumped up from the bed and glared at me hatefully as he came to stand before me.

Was I supposed to be scared? I laughed silently at the thought that I could be scared of this spineless moron. He did not deserve Lucy, but I could have some fun with him since Lucy was no longer here.

I smiled coyly as he continued to glare at me. Putting as much seduction into my tone as I could, I said, "what's wrong, big guy? Don't you wanna play with me?"

The anger left suddenly to be replaced by suspicious surprise. "I thought you didn't like me anymore."

"Lucy did not like you," I said, running my finger up the middle of his stomach and chest and then slowly bringing it back down. "I never said that I did not like you."

Greg opened his mouth to respond, but he was shoved away by a strong arm, and Waller stepped into my view.

"Stay away from my son," Waller seethed.

I smiled up at the towering man and stepped closer. I smiled wickedly as he stepped away from me, but I continued to advance on him.

"What are you so afraid of, Waller? It isn't as if I want to take over his mind. I just want to play with him a little."

"I do not trust anything that comes out of Lucy's mouth when you are in charge," Waller said, but he stopped backing away.

I sighed. "I told you, Waller, I care for Lucy too. Yes, I wanted to get rid of Lucy at one time so that I could have this body, but my priorities have changed."

Waller frowned at me suspiciously and asked, "What do you mean?"

"I mean," I said as a terrifyingly vicious smile spread across my face. "That my new focus is taking down both agencies, WAMB and MDRT."

Waller laughed disbelievingly. "How are you going to do that?"

"I may have something up my ruthless little sleeve, and I am going to need you to do it," I answered as I held the malicious smile. I winked one bright blue eye.

Waller eyed me suspiciously. "What do you need me for?"

"I have a question for you, my fellow mental," I drawled as I stalked around Waller, giving him plenty of room so as not to make him nervous.

Waller's eyes followed me, his eyebrows rising curiously as he asked, "And what question would that be?"

"I know you can use your ability to draw you toward the mutated DNA and find them."

I paused, but Waller remained silent. It had been a statement, not a question. He gazed at me expectantly and waited for the question.

"My question is…can you draw them to you?" I stopped pacing and turned to Waller with an intriguing look.

Waller frowned for a moment before answering, "I don't know. I have never tried."

"Well…try," I said with a cunning smile. "Draw as many of them to us as you can. We are going to need all the help we can get."

*** MDRT HEADQUARTERS: THE NEXT DAY ***

"Would you please stop fussing over me?" Dianna said frustratingly. "It was just a little shock."

"A little shock?" Chris exclaimed with raised eyebrows. "Doc said you were lucky it didn't fry your organs to a crisp, and you were out for the entire day."

"Well, I am awake now, and I feel fine. We have to go find Lucy."

"You are not going anywhere," Chris said firmly. "I am being serious, Dianna. You need to stay in that bed. Blake and I will find Lucy."

"Blake is devastated. He will never be able to do anything in his shape. He is ready to rain down hellfire on the entire planet if we don't find her soon."

Chris threw his hand up in the air in frustration. "What can we do? I am trying to take care of you and calm Blake down. I don't even know where to start looking..."

Chris continued to rant as Dianna's heart grew heavier, and her eyes filled with tears. She turned her head to hide them from Chris.

Chris had always been the comedic relief of the group and had never spoken like this before. Dianna did not know how to handle Chris's optimistic attitude falling into despair. If Chris was distraught…

Dianna felt the bed shift under Chris's weight, interrupting her thoughts, and Chris's finger slid under her chin and gently turned her head toward him.

"I miss her too, Dianna. We will get her back somehow," Chris said gently, and Dianna fell apart in his arms…

"Tell me how in the hell this happened!" Bellowed Doctor Sheppard as he paced in the middle of the cafeteria.

"I told you, dad. Dianna and Lucy went to get the groceries while Chris and I went to get the rest of the supplies. We thought it would save time…."

Blake's words were cut off by his father. "You thought…you thought…" he mumbled to himself before turning to his son in a tirade. "You were *told* to stay by her side at all times. You were not told to think!"

Blake shrank back from his father's harsh words and tone. He had never spoken to him this way before. Blake decided his father had finally lost that never-ending patience he always seemed to have, and he could not blame him. Blake felt as if he would explode with fury at any moment.

Taking a deep breath, Blake continued. "Chris and I were shopping when I realized I had left my wallet in the car. I was leaving the store to get it when I saw Greg. I thought it was strange that he was here, but then I saw Lucy lying at his feet.

I called for her, but Greg picked her up and ran off with her. I chased them out the door, but he loaded her into one of WAMB's vehicles and sped off."

Blake paused, clenching his hands into fists and pounding one on the table where he sat. He squeezed his eyes shut to try to calm his racing heart, running a hand through his hair to pull it back from his face.

He had no clue that Greg had been working with WAMB. It made no sense. How long had WAMB been on their tail before that fateful trip?

His father was looking at him expectantly, so Blake continued his story. "I went to find Chris but was stopped by a commotion at the women's restroom. That is when I discovered that Dianna had been hurt. They said she had been electrocuted but could not determine how. We went to the hospital, but Megan had already been contacted since she was listed as Dianna's next of kin.

When we discovered that you and Megan had transferred her here, we came back here, and you know the rest. You told me to stay and wait for your contacts to find something, so I stayed. I should be out there right now trying to find her, not waiting around here for answers."

Doctor Sheppard had been pacing around the table as Blake had finished his story. He stopped suddenly and pierced Blake with an angry glare.

"You already know where she probably is," Doc said, but his tone had mellowed. He sounded tired and defeated as he plopped down into the chair across from his son.

"But, it makes no sense. Lucy claims that she saw Waller at the airport after we had landed during her birthday trip, and now I see Greg loading her into a WAMB vehicle. She had been dating him for months, dad!

How long has WAMB been onto us, and why have they waited until now to make their move?" Blake ran his hand through his hair again as he blew out a frustrated breath.

"Greg is Waller's son," Doctor Sheppard said softly.

Blake's glare jerked up and connected with his father. "What?! Why didn't you tell me before now? I reported to you every week about what was going on in our lives. You knew she was dating him."

Doctor Sheppard sighed before answering. "I only recently found this out myself, Blake. I would have told you if I had known. One of my new staff members here used to work closely with Waller and his son when we were all still back at WAMB, so she recognized Greg from the pictures you sent us.

She just walked into the room while we had the photos out one day and asked why Lucy was with Waller's son. By then, you were all already on your way home, and Greg was gone, so I did not feel it was worth mentioning unless Greg showed back up at school. I figured it would only upset Lucy more."

Blake shook his head in frustration. "This is all completely messed up. I will burn that place to the ground to get her back!"

He banged his fist on the table again, causing Doc to jump, and shot up from his seat. He started for the door, but Doc's words stopped him in his tracks.

"You must get her back," Doc said, and his tone sent chills through Blake's body. "She is the most important part of my research."

Blake swung around suddenly. "What do you mean, dad?"

Doc cleared his throat and schooled his features. "The research with the embryos that we discussed."

"You mean to get rid of Lily, right?" Blake asked with a suspicious frown.

"Yes, to get rid of Lily," Doc answered and then fell silent again.

Blake turned and stalked out of the room as his mind raced with bad thoughts. His father seemed extra strange today, and Blake felt that he was not being completely honest with him.

He had always been wary of his father's research and often got into heated arguments with Doc about it. Blake felt the same way Lucy did about it and always had. His father had said he left WAMB because he was tired of how the DNA-mutated children were treated.

But then, Doc had built a facility that basically did the same thing, only with embryos. How was that any different? It was still a life, even if it was grown in a lab and destined to fail since it could not live in a dish for long. It still seemed cruel to Blake.

And now his father was angry, not because he cared for Lucy, but because she was important to his research. Blake had thought his father cared for the woman he loved, but now he was unsure.

It did not matter, however. Blake would not let anyone use or experiment on Lucy anymore, not even his father. When he got Lucy back, he would take a stand with her by his side. He would tell all of them where they could stick it.

Lucy would no longer be the focus of anyone's studies, research, or experiments. Blake would take her to another country if he had to. He did not care who got in his way.

Blake came to his bedroom door and glanced forlornly at the other side of the hallway. The door to Lucy's room was closed, but it wasn't locked. Opening the door slowly, he walked inside and sat on her bed. She had not even gotten the chance to sleep in it yet.

He sighed and closed his eyes, remembering the feel of her lying beneath him as they had camped out under the starry sky. He could almost still feel the softness of her skin, smell the wonderful floral scents of her hair, and feel the sensation of being buried deep inside her walls for the first time.

His heart began to beat rapidly at the memories and the sensations that the memories evoked. His eyes filled with tears, so he opened them and blinked rapidly to prevent them from falling.

He vowed to find a way to bring her back home no matter the consequences and woe to anyone who got in his way.

*** THE DILAPIDATED FARMHOUSE *** *** TWO HOURS EARLIER ***

"This is all you could get?" Lily asked disgustedly, rolling her eyes. "Big, bad Waller could only get ten people, half of them children, to follow him? I way overestimated you."

"He is only 'big and bad' when he gets angry," Greg whispered in Lily's ear.

Lily laughed silently, shaking her head as she watched Waller.

Lily and Greg sat side-by-side on a rickety porch swing that hung from the dilapidated porch of their squat house. Three mutated DNA teenagers stood in the yard, along with three mutated young children and four mutated adults. Lily looked up and down the ranks shaking her head in disappointment.

Waller paced back and forth on the porch in front of the swing, being careful where he placed his big feet on the breaking boards of the porch. He stopped and shot Lily an exasperated look.

"I have never used my ability this way, so you can't expect me to be perfect." Waller was frustrated, and it came out in his tone.

How was he going to get his sweet Lucy back? It was not as if he completely hated Lily. On the contrary, he loved her cruelness and snarky attitude. It reminded him of himself.

But she had made him kill his men, which was something that he could not abide by. He may betray that damn organization he worked for, but those men had counted on him to lead them. Some of them had families and children, or at least they did.

No, Lily was just a bit too cruel for his taste, and now she was an adult that could cause way more chaos than she had caused as a child.

However, he would let her carry out her crazy scheme because if anyone could do it, it would be her. Then, he would find a way to get Lucy back.

He would take Blake and Doc Sheppard hostage. They were the closest to Lucy. If he could not force the Doctor to find a scientific solution to bring Lucy back, he might force Blake to coax her back by playing to her emotions.

If that worked, then he would force Blake to keep her happy forever. Blake deserved to be a prisoner forever because of how he had used Lucy.

"Well, I guess they will have to do for now. But not the children. Send the children back home." Lily's face twisted with compassion, and Waller took a surprised step back to see that look on Lily's face.

Lily glanced up at him and quirked an eyebrow. "What?"

Waller shook his head. "Nothing. I am just not used to seeing you care."

"Hmph," Lily grunted. "Lucy would care, and I do not want Lucy mad at me when she returns."

Waller frowned. "I thought Lucy was lost to us. That is what you said."

Lily returned Waller's frown, her voice derisive as she shot back, "I thought you said you would do whatever it took to bring her back."

Waller nodded. "Yes, I did say that, and I meant it."

"Well then, I must keep her happy so we can come to some kind of agreement when she gets back," Lily said matter-of-factly.

"What do you mean by that?" Greg asked curiously.

Lily shrugged. "I figure we can't keep fighting each other forever over this body. Maybe there is a way we can share it."

"Share it?" Greg said, raising his eyebrows questioningly.

"Yeah," Lily answered simply. "I love Lucy, and she loves me. Even though we both say that we want to get rid of the other, we don't really mean it. Maybe we can both be happy if we can work something out."

"I would like to see more of you," Greg said, smiling slyly at Lily.

Waller stopped, looming over them with his massive arms crossed over his chest. His voice was low and dark as he pointed at Lily and spoke firmly.

"This one is too much for you, son. You may share some of my cruelness, but ultimately you are too kind for Lily."

Greg looked at Lily with a glint in his eyes as he said, "Well, damn. That just makes me want her more."

Lily giggled, not maliciously but delightedly, a sound that was as foreign to Waller's ears as his happy laughter. The only time Waller had ever laughed happily was before his wife had been decommissioned.

Widening his eyes in surprise, he shifted his gaze back and forth between the two. "Or maybe," he whispered to himself. "Maybe Greg will be too much for Lily. Maybe Greg can be good for Lily."

"What did you say?" Greg asked, moving his attention up to his father's pacing form.

"Nothing, son. Nothing at all," Waller answered with a rarely seen smile stretching his face.

CHAPTER 25: Preparations

Lily paced in front of the line of the four mutated adults Waller had gathered for their army. The teenagers and children had been sent back home to their parents with explicit instructions to never trust anyone from any organization that promised schooling for their 'special' children.

Of course, they needed no such instructions. Waller had already visited the parents of these children in the past and given them those very exact instructions. They already knew to be cautious.

Lily was confused about how these people had scraped by WAMB without notice, but Waller explained that to her. His explanation had convinced her even more that the organization had to be taken down, and he had gained a little bit more of Lily's trust.

"WAMB chooses its victims based on a certain scale," Waller explained when Lily asked him about it.

"The scale measures certain things such as the powerfulness and rarity of the ability, the child's intelligence, and the genes' pureness. Some of these things cannot be measured until the child is older, but the gene chart is taken into consideration upon birth."

"What about the ones that are…ummm…you know…," Lily could not even say the word. She had no qualms about killing if it suited her purpose, but killing a baby was off the charts for even her.

"You mean the babies that I have killed?" Waller asked as if it were the most ordinary thing in the world for him to go around killing babies.

Lily shot him a furious glare as she said, "yes, the babies. Their genes did not fit the charts?"

"Exactly. The organization has no use for the ones that do not fit the charts."

"So, they send you to take care of them," Lily seethed. "So, how did these people slip by your baby-killing, child-stealing ways?"

Waller chuckled, still surprised at the uniqueness of his laughter, and answered, "Maybe I don't kill as many babies as you think I do."

Lily's brows furrowed in confusion for a moment, and then her eyes grew wide in astonishment as she stuttered, "You mean…those are…how?"

Still smiling the smile that did not seem to fit his severe features, Waller responded, "Yes, Lily. I do not kill the babies. I speak to the parents, explain the situation, relocate them secretly with new identities, and then teach them how to stay in hiding by not drawing attention to themselves.

I provide the organizations with the proper death certificates to get them off WAMB's radar, and then the babies and their families are free."

He shrugged as he continued, "I check on them now and again just to ensure they are behaving and staying safe."

Her face fell into a scrutinizing gaze as she looked Waller up and down. She quirked an eyebrow as she said humorously, "Well, well. Big bad Waller isn't the baby-killing monster everyone thinks he is. If I did not know better, I would say that you are just a big scary teddy bear."

The strange sensation built inside Waller's chest, and suddenly he was throwing his bald head back in a full-blown, gut-wrenching laugh that shook the walls of the rundown farmhouse. The sound surprised even him, and his son came running in from the other room in alarm.

Greg's eyes were wide with trepidation and concern as he skidded to a halt in the middle of the room that had taken him two entire days to clean. Lily sat on the bed with a humorous smirk on her adorable face, and his father was on the sofa laughing.

LAUGHING!

He had never heard his father laugh like that in his entire twenty-one years. The sound was strangely frightening. His eyebrows furrowed in confusion as the laughter died, but his father's face was still set in a happy smile.

He had never seen his father smile like that. There were a lot of things happening that he had never seen from his father, and he felt that it had to do with a particular female sitting primly on the bed.

Waller caught his son's gaze, and his face instantly sobered as if embarrassed to have been caught smiling. Waller had gotten up, stalked out of the door, and Greg had not seen his father after that until now

Now, his father stood and watched Lily pace in front of the line of four people who had volunteered to stay and help take down the organizations. His features were hard and stony as usual, and he stood straight with his hands folded behind his back, which was his normal at-attention stance.

Greg watched him, wondering if he had just had a strange dream in which he had seen his father laugh and smile with joy. If Lily, whom his father had said he was wary of, could have that influence on his broody father, How much more of an effect would this woman have on his father once Lucy, the true owner of that gorgeous body, was alert and back in charge?

Greg was very interested to find out.

I was still floating in darkness, nestled snuggly into the abyss, as I watched the world pass by outside. Lily was behaving, so I felt justified in staying right where I was. I had given in to oblivion for a while, but a strange sound had awoken me from my slumber.

Waller was laughing. The sound elicited memories inside of me from when I was a child. I ran obstacle courses, went through training exercises, and even took a few martial arts classes taught and led by Waller.

I saw him at least twice a week, sometimes three times a week, and I always dreaded those days. I would endure them with a smile, however. Especially the martial arts classes. I liked those.

Waller had been a good teacher, and I made it my personal mission to make that stony-faced man smile at least once during our sessions. If I could make him smile, then I could make anyone smile.

However, the one thing I had never been able to accomplish was to make him laugh. Sure, he had laughed, chuckled, and smirked at my behaviors in the past, but I had never heard him laugh such a full-bellied laugh that had come out of him just then.

It had made me smile deep down inside this cold, dark abyss where I now stayed, and it had diminished that void that still reached out for me. The pain and suffering it promised weakened somewhat as I felt the smile stretch across my face.

It still stretched and reached for me with its icy talons, but its power had lessened to the point that I could breathe in its presence. Perhaps someday, the agony-filled void would shrink to a manageable size, and then I could come out without fear that it would overtake and suffocate me.

Maybe, I would be able to survive the void's embrace after all.

Lily stumbled a bit when she felt Lucy stir. It surprised her. She had not been hiding in the abyss long enough to feel safe, but she had awoken at the sound of Waller's laughter.

Lily felt the smile stretch across her face at the sensation, and she knew that the smile had come from Lucy. Her heart pattered with nervousness.

It was not as if she never wanted Lucy to return. She had been serious about trying to coax Lucy back after this entire mess was over. But Lily was not ready to let her back in the driver's seat yet.

Lucy did not have what it took to win this war that Lily was about to start. Lily needed to stay in charge long enough to complete her plan, but afterward…

Afterward, Lily was prepared for Lucy's return and welcomed it. Lily realized that she would never be able to survive without Lucy, and Lily planned to convince Lucy of the same.

Lucy needed her and always would, and Lily needed Lucy as well.

Lily's smile vanished as she felt Lucy's influence slip back into the abyss.

Lily shook her head and pulled herself from her thoughts. Looking at the troops, she started the speech that she had prepared.

"This mission will be hazardous for all of us," Lily said as she paced in front of their line. "I know you have refrained from using your abilities as little as possible, but that is going to change. We need your abilities strong and ready to use, so one at a time, show me what you can do."

Lily stopped pacing and stepped back from the line, motioning for them to start.

The first one, a blond lady called Felicia, stepped forward and held out her hand. She aimed her palm towards a target Waller had made and hung onto one of the many large trees that grew in the farmhouse's yard.

Her eyes began to glow an intense red color, then fire flew from her palm and hit the target, igniting it into flames that threatened to catch the entire tree on fire.

That was Greg's cue and why he had been standing by. He picked up the hose on the ground in front of him and began spraying the target with water. The fire went out, and Greg dropped the hose back to the ground.

Greg then took down the ruined target, which was pretty much ashes since it was made from paper, and hung a new one.

Lily nodded approvingly. "Good. Fire. It is a common ability but useful. Next."

The brown-haired man named Joseph stepped up next. He did not even look at the target, nor did his eyes glow. He simply held his hand out palm up, and a swarm of bees, wasps, and hornets covered the target. Their angry buzzes filled the air for a moment, then they flew away and disappeared.

Lily walked close to the target, bending down to get a closer look. Millions of tiny holes littered the new target's paper surface, and Lily's impressed eyes took in the young man.

"That was good, but don't they die after they have stung someone?"

"Only the honeybees, and I usually do not call on those. No need to die needlessly when other more venomous stingers are out there."

"Well, thank you for that piece of useless information," Lily said sassily. "Next."

Greg tried to hide his chuckle behind a cough as Waller's eyebrows furrowed over his stormy eyes.

"I apologize. Lily is a little rough around the edges," Waller said to the group.

Lily jerked her head around. "Do not apologize for me," she said sternly.

Waller did not seem impressed by her outburst. He stared at her with an unflinching glare until Lily finally turned back toward her tiny army.

"Who is next?" she asked.

The second lady with fiery red curls that reminded Lily of Dianna stepped forward. She eyed the target with a bright glow in her emerald eyes as she held her hand toward it.

Lily watched in satisfaction as the target was encased in ice, so clear and pure that the target could still be seen, glasslike and sparkling, inside the thick coating of ice.

The redhead closed her fist, and the target shattered along with the ice. Lily clapped enthusiastically.

"That was very good," she said excitedly. "What was your name again?"

"Bonnie," the woman said before stepping back in line.

"We saved the best for last," Waller said as he stepped beside Lily. "Tyrone, show Lily what you can do."

The large, muscled man that had been standing in line silently stepped forward. His broad chest was bare, and his muscles rippled under his chocolate-brown skin. His black hair was cut short and curled close to his scalp, emphasizing his round face with its robust features.

The most startling thing about him was his eyes, which were large and round with the thickest lashes Lily had ever seen. What stood out the most, however, was the color. His eyes were the most beautiful shade of topaz brown and shone with a kindness that made Lily smile.

It reminded her of Lucy.

In the past, that information would have made her sick with envy, but now she welcomed anything that reminded her of her sister.

"Just a bit longer, and then I am bringing you back," Lily whispered to that spot in the back of her mind and was surprised to hear an answering whimper of fear.

No. I did not want to come back. I heard Lily's voice floating through the abyss, saying she would bring me back soon. Was this some kind of trick? Did she want me to die of a broken heart?

Maybe that was her plan, to force me back out and crush me with that void that wanted to wrap me up in its shattering embrace and smother me to death.

I whimpered in fear and climbed further down into the abyss. I began climbing closer to the surface after hearing Waller's laughter. I had started to grow curious about what was going on outside. But now I felt safer retreating back into the abyss and away from the void that seemed to loom between me and the front of my mind forever.

"Dammit!" Lily exclaimed aloud.

She had been distracted by Lucy's whimpers of fear inside her mind and had not been prepared for the shaking of the earth under her feet.

Tyrone had stepped forward with golden glowing eyes and aimed his hands at the ground, and the earth had begun to shake ferociously. It had shaken so violently that it had caught Lily unprepared and knocked her to her ass.

However, it had been more than that.

Lucy had fallen deeper into the abyss, even though she had come closer to the surface earlier that day. She had been curious about Waller's laughter and crawled toward the abyss's opening, but now she had curled right back into the darkness.

Lily stood up and dusted herself off, then smirked in satisfaction when she realized she was not the only one who had been put down.

She walked over to Greg and held her hand out to him, smiling sardonically. He took her hand, and she hauled him to his feet. He smiled at her in thanks, and then something happened that had Lily ready to run back into the abyss with Lucy.

She felt an odd sensation deep in her gut as if butterflies fluttered around her stomach. Her heart beat as if it were trying to keep up with the butterfly wings, and she felt heat rising up her neck and into her face.

The beautiful hazel color of Greg's eyes, the handsome features of his face, the full kissable lips, and the way his hair hung down into his eyes caught Lily's attention, which caused these strange sensations to build inside her.

It startled her and had her backing away from Greg as if he had the plague. She had been in the abyss and caught these types of sensations running through Lucy's mind whenever she had been near Blake, but the experience of those sensations while Lily rode in the forefront was completely different than just hearing them in thoughts or feeling them in the background.

Lily turned away from Greg quickly and pulled her attention back to the troops, and Greg smirked knowingly as he caught the blush on Lily's face before she turned around.

"That was impressive, Tyrone," Lily said, ignoring the sensations that still roared through her. "Waller will take you all on a few drills before we all set down and plan our attack."

Lily stormed back into the ramshackle house and returned to the cleaned and restored bedroom. She only hoped that no one noticed how much Greg had just affected her.

*** MDRT HEADQUARTERS: NOW ***

"I think I know where Lucy is," Dianna said as she stormed into the room.

Blake jerked his head up from his hands. He had stayed in that position for a while, sitting on Lucy's bed with his head in his hands. He had been trying to devise some plan to rescue her from WAMB's clutches but had been coming up empty. He did not even know where she was, much less how he would rescue her.

His heart leaped with hope at Dianna's words as she came into the room with Chris hard on her heels.

"How? How do you know?" Blake asked, and he could hear the desperate hope in his tone.

"Now, it is not a guarantee, so do not get too worked up," Chris said as he sat on the bed beside Blake and gave him a comforting pat on the shoulder. "But Dianna and I think it is a very good possibility."

"Stop beating around the bush and tell me," Blake said frustratingly.

"Okay, okay," Dianna said as she made calming gestures with her hands. "You know I have certain animal spies due to my animal abilities that let me know if anything strange is happening around us."

It was more of a statement than a question, so Blake did not comment. Instead, he nodded and made an impatient gesture for her to continue.

"Well, I have a very annoyed hive of wasps that live somewhere on the grounds. They told me they were summoned to some old abandoned farmhouse on the top of the mountain to punch holes in a paper target."

Dianna stopped speaking, and Blake looked at her with a confused expression.

"Is that it?" he asked after a few seconds of silence.

Dianna stuttered, "Well…ummm…yes."

"What does that have to do with Lucy?" Blake asked.

Dianna huffed impatiently. "Come on, Blake. Use that brain of yours. If WAMB has her, they will want to hide her until they can safely travel with her. Of course, they would have soldiers with them, and you know that they use mutants sometimes for soldiers.

What better place than an old abandoned farmhouse to hide Lucy, and who else would be brave enough to use their abilities but a soldier practicing their gifts while waiting on orders from their boss?"

Blake's heart filled with optimism, but he tamped it down. He could not afford to become too encouraged, only to have his hopes dashed when he found that Lucy was not there. It would completely devastate him.

"Well, can't you send out some of your animal spies to see if Lucy is really there?" Blake asked.

Chris stood up and placed his hands on his hips as he said, "I figured you would want to go check it out yourself. What if she is there, and we waste time sending the spy and wait for the spy to get back to us, only to find they moved her before we could get there."

"That is still possible if we stand here discussing it all day," Dianna said as she moved for the door. "Come on, you lug-heads. We have to go get our Lucy back."

Blake took a deep breath and stood as Chris followed Dianna out the door. He thought about alerting his father but then decided against it. Something did not sit right with Blake where his father was concerned.

He could not put his finger on it, but he was beginning to believe that his father could not be trusted with Lucy's safety. Blake would do anything to keep Lucy safe, even if it meant going up against his own father.

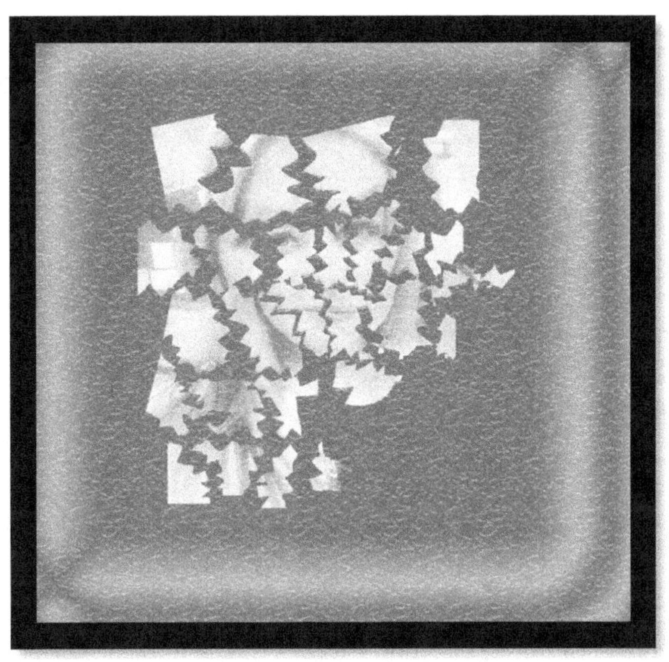

PART SIX

BROKEN

CHAPTER 26: The Confrontation

*** THE FARMHOUSE: TWO HOURS LATER ***

"I think father may be done running drills," Greg said as he entered the room.

Lily shot up from the bed where she had been lying, trying to get some rest after the wearisome day. She had not been able to sleep because the sensations she had experienced with Greg earlier had run through her head and refused to let her rest.

As if she had conjured him with her mind, Greg came barging into the room, announcing that Waller was finished with her tiny army.

Lily sighed as she walked toward the door, ignoring Greg and hoping he would not press her for conversation.

Lily was disappointed.

"Are we going to talk about what happened earlier?" Greg asked as he came up beside Lily.

Lily kept walking as she responded, "What do you mean? Nothing happened earlier."

Greg smirked. "I saw your blush when you helped me up, and I felt your shudder when you looked into my eyes. Admit it. You are into me."

Lily rolled her eyes and kept walking. "I did not blush, I did not shudder, and I am certainly not into you."

The sardonic smirk remained on Greg's face as he said, "liar. You want me."

Lily scoffed. "I want you to leave me alone."

She had almost reached the outside door when Greg grabbed her arm and jerked her roughly around to face him. She turned angry eyes up to his face as he grabbed her other arm and pulled her up to him.

His face was scrunched into a glare, and his voice was harsh with fury as he seethed into her face, "I know what I saw, Lily. You can deny it all you want, but I will never leave you alone. I will prove it for you."

Lily's heart beat furiously inside her chest, but a warming, blissful sensation coiled through her body, and she was not sure if her heartbeat had sped up from anger or something else.

Her eyes narrowed in fury as she shot back, "Yeah? How are you going to do that? I could make you leave me alone if I wanted to bad enough."

Greg moved suddenly, moving forward quickly and shoving Lily back. She felt her back hit the wall hard, and Greg was suddenly covering her body with his, pinning her to the wall.

He brought his face so close to hers that their noses were almost touching as he said in a harsh whisper, "No, you can't. I know how to shove your pitiful little mind tricks back inside you and shock your system until you are writhing in my arms."

His face softened into a seductive smirk, and his tone went deep and caressing as he added, "Or I can make you writhe in pleasure underneath me. Either way, I will enjoy it."

Lily's eyes went wide with surprise at his threat. She was not surprised at the brutality of this man. She was surprised that she liked it. Of course, Lily would not give in to him that easily.

Schooling her features, she returned his seductive smile with one of her own. Pushing forward against his hold, she leaned into him and brought her face closer. She saw the victorious gleam in Greg's eyes as she moved closer.

Her heart beat furiously, and her breathing became ragged as she thought about what it would be like to kiss him. The thought sent that pleasurable sensation shooting through her once more, but she ignored it. She would not fall victim to pleasure.

Lily wanted to play, and she liked to play rough.

She brushed against Greg's lips with hers softly at first and then pressed into him with intent. She heard a triumphant growl of pleasure rumble through Greg's chest as he pushed her back toward the wall.

She smiled deviously as she sucked his bottom lip into her mouth and then bit down hard. The taste of blood exploded on her tongue at the exact moment that fiery desire licked through her veins.

Greg gasped in surprised pain but did not try to pull away as Lily thought he would. Instead, he growled with pleasure again and pressed even harder into Lily's body. The growl vibrated through her chest, igniting the fire running through her into an inferno that threatened to burn her up and leave her a puddle on the floor.

Lily's plan to impress Greg with her vicious play had backfired, and Lily was now a prisoner to the sensations he was eliciting from her soul. Fear coursed through her, but the desire overrode it as she felt Greg's hands grab either side of her face in a rough embrace.

He ran one hand behind her head, grabbing a handful of her hair so hard that she thought he would pull it out of her scalp. The pain mixed with the pleasure coursing through her threatened to be Lily's downfall.

She released his lip from her teeth, and he shoved his tongue into her mouth, pressing his lips so tightly against hers that she thought he would cut into her lips with his teeth. He suddenly tore away from her mouth and glared at her with a lustful gleam in his hazel eyes.

"I knew you wanted me, and I told you I would prove it. I hope you are ready for it," he rasped between ragged intakes of breath.

He released her hair and face to grasp her hips and lift her against the wall. He slid his hands to her thighs and lifted, forcing her to either fall or wrap her legs around his hips.

She grabbed his shoulders for support, staring into his lust-filled eyes with surprise and curiosity. He ran his hands back up to her face with a smirk, pulling her face closer to his.

"Now, tell me you do not want me," he rasped.

Their faces were so close together that her nose rubbed against his as she shook her head in denial. She swallowed hard as he grasped her hair, pulling her into a rough, passion-filled kiss as he thrust his hips into hers and pinned her to the wall with his body.

She cried out in lustful surprise against his lips, gripping his shoulders so tightly that her fingers dug into his skin. He ground his hips against her over and over, pressing her backside harder into the wall with every thrust.

With every thrust, he grunted in pleasure against her lips as her fingernails dug into his shoulder, sending rivulets of desire coursing through her veins as tiny lines of blood oozed down his arms.

Lily gasped as she felt his stiff shaft grind against her through their pants. She thought her heart would burst from her chest as she breathed fast and furiously with every movement of his hips against hers. His massive erection was so hard, and Greg pushed so violently that even through their clothing, he could rub himself over that sensitive spot right above her opening with every thrust and grind.

A delicious coiling of pleasurable sensation began to build in her groin as his hardness abused the sensitive spot between her legs. An ocean of desire threatened to burst from her dams at any moment, and the pressure grew with each thrust and grind.

He pulled at her hair, pulling her head back to nip at her exposed neck with his teeth as he ground into her, moving up to her ear and whispering raggedly, "Tell me you do not want this. Tell me you do not want me to fuck you this way."

Lily could not speak. All she could do was feel. The delicious pressure pushed her further and further toward the edge, and she could do nothing but hold on and ride the pleasure.

He pulled at her hair again and bit down on her neck harder, and a scream of pain mixed with desire escaped Lily's open mouth. The pressure built inside her even more with each nip of Greg's teeth and each thrust of his grinding hips until Lily felt it would spill over at any second.

Lily's moans of ecstasy became ragged and gasping as she reached the precipice of orgasm, and then suddenly, Greg stopped. He stilled his hips and released her hair, then sat her down and moved away from her so suddenly that Lily stumbled and almost fell to the ground.

Greg caught her, grabbing her upper arms and pulling her to his chest. Lily's eyes fluttered closed as the sensations tearing their way through her body went unfulfilled, leaving her shaky and breathless with intense need.

"Look at me," Greg said and shook her roughly.

Lily forced her eyes open and looked up into his face. He smirked wickedly, licking the blood from his lips and then saying in a harsh tone, "You do not get to cum until we do that naked."

He shoved her away, and her back hit the wall again. She stayed on her feet this time and leaned back against the wall for support. She glared at him with a sardonic smile plastered to her face and then spat blood onto the dusty wooden floor at his feet.

He stared down at the blood, smirking in victory as he casually brushed the blood from his arms with the backs of his hands, and then walked out of the door and left her standing alone, unfulfilled, frustrated, and confused.

She had underestimated his viciousness, and she liked it. She would have to try harder next time.

As she stood against the wall and let her breathing and heartbeat slow to a normal rhythm, she admitted to herself that she looked forward to next time. She also admitted to herself that she hoped she lost the next time, which would actually be a win if that building pressure she had felt was any indication.

What would it be like when it spilled over and took her into a blissful oblivion of painfully delightful sensation? She was excited to find out but scared at the same time.

Lily was afraid that she had finally met her match.

*** THE WOODS AROUND THE FARMHOUSE ***
*** NOW ***

"I don't see her anywhere," Blake whispered to Dianna.

"Neither do I, but she could be inside," Dianna whispered back as she crouched beside Blake behind some bushes next to the old farmhouse.

They had seen Waller with four other people, exercising and running drills in the yard surrounding the old house. They had no idea who the people were since they were dressed in regular clothes, but they knew that none of them were Lucy.

"Send one of your spies in there," Chris whispered from the other side of Dianna.

Blake turned suddenly at the sound of Dianna's surprised gasp. Her eyes were wide as she pointed forwards, and Blake's gaze followed the direction of her gesture.

Greg came walking out of the house as Waller came around the side with the four people. Greg had blood smeared over his upper arms, and his lip was swollen and red. Blake surveyed the nail marks on Greg's arms and his bitten lip, and an intense rage swept through him as his mind concluded what could have happened.

Dianna heard the furious growl, and before she could do anything about it, he stood up and stalked toward the house.

"Blake, no!" Dianna said as she grabbed for him, but he was already too far away.

Moaning in frustration, Chris ran a hand through his brown hair before standing up and following reluctantly.

"I guess I have to go follow the idiot before he gets himself killed," Chris said, and Dianna heard the quivering fear in his tone even though she knew he had tried to hide it.

Dianna sighed shakily and stood to follow as well. She may as well follow too. Her boys would probably need a hand, especially since Blake had just made a kamikaze move toward the house.

She turned her attention back toward the scene as she came out of the tree line, and she saw the surprise on Waller and Greg's faces when Blake came charging out of the tree line.

Chris was not far behind, but everyone's focus was on Blake.

He went straight for Greg.

Pain mixed with pleasure swirled into the abyss, where I lay dormant and almost asleep. I had tried to fall asleep and be blissful and content in the cold dark, but the intense sensations my body was experiencing kept leaking into my domain.

I felt the opening of the abyss and wondered why Lily had not closed it yet and trapped me in here. She had said she wanted to bring me back out, but she had not yet tried.

What was her game? Did she want me out or trapped inside?

Another swirl of desire came floating into the abyss…desire?…what was going on?

Curiously, I moved to the top of the abyss and peeked outward. Gasping in surprise, I saw Greg. He was holding us against the wall and…damn…Lily really liked it rough.

And Greg seemed to like it too.

Well damn.

I felt so guilty about hurting Greg until I discovered he was Waller's son. Even then, the fact that I had led someone on even though I had feelings for someone else had not sat right with me. Now, I wondered if there was something to my body's reactions to Greg after all.

I concentrated on the sensations that my body was feeling. Pain, pleasure, fear, and frustration. Yep, that seemed to expand everything I had felt for Greg over those months we dated.

Well, except for the pain. Greg had always been gentle with me during our kissing sessions, but we had never gone further than that. I had always chickened out and never understood why I had been so afraid of Greg's lovemaking.

Now I knew why. I did not like it that rough.

I felt the frustrated satisfaction as Greg teasingly left Lily unsatisfied and standing alone against the wall. Lily liked that. I laughed at the absurdity of the situation and noticed the void shrinking again.

It still reached for me and wanted me, but it was not as scary and large as before. It still promised a multitude of pain and suffering, but it did not seem as unbearable as before.

I still did not want to come out and face life, though. Lily was doing a fine job, and she had found someone to play with.

I was just fine where I was.

Lily felt Lucy stirring again, but she also heard shouting from outside. What was going on? She still leaned against the wall beside the door, but her legs felt sturdy again. Picking herself off the wall, she walked hurriedly toward the door to find out the source of the angry voices, vowing to check on Lucy later.

Greg strutted out of the house, smirking and proud of himself for handling Lily. A couple more bouts of play like that one, and she would be putty in his hands. He could not wait to do that to her for real. He would fuck her until she was begging him to stop.

Or to never stop.

The thought made his member throb again, and he almost turned back into the house, but his father came to the front of the house with Lily's mini army in tow.

"Greg, what has happened to your…oh, son, what the hell have you done?" Waller saw the blood on Greg's arms and became concerned, but then he had seen the patterns of fingernails dug into the skin of his shoulders and the teeth marks on his lip.

He had been playing with Lily, and judging by the look on his face, he had liked it. He watched the smirk on his son's face as he came off the porch and met Waller in the yard, and then a look of dread filled Greg's face.

Greg's gaze was focused on the tree line in the distance. Waller watched as the dreaded look drew down into an intense fury that had even Waller backing away. Waller turned to follow his son's gaze, and his stoic demeanor crumbled.

"What have you done to Lucy?" Blake screamed furiously across the yard. "Where is she? I swear I will kill you with my bare hands if you touched her!"

Blake's strides became hurried as he charged toward Greg, and Greg began stalking toward Blake to meet him.

"Like you care," Greg yelled back. "You crushed her and sent her away because she could not deal with your betrayal!"

Blake stumbled to a halt. "What?" he seethed furiously.

Greg did not stop. He was close enough now that he did not have to yell to be heard. His smirk grew wider as he tauntingly said, "I guess I should thank you. Lily is such a delicious surprise."

Blake growled in fury and charged, bending low to tackle Greg to the ground. Greg met his charge with his eyes glowing a molten gold color. He was about to unleash his wrath on Blake when he heard his father bellow fiercely.

"Do not do it, son."

Greg froze as he went down onto his back with a loud "oomph!"

Blake straddled him and rose over him like some dark, vengeful angel. His eyes did not glow. Blake drew his fist back, preparing to pummel Greg into the ground with his bare hands. Greg bucked upward with his entire body so suddenly and powerfully that he threw Blake off and to the side.

Waller ran toward the fighting couple when he saw Chris break through the tree line and run toward the fight.

"Well, fuck!" Waller exclaimed. How was he going to diffuse this situation?

He did not want to kill anyone. Lucy may never return if all of her friends were dead, and Waller had no way of knowing which ones were in on the scheme and which ones genuinely cared for Lucy.

He could only try to break up the fight, tie them up, and interrogate them until he could determine what to do with them.

Lily stepped onto the porch to see Greg running toward someone in the distance. Lily narrowed her eyes at the running figure, and her heart dropped to her feet. She heard screaming but could not make out what they said.

They were no longer screaming.

They looked as if they were ready to kill each other.

She heard Waller tell Greg to stop as he tackled Blake to the ground, and then she began to run toward the fighting couple. She had no idea what he would be able to do, but she could do something.

Stepping off the porch, Lily ran toward the fight.

I was observing everything going on now. This was getting interesting. Lily had heard screaming coming from outside and was going out to investigate. Greg was running, and someone else was approaching the house from the distance.

Lily turned her gaze to the figure, and I felt my body stumble, and my heart stutter.

Greg would kill Blake as he had possibly killed Dianna.

No.

Blake had betrayed me, torn my world apart, and shattered me in ways I may never recover from, but I could not watch him die. I could not watch Greg kill him.

I surged forward, ready to take back my body, and beg Greg to stop when the void caught my attention. If I climbed out of my hiding place, that void of emotion would overtake me and claim me for its own. I did not know if I was ready to handle that pain overload.

But I could not let Blake die.

I moved forward a bit more when I heard Waller call for Greg to stop. I froze and watched.

Blake tackled Greg to the ground, but nothing happened. There were no convulsions or jerks of Blake's body. Greg was not electrocuting him.

Frowning in confusion, I watched as Greg flung Blake off his body and attempted to hold Blake down on the ground as Waller stalked closer to them.

Then, I heard Lily's intent as she stalked off the porch and charged toward the fight.

Good. Go get them, sister, and while you are in that pretty little head of his, find out why he thought it wise to tear my world apart.

Lily stumbled as she heard her sister's words inside her. She paused for a moment to probe her brain and was delighted to find Lucy so close to the surface of the abyss, closer than she had ever been since she had hidden three.

Hope filled her heart as she charged forward once more. The closer she got to Blake, the further out Lucy came.

"While you are in that pretty little head of his, find out why he thought it would be wise to tear my world apart."

Lucy's words repeated in her mind and spread a devious smile across Lily's face. Lily's sister was beginning to sound more like her.

"Oh, I will, Lucy, I will."

Lily came closer to the fight as Greg straddled Blake, holding his arms down on the ground. She saw the muscles in his arms bulging with effort, and she smiled wickedly as she watched the blood drizzle from her nail marks.

"Stay back. We mean him no harm!" Waller screamed, and Lily raised her gaze from the fight to see Chris striding across the yard.

Chris's eyes were locked on Lily, and they narrowed in suspicion.

"Lucy?" Chris cried out uncertainly.

Blake suddenly froze, stopping his struggles and turning his head to look where Chris was looking. Greg held him, unwilling to let him go just yet, but made no further move to hurt him.

Lily's eyes locked with Blake's, and the look on his face made Lily wonder where Blake had learned to act so well. He looked as if he was relieved to see her and, at the same time, was ready to murder everyone here if they had hurt her.

"Lucy…did Greg…did he…?" Blake trailed off as if he were afraid to finish the sentence, and the dark light in his eyes flickered.

Lily laughed. She could not help it. It was just too funny that Blake deduced the scratches and bite on Greg's lip were from…

Greg bent closer to Blake and harshly spat out, "I did nothing to her that she did not like. She loved every second of it."

Lily's laughter died away as she watched Blake's eyes shut down, and the beginnings of his glow faded to nothingness. She watched his face go slack. She watched his body go limp, and she knew what those signs meant.

She watched as Blake's heart shattered into pieces, and she smirked. How does it feel, asshole?

But wait…he had not loved Lucy…had he? Why was his heart breaking right now if he had not really loved her?

Blake…
His heart was shattered at Greg's words.
I watched him and knew his world was falling apart, but why?
He had not really loved me, had he?

I felt the uncertainty draining into the abyss. Lily was not sure either. I noticed something outside my hiding spot, and my eyes widened.

A shining beacon in the center of the void ate up the darkness and shrank it even more. The bright light beckoned me, promising that the pain would not be as suffocating if I came out now.

What was this light?

It was hope.

Hope that maybe Blake had not known about any of Doc's plans. Hope that Blake had loved me after all.

Hope.

I pulled myself forward, but this time instead of forcing my way out, I asked for permission. After all, I had given Lily control freely, so I figured it only polite to ask for control back.

If she said no, then I would deal with a fight.

Lucy wanted out. Lily felt her leave the abyss, face the void, and now she was asking to come out. Lily frowned in confusion. Lucy had never before asked for permission.

Hope filled Lily's heart. Hope that she and Lucy could work something out after all. Of course, Lily would comply, and maybe, just maybe, Lucy would let her back out to play again.

Lily gave Greg a sad smile and a slight nod, and Greg's smirk disappeared. He shook his head, his eyes begging Lily to stay.

"I'll be back soon. I promise," Lily said to him, and then she slid back toward the void.

"Thank you," I whispered to my sister as she slid back toward me, toward the abyss.

I soldiered forth toward that void that wanted me so badly, but I concentrated on the light instead of the pain.

The void surrounded me, wrapping me up in its embrace. The crushing pain in my chest was suffocating, but I reached for that light in the center of the void.

It came, filling me with hope.

I took a deep, cleansing breath, and the pain in my chest lessened. The light covered my heart as I opened my eyes and met Blake's gaze.

CHAPTER 27: Secrets Revealed

PART ONE

Greg was no longer holding Blake down. He was sitting on top of Blake as Blake lay docile and immobile underneath him, but Blake's eyes were all for me.

"Lily," Greg whispered longingly.

"She'll be back," I said comfortingly. "We sort of have an understanding now."

Greg looked up and met my gaze with raised eyebrows. I smiled softly and nodded, and Greg returned my smile.

"You cannot be rough with me like that, though," I said, pointing a finger at him sternly.

Greg chuckled as he moved off of Blake. "I would not want to. I like you and all, Lucy, but Lily is who I burn for."

Chris and Dianna came up to us with confused looks, and my heart soared at the sight of Dianna.

She was alive! Greg had not killed her!

My focus returned to Blake as his angry gaze moved between Greg and me.

"What the fuck is going on?" Blake asked. "How the hell did Lily get back out?"

"Umm…well…" I sighed and shook my head as I said, "It's a long story."

He jumped up from the ground and came up to me, his brown eyes blazing with fury. He touched my neck with a fingertip, and I flinched as a spark of pain ran through me at his touch. Blake's angry scowl darkened dangerously as he looked me over.

He took in my mussed hair, the bite marks on my neck, and the rumpled mess of my shirt as his face grew more furious.

"You may as well look at my back, too," I said softly. "But, before you do, you should know that Lily was in charge when all of this happened."

With an angry growl, Blake turned me around gently and lifted my shirt. I heard his sharp intake of breath as he looked at my back, and I knew it was bruised up from being banged against the wall.

I knew because I had felt the small radiations of pain from my back when I finally came back to the forefront of my mind and took control of my body.

"Did he do this to you?" Blake asked furiously, yet there was a softness to his tone because he was not angry with me.

"No," I said as I turned back around to face Blake. "He did this to Lily, but she liked it. She likes Greg."

I heard Greg's chuckle of victory, and I felt Lily's irritation. She had not wanted Greg to know she liked him back. She had wanted to play hard to get, but I knew I would have to tell her secret to diffuse this situation.

Blake turned toward Greg, but his visage was still dangerously dark. "You can't have her, you know. I would have to give up Lucy, and I will never do that."

I touched Blake's arm gently, bringing his attention back to me. I tried calming my rapidly beating heart by taking slow breaths. I schooled my features to a composed manner and hoped my voice did not shake too much as I attempted to explain.

"Blake," I began, looking him right in his deep, brown eyes. "We have a lot to talk about, and I have questions. Lily was woken up because Greg gave me a little shock when he was kidnapping me."

Blake's scowl deepened even more, and he started to turn toward him, but I grabbed his arm again and turned him back to me.

"Just listen," I said, a bit harsher than I meant to. I was still hurting and angry, but I was trying to remain calm. I still did not know if Blake was sincere or still playing his part. He did not yet know that I knew of his father's plans.

Blake's angry visage calmed a bit, and I took a deep breath. "When Greg zapped me, he shorted out the chip. Lily did not come out right away, though. She stayed in the abyss for a time, but then…."

I trailed off as a sob gathered in my chest. I tried to hold it at bay, but it choked out of my throat as a tear fell down my cheek.

The anger in Blake's features melted away to be replaced with confusion and concern. He gathered me into his arms, careful of my bruised back, and held me to him.

I stiffened in his arms. I could not help it.

Blake released me and looked into my face, his brows drawn down in confusion. "Lucy, what is wrong? Tell me what has happened."

His voice was soft and deep, and he seemed so sincere. Another sob built inside me and escaped my lips, and I could feel the dam holding the emotions inside the void weaken.

The light that I had held onto weakened and began to sputter, and Lily's voice came through the darkness that had begun to overtake me again.

"You can do this, sis. Hold on to that light. I will be here if you need me, but you must take that pain. You can do it."

Lily's encouraging words tumbled through my head as the dam burst and filled me with the pain that it had held. The pain burst through me, pouring out through my sobs and tears.

I felt warm arms surround me, but they were not Blake's. I looked out through tear-filled eyes to see Chris's face. Another set of arms wrapped around me from the side, and I turned my head to see Dianna.

Strong arms wrapped around us all, and I could feel Blake's heat at my back. I did not stiffen this time, but I wanted to. I was wrapped up in the friends I had grown up with for my entire life, and I was unsure if I even knew them.

I let them hold me, though. I let them embrace me as I cried out all the pain, anger, and hopelessness from the void inside me. I felt Lily stir inside the abyss, smiling proudly at me as I took all that emotion and dealt with it in my own way.

I was unsure how long we stood there like that as I cried out my grief and agony. Afterward, my chest felt lighter, and I could breathe easier. The pain was still there, but it no longer threatened to consume me and crush me into nothing.

I could do this. I could function with the pain as I held onto that light of hope. However, if I found that Blake was just acting a part, then Lily would probably have to take back control.

I could deal with the possibility, but I was not sure I could handle it if it became a reality.

Waller had ushered us into the house, and we all sat in the clean bedroom. Blake sat on the sofa with Dianna and Chris, Greg sat on the bed, and I stood in the center of the room, facing all of them with Waller by my side. Lily's mini-army stood outside, guarding the house.

I had just told them everything I had learned with Waller's help. He filled in some of the blanks since I had forgotten a few details due to my breakdown and Lily taking over.

Blake's face was set with fury, and Dianna and Chris stared at me in disbelief. Greg gave no reaction since he had already known the truth. I waited tensely, holding my breath as I stood silent and gave them a chance to speak.

"How do we know this is not some ploy by you to get Lucy on your side? How do we know that you will not just take her back to WAMB as soon as she trusts you and lets her guard down?" Blake asked, piercing Waller with his furious gaze.

Waller walked over to the bed and bent down, pushing Greg's legs to the side. Greg moved over, and Waller pulled a box out from under the bed.

"I was prepared for this," Waller said as he dragged the box to the middle of the floor. "I knew you would not believe me, so I copied all the files. You can read the truth for yourself."

Blake, Chris, and Dianna sat on the floor around the box and began to go through the files. Their faces fell as they silently read through some of the files.

After a few minutes, Blake threw the files he had been reading back into the box and stood up. He paced the floor furiously, running his hand through his black hair as he seethed.

"I knew something strange going on with father's research," Blake muttered angrily. "I have been suspecting something all along, but I never thought it was this bad."

Dianna's face crumpled as she quivered, "Do you think my mom is in on it too?"

Chris covered her hand with his. "I am sure she is not. I refuse to believe that. Besides, her name is not on any of these papers."

"I never thought Doctor Sheppard would do something like that either," Dianna said as tears trailed down her face.

I grasped at the light of hope in my chest as I asked, "So, none of you knew of this?"

"No," they all said together.

I looked at Blake. "Not even you? Your supposed love for me was never some ploy to entrust me to you and your father so you could use me?"

Blake's eyes looked tortured as he returned my gaze. "Is that what you think, Lucy? After everything we have been through together, you would believe that of me?"

"What was I supposed to believe, Blake?" I asked harshly. "He is your father."

Blake's eyes filled with a fury that I had never seen before, not even when he had thought that Greg had hurt me. He looked at the faces around him, and then his gaze settled on Waller.

"He is not my father anymore," Blake hissed. "The man he has become is not my father. My father is dead to me."

I sucked in a breath, hissing it through my teeth as I covered my mouth with my hand in disbelief. Dianna crumpled into sobs, and Chris gathered her to him, holding and rocking her soothingly as they sat on the floor.

Blake stopped his pacing and came over to me. His eyes pierced mine with a remorseful gaze. "How could you believe that of me?"

I removed my hand from my mouth. "I...I...I don't," I stuttered. I shook my head as a tear trailed down my face. "I'm sorry."

Blake's jaw worked as he gritted his teeth. His eyes trailed over my face as they grew hard and cold, and my heart sank in my chest. His words hit me hard, stealing the breath from my lungs and stopping my crumbled heart.

"I'm sorry too. I guess our love is not as strong as I thought it was."

He brushed past me and stormed out of the room, and I crumpled to the ground. The light I had held onto faded and died, and the blackened void consumed me. I sank back toward the blissed numbness of the abyss, and everything went dark.

Chris held Dianna as she sobbed on the floor, and she jumped as the door slammed behind Blake. She picked her head up from Chris's shoulder and wiped the tears from her face.

"Just give him some time, Lucy. He is just hurt, but he will get over it," Dianna said.

Lily picked herself up from the floor and glared at Dianna. "He is hurt? And what of Lucy? She loved him for years but held him back because she was afraid of exactly this."

Everyone stared at Lily with wide eyes except for Greg, who was smiling broadly. Chris shook his head with a disappointed look on his handsome face. He ran a hand through his coffee-brown hair as he sighed.

"Lily saves the day once again. Lucy will never learn coping skills if you are always interfering." Chris's tone sounded defeated as he shook his head.

Lily's hateful glare turned on him. "She has coping skills. I only take over if it is too much for her to bear. She puts up with much, but this she cannot handle on her own."

"She will probably never come back out now," Dianna said morosely.

Lily shook her head. "Probably not. The only person that will be able to pull her back out now is Blake."

Blake paced back and forth in front of the house. He was beginning to regret his words and harsh actions, but Lucy had shattered his heart. How could she think that of him? How could she believe that he would ever do anything to hurt her when he had protected her and kept her safe her entire life?

He should not have been so hard on her, though. Lucy had always been mistrustful of his feelings for her. She had always held him at arm's length for fear of losing him, and now instead of putting her worries to rest, he had fueled them.

Sighing in defeat, Blake turned back to the house to apologize and beg Lucy's forgiveness when he was stopped by one of the four strangers that had been watching the house while they had had their talk.

He was huge and dark with the strangest topaz-colored eyes that Blake had ever seen, but his eyes held a kindness that made it impossible to be afraid of his large stature.

"Sir…er…what was your name?" he sputtered as he blocked Blake's passage back into the house.

"My name is Blake." Blake offered his hand to the big man as he spoke.

The man accepted, shaking Blake's offered hand firmly as he said, "Blake. I am Tyrone."

"Good to meet you," Blake said. "What can I do for you?"

"Well, Blake, I just wanted to let you know that I can feel two vehicles coming up the mountain road toward the house," Tyrone said in his deep tone.

"What do you mean feel them coming?" Blake asked, frowning in confusion.

"I have an affinity for the ground. I can control the earth." Tyrone's eyes looked worried as he explained.

Blake nodded. "Thank you for telling me. I will alert the others."

Tyrone nodded and turned back toward the road, scanning the area as he called the other three strangers over to him.

Blake turned, rushed back into the room, and then froze when he opened the door. Lucy stood in front of Greg with a flirty smile on her face. Greg was staring at her with a lusty hunger in his eyes and a cocky smirk.

"Shall we find somewhere private to pick up where we left off?" Greg asked her with a seducing growl.

Waller stepped in front of Blake when he saw the fury darken his gaze. Holding out a hand toward Blake, he turned to his son and said firmly, "Stop messing with Lily and clean up that mess."

He pointed toward the ground where some of the files had been scattered out of the box. He turned back to Blake with an apologetic look.

"I am sorry, Blake. Lucy went back into hiding when you stormed out of the room." Waller dropped his hand and stepped back, allowing Blake access to the room.

Blake stepped into the room with a defeated sigh. "I was just coming to apologize to her, but now there is no time."

Chris stood up from where he still sat on the floor. He dropped the file in his hands back into the box and asked, "What do you mean? What's happened?"

Blake ran a hand through his hair. "Tyrone told me that he felt two vehicles coming up the mountain road."

"Fuck!" Waller exclaimed loudly. "Who in the hell found us, and how?"

"What do we do?" Chris asked as he pulled Dianna up from the floor.

Greg put the last file back into the box and slid it back under the bed. "Father and I will find out who it is, and you four hide in here."

"It is most likely WAMB," Waller said as he rubbed his bald head in irritation. "They always find me somehow."

"They probably have a tracker on you as we have on Lucy," Greg said as he shrugged nonchalantly.

"What?" Lily seethed, darting Waller a fierce look.

Greg squeezed his eyes shut and said, "Shit."

"You and your fucking mouth," Waller exclaimed.

Lily fisted her hands and placed them on her hips. "You had a tracker on me this entire time? And here I thought you kept finding me because I used my ability."

Waller shook his head in disappointment. He gestured toward Lily's arm, and she raised her eyebrows questioningly.

"What?" she asked.

"It's on your arm," he said. "On your wrist, to be exact."

Lily frowned. She lifted her arms, looked at her wrists, and then gasped.

"You mean the charm bracelet?"

Waller nodded, and Greg pulled a small box from his pocket, shaking it at Lily with a guilty look. Waller walked over to his son and smacked him on the back of his head as he took the box from him.

"You cannot be trusted with this anymore," Waller said as he tucked it into his pocket.

Lily sighed. "I would like to be angry with you about that, but who knows what situation I would be in now if you had not chased Lucy."

"How did you get the tracker on her in the first place?" Chris asked.

"I had a spy that escaped with you all," Waller said. "She was Lucy's assistant nurse. She told me where Sheppard hid Lucy so I could keep an eye on her. But, when Greg told me about Lucy's surprise birthday trip to the mountains, I had Greg put the tracker on Lucy so I would not lose her."

"Are you talking about my mom? Was she your spy?" Dianna asked.

Waller's eyes held a strange look as he answered, "no. I am talking about Debbie."

Dianna frowned. "I remember her. I wonder what ever happened to her?"

Waller started to answer but was interrupted.

"We got company!" a loud, booming voice shouted through the house.

"That was Tyrone," Lily said.

"You all stay here," Waller said firmly. "Come on, son. Let us go see who is here."

Greg hurried to keep up with Waller as they left the room, and Lily sighed as she sat on the bed.

She was disappointed with being back in charge, but it could not be helped. If Lucy went down, she had to be in control. There was no way they could be in the abyss simultaneously.

Lily was not worried, however. She knew Lucy would come back out eventually when things had calmed down.

Besides, Blake would not allow Lucy to be away from him for long.

CHAPTER 28: The Takedown

"We should be out there," Lily said sourly as she sat on the bed with her arms crossed over her chest.

Blake sat on the sofa with Dianna and Chris, glaring at Lily hatefully. "Haven't you gotten Lucy into enough trouble?"

Lily narrowed her eyes at Blake. "This is all your fault. She would still be in charge if you had not walked out on her."

"I was angry," Blake said, his voice becoming louder. "I was coming back in here to apologize."

"Shhh!" Chris seethed. "You two will give us away if you keep shouting."

"Whatever," Blake muttered, mirroring Lily as he crossed his arms over his chest. "I'll get her back one way or another."

Lily stood up and stalked toward a door at the side of the room. "I'm going to the restroom," she said.

Lily stood in front of the mirror staring at her reflection… well…at Lucy's reflection that was beginning to look more like Lily. She stared wide-eyed at her formally raven black hair; the blond streaks had grown and multiplied so much that it looked as if her hair was blond with black streaks instead of the other way around.

Her eyes had lightened to a shade of baby blue so bright that they almost glowed under the mirror's lights. Her cheeks looked slimmer, her nose thinner, and her chin seemed sharper.

It seemed as though their appearance changed a bit every time Lily came out. How much more could it change before it settled to a more permanent state, or would it change as they changed?

She startled as the bathroom door opened, and Blake stepped in, coming up behind her and placing his hands gently on her shoulders.

His eyes met hers in the mirror, and the agony in his gaze made Lily's heart skip a beat…or was it Lucy's reaction? Looking deep inside her mind, Lily reached for the abyss and found Lucy buried deep within, still asleep.

Nope.

This reaction was all her. She was becoming soft.

Damn her bleeding-hearted sympathy and Blake's effect on her. Blake did not deserve it, yet he had pulled it from her icy heart.

"I like the hair," Blake said softly. "And you look different somehow, good different. Will Lucy be angry with you over the changes?"

Lily narrowed her eyes. "What do you care if Lucy is angry with me? You wanted me gone as bad as she did."

Blake sighed dejectedly and ran a hand through his hair. His tone sounded tired and sad as he said, "Can you blame me, Lily? Do you have no remorse for your actions?"

Lily's eyes softened, and she drew her gaze away from the mirror as she spoke. "I am not sorry for anything I did while trying to protect my sister."

"I don't mean when you protected her, Lily. That was the only reason I put up with you as long as I did."

Lily started to get angry, but Blake slid his hands from her shoulders in a defeated sigh and lowered his head. He rubbed both hands over his face before raising his head back up. He stepped up beside Lily and turned to face her.

"Lily, Lucy said she wanted to try to make it work between you two, so I am willing to make it work as well. I love her more than anything in this world, and I will do what it takes to make her see and understand that." Blake's voice was low and sincere; at that moment, Lily knew that Blake was telling the truth.

She felt a spark deep in the back of her mind as Lucy stirred, but she remained asleep. Hopefully, she would wake up soon after she had rested from her mental breakdown, and then Lily would try to coax her out with Blake's help.

First, however, she needed to get on board with Blake. Blake was right. She needed to start getting along with him to be a part of Lucy's life.

And share her body.

Lily turned to Blake, away from the mirror, and looked into Blake's eyes before saying, "I am sorry for what I almost made you and her do. That was wrong of me, and I am sorry. I am glad Lucy was able to stop me."

Blake stared at Lily in surprise, his eyes widened, and his eyebrows raised. "I accept your apology," he said, and his tone reflected the look on his face.

Lily smiled. "Thank you."

Blake made a disbelieving sound and turned to leave the bathroom, but Lily stopped him by grabbing his arm. He turned back to her with questioning eyes.

"When she starts to stir again, I will let you know so you can help me bring her out."

Blake nodded.

"And do not get mad at her for anything I do while I am in charge."

Blake frowned.

"What are you going to do, Lily?" he asked suspiciously.

"Just promise you won't be mad at Lucy," Lily demanded.

"You're gonna fuck Greg, aren't you?" Blake asked, but he sounded more defeated than angry.

Lily shrugged. "I was thinking about it. I do like him, but don't tell him I said that."

"I just…I can't…it is Lucy's body. I can't think about her being with Greg. I already had to deal with that once when they were dating. I just can't go through that again." Blake's tortured tone tore at Lily, but if she and Lucy were going to make this work, then the men in their lives had to be on board as well.

"Blake, it is me, not her. We share the body, yes, but we are two separate people. Just pretend we are identical twins in the traditional sense, and I am the twin. You even said I look different, so start seeing me as a different person, which I am."

Blake frowned. "Huh. I never thought of it that way."

"Well, you might as well get used to it if Lucy and I are going to make this work," Lily said, echoing her earlier thoughts.

Blake sighed and said, "I'll try, Lily. Just try not to abuse her body too much."

Lily smiled that sly smile that Blake had always dreaded because he knew it meant trouble. Her eyes, which were a different color blue now, sparkled as she replied, "I make no promises."

Blake groaned in disappointment, then Blake and Lily both jumped violently at the sound of the bedroom door crashing open. Hurrying out of the bathroom, they saw Waller charging into the room with Greg on his heels.

"They fucking found me again," Waller exclaimed. "We have to find another hiding spot."

"I know a place," Chris said as he stood from the sofa where he had been sitting with Dianna. "Megan used to take us there when we were with WAMB, just to get us away for a while."

Dianna's eyes widened. "Oh, yeah, I remember that place! She used to say that WAMB would never be able to find it because it was hidden by magic."

Waller's eyes turned to Dianna in surprise. His eyes were so wide that Dianna thought they would pop out of his head. His voice was barely a whisper, so Dianna had to strain to hear.

"That's impossible," he said.

Dianna frowned. "What?"

Waller shook his head as if to clear it and said, "Never mind. So, where is this place?"

"It's miles from here, maybe about a five-hour drive. It's in a place called Daisville, Kentucky. If you can get me to Daisville, I can show you the way from there."

Lily laughed, and everyone turned to her. "The class that I joined on the top of the mountain after my escape was from Daisville Elementary School," she said when she saw the questioning looks.

"Well, isn't that a funny little coincidence," Dianna said sarcastically.

Lily rolled her eyes as she strolled from the room.

Everyone followed her as she made her way outside. "What are we going to do with these four?"

Waller shrugged, coming up behind Lily, and said, "Whatever they want to do. If they want to join our cause, then let them."

"What is going on?" Tyrone asked as Lily stepped down off the porch.

"We must leave for a new hideout, which is miles away."

Tyrone nodded. "I'm in."

The other three stepped up with worried glances.

"Umm…I have a child to care for," Felicia said, staring fearfully at Waller. "Please do not make me leave my family."

"No one is being forced to leave," Waller said calmly. "Any of you who want to return to your homes are free to do so."

Felicia sighed with relief as she looked around uncertainly.

Joseph said, "I would like to stay, but I am the only one that drove here. The others rode with me. Can you wait for me to take Felicia home before you head out?"

Waller nodded. "Sure, just do not take too long. We need to leave as soon as possible."

Joseph took Felicia's arm and led her to his truck, and Lily stepped beside Waller.

"I have an idea to keep us busy while we wait," she said to Waller.

Raising his eyebrows, he looked down at Lily and asked, "Oh yeah? What might that be?"

Lily smirked an evil little smirk, and Waller groaned in dread. He knew that smile.

"I think it is time that Blake confronts his daddy," she said, and the evil in her tone matched her smile.

Waller ran a hand down his face as he whispered, "What the fuck have I gotten myself into?"

Blake stepped up beside them and said darkly, "She is right. I need to hear it from him."

"Fine," Waller said dejectedly. "Let's go."

** MDRT HEADQUARTERS, ONE HOUR LATER **

Lily, Waller, Greg, Blake, Dianna, and Chris pulled into the tiny parking lot, crammed into Waller's SUV.

Waller turned in the driver's seat to the four people scrunched into the backseat. Lily was pressed against the passenger side back door with Chris in the middle. Dianna was perched up on Chris's lap, and Blake was against the back driver's side door.

"Greg and I will wait here unless we spot trouble," Waller said.

"Which translates to, if dad feels powers being called," Greg said with a smirk.

Lily opened her door and practically fell out of the SUV. She caught herself before she fell and steadied herself on her feet.

"We need a bigger car," she groaned as she brushed herself off.

"I'll grab some keys to one of dad's cars," Blake said after climbing out and coming around to Lily. "We can have more room with two vehicles."

"What are you going to do, Blake?" Dianna asked as she climbed off of Chris's lap and climbed out of the car.

"I'm going to talk to him," Blake said simply. "I will go from there depending on his answers."

Chris climbed out behind Dianna. "Blake, do not get too angry and do something you might regret."

Blake's eyes darkened as he strolled toward the doors to the facility. "I don't know if I will be able to control my temper. That's what I have you all for."

"Don't count on me," Lily said with a devious smile. "I am all for chaos and destruction."

Dianna rolled her eyes as she hurried to keep up with Blake's huge strides. "I guess I will have to do it," she sighed.

Blake put his code into the panel and pushed open the front doors. He walked straight through the reception area and toward a doorway to the right instead of heading straight for the cafeteria.

"I have not yet been down this hallway," Chris said as he followed the group through the building.

"This is the way to the main lab," Blake said. "Dad is usually working at this time of the day."

He followed the hallway to a set of double doors at the end, bursting through the doors and into the large lab. Four sets of eyes looked up at his hurried entry.

Two of the people Blake did not know, but he narrowed his eyes dangerously at one of the other two.

"Mom!" Dianna exclaimed and ran over to Megan, throwing her arms around her mother's neck.

Megan gasped happily at the group's intrusion into the lab and held her arms out for her daughter. She wrapped her up into a firm hug, kissing the side of her head happily.

Blake stood and continued to stare furiously at his father.

"Blake," Doctor Sheppard bellowed in welcome, ignoring the fact that his son was staring at him as if he were ready to shoot fire into his face.

"I see that you have found our Lucy." He stepped around the table he had been sitting at, which housed many beakers, vials of liquid, dishes, and other things, and walked toward Lucy with his arms held out in welcome.

The open-hearted smile on Doctor Sheppard's face made Lily want to gag. She stepped away from Doctor Sheppard's advancement just as Blake stepped protectively in front of her.

"You do not get to touch her ever again," Blake ground out furiously.

Doctor Sheppard stopped suddenly, frowning in confusion as he glanced around Blake's body at Lucy, or what he thought was Lucy. He took in the lightening of her hair and the crystal blue of her otherwise darker blue eyes. Her face was slightly different than last he remembered it.

Could this be…?

"Blake, I am afraid that is not Lucy," Doctor Sheppard said carefully, wondering how Lily had gotten back out.

"Well, duh," Lily said as she rolled her eyes.

Doctor Sheppard began to advance again, slower this time, and said calmly, "Let me take her, son. I will fix this."

Blake put an arm behind him, wrapping it around Lily and drawing her closer to his back as he said, "I know this is Lily, and you don't get to touch her either."

"Well damn," Lily thought to herself. *"Blake has never been protective of me before. What the hell is going on with him?"*

Lily felt a spark in the back of her mind and was instantly drawn toward the abyss. She felt for signs of life and found Lucy stirring at the sensation of Blake's touch and protective tone.

Lily had not paid attention to the swelling of her heart as Blake held her protectively and defended her against his father. However, Lucy had felt them deep down inside the abyss, and it had stirred her.

Not enough to wake her, but still, it was a start.

Doctor Sheppard was frowning harder as he stopped his advancements and stared at his son.

"What do you mean, Blake? Do you not want Lucy back? My research is almost complete, and we will be rid of Lily soon. Let me take her to the prep room and keep her there until we perform the procedure."

Blake began to laugh, a dark, sinister laugh that sent chills of apprehension slithering down Lily's spine. She shivered delightedly. She loved that feeling. If Blake continued to laugh like that, she might consider stealing him away from Lucy.

Nah, on second thought, Blake was too soft for her.

Lily turned her attention once more back to Blake and Doctor Sheppard. Blake's chilling laughter had died away quickly, and he stood, still holding her to his back, and faced off with his father.

"I know what you are up to, father. Waller told us everything."

"What do you mean, son?" Doc asked, his brows drawing down in confusion. "Did you see Waller?"

"I saw him alright," Blake answered hatefully. "Saw him, spoke to him, saw the damn files. I knew your refusal to give up your research was suspicious. Even though you acted as if you wanted to do away with the cruelty put onto these children, you still kept to your old ways even after you left WAMB. I knew something was not right."

Still holding onto Dianna, Megan glanced up at the conversation and asked, "Sheppard, what is Blake talking about?"

Dianna grabbed the collar of her mother's lab coat and pulled her down so that her face was close to Dianna's. She began to whisper in her mother's ear.

"Do not believe the children," Doctor Sheppard said as he turned their way. "They have been brainwashed by Waller."

"Yes, we have been brainwashed," Blake said. He released Lily and pulled her around to his side. "We have been brainwashed by you all these years."

Megan's disbelieving gasp was so loud that it filled the large lab room. Doctor Sheppard's faux look of confusion dropped away. His true face emerged, furious and cruel, and a harsh gleam glittered in his faded blue eyes.

Megan shrank back from that look, holding her daughter protectively as she said, "Doc, how could you?"

"How could I not?" he seethed. "We were all in the same class, Megan. Waller, you, and me. We were all held at WAMB, even though you do not remember. You were decommissioned and have been given new memories, but I remember everything.

They raised us to be their lap dogs. They trained and schooled us to use us for their own devices, all while pretending they cared. They allowed us a life, family, and children, only to take them away from us later when we refused to be their lap dogs.

They did it to Waller and to me. I tried to convince Waller to join me when I left WAMB, but he would not come. I assumed his obsession with Lucy would make him want to come, but now I know why he did not come.

He knew of my plans, snooping around in things he should not be messing with. But, no matter. I have the very thing that will get him on my side, even if it is by force. I need his skills to find others like Lucy."

"What are you babbling about?" Blake said as he stepped further into the room, moving toward Megan and Dianna.

"I am speaking of you, Megan. You will help me convince Waller to join us." Doc moved closer to Megan and Dianna just as Blake moved up onto his father from behind.

Megan moved in front of her daughter, pushing Dianna protectively behind her. "What are you talking about? Why would Waller listen to me?"

"Oh, I am sure he will listen," Sheppard said. "You will have to trust me."

"Trust you?" Megan shouted sharply. "I have trusted you all of these years. I have followed your lead, thinking that you were trying to help these children, not turn them into some kind of army for your crazy schemes."

"You will do this willingly or unwillingly. Either way, this is happening," Doc said wickedly. "You will all follow me, or you will die."

"Father, what are you going to do?" Blake asked angrily.

"You do not have to worry about that," Doc said as he turned to Blake with his evil grin. "You will be locked in your room until you learn respect."

Blake's eyebrows rose in surprise. "Father, what has happened to you? This is not you.'

"This is me, Blake. This has always been me, and thank the universe, I no longer have to act like a sniveling simpleton." Doctor Sheppard turned back toward Megan and Dianna.

"I will deal with you first, then with my son and his friends."

Lily looked toward the two other men that had been in the room. They were hunkering fearfully under one of the tables by the door beside where Lily stood.

"Go," she whispered at them furiously, and they bolted from the room.

Lily turned back to the room as chaos ensued.

Blake yelled, "Leave them alone!" as he raised his hands toward his father, and the glow of his eyes flared to life.

"Blake, no!" Megan shouted, raising her hands toward Blake.

"Mom, what are you doing?" Dianna shouted as she grabbed one of her mother's arms and began to pull. "You do not even have any powers."

"I got your back!" Chris yelled as the silver glow of his eyes lit up his face, and he pointed his hands toward a metal table at the back of the room.

Wind shot out of Blake's palms with enough force to knock Doc from his feet, but somehow Doc stood his ground, hunkering forward with his hands held out toward his son.

Chris's ability liquefied the metal table, and the liquefied metal flowed toward Doc's feet, but Doc turned toward it and pointed his hands toward it.

The metal became solid once more, turning into a disfigured metal sheet lying on the floor, and Doc turned again toward his son.

"Dad?" Blake whispered uncertainly.

"He's a null," Lily whispered. "His power stops all other powers. That's why his eyes don't glow."

"That's right, girl. None of you can touch me," Doc shot back hatefully.

Lily smiled wickedly as she sauntered fearlessly toward Doc. "Oh, but that is not completely true now, is it? Mental powers work on nulls with physical touch."

Doc backed away as Lily strode closer, holding his hands up in a gesture of defense this time. "Stay away from me, you wicked girl," he exclaimed.

Lily ignored him, grabbing his arm and pulling him toward her as her eyes lit up with a bright blue light. Sheppard tried to tear from Lily's grip, but Doc was thin and weak, and Lily was strong. The tingling began in her fingers where her tight grip held onto Doc's arm, but before she could take his mind, Blake grabbed her other arm and pulled her back to him.

"Don't," he said as the golden light in his eyes pulsed in time with his heartbeat. "He is mine."

"Blake, you don't understand. Not only do nulls stop all powers, but they absorb them as well," Lily said worriedly.

She could tell Blake was not listening, so she released Doc to keep Blake from pulling him with her. Blake pulled her back to him and placed her behind him as he raised his hands toward his father again.

She pulled on Blake's arm, begging him to turn and listen to her, but before anyone could react, Doc raised his arms toward Blake at the same time that Blake raised his hands, and The forceful wind that Blake had shot from his hands earlier came from Doc's hands this time and headed straight for Blake.

He only had time to squeeze his eyes shut and brace for impact, hoping that Lily had enough time to get out of the way before he was flung backward, but the impact did not come.

Blake cracked his eyes open and saw a shimmer just as he heard Lily and Dianna gasp in surprise.

"What the hell…?" Chris exclaimed.

Blake opened his eyes the rest of the way and saw a shimmering globe surrounding him, protecting him from the gust of wind hammering against the outside of the shield.

"Woah!" Blake exclaimed.

His eyes roamed around the room, looking through the shimmering glass of the shield held around him. He met Megan's relieved gaze as her eyes glowed with emerald light. She still had her hands held out toward him.

Raising his eyebrows in surprise, he said, "Is this you?"

Megan smiled and nodded.

A furious, booming yell belted from Doctor Sheppard's mouth as he dropped his arms. He turned furiously toward Megan, his blue eyes burning with rage.

"How is this possible?" he seethed.

Megan's glowing eyes narrowed. "I never lost my memories. I just acted as though I did to protect my family. I took an antidote right before they shot that vile fluid into me."

"Mom?" Dianna whispered uncertainly.

"I'll explain later, honey," Megan whispered back, shoving Dianna behind her as she glared at Doc.

"No matter," Doc Sheppard said. "You will still be useful."

"You are outnumbered," Chris said. "We may not be able to use our abilities on you, but we can overpower you."

Doctor Sheppard chuckled. "Do you think that I would leave myself unprotected?'

He turned to the lab's still-open door and shouted, "Guards!"

All eyes turned toward the door as everyone's hands shot up, preparing to take out whoever entered the door.

Doc Sheppard moved quickly toward the door, but Blake tackled him into one of the tables as he ran by. Both men and the table crashed to the floor.

The metal table clanged loudly as it crashed to its side, Doc landed on his back, and Blake landed on top of his father. Blake twisted quickly into a sitting position, grabbing his father's arms and pinning him to the floor.

Blake was a big man with muscular stature, and his father was tall and thin. He did not have the strength to wrestle from Blake's grip, but he struggled underneath Blake's hold.

"Guards!" Doc shouted even louder as he struggled.

Lily moved quickly to shut and lock the door, but before she could, a massive body moved into the door frame.

"I am afraid that your guards are incapacitated, Doctor Sheppard," Waller said smoothly as he entered the room.

Greg sauntered in behind him with his eyes blazing golden light, throwing a playful wink at Lily and saying, "Hey, babe. Did ya miss me?"

Lily rolled her eyes even as her heart fluttered happily.

Waller's eyes roamed the room, taking in the situation. His eyes landed on Dianna and Megan, and a momentary spark of grief and loss flowed through his gray depths so quickly that one would have thought they had imagined it if they had seen it.

He glanced at Chris, standing on the other side of the room with a saddened look. Waller felt pity for the boy. His parents had been decommissioned long ago. Only his power over metal, a scarce ability, had kept him from being decommissioned at a young age.

He looked over toward Blake, who had his father pinned to the floor, glaring down at him in resigned hatefulness with a touch of loss. Waller was sure that Blake would have a hard time working through this. Blake had been close to his father when he was younger.

Finally, his eyes landed on Lily, who had sidled up to his son's side. He took a deep breath and ran a hand over his bald head. He had no idea how he would deal with her and Greg or how he would get Lucy back.

"I think we need to burn this place to the ground," Chris said as he stepped forward. "If we eliminate all his research, he will have nothing left to go on. WAMB already raided and burned the other lab, and this is the last one."

"Is there anywhere else that you know of where he keeps his research?" Dianna asked her mother.

Megan started as if she had forgotten where she was for the moment. Her fearful gaze had been locked on Waller. "Umm…what did you say?"

Dianna smiled comfortingly. "Do not worry, mom. He is on our side. He's rough around the edges, but I doubt he will hurt you."

Megan turned her full attention to Dianna and said, "Yes, I am sure you are right."

Dianna asked her question again, and Megan responded, "Not that I am aware of. This was the last place he had, and he also lived here, so all his personal files are here."

Doctor Waller lay on the floor under his son's crushing weight, screaming in rage and threats. Blake ignored his screams and pleas not to burn the lab as he hauled his father up from the floor.

"Here," Waller said to Blake, pulling a set of metal cuffs out of his tactical vest. "Put these on him. They have nullifying effects that prevent the use of abilities.

"Give them to me," Megan said, reaching her hand out for the cuffs.

Waller frowned and handed them to her, watching her curiously as she held them in her hands. A bright light radiated from her hands, flowing into the cuffs and bathing them in shimmering sparkles. The light settled into the cuffs, giving them a shine that they had not had before.

"That should make the nullifying power stronger," she whispered as she moved toward Blake and handed him the cuffs.

Her gaze turned toward Waller, and she smiled softly.

His eyes were tortured, his visage twisted into a look that Lily had never seen on his face before.

"You remember," he whispered roughly.

Megan only nodded and moved toward the door, where the others were slowly moving.

Blake snapped the cuffs onto his father and led him from the room. "I will sit with my father in the cafeteria while you all gather supplies and snag some keys. We will probably need another two vehicles for our trip."

"Where are we going?" Megan asked curiously as she came out of the lab behind Greg and Waller.

Dianna came out behind her mother and answered, "Your special place."

Dianna turned to her daughter with a surprised look. "You remember that place?"

Dianna nodded. "Of course. I always felt safe there."

"I remember it too," Waller said low enough for only Megan to hear as he bent down close to her.

"I guess I have a lot of explaining to do when we get there," she whispered back.

Waller only nodded as he moved back from Megan and went to explore the place for supplies.

They loaded four vehicles down with supplies. Blake drove the little red sports car with his father cuffed and tied in the back. Greg drove another vehicle, and Lily offered to ride with him even though Blake glared at her.

"Go with them," Waller told Megan, and Blake chuckled in victory as Greg shot his dad an exasperated look.

Waller drove his own vehicle, and Chris and Dianna drove the fourth and final one. Three SUVs with black tinted windows and a tiny red sports car, which belonged to Doctor Waller, sped out of the hospital parking lot and back down the mountain toward the interstate.

Lily gazed into the side view mirror, looking back at the flames that licked the air, burning out of each of the open windows of MDRT's last standing lab that had been lit on fire by Blake's hand of power.

She flinched at the booming sound of an explosion from inside the building, which lit up the structure even more. She watched it burn in satisfaction as they drove away until the burning building was out of sight.

The Mutated DNA Research Team was no more.

CHAPTER 29: The Chase

With Waller's car in the lead, four cars pulled up in front of the farmhouse. The three remaining mutants watched as everyone piled out of the vehicles.

"Get the supplies from the house, and then pick a car. We are leaving this place," Waller said commandingly as he stepped into the yard.

Megan came up to Waller, her coffee-brown hair shining in the setting sun. Waller looked into her serious green gaze, and his heart pattered fiercely inside his chest.

She was one of the many reasons he had not burned MDRT to the ground before. He never wanted to take the chance of hurting her. It had been hell seeing her every day before she escaped from WAMB, and it had been a relief to know that he did not have to see her again and yet know that she was safe.

"Can we talk before we leave?" she asked uncertainly.

Waller nodded and gestured for her to follow him. He led her to the back of the house, where a small bench sat in front of a miniature flower garden. A tiny, weathered birdbath sat in the middle of the garden, surrounded by crumbling stones and filled with weeds that choked out what little flowers were left living.

He sat on the bench and gestured for her to sit beside him. His tortured gaze fell on her as she opened her mouth to speak.

"I had to, Gene. I had to pretend that my memories were gone," she whispered softly.

Waller closed his eyes, squeezing them shut against the pain that filled his heart as he asked, "why, Megan?"

"If WAMB had discovered that I still had my memories, they would have killed the children and me." Megan bowed her head, lowering her gaze to her lap.

Waller opened his eyes and said, "Why didn't you tell me after you escaped WAMB?"

Megan sighed. "We had won. We were off their radar. They were more interested in Lucy than us, but if they had found out that I had lied, they would have strengthened their search to keep a hold over you."

"I could have protected you, Megan like I did Lucy," Waller said, and his voice began to grow angry. "Do you know what I went through? Seeing you every day and not being able to touch you, kiss you? Not being able to tell my baby daughter that I was her dad and watching her grow up from afar?"

Megan lifted her gaze, and tears began to flow down her cheeks. Her eyes were filled with agony as she responded, "I know, Gene. Don't you think I suffered too? I had to watch my baby boy grow up from afar, but I did it to protect the children.

I would have gladly died for you so that you would not have to live with the pain of seeing me every day, but I could not bear the thought of losing Greg and Dianna. I was just thankful that they at least let you keep Greg. At least I knew that you had something to keep you human."

Waller took a deep breath and released the pain with his exhale. Megan was right. She had done the right thing by keeping their children safe.

"If I had known that you had been protecting Lucy and her friends, I would have reached out to you. I would have…."

She choked on a sob, stopping her from speaking.

Waller tenderly wiped the tears from her cheeks as he said, "Alright, baby. Don't cry anymore. We will figure this out, and I will keep you all safe as I have done for years."

Megan's throat worked as she swallowed the lump that had formed in her throat. She smiled softly at this man who had captured her heart despite his dark soul. He had a good heart deep, deep inside, and he had always been soft and gentle with her.

Except in bed, but Dianna loved a little pain with her lovemaking.

She watched as the snake tattoo that had always turned her on writhed on his neck as he swallowed. He was so dark and dangerous, which had always lit Dianna's loins. She had missed him so much.

Waller had missed her as well. He bent his head and softly captured her lips with his, wrapping one arm behind her back and sinking his other hand into her mass of brown curls.

He had always loved her hair, shiny and soft and so easy to pull.

He nipped her lip roughly, causing her to moan with desire as she climbed up to straddle him. She grasped his shoulders, breaking the kiss to throw her head back and give him access to her neck.

"God, I missed you," she rasped roughly as she pushed her hips forward, grinding herself against him and gasping with pleasure as she felt his hardness through her pants.

Waller licked up her neck to her chin and groaned as she ground into him. He wanted to bite into her neck so fucking bad, but…

"I missed you too," he rasped back in a tortured tone. "But, we cannot do that here, and not until we explain things to the kids."

Megan drew her head back down, her green eyes hooded with passion. "They are not kids any longer, Gene."

"I know, but…."

"What the hell is going on back here?" Lily said. A mischievous smile was stretched across her face as she skipped around the side of the house.

Megan shot up from Waller's lap, shakily smoothing her shirt back down and running her fingers through her mussed hair. Waller sat still with his hands in his lap, covering his erection.

"Lily!" Megan exclaimed, trying to keep the guilt from her voice. "Did you need something?"

Lily twirled a piece of her hair around her finger as she glared at the pair in suspicion. "I was looking for Waller to tell him that we are ready to leave, and Dianna is still looking for her mother. I wonder what she would say if she found you out here with Waller?"

"Lily, please do not do that. This is a sensitive matter, and we would rather they found out from us," Waller said sternly.

"They?" Lily asked, her blue eyes sparkling with mischief. "Hmmm…this just keeps getting more and more interesting."

"Lily…," Megan began, but Lily cut her off.

"Alright, alright, I won't tell since you said please." Lily smiled and turned, skipping off back around the front of the house.

Megan sighed in relief. "We better tell them soon."

"The sooner, the better," Waller said, still suffering from a massive erection.

*** SOMEWHERE IN KENTUCKY ***
*** TWO HOURS LATER ***

"We should stop somewhere," Megan said from the passenger seat.

She was riding with Waller in his vehicle, which was in the lead on the interstate, with Tyrone in the back seat. They were only two hours from their destination, but it was dark, and Megan was tired after the very trying day.

"We can stop at a rest area, but I want to get there as soon as possible. I do not want to stop and waste time." Waller glanced at Megan apologetically before turning back to the road.

Megan sighed. "Okay, I guess you have a point."

Megan leaned her head against the back of the seat just as she heard tires screeching. Her head snapped up to see Waller's face crumple in anger and fear as he glanced in the rearview mirror.

Waller braked suddenly, skidding the large SUV sideways across the lanes. Megan gritted her teeth and held on to her seat as they lurched across the road, coming to a quick halt on the shoulder.

Waller jumped from the truck as soon as he had slammed the gearshift into park, running back toward the other three cars that were pulling off to the side as well.

Tyrone climbed out of the back seat and began running, and Megan jumped out and ran too. She was unsure what was going on, but her heart skidded with fear. She ran harder when she spotted the little red sports car flipped up onto its side.

Blake…oh god…Blake and Doc had been in that car.

She ran past one of the SUVs that had been following Waller's SUV as Chris and Dianna jumped out and began running alongside her. Bonnie and Joseph came out of the back and joined the fray.

331

Lily's heart was hammering in her chest as she jumped from the third SUV before it had even come to a complete stop. She saw the others at a dead run, running up the shoulder of the road toward the flipped car.

Fuck! If something happens to Blake, Lucy will never come out," Lily thought to herself as she ran for the flipped car.

She spotted Waller running ahead; he was almost to the car when she heard the first gunshots.

"What the fuck!" Greg exclaimed as he stumbled and looked around for the source of the sound.

Lily kept running, keeping her eyes glued to the flipped car as she watched the wheel that kept turning around and around as if it were still trying to drive away despite being flipped up on its side. It had been flattened, probably shot flat judging from the gunshots, which explained why the car had lost control.

Her heart leaped with relief when she saw a black-haired figure climbing up and out of the car, but her relief was short-lived when another gunshot rang out, and Blake fell from the window and slid to the ground.

"Blake! God, no!" Lily screamed and ran harder.

Waller pulled a gun from his vest as he ran, and when he reached the car and Blake's still body lying on the ground, he knelt beside Blake and aimed his gun out into the darkness of the interstate and the passing cars. He searched the area, the tip of his gun following his eyes as he searched.

Lily slid to the ground, stopping beside Blake as she lifted his head from the ground and placed it in her lap.

"Blake, please," she whispered shakily as tears built in her eyes.

What the hell was this? Lily was not used to feeling pain that she did not like, and she sure as hell was not used to crying.

"Blake, dammit, you cannot die. Lucy will be furious with me if I let you die." Lily smoothed the hair back from Blake's face as another gunshot rang out in the dark.

She heard a grunt of pain, and Waller screamed out, "No!"

"Joseph!" Lily heard Bonnie yell.

"Joseph, no," Bonnie sobbed, and she could tell from the tortured tone that it was probably bad.

"Where the fuck are they?" Greg yelled as he came to a halt and knelt beside Lily.

One of the SUVs backed up, shielding Lily, Blake, and Greg from the road and the many passing cars.

"The shots are coming from the other side of the interstate," Megan said as she rolled the SUV window down. "Come on and get him in here and leave the car."

"What about Doc?" Lily asked.

"Screw him," Greg spat vehemently. "The world is better off without him."

Blake groaned, catching Lily's attention. "Thank God," she breathed in relief.

"Lily, we have to get him to a hospital," Greg said, his voice quivering.

He held up his hand that had been resting on the ground beside Blake, and it was covered in blood. Icy dread crept its way up Lily's spine as Blake was lifted from her and placed in the truck by Waller.

"He is bleeding badly," Greg said to his dad. "We have to find the wound and stop the bleeding."

"You do it, son. You know first aid. I'll drive." Waller ran to the driver's seat, ducking down when another gunshot rang out.

Greg climbed into the back, being careful of Blake, and reached into the back compartment and pulled out a first aid kit.

Lily started to climb up, but Greg stopped her. "No room. Get in the passenger seat."

Lily did as Chris and Dianna came up beside the SUV.

"Blake is shot," Lily said. "And Doc is still in the car."

Dianna and Chris looked over at the car, but before they could react, Megan came running around the SUV to Dianna, grabbing her arm and saying, "Chris, take Waller's car, and Dianna, go with me to the other truck.

Dianna and Megan ran off toward the second SUV as Chris followed, heading for the lead vehicle. As soon as they left the SUV cover, another shot rang out, and Chris went down, screaming in agony and holding his leg.

"Fuck this shit!" Waller exclaimed as he climbed back out of the vehicle with his gun drawn and ran across the busy road.

"Everyone meet up at the Motel Seven, two exits down!" he yelled as he ran across the median that separated the two sides of the four-lane interstate and disappeared into the darkness.

"Gene!" Megan called out, but she did not dare follow. Instead, she kept running for the SUV with Dianna in tow.

Tyrone helped Chris from the ground and took the keys from his hand. "Hold pressure on your leg. I'll drive."

Chris nodded as Bonnie came up to help him into the SUV.

"Joseph is dead," she choked out miserably. "They got him in the head."

Chris, Bonnie, and Tyrone climbed into the SUV, slamming all the doors as Tyrone merged into the traffic and sped off down the road.

Megan and Dianna reached the other SUV as a multitude of gunshots rang out across the median on the other side of the interstate.

They dove into the SUV, but Megan did not drive away. Instead, she ducked into the seat, pulling Dianna down with her.

"Mom, we have to go," Dianna said.

"Not until I know he is safe," Megan replied shakily.

"Why are you so worried about Waller?" Dianna asked. "I mean, I know he is kind of on our side now and all, but he has chased us and tried to kill us."

"He would never have killed us," Megan said with surety. "There is much you do not know, but now is not the time."

"The gunshots have stopped," Dianna whispered.

Megan listened for a long minute, but there was only silence. She carefully raised her head and peered out of the window towards the other side of the interstate, and her heart shuddered with fear and hope.

A figure loomed out of the darkness, stalking along the median and running across the road. No shots rang out. Megan strained to turn and look at the other SUV, still sitting on the side of the road with Lily standing in front of it. Her eyes were glowing brightly with her arms flung out toward the other side of the road.

Megan breathed a sigh of relief when she saw the moonlight glint off Waller's bald head, and she sat up, started the truck, and sped off down the interstate.

"Good job, Lily," Waller said as he approached her, standing in front of the truck. "They were all docile by the time I got over there."

"Yeah, I should have thought of that sooner, but I was worried about Blake," Lily said regrettably.

"We should get him to a hospital," Greg yelled from the back of the vehicle. "I have the bleeding stopped, but it is bad. We need to go."

"Come on," Waller said as he climbed in, and Lily ran around and climbed into the passenger seat.

She glanced back at Blake as she slammed her door, and her heart skidded with fear as she looked upon Blake's slack features. His usually pale skin was even paler, his face drained of all color, and his eyes were closed and seemed sunken into his face.

Sweat beaded out along his forehead, and his groans of pain filled the car as they sped down the interstate. Suddenly, the car lurched as it was hit from behind, and Waller struggled to keep control as they careened toward the exit coming up on the right.

"What now?" Greg groaned as he turned to look out the back window.

A black truck was barreling down on them, ramming into the back of their vehicle. Waller's massive arms bulged with strain as he struggled to stay in control, and Greg let out a string of curses as he climbed into the main back compartment of the SUV.

"Climb back here and hold this on Blake's side," Greg said, holding out a rag to Lily.

Lily grabbed the blood-soaked rag and climbed into the back, raising Blake's head gently and placing it in her lap. She searched for the spot on Blake's side and gasped in horror as she saw the gaping hole.

"Lily, don't panic. Just hold the rag on the wound and put pressure on it. Can you do that?" Greg's voice was low and soothing, and Lily nodded as she took a calming breath.

She sobbed as the vehicle lurched again, and Blake almost fell from her lap. She clutched onto him, firmly pushing the rag onto the hole in his side and holding onto him tightly.

Greg nodded in approval, then turned and climbed into the back of the SUV.

Lily sent her senses out, searching behind them for the driver of the chasing vehicle. The tingling in her arms was growing weaker due to her tired state, but she pushed on. She growled in frustration as her power fizzled out. She had taken on too many back at the shooting sight. Twenty men were shooting at them, and Lily had subdued them all as Waller had taken them out.

That was a lot of minds to take. The last time she had done that had been on the mountain, when she had taken over a busload of kids and five adults. That one almost cost her her life and would have had Blake not saved her.

She turned to see Greg shooting lightning from his hands out of the back window. She heard the screeching of tires and crunching metal, and then the lurching of the car stopped.

She breathed a sigh of relief and laid her head back on the seat as Waller took the next exit and left the interstate.

CHAPTER 30: Secrets Revealed

PART TWO

Lily sat by Blake's bed, watching the monitors and listening to the steady beeping, indicating that his heart still beat. She was holding his cold, limp hand in hers as she reached out to Lucy, still curled in the abyss.

"Lucy, please come out. Blake needs you."

There was no response except a faint blip of remorse, and Lily sighed in disappointment. Blake had not woken up since he had lost consciousness in the truck's back seat, and Lily was beginning to get worried despite the doctors' assurances that Blake would make it.

The bullet had lodged in his side, missing any vital organs but tearing muscle and tissue. They had extracted the bullet, cleaned the wound, and packed and bandaged it. They hooked him up to fluids that would replace the blood loss and rehydrate his body.

Lily had to admit that he looked a bit better this morning. The color had returned to his cheeks, and he was no longer sweating. He lay peaceful and still in the bed as his eyelids fluttered in dreams.

She released his hand and got up from her seat to stretch out her aching muscles, pacing around the room to work the soreness from her legs and back.

She thought about the sad call Waller had made to Joseph's family. The entire scene had been cleaned and covered up by WAMB, so his family would not have a body to bury. Lily felt pity for the family, but this was another reason to take down the agency that had ruined many lives.

There was a knock on Blake's hospital room, and Lily walked over to open it just a crack, peering out to see who was outside the door. Greg's smirking face stared back at her, and she relaxed as she opened the door.

"How is he this morning?" he asked as he entered the room, closing the door behind him.

"Better, I think," Lily said uncertainly.

"He looks better," Greg said, coming over to stand by the bed. "That was pretty close. It could have been worse."

"I know," Lily sighed. "I just wish Lucy would wake up. He is gonna need her when he wakes up and finds out that we lost his dad."

Greg grunted angrily. "Blake deserves better. We have our differences where you and Lucy are concerned, but he is a good man."

Lily widened her eyes in surprise. "I didn't think you two liked each other."

Greg shrugged. "He was jealous of Lucy and me, but I did not hate him. Since you and Lucy are working out your problems, maybe things can change."

"He took Lucy's virginity," Lily said softly.

Greg's gaze shot up to Lily. "When?"

"After you left, when they were running from your dad in the forest," Lily answered.

Greg's gaze softened as he nodded. "Yeah, I figured. We were already broken up by then. Lucy is not the cheating type."

Lily chuckled. "No, she isn't."

"Are you?" Greg asked curiously. There was no allegation or anger in his tone, just simple interest.

Lily shook her head. "I am not even the relationship type, so there would be no reason for me to cheat."

Greg moved closer to Lily as he said, "I bet I could change your mind."

Lily smirked as she matched Greg's movements, moving closer as he moved closer until their bodies touched. She had to raise her head to look him in the eye, which she did, staring into his hazel eyes with the smirk plastered on her face.

"Is that a challenge?" she asked softly, lowering her voice seductively.

"Yes," he answered simply.

He lowered his face to hers, leaning his forehead against hers as he smiled and whispered, "Lucy is no longer a virgin, but are you still a virgin?"

She jerked back from him quickly, stepping back and putting distance between them as she hissed, "that is none of your business."

The smile never left his face as he replied, "that means yes."

A sound of rage came out of her mouth as she turned and stalked from the room, and Greg sat in the chair beside Blake's bed, chuckling.

"I love how you can get to her. I never could do that," a raspy voice came from the bed.

Greg jerked his attention to Blake and said merrily, "You're awake! Can I get you some water or something?"

"Water," was Blake's hoarse reply.

Greg jumped up and poured water from the plastic hospital pitcher into a cup. He found a straw in the bedside drawer, placed it into the cup, and helped Blake take a sip.

Blake gulped down the cool water, appreciating how the coolness relieved the scratchiness of his throat. He drank until the straw began slurping, indicating that the water was gone.

"Thank you," he said to Greg, and his voice sounded better.

"You are welcome," Greg said as he sat the cup down and sat back in the chair. "Dad sent me to keep an eye on you while you recover. The others are at the safe house preparing for the raid."

"The raid?" Blake asked.

"Yeah, the raid on WAMB. We are going to take down their facility like we did MDRT."

Blake tried to sit up, but agonizing pain shot up his side. He groaned and lay back down with an irritating huff.

"You shouldn't try to sit up yet," Greg said. "The doctors say it will be a few days before you should try to move around."

"You all can't raid WAMB without me," Blake said.

"We are going to wait til you are better; don't you worry," Greg said.

"My father," Blake said weakly, his voice quivering slightly. "My father did not make it. He was dead when I climbed out of the car."

Greg did not know what to say other than, "Sorry, man. Sorry for all of it. Sorry that he died, and sorry he was such a shit."

Blake squeezed his eyes shut as he said, "Yeah, I suspected he was up to something. I just had no idea it was that horrible."

They sat silently for a moment before Blake asked, "What happened? I remember my car having a blowout, and I lost control, and then someone started shooting at us….that's all I remember."

"That was pretty much it. It was WAMB. They were after my father, it would seem. When they came to the farmhouse, they wanted dad to turn in a full report on what he had been doing for the past weeks. When my father didn't show up for the meeting, they came looking for him and intercepted us on the interstate. My father thinks they have some sort of tracker on him, but he has yet to find it."

Blake nodded against the Pillow. "That has to be it. There is no other explanation for how they keep finding him."

"He will find it. He told me that he is not returning to WAMB, so they will be looking for him. He thinks they will try to decommission him." Greg leaned back in the chair, and silence ensued once more.

Blake's eyes fluttered closed. He was so tired. He felt he could sleep forever, which is what he wanted. His heart was heavy with loss, confusion, and a sense of betrayal that threatened to take the wind from his lungs and suffocate him.

He missed Lucy. He needed to feel her comforting touch. He wanted to hold her in his arms. He needed to see her writhing underneath him as he sank into her delightful depths and lost himself to the sensation of being inside her.

Sleep dragged at him as he continued to think of Lucy and all that had happened since she had regained her memories. If only she had stayed unwitting and happy. But then she would still be with Greg, and Blake would be stuck wanting her from afar.

Of course, Greg was not bad, and Blake would have to share Lucy with him now anyway. Well…not Lucy…just her body. But, hell, that was bad enough.

He would have to learn to deal with it, though.

Blake took a deep breath and settled into the uncomfortable hospital bed as his eyes grew heavier and sleep dragged him under. His dreams were filled with a raven-haired, blue-eyed beauty that had stolen his heart and his soul.

*** SOMEWHERE IN DAISVILLE, KENTUCKY *** *** ONE WEEK LATER ***

Lily sat on a stump in the wooded area around the home. The land around the house was large, with an outdoor pool, a trampoline, a fire pit area, and a cookout patio, complete with an outdoor dining table and two large outdoor grills.

The woods around the home were not deep. Through the wooded area were wheat fields to one side and behind, and a cow pasture on the other side.

The neighbor's houses were far away enough that they could not be seen from the sprawling backyard. From the front yard, one tiny house could be seen far away across a large pasture that housed one horse. If anyone was out in the yard of the other house, they were too far away to see.

The place was virtually private, and no one except Megan, Waller, and Lucy's friends knew about it.

Lily sat on the stump, staring out into the distant wheat field, pondering everything she had learned over the past week. Blake had come here after only three days in the hospital and was still healing. Lily could tell he was still in immense pain, but he never complained.

Soon after Blake had settled in, Waller and Megan gathered everyone together and told them a very long, sad story. Lily sighed as she remembered the tortured looks on their faces as they told the story and then the anger and surprise from Dianna and Greg when they found out they were brother and sister.

"But why, mom? I understand you were trying to protect us, so why did you give Greg up?" Dianna had asked angrily after hearing the story.

"They would have had to decommission him since he was old enough to remember certain things, and I did not want to put him through that. We decided it would be better if your father took Greg and kept him away from me. I got to keep you as part of my 'new memories' since you were too young to remember anything," Megan had explained.

"That is why I had a home of my own instead of living at the facility," Waller had added, speaking to Greg. "It allowed me to raise you away from your mother."

"I barely remember having a mother, but I remember small things like bedtime stories and such." Greg paused and then asked sullenly, "Why did they do it? Why did they take you, my mother, from me?"

"That was my fault," Waller answered. "When I was first placed into my role in the facility, I was told that I had to…kill babies." His tone was disgusted as he continued, "They said that if I refused, I would lose everything they had given me.

I thought they meant they would take away my home and paycheck, which I could deal with. I could find work somewhere else. I had no idea they indicated they would take away my family as well. I am lucky that they agreed to let me keep you," Waller said, looking at Greg, and then his gaze moved to Megan.

"What I do not understand," he said with a questioning look. "Is how you still maintained your memories after they supposedly decommissioned you."

Megan swallowed and cleared her throat. Her eyes flicked to Blake momentarily before she answered, "I took an antidote solution that I had been working on. I have been working on many things to combat the decommissioning, but this serum only works if you take it right before they give you the decommissioning drugs."

Her gaze saddened as it flicked to Blake once more. Her voice was barely a whisper as she added, "I was working on the serum a long time before Lucy was decommissioned. I would have given it to her had I known it would work. Back then, it was in the early stages.

Later, after I had perfected it, I would have given it to her had you let me instead of waiting until we had no other choice."

"I understand, but I did not want Lucy to be someone else's science experiment," Blake had said furiously, gripping his side and wincing in pain as he leaned up on the couch.

Megan looked away guiltily. "I know. Dianna told me that was what you had said, and I understood. It makes me no better than WAMB, I guess. I feel horrible for the children that suffered from the bad batches."

"No, mom, do not think that way," Dianna said. "You were trying to help, unlike WAMB, who only seeks to destroy."

"We have to take out WAMB, so this does not happen to other families," Blake said through gritted teeth as he winced in pain. "But we have to be careful, and we have to be smart."

No one disagreed with Blake's statement.

Lily sighed as she wondered about the implications of her plan. WAMB was a large secret organization with governments, billionaires, and law organizations backing them. If caught, they could be subject to punishments worse than death.

They had to be careful and smart, as Blake had said, and Lily would have to be in charge when things went down. Lucy was too soft for this kind of war.

"Is this seat taken?" Greg asked, bringing Lily back to the present.

His voice made Lily shiver in ecstasy, and the look on his face when she looked at him threatened to turn her into a puddle at his feet. She scooted over to give him room to sit, swallowing hard as her heart leaped into her throat.

They had teased each other mercilessly for the entire week, and he had left her empty, frustrated, and wanting. She knew he was doing it on purpose, and she had not once gotten the upper hand on him.

She knew that he was leaving himself unfulfilled as well, but he had always gotten in the last move, and he had always been the one to stop it before it went too far.

"So, you have a sister now," Lily smirked.

Greg chuckled derisively. "Heh, yeah. I guess I need to learn how to be a big brother."

Lily shrugged. "Just love and protect her, like I do my sister."

Greg scooted closer and kissed Lily's shoulder, whispering against her skin as he said, "Yeah, but that's different. I don't share a body with my sister."

Lily shivered with desire as his kisses and warm breath caressed her shoulder as he added, "And what a beautiful body it is."

Lily reached over and ran her hand up his leg, stopping just short of his groin as she said, "You're not so bad yourself, you know."

Greg grabbed her arm before she could take it away and forced her hand toward his groin as he bit into her shoulder. Lily grunted in pain and delight as her hand found him massively erect and wanting.

Greg licked the spot he had bitten before trailing kisses up to her neck and nipping her earlobe.

"I am tired of playing, babe," he whispered roughly as he pressed her hand tighter against his hardness. "I want to fuck you for real this time."

Lily was tired of playing too. She had tried to win this game, but her body burned at the idea of losing. She wanted that massive hardness inside her instead of just in her hands.

Lily turned her face into his, pressing her lips against his and whispering, "Then fuck me."

A lustful growl issued forth from his mouth, vibrating against her lips and eliciting a seductive moan from her throat. Greg grabbed the back of her head, balling his hands into her hair, and kissed her roughly.

His teeth grazed her lips as his tongue delved deeply into her mouth and almost touched her throat. His other hand released her arm to grip the waistband of her pants and jerk them roughly, breaking her button snap and ripping the zipper down.

Her body jerked with the force, and she gasped with pleasure, bringing her hands up and balling them into his button-up shirt. She jerked it open, spilling buttons across the forest floor, and ran her hands along the rippling muscles of his bare chest.

Greg stood up and pulled her up with him roughly, never breaking the ruthless pressure of his lips on hers. He broke away to pull her tattered pants down to her knees, biting at her breasts along the way.

With a growl of frustration, he raised his hands and tore her shirt open, spilling her bare breasts into his waiting mouth. He bit, licked, and sucked each nipple while Lily held on, balling her fists into his hair as he ravaged her breasts with his mouth.

That delicious pressure built in her groin as coils of passion licked her nerves with each painful bite and soothing suck, and she cried out in ecstasy.

Greg pulled her pants down to her ankles and ran his hand up the inside of one leg. He looked up into her eyes as his fingers found her folds, and he slid two fingers into her opening.

Lily threw her head back as the sensation of his fingers lit a fire inside of her, licking her veins and burning her up from the inside. The pressure built as she rocked her hips against his hand, begging him to go deeper, harder, and he obliged as he rose up and began ravaging her breasts once more.

He stood further, grabbing a handful of her hair and forcing her head back toward him.

"Look at me, Lily," he said roughly, pulling her hair as he continued to assault her sex with his fingers.

Her eyes fluttered open, and the intense look on his face caused her to gasp with the promise of torturous pain and tremendous pleasure.

The pressure built to a crescendo, and she tensed in preparation for it to crash over, but then Greg removed his fingers from her and let go of her hair.

Groaning in confusion, frustration, and anger, she was only half aware of what was happening when Greg turned her around and shoved her roughly.

She cried out in surprise as she fell forward, landing on her stomach over the huge log where she had been sitting. She felt Greg's hands on her hips, positioning her over the log, and then heard the zipper of his pants.

She swallowed hard as the pressure subsided somewhat. The log bit into the bare skin of her stomach and breasts as he pressed her down onto it, then slapped her hard on her ass.

She cried out, tears stinging her eyes as the pain mixed with the pleasure coiling around inside of her.

"Tell me you want me," he said.

She shook her head, and he slapped her harder, this time on the other cheek. Tears fell from her eyes as the intense pleasure/pain coursed through her.

"Tell me you want me," he said louder.

Lucy swallowed and said, "I want you."

He slapped her once more. "Louder."

"I want you," she yelled.

"Good girl. Now, tell me to fuck you." Another slap and Lucy cried out as another coil of pain and pleasure ran through her.

"Fuck me," she said in a whisper.

"Bad girl. Not loud enough." Her walls began to pulse with a wanton longing as he slapped her ass, taking turns between cheeks until she could no longer tell the difference between the pain and the pleasure.

"Fuck me!" she cried out when she felt she could no longer take the pain/pleasure of his slaps.

The slaps stopped, and she felt his hands grasp her hips roughly. Without warning, he shoved himself into her, stretching her walls and shoving her roughly against the log. The tip of his member hit the end of her hard, and a piercing pain/pleasure shot through her and brought a scream from her throat.

"Fuck, baby," Greg cried out in a harsh tone. "You are so wet and tight."

The pressure began to build as he pulled out and then shoved into her again, harder this time. Her walls pulsed around him as he hit the end of her again.

"Damn, you feel so good," he said as he pulled out again and slammed into her so hard this time that it elicited a grunt from his chest and a scream from Lily's throat as he hit her end even harder than before, sending the piercing pain/pleasure crashing through her core.

"Shut up and fuck me," Lily cried out with his member buried deep inside her and her walls pulsing around his massive hardness.

"Mmm…alright…hold on, baby."

His hands dug into her hips, holding her firmly against the log as he pulled out one more time, and then he fucked her. Pulling out and ramming into her fast and hard, over and over, until the building pressure inside her finally broke with overwhelming sensations.

She held onto the log with both hands, digging her nails into the wood as she screamed and screamed with every pulse and wave that coursed through her walls and filled her entire body.

Her naked stomach scraping against the log, the end of Greg's massive shaft ramming the back of her core, and the pain/pleasure of it all coursing through her body caused the pressure to build again.

His thrusts became shorter and faster, and she could hear his breathing stutter as the sensations spilled through her once more, and she couldn't tell where one orgasm had ended, and the other began.

Finally, Greg cried out as he continued to slam into her, and her orgasm continued to ride through her. "Fuck, baby…dammit…Lily…oh god,"

He slammed into her one last time, and she felt his shaft pulsing inside her as hot liquid filled her. His throbbing shaft pulsated against her throbbing walls as they shared their orgasm, and then Greg collapsed onto her back, shoving her down onto the log.

Her heart beat furiously against her chest, and she could feel Greg's heart beating against her back. They were both breathing fast and raggedly, and it took more than a minute for their breathing and heartbeats to slow to a normal pace.

Greg eased himself up from Lily's back and pulled himself out of her. He stroked her back as she lay still over the log.

"Did I hurt you?" he whispered worriedly. As he spoke, he stroked her bare ass, and Lily flinched as a stinging sensation shot through her.

She smiled and said, "Yes, but I liked it."

She heard Greg chuckle. "Just liked it?"

Lily pulled herself up from the log, flinching in pain with every movement of her sore, abused body. She turned and smiled into Greg's eyes.

"I loved it," she said, then doubled over in pain. Shooting cramps shot through her stomach, and Lily sank to the ground, groaning.

Greg pulled his pants back up, fastened them quickly, and knelt beside her worriedly.

He rubbed comforting circles over her bare back as he asked, "Lily, how many times did Blake and Lucy make love after he took her virginity?"

Frowning, Lily croaked out, "Just twice I think; why?"

"Oh, Lily," Greg said as he rubbed circles on her back. "God, I am sorry. I had thought they had been together more times than that. Your body was too inexperienced for a fucking that hard. Had I known, I would have been gentler."

"Fuck that," Lily bit out, fighting through the pain. "It was worth this pain. That was absolutely incredible."

Greg laughed and shook his head. "Dammit, woman, but you are amazing. Next time, though, I will take it easy on you."

The pain subsided, and Lily stood shakily on her feet.

"You better not," Lily said as she wobbled slightly. She tried to take a step forward but stumbled as the shooting pains hit her again.

"Come here, you wanton vixen," Greg said, chuckling, and he scooped her up into his arms.

He stooped down with her in his arms and grabbed his torn shirt from the ground. He stood back up easily as if she weighed nothing and then carried her like a baby, covering her nakedness with his torn shirt.

Lily leaned into him, laying her head onto his hard chest as her eyes fluttered close. The pain had gone, but her body was still weak and shaky. Lovely little aftershocks shot through her as Greg carried her across the backyard and toward the house.

He snuck her into the back door and tread quietly down the hallway to her room, hoping that Dianna was not there since she and Lily were sharing a room.

Thankfully, the bedroom was empty, and Greg carried Lily over to her bed and laid her down gently. He pulled the blankets out from under her, then draped them over her, firmly tucking them under her chin.

She had fallen asleep in his arms as he had carried her, and Greg gazed down into her sleeping face. A feeling of blissful dread washed over him as he stared at her and wondered how in the world he had fallen so hard for her in such a short amount of time.

Lily had melted his frozen heart and claimed his dark soul for her own.

PART SEVEN

RESTORED

CHAPTER 31: Lucy's Return

*** THE HIDEAWAY, THE NEXT DAY ***

Blake came storming into the room that Greg shared with Tyrone and dragged Greg from the bed by his pajama shirt, tossing him to the ground and standing over him.

"What the hell, man," Greg groaned as he rolled over and looked up at the massive hulk of furiousness glaring down at him.

"I told you not to abuse her body!" Blake yelled down at Greg. "If I did not have huge respect for your dad, I would kill you with my bare hands!"

Greg raised his eyebrows. "Since when did you gain respect for my old man?"

Blake kicked him hard, causing Greg to grunt and curl up in pain. He laughed and said, "Is that all you got?"

Blake kicked him again harder, and Greg grunted again. He wasn't laughing any longer.

"She has scratches all over her stomach and bruises all over her ass. Not to mention the bite marks all over her breasts."

Greg rolled onto all fours, his head down as he breathed through the pain. His sandy blond hair hung down over his face as he rasped out, "I take it Lucy is back."

"No," was Blake's only reply.

Greg's head shot up, and he pushed back so that he was sitting on his knees. He pierced Blake with a furious glare as he asked, "Then what the fuck were you doing looking at her bare tits and naked ass?"

Blake rolled his eyes as he answered, "First off, I can look whenever I want because it is my girlfriend's body, and secondly, I was not looking. Dianna told me."

"So, when Lucy returns, I am allowed to look at her naked since it is my girlfriend's body too?" Greg asked, then flinched inwardly when he realized what he had said.

When had he begun to think of Lily as his girlfriend?

Blake hung his head, his black hair dropping into his eyes as he said, "Alright, you have a point. But I didn't look at her naked."

Blake ran a hand through his hair, picked his head back up, and glared at Greg. "Since when did you and Lily become a couple anyway? I thought you just wanted to fuck her."

Greg laughed as he shook his head. "I was just asking myself that same question."

Blake stared at Greg for a minute and then laughed. Greg looked indignant at first, and then he joined in the laughter.

"Does Lily know that you want a relationship?" Blake asked as the laughter subsided.

"I mentioned it to her, but I was teasing her…or at least I thought I was teasing," Greg said.

"I want to be there when you tell her. It's going to be hilarious to see you get your ass kicked by a girl," Blake said.

Greg let out a short, barking laugh and said, "Not likely."

Blake shook his head. "I'm still mad at you for what you did to her body."

"I'm sorry, man. I just like it rough sometimes, and Lily liked it too. I didn't do anything she didn't want me to do." Greg stood up and then sat on the bed as pain shot through his side.

"Dammit, man, you kicked me hard," Greg complained, rubbing his side.

"Remember that next time," Blake said, but the corners of his lips lifted as he turned and left the room.

He suddenly stopped outside the door as Lily came down the hallway, her eyebrows raised in a questioning look.

"I heard screaming, and then I heard you laughing," she said.

"I was having a little talk with Greg," Blake said, quirking one eyebrow.

Lily groaned, her features twisting into a disappointed look as she said, "Dianna told you."

Blake only nodded and reached down for the bottom of her shirt. She slapped his hands. "It is not that bad, Blake. Damn, I am never getting dressed in front of Dianna again."

Blake sighed. "Just let me see a little."

Lily blew out a frustrated breath as she rolled her eyes, pulling her shirt up to show her stomach. She heard Blake's sharp intake of breath as he gently traced the scratches with the tip of his finger. Lily flinched.

"Ouch," she said sharply.

Blake's eyes darkened in anger as he grasped Lily's arm and said, "Come with me."

Blake was stopped suddenly by a hand gripping his arm.

"Let go of her, man," Greg seethed.

Blake did not let go. Instead, he turned and gave Greg the total weight of his furious stare.

"I am going to clean her wounds, but I am not against kicking your ass before I do it," Blake said. His voice was calm and controlled, but Greg could hear the undertones of anger.

Greg gave Blake a considering look as he hesitated for just a moment. Finally, he released his hold on Blake's arm with a shrug.

"Fine. I don't feel like cleaning up the blood anyway," Greg said.

Blake turned, holding onto Lily as he pushed her from the room. Lily tried to pull away, but Blake's grip tightened as he pulled her down the hallway and pushed her firmly into the smaller bathroom.

"Sit," Blake said, pointing at the tub.

Lily sighed and perched on the tub's edge. She watched as Blake pulled a tube of salve, a washcloth, and a bottle of peroxide from the tiny cabinet above the toilet.

"Do you have on a bra?" he asked.

Lily nodded, pouting her lip as she whined, "Why?"

Blake chuckled. "That look only works on me when it's Lucy, and I asked because I'm going to need you to take off your shirt."

Lily huffed as she pulled her shirt over her head and tossed it to the floor. Blake frowned as he observed the scratches over her stomach and the bite marks on her breasts. He turned her gently to look at her back, but the skin there was smooth and perfect.

"Lean backward over the tub," Blake demanded, and Lily complied.

She hissed in pain as Blake poured the peroxide over her stomach, watching as it bubbled up over the scratches. Blake let it bubble for a moment and then wiped the remaining peroxide away with the washcloth.

"You can raise up now," Blake said softly, helping her sit up with his hand on her back.

He poured more of the cool, slightly stinging liquid over her breasts, holding the cloth under so it did not run down into her bra. He repeated the process of letting it bubble and then wiping it away from the tops of her breasts and the bite marks.

"Now, stand up," Blake said.

Lily stood, and Blake knelt in front of her. He put some of the salve onto his fingers and gently rubbed it over the scratches.

Tiny spasms of pleasure coiled through the abyss and woke me from my slumber. I did not know how long I had slept down here in the cold darkness, and I did not care. Now, however, I felt the tiny tendrils of desire reaching for me, coaxing me out of my hiding spot and promising to bring pleasure.

I had felt some backlash of pleasure earlier and knew it had been from Lily. This pleasure that was coalescing in the abyss with me now was mine. I did not want to face the pain of coming out of my hole, but it was calling to me, reaching out for me, and wrapping me in a cocoon of delightful sensation, promising more if I would only come out and play.

Lily gasped, but not from the pain. She felt her sister. Lucy was waking up. The more Blake caressed her bare skin, the more Lucy stirred.

Blake looked up from his work, frowning. "Am I hurting you?"

Lily shook her head. "No. Don't stop, Blake."

Blake quirked an eyebrow as he stood and looked down at her breasts.

"I only have a few more to go," he said as he stared into Lily's blue eyes.

Lily sighed, closing her eyes and nodding her consent.

He put more ointment onto his fingers and began massaging it into the bite marks at the top of her breasts.

Lily's eyes flew open as she felt the stirring in the abyss once more.

There it was again, that tendril of pleasure coiling through me, stirring me from rest. It was stronger this time and more intense. There was no way I could sleep anymore if these stronger sensations kept disturbing me.

Giving up trying to rest, I curiously came to the surface of the abyss to see what was going on. I froze at the very edge as I stared into Blake's face. He was looking down, stroking the tops of our breasts...my breasts...Lily's breasts?

Why was Blake touching her?

Anger and jealousy flowed through me, and I came fully awake and enraged.

"Calm down, sis. He is just rubbing ointment on a few scratches," Lily's voice floated down to me as I climbed out of my hole.

"He should be rubbing it on me," I said sternly. "He should be touching my breasts."

"Gladly. I have been trying to get you to crawl out of there anyway." Lily shot back.

"You should know, sis, before you come out fully. Things have been...well...hard." Lily said as I moved closer to the surface.

I stopped. "What do you mean?"

"Come back to us, and I'll show you. Just, please do not run back inside." Lily said as she came toward me.

Fear shot through me, and I shrank back.

"No, please don't run away again. Blake needs you, Lucy."

I stopped. Blake needed me. I thought back to all of the times when I had been depressed, lonely, sad, or scared and how Blake had always been there to pull me up and put me back on my feet.

Those times were precious to me, and I owed it to Blake to return the favor if I could, even if he was still angry with me. Even if he no longer wanted me because I had hurt him so badly, I could not abandon him.

Blake needed me.

With those words pushing me forward, I came out of the abyss as Lily floated happily down, blowing me a kiss on her way into the hole.

Blake's fingers on my breasts sent shockwaves of pleasure coursing through me as I came fully in control, but there were also tiny stings of pain mixed with the pleasure that made me gasp and shrink back from his touch.

Blake looked up from his work, glancing into my eyes with a frown before returning his gaze to my breasts. "What is wrong with you, Lily? You were taking it like a champ before. I only have a small bit left."

He continued to rub the salve on my breasts but was gentler this time. I looked down at my breasts and sucked in a breath as I saw the bite marks on my skin.

"What the hell did Lily do to my body?" I asked.

Blake's fingers froze, and his body stiffened. He looked up at me slowly, and his brown, hope-filled, tortured gaze tore at my already sensitive heart.

I saw his throat work as he swallowed, and his choked voice whispered, "Lucy?"

I could not answer, however. The memories of the past few weeks tore into my head from Lily, and I grasped my head in both hands as I cried out in agony.

Blake gently grasped my shoulders. "Lucy? Lily? What is going on?"

Greg came storming into the door, shoving Blake back against the wall and screaming, "What are you doing to her? Get away from her!"

"I didn't do anything," Blake yelled back. "You need to let go of me now."

"I will do more than just kick your ass if you hurt her," Greg seethed as he held Blake against the wall.

"Stop it, both of you," I screamed as I held my head in agony. "It's Lily doing it."

Greg froze and turned his gaze to me. "Lucy's back," he whispered in disappointment.

"Yes, you moron, now let go of me," Blake said, pushing Greg away.

The pain subsided quickly, and I sucked in a deep, ragged breath.

"Dammit, Lily, that hurt!" I yelled.

"Sorry, Lucy. It always hurts when you shove them in all at once, but I had to catch you up quickly," Lily said apologetically.

"We really need to find a way for both of us to stay in the loop. That hurts like hell," I replied.

"I have some ideas if you're willing, sis."

"Like what?" I asked curiously.

"Later. The men are looking at us funny."

I let go of my head and looked up to find both men standing over me, staring at me questioningly. "I…I umm…I was talking to Lily. She just gave me a memory overload on what has happened since I have been out, and it hurts when she does it all at once like that."

Greg's face looked guilty as he asked, "Did she show you everything…as in…well…the sex part?"

"Eww…Not that part," I said, scrunching up my nose in disgust. "I don't want to know about my sister's sex life, even if she is using my body."

Greg would not look at me, but I heard his relieved sigh. Blake darted him an angry look as realization dawned on me.

"Wait," I said, glaring at Greg. "Is that what happened to my breasts?"

"It isn't just your breasts," Blake said, pointing at my stomach.

My eyes narrowed in anger as I turned to the mirror and gazed at my body entirely. The bite marks ranged across the tops of my breasts, red and angry, and looked much worse as I stared at them full-on. I gasped as I looked at my stomach.

Red and rough, glaring at me angrily, were deep scratches and minor scrapes all over my stomach, crisscrossing the white, puckered scar of my earlier wound. There were also bruises joined with the cuts, and there were finger-shaped bruises on my upper arms as well.

I turned back to Greg in a fury. "What the hell did you two do?"

Greg shrugged unabashedly as he said, "She likes it rough."

"This isn't just rough," I said, my voice growing louder as I gestured down at my body. "This is abuse. If you took advantage of my sister…."

Greg's eyes shot to mine and narrowed in anger. "I would never do that!" he exclaimed. "No, Lucy. I might be many things, but I am not a rapist."

He paced the small space and continued to rant, "I would never hurt her unless she wanted me to. I love causing pain, but that does not excuse giving it by force to someone you care about. I would never do that to Lily because I am in love with her."

Greg stopped suddenly, and his eyes widened in horror as if he could not believe what he had said. The words hung between us, and I felt Lily startle inside my head. Lily was…processing. That was all I could tell of her reaction inside my mind.

"Dammit," Greg said as he ran a hand through his sandy blond locks. A stream of curse words came from his mouth as he paced the small space in the bathroom.

I heard Blake snickering behind me, which made me want to laugh too, but I held it in as Greg worked out his confused revelation.

"Fine. Yes, I love Lily," Greg said, throwing his hands into the air as he gave in to himself. "And I know you hate me, Lucy, and Blake is not too fond of me either, but I am never going to give Lily up, no matter what you two say."

Blake had stopped laughing, and I looked back at him with raised eyebrows.

I turned back to Greg. "Greg, stop pacing and listen."

Greg complied and turned to me, looking angry and determined.

"I do not hate you. I used to be rather fond of you, if you remember," I smiled encouragingly.

I heard Blake growl in anger behind me and turned on him. "Oh, hush. You know where my heart lies, so stop being so jealous."

Blake looked surprised for a moment, then relieved, and then a slow, huge smile broke out on his face before I turned back to Greg.

"Good," Greg said, crossing his arms over his chest. "That means I won't have to kick Blake's ass and force you to bring Lily out whenever I want to see her."

He stalked out of the bathroom, and I shook my head as I watched him storm out the door. I felt Blake's hand timidly touch my shoulder, and I turned to face him.

"Lucy, I have missed you," he whispered longingly. "I just need to apologize to you for…."

I interrupted before he could say anything else. "Stop, Blake. I am the one who should apologize. You were right. I did not have enough faith in us before, but I do now. Forgive me?"

"Dammit, Lucy," Blake rasped as he pulled me into his arms. "There is absolutely nothing to forgive."

I wrapped my arms around his waist and felt him flinch. I had forgotten about his injury in all the drama with Greg. I had forgotten about the memories that Lily had given me.

I loosened my hold, breathing an apology as I concentrated on the memories, sorting through them in my head and processing them into my thoughts.

Lily had been right.

The past weeks had been hard. It had also been surprising and a bit happy. Greg was Dianna's big brother! And Megan and Waller were their parents? That one surprised me more than anything.

Then the saddest one filtered through, and I strained not to hug Blake tighter to me.

Blake had lost his father.

"Oh, Blake," I said in a strained whisper. "I am so sorry about Doc."

Blake's hold tightened as I lay my head on his chest. My heart constricted painfully, and tears pricked the backs of my eyes. I squeezed them shut tightly. His chest heaved as he breathed in, and I heard a choking sob escape his throat.

Tears fell down my cheeks as I stood in Blake's arms. Doc was almost like a father to me as well. His loss may not have been as hard for me as for Blake, but it weighed heavily on my heart.

"I wish I had known sooner that he was losing it," Blake whispered chokingly into my hair as he leaned his head on top of mine. "Maybe I could have helped him somehow."

"No, Blake. He was too far gone by the time you were old enough to help. Do not go through life blaming yourself."

"There is one good thing that came out of my father's obsession with you," Blake said softly as his warm breath blew through my hair.

"What is that?" I asked.

Blake placed his fingers gently under the bottom of my chin and raised my face to meet his eyes. I raised a hand to gently wipe the tears from his face, and he wiped the tears from mine too.

His eyes were gentle and kind, with a spark of longing deep in the chocolate depths, and my heart pulsed with desire as his deep, trancing voice caressed my ears.

"I got to keep you," he said, and then he kissed me.

The kiss was soft and tender at first, just a bare brushing of lips and a swipe of his tongue across my plump bottom lip, and then grew to something passionate and wanting that sparked an intense desire in my veins.

His hands ran across the bare skin of my shoulder, stimulating goose bumps down my arms and across my back. Shivers of delight ran up my spine as his caressing touch moved down my arms and down to my hips.

He pulled me closer, pressing my hips into him as he deepened the kiss, and a sigh of pleasure vibrated against our joined mouths. An answering moan came from Blake's mouth as our tongues danced around each other.

Blake pulled back and trailed kisses down the side of my jaw to the sensitive spot on my neck, just below my ear, and his hot breath on my skin sent rivulets of pleasure coursing through my body.

His hands trailed around to cup my butt, squeezing gently as he suckled lightly on my neck. He slipped his hands into my loose pajama bottoms and ran his exquisite touch over the bare skin of my ass.

I threw my head back and moaned, wanting him and needing him inside me. My walls pulsed in want for his hardness as the delicious pressure of promised delight built in my groin. I quivered in ecstasy as he pulled the pajama bottoms down my hips and thighs.

He turned me in his arms so that my back was to him, and I watched in the mirror as he pulled his shirt off and tossed it to the floor. He unhooked my bra and pulled it down my arms, tossing it to the floor as well.

He pulled me to his naked chest, reaching around to softly fondle my breasts in his large hands, rolling the hardened nipples between his thumbs and forefingers.

Our eyes met in the mirror as he played with me. His eyes glowed with passion and desire, chocolate fire piercing into sapphire blazes that burned with want and need for him.

"Don't close your eyes. I want to see you as I make love to you," Blake whispered huskily as one hand careened down my stomach, careful of the scratches, to cup my sex in his palm.

I held his gaze as an ocean of hunger swept through my body. I pressed myself into his hand, begging for more, and he obliged. His hand came up to the top of my mound, and he slid a finger into my folds and caressed my sensitive bud.

I moaned in ecstasy as I held onto the sink countertop, holding his gaze in the mirror as he tortured my clitoris with his finger. His eyes blazed with need as he watched my eyes alight with pleasure and longing.

My walls throbbed, and the pressure built as he stroked my clitoris repeatedly, and sharp stabs of pleasure coursed through me when he dipped his finger down and into my wet opening.

"Mmmm," I moaned as the sensations rocketed through me, and I held his eyes with mine as the pressure almost took me over the edge.

He suddenly pulled his finger out of me, causing the throbbing to ebb somewhat, and reached down to pull my bottoms to my ankles. He pulled his flannel bottoms down as well, freeing his massive erection.

He pushed me forward slightly, and I leaned my weight onto the countertop as he parted my legs. He grasped a handful of my hair and pulled ever so gently, forcing my head up to look at him in the mirror.

The raw hunger in his eyes made me gasp as he reached his other hand down to guide himself inside me. The tip of him entered me from behind, and I cried out in pleasure as my walls throbbed and begged for more.

He pushed further into me gently, using his free hand to hold onto my hip and pull me back onto him. I complied, pushing my ass back towards his front, sliding more of his delicious hardness into my throbbing core.

"Ah!" I cried out as he pushed forward to meet my movement, sending his entire shaft deep into me, and the tip of him met the end of me.

It hurt for just an instant, and then the pressure almost spilled over at the intense stimulation of his tip bumping the end of my core.

"Don't close your eyes, and don't look away," Blake rasped in a desperate whisper as he let go of my hair.

He used both hands to hold onto my hips as he pulled himself out of me, pushing my hips to help the movement. As he moved into me again, he pulled my hips to him to help slide himself into me.

He gently bumped the end of me again, eliciting another cry from me, and my walls throbbed with the need for release. His shaft answered my throbs with its pulses, sending intense sensations through my entire body.

He started an easy, steady rhythm using his hands on my hips to help guide me to match it, and together we moved his hardness in and out of me, exquisitely slow and easy.

I held onto the counter, gripping the edge with my fingers until my knuckles turned white. The sensation of his massive muscle moving in and out of me, stretching and filling me, pushed me closer and closer toward the edge of orgasm.

The intense need for release filled my sapphire depths as we held our locked gazes in the mirror, and the lustful hunger of his chocolate eyes as he pumped in and out of me did me in.

I screamed my pleasure as waves and waves of sensation poured through me, and my walls quivered and pulsed around his massiveness. My eyelids fluttered, straining to stay open, fighting to keep my gaze locked on Blake's as I felt his shaft pulse in time to my walls.

His rhythm quickened as my orgasm came almost to an end, and he pumped into me faster and harder as he grunted and moaned in ecstasy. I felt his orgasm fill me, the pulsing of his member inside me, and his warm fluid poured into me in a rush of sensation.

His deep brown eyes locked onto mine, filling with a look of carnal lust and intense passion as his orgasm rode him. My orgasm that had been fading was fueled to life by the sensation of his orgasm flowing inside me. Pulses of pleasure poured through me as our cries of release melded with one another in the small room.

My entire body trembled with the ebbing of release, and my legs became shaky and unsteady. I could feel Blake's body trembling in time with mine as he struggled to stay on his feet. He pulled out of me gently as his climax came to a finish, and his body continued to tremble.

My knees gave out as my orgasm left me, and I collapsed, dragging Blake's unsteady body down with me. We landed on our butts on the cold tile floor of the bathroom, with Blake's back against the tub and me between his legs with my back against Blake's front.

We sat like that for a minute, allowing our pounding hearts to calm and relearning how to breathe. We sat in silence until we had enough breath to speak, and Blake broke the silence.

"We need a shower," he said in a raspy whisper.

"Yes, and we have taken up the bathroom far too long," I said with a chuckle.

"Can you stand up yet?" he asked cockily.

"I think so, but it will be difficult," I said, laughing.

He pulled me to him, nestling his face in the top of my head and whispering into my hair, "I love you, Lucy. I have always loved you. I would never use you. I will always protect you."

I smiled happily as I whispered back, "I love you too, Blake, and I will never doubt our love again."

CHAPTER 32: The Plan

*** THE HIDEAWAY, TWO DAYS LATER ***

The negotiations for a plan to take down WAMB had been insane. It seemed as if none of us could agree on a suitable course of action. WAMB was a worldwide organization with government backing. It would be too risky to attempt to destroy WAMB's entire organization as we had MDRT.

It was much bigger than MDRT had been. It was not some small facility run by one vengeful doctor with suitable contacts. No, the World Against Mutants Bureau would be much harder and more dangerous to take down.

Blake was the one who had come up with the best plan. Blake's plan was not a plan of destruction. It was a plan that would take time. He felt the best plan of action would be to fight fire with fire.

It was a good plan. Even Lily liked it. She thought it was better and safer than storming the compound and starting an all-out war.

We sat in the dining room as Blake stood at the head of the table. All eyes were on him as we waited expectantly to hear his plan. I had already heard it, of course. I was here for moral support.

"We need to build our own organization," Blake began. "We need to build an organization that gives people a safe place to come, where they can be free to live safely and comfortably. The more people we can take away from WAMB, the smaller the organization will become. Eventually, they will not be as powerful as they are now."

"That's a pretty thought," Megan said. "but what's to stop WAMB from destroying everything? They will never leave us alone. Plus, It will give them more time to find a way to destroy the mutated DNA and do away with our kind for good. Do we really want to take that risk?"

"They won't be able to find a way to do anything to us if we take all of their scientists away from them," I replied. "Doctor Sheppard may have been delusional, but many of the scientists did not know that. They respected him, and will follow his son if Blake asks."

"Yes, and they will leave us alone if they fear us enough," Blake said. "I say we let them find us and show them that we can weaken them when they come for us. Make them afraid to ever send anyone for us again."

"Blake, do you know how many soldiers and warriors WAMB has?" Waller asked worriedly. "There are way more than that little scouting party they sent after us on the highway, and they have more destructive weapons than guns."

I winced at the memory Lily had given me of Blake getting shot. I regretted that I had not been with Blake when he had been hurt, but Lily assured me that he was not even conscious through most of it. The shooting and car chase had been intense, so I was glad I was out for that one. Lily was much better equipped to deal with that kind of excitement than I was.

"I am not talking about fighting them, Waller," Blake said. "I am talking about bringing them to our side. Most of WAMB's soldiers are mutants, like us. If we can recruit them to our side, our forces will grow stronger, and they will be weaker. They will fear us, not because of our power to destroy, but our power to take away their power."

"So, how do you propose we do that?" Waller asked, his eyebrows raised in disbelief.

Blake shrugged as if we were talking about the weather instead of a way to take down a vast organization. "Lucy can take their minds to subdue them, and then we will treat them as guests, talk to them, and convince them to stay with us. We give them to Greg and Lily if they get too rowdy."

Lily stirred happily inside me, and Greg smiled maliciously. He gave Blake a nod as he said, "I'm in. I like that plan."

Waller's eyes grew wider, and I could hear the disbelief in his crazy outburst of laughter.

"That is the craziest plan I have ever heard," he said after his short bout of laughter had died.

"What if they do not cause trouble but still do not want to join our cause?" Megan asked.

"You are not planning on going along with this, are you?" Waller asked her.

Megan shot him an angry look. "Just listen, Gene. Blake may be onto something here."

Waller sighed in defeat, ran his hand over his bald head, and then sat back in his seat. He made a gesture toward Blake to continue.

"We hope for that to happen. If some do not want to join us, they will be free to return to the organization. We will, of course, take away all of their weapons and gear when we capture them, but we will give them supplies and a means to return safely."

Blake crossed his arms over his chest and sat back in his chair as he continued. "I believe when more and more of the soldiers return with stories of us, that is when the scientists will start coming to us."

"Tell them about the children," I whispered as I leaned toward Blake.

"There's more to this crazy plan of yours?" Waller asked.

"Waller, just hush and listen," I said, rolling my eyes and giving my attention back to Blake.

"You are beginning to sound like me, sis," Lily's voice in my head said with a snicker. *"That thing we have been practicing may be working a bit too well."*

I smiled inwardly and turned my attention back outwards as Blake began to speak.

"This is where we will need your help, Waller. WAMB had you finding or killing children for them, but we want you to do that for us. Well, not the killing. Your gift is very rare, and WAMB does not have another like you, which is why they are relentless in pursuing you."

Waller leaned forward, placing his elbows on the table and crossing his fingers together. "This is true," he said. "I found that tracker they had on me. It was in my fucking tattoo of all places."

He laughed harshly and shook his head. "Megan found it just yesterday. I had this weird pain in my neck right around the tattoo, and there it was. A tiny little chip under my skin, camouflaged by the tattoo. They won't be able to track me anymore. I will no longer hunt children for them, nor will I ever go back."

"Well, you could do that for us. You could find children and newborns and bring them and their families here where they will be safe," Blake said. "You would never have to kill babies or children again. Instead, you would save them like you already do, but you would not have to keep them hidden."

"We will need a lot more room than we have," Megan said. "We have a lot of land but only one house. We will need more houses."

Blake smiled victoriously, flashing his white teeth as he said, "We have a lot more than that, Megan. We have an entire town."

Her eyes grew wide with shock, as did everyone else's at the table except for Tyrone. Tyrone sat nervously fiddling with his fingers on the table. Blake had already told Tyrone about this plan earlier, and Blake had filled me in on Tyrone's part.

Blake motioned toward Tyrone. "Our new friend here has informed me that he has inherited his father's land. It is more of an entire road of houses that grew into a small town, but it is virtually a ghost town. It has been uninhabited for quite some time, so it will need lots of TLC, but we can all do it if we work together."

Tyrone sat silent as everyone stared at him in disbelief. He cleared his throat, saying, "It has not sat empty for too long, only about two years or so when the last store went out of business."

His honey-colored eyes held a faraway look as he continued to speak. "It was my father's dream for me, and others like me, to have a safe place to raise a family. He got sick with cancer when I was only ten, and he made my mom hold to the promise to keep me hidden, the promise that he had given Mr. Waller when he came for me after I had been born."

Tyrone glanced toward Waller, a look of loss and respect in his eyes, and then continued. "My father built that place for me, and after his death, it went to ruin because my mother was too distraught to care for it. She moved in with family and still collected all the rent until the last person left, and all the rent she collected is still gathered in the trust fund my father left me.

She never spent a dime of that trust fund and never spent any of the rent she collected. She worked hard to provide for me without having to spend that money. When I was old enough, she gave me the trust fund and all the blueprints for my father's plans. I have been holding onto that money until I could figure out how to see my father's vision come true.

I will be your investor. I will give you the trust fund and the land with the promise that you will follow my father's plans for the town."

Tyrone stopped speaking and sat back in his chair. He glanced around the table nervously, waiting on everyone's replies.

"I believe in Blake," Dianna said, smiling proudly at her friend. "I think it could work."

"I would love to have a place to call my own without running all the time," Chris said as he took Dianna's hand.

"We are going to need more people," Greg said.

"Which is why we need your father, and we need to convert as many WAMB agents as we can," Blake said. "That is the entire purpose of my plan."

"I bet Joseph's family would join, especially because of what happened," Bonnie said, her green eyes flashing with anger. "They were told that he died in an interstate pile-up and that his body was burned beyond repair. They sent his mother an urn of ashes instead of a body."

"Where is this town of yours, Tyrone?" asked Waller, shifting uncomfortably in his seat.

I could tell he was just trying to change the subject. He blamed himself for Joseph's death, making him uneasy when we talked about it.

"It is not far from here. In fact, it is just on the other side of that field on the south side of this house." Tyrone pointed toward the back of the house and the field on the other side of the small wooded area with the giant log.

"I was surprised when we arrived and I discovered where we were. It is as if fate sent me here so I could finish my father's work." Tyrone held a faraway look in his eyes as he spoke and turned his gaze to the window.

I turned in my seat, so I could follow his gaze, and a spark of recognition flittered in my mind when I saw the log sitting in the middle of the forested area. Lustful thoughts and memories floated around in my mind, eliciting memories of pain through me from the scratches and bite marks that had been on my stomach and breasts. They were days old now, but the memory of the pain lived on.

"Nope, no, no, no. Keep those thoughts to yourself!" I cried as I turned back around in my seat, and I had accidentally said it aloud in my haste to keep Lily's thoughts from crowding into my conscious mind. Everyone looked at me curiously as my face flamed with embarrassment.

"I was talking to Lily," I mumbled shyly as I slouched down into my seat. I wanted the ground to open up and swallow me. I had seen glimpses of Lily's memories of the big log, and what I saw had mortified me. I now knew how I got the scratches, bruises, and bite marks that riddled my body. I had not been able to keep all of the memories at bay.

My eyes flicked to Greg and then quickly back to the table when I saw his knowing smirk as he glanced out the window toward the forested area at the end of the backyard. Thankfully, my seat was right in front of the window, and my back was to the window. I did not have to look at the log unless I turned back around.

I sank further into my seat, wanting to escape everyone's curious stares.

"I do not want to see memories of your sexual encounters!" I spat in my head, directing my anger toward the abyss where Lily sat, waiting for her turn to be in charge.

"*I'm sorry,*" Lily said remorsefully. *"It caught me by surprise when you looked at that log.*"

"What if someone saw you two?" I said in mortification. *"You can see it perfectly from this window.*"

"Then they would probably learn something. That man sure knows how to...."

"Lucy, are you listening?" Blake said, breaking through my internal debate with my sister.

Thank God.

I gladly returned my focus to the outside world, and my eyes settled on Blake. "I am sorry. I was having a conversation with my sister."

"Lily? What did she say? Did she ask about me?" Greg sat up, shooting questions my way at the mention of Lily.

"I will discuss that with you later," I said impatiently as I gestured with my eyes toward all the other people at the table who did not need to know our business.

Lily had come out yesterday and spent time with Greg; he was still angry that she had not stayed out all night. I had slept in Blake's bed last night.

Greg slouched back into his seat. "Fine, whatever," he mumbled.

"Sorry, Blake, what were you saying?" I asked.

Blake cleared his throat as he shot a warning glare at Greg and then said, "I was just saying that we need a base of operation, and since this house is so close to the future town, I suggest we let this house be the base. We could build a road out to the town through the field."

I nodded. "I agree. I also suggest that the leaders of this little organization we are building be the ones to live in the house."

"And who is going to lead this little group of misfits?" Megan asked humorously.

Dianna answered before I could.

"You and Waller…er…father? Should I call you father now? Or just Waller since that is what I have known you as for my whole life…or I could call you father if you want me to…."

"Dianna," Waller exclaimed loudly, interrupting her rambling.

She stopped speaking instantly.

Waller chuckled and said, "You can call me whatever you want."

"Oh, okay then. As I was saying, I think you and mom should be the ones to lead us." Dianna said, smiling shyly.

"I second that," Greg said.

"Me too," I said.

There were murmurs of agreement around the table, and then Waller stood, silencing everyone as he folded his arms over his chest.

"If I am going to lead this group of rabble-rousers," he began, roaming his eyes around everyone at the table. "Then I will have to start up those obstacle courses you all hated so much."

Moans, groans, and even some excitement from Blake and Greg ran around the table. Waller simply chuckled.

"You are all going to learn how to fight and use your gifts defensively and offensively," he said as everyone continued to groan or challenge each other for dominance.

After the testosterone contest was over and everyone had quieted, Blake stood from his seat and pulled several notebooks stuffed with papers from a box on the island bar that separated the kitchen from the dining room.

"I have drafted some notes over the past week since I could not get out of bed," Blake said as he stood and began passing out the packets of papers to each person.

"These are plans and copies of the blueprints from Tyrone's father and notes on his father's ideas for the place. Of course, all new ideas or thoughts will have to be approved by Tyrone first and then by our great leaders," Blake said, winking at Megan and giving a respectful nod toward Waller before continuing.

"If anyone has suggestions or anything to add, just see Waller or Megan. They will take the approved suggestions to Tyrone for final approval."

Blake wrapped up the meeting, and everyone got up from the table. Blake came to stand by my side, and I stopped Greg before he could leave with a hand on his arm.

"Wait here for one second," I told the men, and they both nodded with curious looks.

I walked over to Dianna.

"We need some privacy," I said, motioning to Blake and Greg. "Would it be alright for me to use our room for about an hour?"

Dianna smiled with a knowing twinkle in her eye. "Sure thing, girl. Get your sex life straightened out, and I want details."

My face flamed with embarrassment, but Dianna only giggled and walked away.

I turned back to Blake and Greg and motioned for them to follow me. I led them to my bedroom, which I shared with Dianna, glad that she had given permission for us to have some privacy long enough for us to resolve this situation. Lily and I had been practicing something, and I was excited to show our men.

I paced the room as the men sat on the bed, looking up at me expectantly. I took a deep breath, sending a signal into the back of my mind to my sister.

"Are you ready for this?" I asked her.

"Ready when you are," came her reply.

"This may seem a bit weird at first," I started. "Lily and I have been trying something new over the last couple of days. We are going to try to share, unlike before, when one was gone. We are going to both try to be in the front at the same time."

"How would that even work?" Blake asked, frowning. "How will I ever be alone with you?"

"Yes, and what if I want to be with just Lily?" Greg chimed in, then quickly added, "no offense, Lucy."

I chuckled and tried to explain once more. "There will be times when one of us will be sleeping to give the other some privacy, obviously. But, for the most part, we will both be present for you."

Greg and Blake glanced at each other and then back to me. They were adorable when they were confused.

"We are going to try something," I said. "Just try to keep up."

I felt Lily come up out of the abyss and fill my sight and senses. I struggled to stay in control as she filled me, working to share the control. We had been practicing this secretly for two days now, and we were quickly mastering it.

"Hey, sis. I think it is working." I smiled as I heard Lily in my head; this time, her voice was closer and easier to hear. It was as if she were standing right beside me.

"Lily is here with me," I said. "She can see, feel, and hear everything from the front with me instead of only getting overflow like before."

Greg smirked and said, "Yeah? Show us."

I closed my eyes as I let Lily take the seat for a minute, and then Lily opened our eyes. I was still in the forefront, not in the abyss, and I could experience everything Lily was experiencing.

She glanced at Greg, who was staring at us in confusion. She smiled seductively at Greg as she sashayed over and sat between the two men.

She placed her hand on Greg's leg and whispered, "I guess you proved me wrong, stud."

"Lily?" he asked uncertainly, and she nodded.

"I guess I am a relationship kind of girl, after all, if you'll have me."

He smiled widely and pulled her into his arms, grabbing her hair roughly and pulling her head back...pulling our head back.

That hurt, and I did not like it, but I could feel Lily's excitement and joy at the rough treatment. It was working a bit too well at this point.

Blake grasped Lily from behind and gently pulled her away from Greg's rough hands, glaring hatefully at him.

"Do not touch her that way again," Blake seethed angrily.

Greg let go of her hair but did not let go of her arm.

"But this is Lily, not Lucy, and she likes it," Greg shot back.

Lily stepped back and let me back in front. The transition was smooth and fast. I glared at Greg, and he let go of my arm as his eyes widened in surprise.

"It is not just Lily; it is both of us. That hurt, and I do not like pain," I seethed. "You can't be rough like that when Lily and I are sharing."

He dropped his gaze and mumbled, "Sorry, Lucy."

I turned to Blake. "You need to let go, too. You need to learn to get along with Greg for this to work. Lily does not like you being so hard on him."

Blake frowned, his visage matching Greg's, and released my arm. "Lily and I are trying to be active simultaneously instead of one of us being pushed to the back. We are stronger this way and can communicate easier. It will be better for us.

I know there will be times when you want to have alone time with one of us, and in those cases, the other will return to the back of our mind and sleep for a time.

Also, I know you may want intimacy throughout the day, such as a hug or kiss. You can touch us, hold our hand, or hold us no matter which of us is in control, and we can switch accordingly.

Finally, you two have to stop this fighting and competition between you. We want you to get along, so neither of us has to lose either of you.”

“Lucy will never lose me,” Blake said.

“And I will never give Lily up,” Greg said.

“Then you have to get along,” I said.

Silence filled the room, and I stood nervously waiting for their reaction. They glared at each other for a long moment, and then finally, Blake sighed and looked away.

“I am willing to try on one condition,” Blake said.

“What condition?” I asked nervously.

Blake darted a glance at Greg as he answered, “Greg needs to go easy on your body.”

Lily came forward suddenly, and I moved back and let her take control. We both felt a sense of elation at how easy it was becoming.

“I like it rough, Blake. You need to learn to deal with that,” Lily said.

Blake’s eyes widened in surprise for a moment, but he recovered quickly.

“It makes it hard for Lucy and me when she has wounds to work around because Lucy does not like the pain,” Blake explained in an imploring tone.

“Blake is right,” I said, stepping back into control quickly and smoothly. Lily sighed in my mind and agreed.

Blake’s eyes widened again, and again he recovered quickly.

 “You two are good at that already,” Blake said with a chuckle.

I smiled. “Thanks. We have been practicing.”

“I knew you and Lily were up to something,” Blake said. “You kept running off and would not tell Greg or me where you were going.”

I shrugged. “I wanted it to be a surprise.”

Lily came forward and added, “And I wanted to keep it a secret a bit longer, but Lucy insisted.”

“It’s gonna be hard to keep up with them now,” Greg said with a smirk, and Blake nodded his agreement.

“I’ll try not to rough up your body,” Greg said. “But if Lily wants to rough me up, she is more than welcome.”

"Oh, I will take you up on that soon," Lily said seductively, leaning toward him for a quick kiss as I hung back until the kiss was over.

I heard Blake growl angrily behind us, and Lily stood back so I could come forward.

I turned to Blake and whispered, "Stop growling like an angry animal. You will have to learn to get used to this."

Blake sighed in defeat, running a hand through his hair as he said, "okay, Lucy. I will try for you."

I smiled and gave him a soft kiss before saying, "thank you for understanding and trying."

"I would do anything for you, Lucy. I have told you that before, and I meant it."

He placed his palm on my cheek and leaned into me, brushing his lips softly against mine.

We got up from the bed and turned to them both, smiling happily.

Blake turned to Greg and offered his hand. "I guess we will need to call a truce, then."

Greg looked down at the offered hand for a moment and then took it and shook it firmly. "Fine, truce, but only where the girls are concerned."

Blake took his hand back, frowning. "What do you mean?"

Greg smiled deviously and said, "When we are on the obstacle course and in training, all bets are off."

Blake's smile was cocky as he responded, "challenge accepted."

We sighed and shook our heads at our wonderful, incredibly sexy, and horribly stubborn men.

CHAPTER 33: New Beginnings

*** THE HIDEOUT, THE NEXT DAY ***

I could see her again as I could before when my memories were gone. I was standing before the mirror in the bathroom, staring at my reflection; and the reflection of the woman beside me.

My sister.

"So, why can I see you again?" I asked. "I could see you before I had my memories because my mind's way of protecting me from thinking I was crazy. So, why can I see you now that I know you live inside me?"

Lucy cocked her head and gave me a thoughtful look. "I am not sure, but it would certainly be handy for me to have my own body."

"Maybe this is just how my brain helps me keep you separate," I suggested. "Since we have been practicing that sharing thing, I feel more and more like we are one person instead of two separate beings. It's getting kind of creepy, truthfully."

Lily nodded, her blond hair shining under the lights of the mirror. Her baby blues sparkled with a mischievous light as her gaze locked on mine in the mirror.

"Maybe you are right. I just wish this was a real body," she said.

She turned and gazed at herself appreciatively. "I like it."

I poked my finger at her, and it went right through her.

Frowning, I said, "It doesn't matter that it isn't real. You will be with me, and we can share this body. I'm not going to let anyone take you away as long as I can help it."

Lily smiled. "Ditto, sis. I still like this body, though."

I returned her smile as I gauged the differences in our appearances in the mirror. The hair was the most significant difference. Hers was blond, and mine was raven black, so black that it had blue highlights in the right light.

While Lily had been in charge during my meltdown, our hair had begun to lighten and developed blond streaks. Now it had changed back to its original black, but her apparition in the mirror had blond hair.

Our eyes were different as well. My eyes were a startling sapphire blue, and Lily's were a light baby blue. My skin was paler than Lily's, and her face was thinner and her chin sharper. If anyone other than me could see Lily's apparition, it would be easy to tell us apart. As it was, however, they only saw me, this body, no matter who was in charge.

"Well, I guess it's time for you to take charge," I said to her.

"Yep. I'll make sure that Blake and Greg do not kill each other today during sparring sessions," she responded with a smirk.

"Alright then. Let's do this."

I had never stood in front of the mirror and watched the change happen before, so it was surprising to see Lily's form step into me and merge with me. I stared wide-eyed as her body dissipated into mine, and then I was looking out from the inside.

We had been practicing this, so I should have been used to it. Even so, I was still in awe of the sensation of both of us being in the front. Always before, I had ridden inside the abyss, able to look out and get backlashes of senses but never right in front of the action where I could experience everything. It was new and different, and I liked it.

I was not prepared for what came next, though.

I was still looking in the mirror but was doing so through Lily's eyes. It was a bit disorienting, and I wished I could see normally. Lily was in control, so my vision was like looking through a window. I wished there was a way that I could be by her side like she had been by my side, and that is when it happened.

Suddenly, I began to feel funny, almost dizzy, and I shut my eyes to catch my bearings. I heard a startled gasp from Lily...

But the sound came from beside me...

My eyes flew open and then widened in horrified shock at what I saw. I saw myself, but I was not in the body. I was standing beside my body in another body that looked just like mine. Then, my real body changed right before my eyes!

My hair went completely blond, my eyes lightened to a baby blue, and my face became thinner with a sharper chin. My body looked like Lily, and the other body standing in the mirror, which was currently me, looked just like me.

Our eyes met in the mirror, and I looked shocked and horrified. Lily did not. She looked calm and a bit amused.

"Oh my God!" I exclaimed. "What is going on? How do I get back in my body?"

Lily laughed and shrugged. "I have no idea."

"Lily! This isn't funny! And my body changed too!" I cried hysterically.

"Yeah, I look like myself now," she said, turning in the mirror and smiling at her reflection…my reflection.

"Wait," I said, taking a deep breath to calm down my racing heart. "Let's try switching back. I'll step toward you as you stepped toward me just now, and you concentrate on giving control back to me."

Lily shrugged. "Alright, we can try."

I took a deep breath and closed my eyes. I stepped sideways toward my body, and the feeling of miasma swirled over me once more. It lasted only seconds, and then I heard Lily laughing delightedly.

I opened my eyes, and I was in my body again, in control, and Lily was standing beside me in her…well…ghost body? That was the only word I could think of to describe it.

I turned to my reflection and watched as my appearance changed, and I was myself again. My shiny, straight black hair, my sapphire blue eyes, and my round face with the high cheekbones were all back.

My eyes drifted to Lily's reflection, and she looked like herself. Her blond, slightly wavy hair, baby blue eyes, and thin, triangular face stared back at me with a delighted smile.

"Well, this is new," I said, but I was calmer now. My heart was not trying to pound its way out of my chest, and my breathing was normal.

"This is awesome!" Lily explained happily. "Now, everyone will be able to tell who we are, and we will be able to experience everything together in separate bodies."

"How did this happen?" I asked, more to myself than anything, but I had spoken it out loud.

"I don't know exactly," Lily answered with a shrug. "I just wanted to talk to you, and I would appear to you. That was before you knew I lived inside your brain, though."

"I wished I could stand by your side moments before it happened," I said as I frowned thoughtfully at my reflection and added, "So, maybe it wasn't only my brain's way of helping me deal. Maybe, this is an actual ability that we have."

"Maybe. Let's try it again," Lily said with excitement.

I laughed as I replied, "alright, but I am not sure how I got out into the ghost body before, so I might not be able to do it again."

"Ghost body?" Lily asked, quirking an eyebrow. The corners of her lips tilted up in humor.

"Don't laugh at me," I said indignantly. "It's the only word I could think of to describe it."

"Well, okay then," she said, but I could hear the laughter in her tone. "All you have to do is the same thing you did before. Concentrate harder this time. See how long you can hold the form."

"Okay, let's do this. Let me try to ride the ghost body," I said, and now I was getting excited too.

Lily snorted with laughter. "Can't we call it something other than a ghost body? It just sounds so silly."

"Well, what would you call it?" I asked irritably.

"I don't know. A mirage, maybe? You know, like in the desert, people see a mirage that isn't there?"

I chortled, and Lily shot me a dirty look. "A mirage? That sounds even sillier than ghost body."

"You are such a loser," Lily said playfully, rolling her eyes at me.

"And you are such an asshole," I shot back.

Lily's eyes widened in mock surprise. "Did the miss perfect Lucy actually curse?"

"Shut up," I said, smiling.

I loved this. Lily and I were getting along like real sisters. I knew that Lily was dark. She enjoyed causing pain and liked chaos, but it was usually deserved. I knew deep down inside, somewhere was a good heart.

I knew this because it was my heart too.

"Alright, let's try to switch again and see if we can get this right," Lily said.

I took a deep breath and nodded.

"Okay, I'm ready," I said, and we did it again.

This time when I felt Lily take control, I concentrated on being apart from her. I focused on the feeling of being my own person, separate from Lily.

The dizzy feeling came, but this time I rode it through. I knew what was happening now, so it wasn't such a shock. I closed my eyes to the sensation, and when the dizziness was gone, I opened my eyes and saw myself standing beside Lily in the ghost body.

I was still going to call it a ghost body.

Our eyes met in the mirror, and we both smiled victoriously, then Lily's smile turned mischievous.

"Wanna mess with the boys?" she asked, waggling her eyebrows.

I quirked one eyebrow up inquisitively and asked, "How?"

"I want to see them freak out when they see us switch places and see our body change," Lily said, smirking.

"You are so devious," I said with a giggle.

"Oh, come on. You know it will be fun," Lily said as she turned to walk out the bathroom door.

I started to turn and follow her out, but the strangest sensation overtook me. It was as if there was a rubber band holding this form to my physical body so that when my physical body walked away, the band stretched out as if it would snap me back at any moment.

I had forgotten for a moment that this form was tied to the body because we were one mind sharing a body, and as soon as I thought that, I began to be pulled back into my body.

I was back inside my head, looking out while Lily remained in control before I could stop it, as if the rubber band had snapped me back in instantly.

"You stopped concentrating on being separate, didn't you?" Lily asked, her voice floating at me where I rode inside my head.

"I got distracted by that rubber band thingy," I said disappointedly.

"Rubber band thingy? You mean the main connection to the physical body?" Lily asked humorously.

"Stop making fun of my analogies," I huffed. *"It is difficult to maintain that form with the connection distracting me."*

I rolled my eyes as I accentuated the word connection, and Lily snickered.

"It does take concentration, but you get used to it." Lily shrugged nonchalantly. *"Just ignore the sensation of the connection and concentrate on keeping up with the physical body."*

"I will try," I said.

I concentrated, and once again, I was in the ghost body with the band connecting me to the physical body. The sensation was strange and eerie, but I did not let it distract me this time. This time, I stayed in the ghost body as we went down the hallway of the big house.

We could hear voices coming from the dining room where Blake and Greg sat at the table with Waller and Megan, discussing the plans for our new town.

"So, what do you suggest we do first?" Waller was saying.

"As I said before," Blake responded impatiently. "We will lure them here by taking down the shields so they can find us. In the meantime, Waller can use his gift to find others like us and bring over the ones he has already helped if they want to come. I said all this before, so I don't know why you want me to repeat myself."

"We are not asking you to repeat yourself," Waller said more patiently than Blake. "We are asking you to help us with the mechanics of the plan. You know, the when, where, and how?"

Greg chimed in. "I think we should train first before the shield is lifted. I know it will take time, but as you said, Blake dad can find others while we train. We can incorporate the training into the reconstruction. There will be lots of physical activity involved in rebuilding the town.

By the time the shields are finally lifted, we will have some of the town built and be stronger and better prepared to fight should the need arise."

Waller nodded. "This is true, but you need to train in hand-to-hand combat, and honing your abilities as well, not just for strength."

"We could split off into groups. One group could work on construction while another group trains in fighting, and a third group trains in magic. The groups can rotate daily," Blake suggested.

"I think that's a great plan," Megan said.

"We need to make up some blueprints for an obstacle course, too," Blake said as we walked into the room.

"We will probably need to…."

His words were cut off as he looked up and saw us. I watched from my ethereal form as his eyes looked upon Lily and widened with incredulity.

Greg looked at Blake in confusion, following his gaze, and then his mouth dropped open as his visage matched Blake's.

Waller and Megan looked stunned as well, but their amazement was not as intense as Blake and Greg's.

I could see Greg's throat work as his eyes roamed up and down my…well, our…body with Lily in charge. I had to admit, she was stunning. Sometimes I envied her wavy blond hair and baby blues, but that was silly to me now.

Blake stood from his seat, and his eyes began to show a bit of fear as he walked toward us. His voice was a whisper as he said, "Lily, what has happened?"

"That is what Lily actually looks like?" Greg asked as he stood from his seat as well. However, he did not approach us and stayed standing by his chair.

Blake turned to Greg and answered, "Lucy used to be able to see Lily before she regained her memories when she thought Lily was separate from her.

It was her brain's way of helping Lucy deal with her twin without the trauma of having her in her head. Lucy told me what she looked like once."

Blake turned back to Lily as I stood in my ghostly form and watched. The looks on Greg and Blake's faces had certainly been worth our cunning little surprise, but when Blake turned back to us, my heart fell.

His face had fallen to an intensely sorrowful look. I could even see the beginnings of tears glistening in the corners of his hazel eyes. His voice was broken and gruff as he asked, "Has something happened to Lucy?"

Shit…I had not thought this through. I did not want Blake to believe anything bad had happened to me.

Lily turned to me with understanding in her eyes and gave me a little nod. I stepped towards my body and breathed through the disorienting sensations of taking back control.

I opened my eyes to find the amazement and wonder back on Blake's face. "Lucy?"

"I am fine, Blake. Nothing has happened to Lily or me. We have been practicing sharing the body, that's all." I brought a hand up to cup the side of his face as I smiled into his eyes softly.

"That's all?" Waller asked in surprise and disbelief. "Have you done that standing in front of a mirror?"

I looked beside me where Lily stood smiling as I answered, "Yes, we have, actually."

"Then, how can you not see just how amazingly impossible you are?" Waller asked.

"Other people in our group have much more amazing abilities than I do," I said modestly.

Lily shot me a dirty look.

"Do not underestimate our gifts," she said crossly. "We can kick ass when we need to. We can make people do whatever we want them to do."

"Within a moral scope," I said firmly. "We cannot go back to the way it was before. You will have to learn morals."

Blake touched my arm, catching my attention, and frowned at me. "Are you seeing Lily separately again? Is that who you are talking to?"

I nodded vigorously, "Yes, and when Lily is in control, I can also appear to her. We only just discovered it. I think instead of our brain giving us a way to communicate, it is actually an ability of ours that we never knew about. I call it the ghost body."

Blake smiled and said, "Ghost body…that is clever."

I shot Lily an 'I told you so' look, and then I heard Greg's booming laughter.

"That is the funniest thing I have ever heard," he said as he laughed.

Lily crossed her arms over her ample bosom and smirked victoriously. I rolled my eyes.

"Lucy, this is amazing," Blake said. "I am so proud of you."

Lily cleared her throat loudly, giving Blake an irritated look.

I laughed. "He can't see you, remember?"

Blake frowned. "What?"

"She is angry that you did not give her any credit. This was actually all her. She is the one that taught me to control it and how to ride around in the ghost body."

Greg snickered, and I shot him an irritated look.

"Oh," Blake said and cleared his throat. "I am sorry, Lily," he said, looking beside me even though he could not see her. "I am also proud of you, and thank you for helping Lucy."

"That's better pretty boy," Lily said sarcastically as she rolled her eyes.

"I guess I am going to have to remember that Lily is always listening now," Blake said, chuckling.

I nodded. "I wanted Lily to have more freedom than before. It wasn't fair that she always had to stay hidden inside unless she had to come out to save me. I was not fair to her."

"I am only glad that Lily took care of you for as long as she did, even though her plans to take your body failed," Blake said with a smirk.

Lily huffed and said, "It is not like I care or anything. I was taking care of the body, not necessarily Lucy herself."

I smiled slyly and said, "Liar."

Lily's smile spread across her face. "Alright, you got me. However, you were right to keep me hidden when we were younger. I did take certain liberties that I should not have."

"No, you should not have....wait." A smile of revelation spread across my face as I looked around the room.

"Lily just gave us the name for our town," I said.

"I did?" Lily asked in confusion.

I gave her a wink, even though I knew it looked like I was winking at thin air. I did not care.

"Yes, you did," I said. "I think we should call the town Liberty City."

Tyrone's deep voice coming from behind me startled me. "I love it. It is a very fitting name."

He entered the room as I moved aside, allowing his massive frame to pass through the hall doorway. His smile was infectious as he looked around the room at all the faces smiling back at him.

Waller slapped the table with his palm happily and stood. "I think that is a fine name."

Everyone agreed, nodding enthusiastically.

"I must go into town for some supplies," Tyrone said as he moved toward the front door. "Does anyone want me to bring them anything back?"

"We are almost out of coffee," Dianna said.

"I will get some," Tyrone said before slipping out the door. "I will be back soon."

Ten minutes later, we were all standing around the dining room chatting and talking. Blake and Greg hovered around me, asking me questions about mine and Lily's new transformation abilities, while Waller and Dianna were talking excitedly about plans for Liberty City.

Bonnie and Chris had joined us at some point and had joined Waller's group. We were all in good spirits, laughing and joking, and glad to finally have peace.

It was short-lived.

Waller had set up surveillance cameras at the end of the road leading up to the property in the first week of us being here, and the monitors were installed in the master bedroom that he was sharing with Megan.

We were all in the dining room. The cameras were not being monitored, and our earth affinity guy, Tyrone, had left the property. So we were unprepared for the sound of vehicles barreling up the gravel driveway to the house. And we were certainly not prepared for the hailing rain of gunfire that pummeled the house, breaking through the front windows of the living room and scattering throughout the open space into the dining room.

Someone screamed, and my blood ran cold as I was thrown to the ground with an overwhelming force. My head hit the hardwood floor, sending shards of intense pain through my head and radiating throughout my entire body. I was suddenly staring at the ceiling, and confusion swarmed in my mind.

I heard Waller's commanding voice shouting for everyone to take cover. Someone screamed my name and Lily's as I tried to regain my senses.

My vision blurred as I tried to turn my head and look around. Spots danced in front of my eyes, and I could not see clearly. My head was clouded with the pain that overwhelmed me, reeling my senses into a miasma of confusion and terror.

I called for Lily, reaching for her through the muddled sensations flowing through my system and finding an empty hole where the connection usually rode. Panicking, I searched deep into my mind, down into the abyss, and she was not there.

Hands grappled my ankles and pulled me across the floor. Strong arms wrapped around my waist, pulling me toward a warm, hard body that covered me and shielded me from the bullets still pelting the dining room walls.

I was frozen with terror and sadness. All I could do was lay there under that body as tears fell down the sides of my face. An overwhelming tide of pain flowed through me as I heard Blake's voice calling me repeatedly, begging me to open my eyes.

I could not. I could not think through the pain and through the terror and fear that filled me over the one thought that ran through my mind repeatedly.

Lily was gone…

Lily was gone…

Lily was gone…

Darkness engulfed me, and the world fell away.

CHAPTER 34: Separation

Lily stared in horror at the scene before her. She was still attached to the body, but Lucy had been shot. Lucy could not transition, and Lily was not about to return to the body just yet.

Sure, she could slip back in and take the death for Lucy, but then Lily would not be able to help Lucy's friends, and Lucy would be extremely pissed off at her if any of her friends died.

How was she going to help, though?

Hell, she could not help anyone if she did not have a body. Lily had no abilities in this form, and she was not corporeal, so she could not touch anything or anyone.

No one except Lucy could even see or hear her.

Lucy's explanation of 'ghost body' seemed fitting now.

Lily felt the pain, fear, and confusion radiating through the bond she still shared with the body, but she pushed it away. Lily was used to pushing away these sensations and emotions. She had learned how to ignore them over the years instead of letting them consume her.

She blocked it out as she knelt by her and Lucy's body. Blood was pouring from her shoulder, where Lucy had been shot once before. There was a hole in her upper outside thigh that was seeping blood, and the most frightening gunshot, the one in her chest, had blood spreading all over her shirt.

Blake, who had just pulled Lucy's body behind the table and to safety, struggled weakly to cover Lucy, bleeding from holes that riddled his body. They were mainly in the leg and arm areas, but none looked fatal unless they continued to bleed his life's blood all over the floor.

He hovered over Lucy and shielded her with his body as he bled all over the floor and yelled at her to open her eyes.

Lily connected to the bond and concentrated on the radiating pain in her chest. She did not think it had hit her heart, but she believed it may have collapsed a lung. She felt the body's struggle to breathe and knew there was not much time left before they suffocated or drowned in their own blood.

Dread coursed through her ghost body, but she blocked it out. She would be unable to think if she let panic take her over. She surveyed the scene while trying to think of what she could do.

They had turned the large dining table over on its side, and Bonnie had coated it in an impossibly thick coating of ice. The bullets cracked and chipped at the ice as they hit, but it held firm. Everyone was huddled behind it, staying as low to the floor as possible.

Waller was on his knees with his gun trained on the large window behind them in case someone tried to come around to the back of the house. Someone had obviously already tried because the window was shot out, and there were dead bodies crumpled on the ground under the window.

Chris held Dianna close to him, huddling next to Blake and Lucy and whispering calming words into Dianna's ear. Bonnie sat next to them, rubbing soothing circles on Dianna's back. Dianna was holding her head in her hands.

Suddenly, Lily heard the sounds of crows cawing outside the window. The sound was loud and eerie, overpowering the sounds of the guns. Screams came from outside, sounds of pain and anger, and the gunfire ceased for just a moment.

The gunfire began again, but the bullets were not shooting into the house now. The dying screams of birds and gunfire filled the air outside.

Lily's connection to the body would not allow her to go very far, so she couldn't go outside to determine what was happening. She could not see very far out from her vantage point in the dining room. The window was too far away.

The bullets flew into the house once more, and a hail of bullets passed through Lily's ethereal form as she ran around and tried to think of how to get someone's attention. Lucy needed medical attention.

She was lying very still under Blake's body. He was still shielding her underneath him, careful not to put too much weight on her, and Greg raised his gun and scoped the space around Blake and Lucy.

Megan was huddled on the floor on her hands and knees, staring at the space between their hiding spot and the hallway leading to the bathroom. Her shield only protected against magical attacks, so it would not be helpful against a rain of gunfire. She felt helpless magically, but there was something she could do physically if she could only get to the first aid kit in the hallway bathroom.

"Waller, cover me," she shouted over the noise of gunfire. "I have to get to the first aid kit. Lucy and Blake have been shot."

"No, Megan. It's too dangerous unless the wounds are deadly," he replied.

"Dad." Greg's voice was calm, frighteningly calm.

Waller turned to Greg, and Greg removed his hand from his stomach.

Lily had not noticed before that he had been holding his stomach with one hand while he held the gun with the other, so what she saw sent cold dread flowing through her, dread that she could not block out this time.

Blood poured from the right side of his lower stomach, thick and gushing, and Greg's face was too pale. His eyes fluttered as if he were desperately trying to hold them open, and his whole body shook with tremors as he tried to keep the gun in his other arm aloft.

"Lucy is worse than I am," he managed to say in a croaking voice.

Panic flowed through Waller's gaze for a split second before he recovered and turned back to Megan. Megan's eyes were wide with panic as she looked upon the blood pouring from her estranged and newly recovered son's stomach.

"Megan," Waller said sternly.

No response.

"Megan," Waller said louder this time.

She blinked rapidly and turned her gaze to his.

"Go get the kit. I'll cover you," he said firmly.

She nodded, her motions stilted and automatic as if in a daze. Greg collapsed to the floor, and Blake's arms quivered as he tried to stay atop Lucy's prone form.

Megan shot into action, crawling rapidly on all fours toward the hallway as Waller stood up and began shooting toward the window. Bonnie stood as well, shooting shards of ice from both hands in the same direction that Waller was shooting.

Megan screamed as a bullet ripped through her calf before disappearing into the hallway. She kept going, gritting her teeth against the pain as she crawled down the hallway toward the bathroom where the first aid kit was kept.

Bonnie coated the table in a newly refreshed layer of ice to keep the bullets out before ducking back behind the table. Waller ducked back behind the table after Megan had disappeared into the hallway, holding his arm and grimacing in pain.

Blood poured down his arm and spread between his fingers as he held on and tried to stop the blood.

"Some of the guns are not metal!" Chris screamed out in frustration. "I can't melt them!"

Greg was still not moving, and he looked paler than death. Blood was pooling on the floor under his stomach, and a slow pool of blood was slowly building underneath Blake as well.

Blake's body suddenly went limp, and Lily felt a smothering sensation as Blake's weight fell on top of Lucy's still body. Lily could not breathe, and she felt herself being pulled back into the body as darkness loomed at the sides of her vision.

No!

This could not be happening!

Lily screamed in anger, frustration, and fear. Loud and long, filling the room and overriding the sounds of gunfire from outside. She scrambled to stay in her ethereal form and not be dragged into the dying body as her scream died.

What the hell was she going to do? If only she could use her power…

As soon as the thought formed in her mind, a slow tingling began to build in her fingertips, flowing up her arms and chest. It chased away all sensations, including the pain and panic, until she could feel nothing but overwhelming power.

Waller's eyes flew around the room as if he had heard her screams, searching for whatever had made that horrible sound. His eyes pierced hers, and recognition flowed into his stormy gray eyes.

"Lily?" he whispered in awe. "But, how. That is impossible."

Lily blinked as the scream died away, and she concentrated on the tingling power filling her entire and, obviously now substantial, body. Bullets were still flying, and she ducked behind the table quickly to avoid them.

She was willing to bet that they would not fly through her now, and she would not take the chance.

She sent the power swirling inside her toward the minds filling the house's front lawn. She counted slowly, checking and double-checking to be sure she had them all.

She swallowed hard as a pulling sensation surrounded her and threatened to take her into darkness. She pushed it away before it could break her concentration.

"Lily, you keep flickering like you're going to disappear," Waller said as he stared at her wide-eyed.

Flickering?

Lily could not think about that now.

She counted ten. Ten alive minds that she needed to take, and quickly.

Megan scampered back into the dining room and quickly crawled back behind the ice-covered table. She began digging items out of the large bag she dragged with her. Resisting the urge to go to her son first, she went to Lucy first. Her son had said that she was worse, and after years of holding to the standard that the worse wounds get treated first, she went to Lucy.

She gasped at the awful wound in Lucy's chest as she gently rolled Blake off her and checked her wounds. She would live from the reopened shoulder wound and the thigh wound if she packed the wounds and stopped her blood loss, but she was unsure about the chest wound.

It was on the left, so she knew it had missed her heart, but it could have pierced her lung. If that were the case, she could drown in her own blood. Megan was comforted by the fact that Lucy was breathing steadily, so she packed the wounds hurriedly to check on her son.

As soon as Blake's body was moved out of the way, Lily could breathe. Her breath came in long, relieving draws of air, and her concentration became better because of it. The tingling in her became stronger, and Lily smiled deviously.

She sent her power out toward the minds outside, taking every one of them one mind at a time. She dug her ability in hard and firm, taking them and commanding them to stop shooting.

"Megan," Lily ground out through gritted teeth, trying to simultaneously speak and keep hold of the minds.

Typically, this would be easy for her, but she was not in her body, and she had no idea how she had been able to conjure her ability in the first place.

Megan glanced up in surprise as if just noticing that Lily was there.

"Do you need help caring for everyone?" Lily asked her as she stared up in wonder.

"Uh…I…it would be helpful," Megan stuttered as she tried to wrap her mind around what she was seeing.

"There is a healer out there, along with two nurses," Lily said. "What should I do with the others?"

Megan just looked confused, but Waller turned his attention to her knowingly.

"Bring in the healer and the nurses. Have the others shoot each other, but spare one of them. We will send him back to WAMB with a message." Waller's eyes were hard and cold as he spoke.

Megan shot him a look, but he shook his head to cut her off. "No, Megan. We cannot afford to be soft right now. Be lucky I am having Lily spare the three to help you heal them.

I know this was not part of Blake's plan, but Blake is lying on the floor right now, possibly dying, along with Lucy and our son. We can't give them the care they need if we continue to be shot at."

Waller turned his attention back to Lily. "Do it, Lily. I know from experience that you have no qualms about killing, especially regarding Lucy's safety."

The sounds of gunfire ceased. The only sounds drifting through the ruined windows now were the moans of pain and the caws of dying birds. Three people entered the front door, two women and a man. They walked through the room in stilted, puppet-like motions and began helping Megan with the injured.

One of the men held his hand to Greg's stomach, and a brilliant light left his hand and flowed into Greg's wound. Lily's eyes widened as she watched a bullet come rushing out of the wound, and then the wound closed right before her eyes.

He still looked too pale, but at least he was not bleeding anymore. Lily wondered if they would be able to keep this healer. He would come in handy.

She turned her attention back to the seven minds outside, still under her control. A dark smile lifted the corners of Lily's lips as the sounds of gunfire cut through the air again, but no bullets entered the house. It only lasted seconds, and then there was silence once more.

Megan shuttered as she glanced back at Lily, but she was no longer there. She had walked over to the now non-existent window. The entire side of the house where the windows had been was shot so full of holes that it looked ready to crumble at any moment.

Lily held her hand out to something outside the window, and another hand grasped Lily's from outside. Lily pulled the figure toward her.

It was a boy, barely fifteen from the looks of him, and his eyes were wide with shock and fear. His orangish-red hair was short and spiked on top. His skin was pale with a light sprinkling of freckles across his round cheeks and straight, strong nose. He was tall and lanky, wearing a simple button-up and jeans with sneakers.

Megan gasped as she spotted Waller roughly drag the boy from Lily's grasp, tie his ankles together, cuff his hands behind his back with the magic-binding cuffs, and push him roughly down into a chair.

Lily nodded at Waller as an understanding look passed between them, and then Lily's form began to flicker violently as she faded away. Waller's eyes grew huge with shock and sadness as Lily disappeared, and Waller turned panicked eyes to Megan.

She looked down at her patients to see the healing man holding his hands over Lucy with the light flowing into her. She was still breathing steadily, and her eyes fluttered as if struggling to open.

Breathing a sigh of relief, Megan turned her gaze back to her husband with a reassuring smile and gave him a thumbs-up. She watched Waller as relief filled his eyes, and he nodded before turning his attention back to the boy.

Megan turned her attention back to her patients as the healer continued to work his magic. He was assisted by the two nurses who cleaned and bandaged the wounds after the healer had closed them.

Megan noticed that they worked in smooth coordination, and their movements were no longer puppet-like. The healer turned to her with clear eyes and a sense of purpose in his features, and Megan gasped as she realized they were no longer being controlled.

"Is there a place where we can take the wounded and set up a makeshift hospital room rather than have them lie on this glass-covered floor?" he asked.

His voice was smooth and sharp without a hint of maliciousness in his tone. His piercing jade eyes held no sign of hate or ill intent. He simply stared at Megan questioningly, waiting for a reply.

"Umm…I uh…we can take them to the master suite," Megan stuttered.

"Good, show me where," he said commandingly, but his voice held a softness as if he were trying to show that he meant no harm and yet insisted on obedience at the same time.

Megan pointed down the hallway on the other side of the room, opposite the hallway where she had crawled from the bathroom earlier.

"It is that way, the door at the end of the hall," she said shakily.

The man nodded. "I am Darius. I will ensure these three get proper rest while their wounds heal. My healing ability will have their bodies completely healed and back to normal in a few more sessions."

Megan was still stunned and surprised at his calm demeanor as she shakily introduced herself and told him the names of Blake, Lucy, and Greg, all three unconscious and resting peacefully.

"I am sure you have questions, and I will be happy to answer them later after I have made sure that my charges are resting comfortably," Darius said, and then he turned and started barking orders to the two nurses.

Megan watched in confusion as her three new helpers made makeshift stretchers from blankets they had found in the hall closet and began placing Blake on one.

She shook her head to clear it, gathered herself, and rose to help. Darius graciously bowed out of barking orders as Megan took charge, and together they all managed to get the three wounded to the master suite.

Megan mainly supervised since the wound in her calf throbbed painfully, preventing her from walking comfortably. Darius took one look at her after they had taken care of their patients and ordered her to sit down and let him look at her leg.

She did as Darius instructed, and he had her leg healed and back to normal within minutes. It took him less time to heal Waller's shoulder wound. Chris, Dianna, and Bonnie had not been wounded and needed no care, so Megan ordered them to try cleaning up the mess as best as possible.

Megan took a deep breath of relief as everyone scrambled with their different tasks. They had all lived…well, so far…through an attack from what she assumed was WAMB soldiers.

It had been bad. How had they found them through her shields? They had discussed letting the shields down, but she had not done it yet.

Megan was unsure if they would survive another attack like that, and she trembled at the thought. How would they survive long enough to reconstruct a ghost town and build a safe place with these kinds of attacks?

Megan thought about Blake's plan to convert agents to their side, bringing her thoughts to the healer and the two nurses. Lily's control of them had vanished when Lily faded away, yet they had continued to help. They had chosen to stay after Lily's influence had freed their minds.

It gave Megan hope that Blake's plan may work after all.

Pain filled me, profound and overwhelming, torturous and agonizing. My eyes fluttered open. All I could see was light streaming into me from a hand that was held over me, and the more light that entered my body, the more the pain eased.

My heart beat with panic and confusion as I called for Lily and found the abyss empty. She was not in the front of my mind with me either, and fear began to overtake me.

I looked up to see a stranger leaning over me, and I wanted to scream, but the calming, soothing light filled my body, numbing me to any sensation or emotion.

Lily's face floated into my mind, smiling and peaceful, filled with a serene calm. I was numb to the sensation of relief that I knew I should feel at seeing her.

Even though I did not feel the sensation, I thought, *'oh, good. Lily is still here. I am glad.'*

The strange feeling of numbness was nothing like I had ever felt before as I watched that light fill my body. I drifted into a strange bubble of numb awareness for what seemed like an eternity. Time seemed to be frozen along with my emotions as I wafted through the fog that was my brain.

My eyes drifted close, and I slipped away from consciousness.

CHAPTER 35: Hope

My eyes burned. Even though they were still closed, I could feel the light stinging my sensitive orbs through my eyelids. I knew it would hurt to open my eyes, so I lay there and kept them closed, trying to use my other senses to determine where I was and what had happened.

"Lucy, are you awake?" Blake's whisper filled the space around me, and it was the best sound in the world to me at that moment.

"I am awake," I whispered back.

I heard his sigh of relief as I added, "my eyes hurt."

"Oh, sorry about that. I thought you might enjoy the sunlight on your skin. I'll close the curtains until your eyes adjust."

Sounds of shuffling came to me for a moment, and the harsh light dimmed. Slowly, I tried to open my eyes a crack, testing for light sensitivity. Even though the curtains were closed, the light in the room was still a bit bright.

Water filled my eyes for a moment as I blinked my eyes fully open, and then the stinging sensation was gone, and I could see. The first image that filled my newly opened eyes was breathtaking.

Blake turned from the window and pierced me with his sultry gaze. His black hair had fallen into his eyes as it always did, and he raised a hand to brush it away. His chocolate brown eyes held a desire so intense that it made me quiver with delight. He was shirtless, and his muscles danced under his fair skin as he strode toward the bed where I lay.

I tried to sit up and hold my arms out to him, but a sharp pain radiated through my chest, and I fell back onto the soft pillow under my head.

I gasped in agony and tried to bring up an arm to grasp my chest, but it sent another stab of pain through me, and I groaned miserably. I closed my eyes again and tried to breathe through the pain in deep, even breaths.

"Lucy, are you okay?" Blake asked, and I could hear the concern in his tone.

The bed shifted, and I felt Blake's touch as his hand covered mine, which still lay at my side since it hurt to lift my arms.

"I tried to sit up, and it hurt," I ground out through gritted teeth.

"Just hang on. I'll go get the healer," Blake said consolingly, and his weight left the bed.

"Healer?" I asked curiously. "When did we get a healer?"

"It's a long story," Blake said. "Let me take care of you, and then I will tell you everything."

I kept my eyes shut as I nodded slowly, not wanting the stabbing pains to start again. They had mostly faded, and I could breathe easier, so I lay still and quiet to keep the pain at bay.

After a few moments, the sound of footsteps entering the room had me opening my eyes again, and Blake's concerned features filled my vision.

I smiled softly, and Blake returned my smile, but it was stilted with worry. I turned my gaze to the man that had followed him into the room.

His tall body was thin, yet I could see toned muscle under his tight t-shirt. His face was round with deep-set, jade green eyes that shone with kindness, a strong, straight nose, wide, full lips, and dark brown, thin eyebrows that matched his military-style cut hair.

He smiled kindly and nodded toward me, and the smile and his soft, comforting, deep-toned voice had me relaxing instantly in his presence.

"Hello, Lucy. I am Darius," he said smoothly.

I returned his infectious smile and said, "Hello, Darius."

"I understand you are still in quite a bit of pain?" His smile vanished and was replaced with concern.

I nodded slowly as I answered, "Yes, it hurts to move. I could if I wanted to push through the pain, but I do not do so well with pain."

He chuckled humorously and answered, "I would imagine that no one does so well with pain. Some of us are just more skilled at ignoring it than others."

"Well, then, I suppose I am not good at ignoring it," I said sarcastically.

This made Darius laugh, which caused me to smile. His laugh was deep and musical. It made people want to laugh with him. I liked this man very much. He had an excellent bedside manner. Where had we found him?

"I am going to perform another healing session on you, and hopefully, it will help ease the pain somewhat. Will that be okay with you?" he asked.

"Am I right to assume that you already did this to me while I was unconscious?" I asked curiously.

He nodded with that comfort-inducing smile on his face. "That is correct, but I prefer to ask permission when one is awake, and it is not life-threatening."

"That is very kind of you," I replied with a raised eyebrow.

"I try to be kind," he responded, and then his smile widened as he added, "I find it much easier to do so here, which is why I stayed."

"What?" I asked. His statement piqued my curiosity, and I began to suspect where the healer came from.

The thought made my nerves prickle with anxiety, and my eyes widened in fear. I swallowed hard as he moved closer to me, but the kind look in his eyes and the gentleness of his tone had my panicked terror draining away once more.

"Please, Lucy, do not fear me. I would never want to hurt anyone. I was forced to." He shuddered as a look of disgust caused his brows to furrow over his warm, jade-colored eyes. "When your sister commanded me to heal instead of kill, I knew I had found my place. I do not have to be forced to heal."

My sister? At the mention of Lily, I remembered what had panicked me before I had lost consciousness. I had not been able to find Lily. Her face had drifted to me while I had been numbed by, what I now assumed to be Darius's healing light, but I was not sure if that had been a dream or reality.

Taking a calming breath, I searched for her, reaching into the empty abyss and finding it…gone…the abyss was gone! I scrambled through my mind, but there was no sign of the abyss or my sister. Frantically, I looked around the room for her ghost form, but there was no sign of her anywhere.

My heart raced with panic as my body filled with sorrow and loss. What had happened to her while I had been hurt? She had been in the ghost body when I had felt the bullet rip through my chest, but I had felt her being pulled back to me right before I had lost consciousness.

Had she taken the pain for me? Had she died to protect me? I could not lose her. Not now, when we had only just learned how to co-exist and love each other without fighting. A sob escaped me as I realized I may have already lost her while I had lain shut off from the world. Grief and misery consumed me as I shut my eyes.

"You did not answer my question," Darius said softly, his voice pulling me from my dark thoughts.

"Yes," I said in a flat, breathy voice. "You may heal me."

I felt warmth spread through me. It soothed the physical pain of my wounds, but it did not comfort the heart-wrenching pain I felt inside. Tears fell from the corners of my closed eyes as I lay and let Darius heal my wounds.

The bed shifted by my head, and Blake's electric touch was on my cheeks, wiping away the tears and brushing my hair from my face.

"Why are you crying, love?" Blake asked in a whispered voice. "Isn't the healing helping?"

"It's not that," I croaked through tears and sorrow. "Lily is gone. I cannot find her. I fear she may have died to save me from death."

"Oh, baby," Blake said softly, and strangely I heard happiness in his tone. "Lily is not dead."

Hope lifted my soul and eased the pain in my heart. Did he know something I did not, or was he speaking from the hope that I was mistaken somehow?

"Then why can't I feel her?" I asked. "Not only that, but that space inside my mind where Lily lives is not even there anymore. Every sign of her is completely gone."

Blake laughed and said, "Good."

My eyes flew open, and I frowned as anger began stirring in my gut. Blake was holding my hand, smiling at me in what I could only read as pleased humor.

"You are glad she is dead?" I asked as the anger rose inside of me.

Blake's smile turned comforting, and he squeezed my hand reassuringly. "Lucy, I told you she is not dead. She is with Greg as we speak."

My eyebrows rose in confusion and disbelief. "She… what… how?"

Blake's visage twisted in thought, and his gaze shifted to the wall behind my head. "Well…the way she described it to us is that the ghost body is no longer a ghost body, but more of a vehicle body. It is substantial and yet not. We can see it and hear it but cannot touch it. It will afford you privacy and vice-versa depending on who needs the physical body."

His gaze drifted back to mine, and the thoughtful confusion left his face as he asked, "Does that make any sense to you?"

I thought about it and nodded. "Yes, some of it does."

"So, when I asked Lily to give us some privacy while I checked on you, she appeared beside me and said she would sit with Greg for a while and give us privacy. I freaked out, and she tried to explain, and that is what she told me." Blake shrugged as he finished speaking.

"Oh, so that is why you said it was good that she was completely gone," I responded in understanding.

"Yes, of course," Blake answered. "I would never wish Lily dead…well…I mean, not now I wouldn't."

I laughed and then realized that it had not hurt. I looked up at Darius, still standing with the light streaming from his hands into me.

Gingerly, I moved my arm upwards, and it did not hurt. I shifted my weight slightly to sit up, which did not hurt either.

I smiled up at Darius. "I think it worked. You can stop now."

Darius lowered his hand as the light stopped streaming from his hand. "You feel better?"

I nodded, braced myself, and sat up quickly. A slight flicker of pain shot through my chest and shoulder, but it quickly disappeared. I took in a deep breath and let it out slowly.

"I feel fine now. Thank you so much, Darius, and I will be sure to tell my sister about you when she returns." I smiled at him, and he returned my smile.

Darius chuckled and said, "I assure you, she already knows about me. However, be sure to thank her for me. Tell her I am not angry that she took over my mind. It was refreshing to be forced to heal for a change."

He gave a slight nod to Blake and smiled at me as he bade us goodbye and left the room.

I raised curious eyebrows at Blake. "So, Lily took over his mind and had him heal me?"

Blake nodded. "Yes, it would seem that she was still at work even though we were all unconscious…."

I interrupted his explanation. "We?"

"Umm…yeah….you, Greg, and me. Greg was hurt pretty badly, and he is still sleeping. I was not hurt as badly. I lost a lot of blood from multiple gunshots, but they were mostly in my arm and legs." He shrugged as if it was no big deal that he had been riddled with bullets, but my heart cringed at the thought of how frightening and painful it must have been.

Blake's smooth tone continued. "Waller and Megan were shot, but only once each. Lily took over the minds of all of the soldiers outside. She realized that one was a healer and two were nurses, so she commanded them to help Megan with us."

Blake's eyes crinkled with worry as he said, "I am afraid we may not have made it without Darius's healing. We had all lost a lot of blood, and there is only so much that Megan could do without magic healing to assist her."

"So, you are saying Darius saved our lives under Lily's influence?" I asked in surprise.

"No. I am saying that Lily drifted away in the middle of it all from exhaustion, and Darius continued to heal us without her influence," Blake said calmly.

"So, Lily stuck to your plan in the middle of a gunfight, and it worked?"

Blake nodded. "Yep. Crazy, huh?"

"Crazy does not begin to cover it," I mumbled.

My mind whirled with confusion at everything Blake had told me, but one thing held firm. Darius had stayed with us even after Lily's control had vanished from his mind. He had made the conscious choice to continue to help us, even when he had not been forced to do so.

I smiled proudly and triumphantly at Blake as I said, "Your plan is working. We have already gained three new people."

Blake's happy visage faded as he said, "Yes, but we almost lost lives doing it. I don't know if we could survive another attack like that."

He was right, but I refused to give up hope. "You may be right, but surely there is something we could do to prevent it, some way to get close enough to take over minds safely before they attack."

Blake regarded me with a considering look. "I would say that it could be done if you and Lily could figure out how to control that other form that you two have discovered. If you could learn to control when it was visible and when it was not, then one of you could take the form invisibly and sneak up on anyone that tried to come here. Also, we could strengthen our security, maybe install a gate and a fence around the grounds, more cameras, and other things."

A slow smile spread across my lips as I said, "I think it could work. I will speak with Lily and try to see if we can control the ghost body."

Blake smiled widely as he said, "Well, Lily is calling it a vehicle body now."

I laughed. "That's just silly."

"Not any sillier than ghost body," said a voice from the doorway.

I whipped my head around to find Lily in the doorway with a humorous smile on her sharp features. Her long, blond hair flowed around her as she drifted into the room, piercing me with her baby-blue eyes that were twinkling with suppressed laughter.

My smile brightened, and gladness filled my heart at the sight of her. "Lily! I was so frightened when I awoke and couldn't feel you."

Her eyes softened with regret as she said, "Yeah, sorry about that. I was so worried about Greg that I did not think about how you would react when I wasn't there."

"No," I answered quickly. "It's alright. I'm just glad that you are okay."

"Me too," she said as she came to the side of the bed opposite Blake. "I would hug you, but apparently this body is not totally corporeal."

"We have never been able to give each other a physical hug," I said with a twinge of sadness.

Lily smiled and said, "We will figure it out."

I nodded. Yes, we would. We had to. If we could figure out these strange new abilities we seemed to be gaining, we would be able to help in outstanding ways. The thought gave me hope, and we all needed hope we could get…

And maybe just a tiny bit of luck as well.

PART EIGHT

JOINED

CHAPTER 36: Henry

I was feeling much better after my latest healing session with Darius. It was amazing how much faster one could heal when a magic healer was handy.

The hole in my chest was only a tiny, pink mark now and matched the small scar on my thigh. My lung had collapsed, but that had been healed during the first session. Darius had explained that it had been of the utmost importance to heal that first so that I could breathe.

No oxygen, no life, dead me. That was not acceptable.

The torn shoulder wound had completely healed with only a puckered, white scar where an angry red hole used to be, and I was glad that it would not be able to be reopened, short of someone shooting me there again.

That was not acceptable either.

I felt healthy and strong again, and Lily regained residence inside my mind. She needed rest to restore all the energy she had lost by drifting around on her own in our other ethereal body. The abyss no longer existed, so she rested in the forefront, floating peacefully there where I could keep an eye on her.

She was sleeping now, and as long as I had no extra loud thoughts or emotions, she would rest until her energy was restored.

It was strange not to have the abyss inside my head any longer for Lily to hide in. Not that I minded her company, but it was unnerving to be so hyperaware of her presence when it had been so easy to ignore her existence before.

Blake's wounds were completely healed, and he felt strong and restored. He had stayed by my bedside for the past two days but refused to share my bed for fear of hurting me or reopening any wounds.

Greg was feeling better as well, but he was still bedridden. His internal injuries had been healed, but it would take a few more sessions for him to be at full strength. At least the wound was no longer bleeding, and he was conscious again.

Lily had come back into my body before he had awoken, but he was happy when Blake told him that she had stayed by his bedside as long as she could before she had to restore herself.

Tyrone had spent the last two days moping around the house and apologizing to everyone that he had not been here to defend us. We had all told him multiple times that he was forgiven, but the sadness on his face when I looked at him told me that maybe he needed to forgive himself.

There was no way he could have known that this would happen. I had decided that Lily and I would talk to him later and try to help ease his mind if we could.

I sat at the dining room table, drinking my coffee and nibbling on a buttered bagel. Blake had gone to shower and check on Greg. I did not know where anyone else was, but it was good to have a moment to myself.

That moment did not last long, though, because, in a few short minutes, Waller shuffled into the room. He smiled when he spotted me sitting at the table, and I returned his smile hesitantly. I watched as he poured himself a cup of coffee from the coffee maker that sat on the island bar that separated the dining room from the kitchen. He plopped down at the table across from me, and I could tell he was not feeling his best today.

"You look tired," I said sympathetically.

Waller grunted. "That is an understatement, dear Lucy."

"Have you not been getting enough rest?" I asked, still trying to be considerate.

"There is still so much to do and many things going on that need my attention," Waller said, and I noticed that his deep, gruff voice was even rougher with fatigue.

"There are plenty of people here to help, Waller. Get someone else to help with the work. You need rest."

Waller glanced away from me as he said, "It is not that simple. There are things that you do not yet know."

I shrugged. "Well, inform me then. I will help if I can."

Waller started to say something, and then his eyes flickered as if he had just thought of something. His gaze drifted back to mine with a contemplating look.

"Maybe there is something you can do for me," he said mysteriously.

"What is it?" I asked and took another sip of coffee.

Waller took a sip of his own coffee before answering, "There is someone I would like for you to read if you get my meaning."

I narrowed my eyes. "You mean to take over their mind and discover all of their secrets?"

He did not answer and only nodded.

"Who?" I asked suspiciously.

"First, answer a question for me," Waller said, and I swear I saw a nervous glint in his stormy gaze.

It also made me nervous, and my heart began to pound in my chest. I took another nibble of my bagel, chewed, and then took a sip of coffee.

I swallowed it all down and said, "Ask away."

"What do you think happened to the other soldiers after Lily took over the healer and the two nurses?" Waller asked, and I could see him tense as he took another sip of his coffee, trying to act nonchalant.

I was not fooled.

Chills ran up my spine as I thought about what could have happened and what Waller was trying to tell me. What had Waller done to the other soldiers?

"I had not thought about it," I answered carefully. Queasiness settled in my stomach as Waller pierced me with his stormy gaze.

His voice was low and dangerous as he asked, "what would you have done to them if you had been conscious?"

I swallowed the bile that threatened to rise into my throat and took a calming breath to still my rapidly beating heart. "I would have done what I had to to keep us safe."

"Would you have been able to kill?" he asked.

I was already shaking my head before the words left his mouth. I knew what he was going to ask on some instinctual level, but hearing the words made it so much worse.

"I...I don't...," I stuttered, trying to deny that I would kill anyone, but was that true?

I would do anything to protect my friends...no, my family...even if it meant that I would have to do something that could break me at a soul level.

This is what I had Lily for. She did the things that I could not do. She took the hits for me because her moral compass did not point the same way mine did. She could do things I would regret forever without tainting her soul, and yes, I did believe that her soul was separate from mine. We might share a body, but our souls are different. Connected, yes, but different.

Waller was still staring at me expectantly, so I cleared my throat and admitted the truth. "I would not be able to kill, but Lily can. I would have given over control and let her do the job.

It is not as if I would not do it because I would. It is just that it would kill something inside of me that would never be able to be repaired. I would break myself to protect my family if I had to, but as long as I have Lily, I do not have to."

Waller nodded in understanding as he said, "I am glad to hear you say that because Lily is the one who saved us. She took over the healer, the nurses, and seven other soldiers outside the house. She kept one alive and made the others shoot themselves."

I shuddered at Waller's words, but he kept speaking as if I had not just reacted. Bile rose into my throat again, but I kept breathing slowly and steadily. I would not throw up.

"The one she kept alive has been neutralized, and we have been taking care of him. I want to learn what he knows and send him back to WAMB with a message, like Blake's plan."

I did not respond at first, and Waller remained silent as well.

Finally, Waller broke the brief silence. "I told Lily to do it."

"Why would you tell her to do that?" I asked in a whispering voice.

"Because I watched her form fading and saw it flickering as if she would disappear. I knew she would lose energy soon, and there was no way I would have been able to deal with that many soldiers alone if her influence was gone from their minds. It was the only thing I could think of to do."

I closed my eyes briefly as I took in everything he had said. I could understand why he had done it and Lily's acceptance of the task. My nerves calmed as the nausea faded. I could not be angry with her or Waller for protecting us.

"I understand your decision, and I am not angry with anyone. I am glad that you and Lily were able to keep us safe," I said calmly.

"You will be proud of her when you see who she decided to save out of all of the soldiers," Waller said, causing me to lift my brows in curiosity.

He did not wait for my reply before trudging along with his explanation.

"They brought a kid with them, a boy of only fifteen." He paused, and I saw his jaw clench tightly before he continued.

"He is a mental, sent with the soldiers to steal information from us and find out what we know. His powers feel close to yours."

"How do you know that?" I asked curiously.

"I can feel it. He initially tried to use his gift on me until he found out he couldn't, and I felt his power."

I blinked slowly as I asked, "Did he tell you that he had been sent to gather information?"

Waller nodded. "Yes, and that is why I would like you to meet him. I want to see if you can discern if he is being truthful. Lily could do it if you do not want to."

"It isn't that I don't want to," I said with a hint of frustration. "I just don't know if I…if we can. A mental trying to read another mental, especially if their powers are similar? I just don't know."

"Will you at least try?" Waller asked hopefully.

I sighed. "Sure, I will try. What can it hurt, right?"

We finished our coffee in silence. I did not eat the rest of my bagel. I was not sure if my stomach could handle it. My nerves had begun to act up again with the thought of meeting another mental.

It was not as if I did not know other mentals. There had been mentals in my class when I was younger. Megan's gift was considered a mental gift, and so was Waller's, which is what made me nervous.

I had never been able to read or control him without physical touch, which was Lily's doing. She had never been able to control his mind without contact, even when he was not wearing his protective band.

The thought that Waller's ability was nowhere close to mine and I could not read him, and this kid's ability was almost the same as mine, led me to believe that I would not be able to read him at all, physical touch or not.

But, I had promised to try, and try I would. What made me super nervous was that this kid may be better than me because he had had more training. I had been taken out of WAMB…well, broken out was a more correct term…when I was only six years old, and this kid was fifteen.

He would probably be better at controlling his gift than I was, which meant that this meeting could go the other way. The kid may end up reading my thoughts instead of me reading him, and then he would have his information.

My stomach fluttered with apprehension when Waller got up from the table with his coffee cup in hand. He reached over and took my cup and half-eaten bagel as well, and took it all to the sink and sat it on the counter.

"We will clean up later. Are you ready?"

No, I was not ready, but I did not say that.

Instead, I simply nodded and stood up from the table. A wave of nervous nausea flowed through me, but I breathed deeply and chased the sensation away as I stepped away from the table and followed Waller toward the small doorway hidden in an alcove in the living room that led down to the basement floor.

Were they keeping the kid in the basement?

The basement was fully built-in with a recreational room that featured a large billiards table, two sofas, and a couple of lounge chairs. The other rooms in the basement consisted of three extra bedrooms, a bathroom, and a small mini-kitchen with a small refrigerator and a microwave oven.

Waller led me to the last door at the end of the small hallway that led off the rec room and knocked soundly on the door.

"Yes?" a young voice called out.

The voice was scratchy, caught somewhere between a high-pitched tenor and a low-pitched tenor as if his voice was in that stage of adolescent change.

"It is Waller. I have brought someone I think you should meet," Waller said in a deep, commanding tone.

"Well, bring them in then," the voice replied impatiently.

Waller lowered his voice and looked at me before entering. "His personality is not exactly likable."

I shrugged and whispered back, "I can handle it."

Waller turned back to the door and unlocked a master lock that had been attached to the door. Turning the knob, he opened the door slowly. He stepped back, allowed me to enter, and closed the door behind us.

My gaze surveyed the room slowly.

Only one window sat very high up on the wall, almost touching the ceiling. The window was too small for a body to fit through, but it let a lot of light into the tiny room.

The small, twin-size bed sat to one side of the room and was scooted against the wall. There was a small bedside table with a lamp for extra light during the night. One small dresser sat on the other side of the room against the wall, and there was a small throw rug that covered the hardwood floor between the bedside table and the small dresser.

A rocking chair sat on the throw rug, and in the chair sat the teenage boy, regarding me with suspicious, light-brown eyes. His orange-red hair was cut short and parted to the side. There was a light spattering of freckles across the bridge of his small nose and another patch of freckles along his forehead and cheeks.

His light skin was a contrasting background for the freckles that dotted his face and made the golden brown of his eyes stand out drastically. His young face was oval-shaped with a sharp chin and a jawline that promised to be strong when he was finished developing.

As Waller introduced us, he looked me up and down with his suspicious gaze.

"Henry, this is Lucy. Lucy, this is Henry." Waller gestured to each of us in turn as he spoke our names.

I nodded in greeting as I said, "It is nice to meet you, Henry."

He narrowed his eyes as he responded sarcastically, "Likewise."

He certainly did not look or sound as if it was nice to meet me, but I did not say anything. Instead, I smiled a friendly smile as I stood awkwardly in the doorway.

He did not return my smile. His gaze became even more intense, and I felt a funny sensation fill my head. It was as if a gentle breeze was blowing around me, but instead of caressing the outside of my body as normal wind does, it tickled the inside of my head.

The warm and inviting breeze blew against my brain, encouraging me to open up and let it in, promising me that it would blow away all of my fears, worries, and pain.

Lily stirred inside my mind, opening her eyes and staring into the space where the wind-like sensation requested entrance. Her eyes narrowed in anger as she fully awakened. Her presence filled me as she stood large and firm against the intrusive manifestation, standing with her arms crossed over her chest intimidatingly.

I was still in control, but her presence stood against the warm, inviting sensation. She was not fooled by its gentle, inviting caress.

"What the hell is this?" she asked fiercely inside my mind.

"I think this kid is trying to read our mind," I answered as I focused my eyes on Henry so that Lily could see him.

She gazed out of our eyes in contemplation as she kept the intrusive energy at bay. She scoffed in irritation as she pushed the power away even further.

"He is not a very strong mental if that is all of his power. His eyes do not even glow," she said, and she waved her hand dismissively.

The invasive wind flew out of my head and was thrown back toward Henry with such force that he gasped aloud and was flung back into the chair, causing the chair to tilt back precariously.

Henry recovered quickly and leaned forward, bringing the rocking chair back upright before it could totter backward and spill him to the ground. His visage became fierce as his eyes narrowed even more.

"I tried to be nice about it," Henry said, and his tone had grown cold with anger.

My anger, mixed with Lily's, surged inside me violently, so my answering tone was fiercer than his. "That was nowhere near nice, Henry. You did not even ask permission first,"

"Oh, like you asked permission before taking over my mind and forcing me to become your prisoner?" he spat.

I felt Lily shift, reaching for that other form we carried, and suddenly I understood what had happened to the abyss. I felt our ethereal body forming, felt the sensation coming from that spot that had previously held the abyss.

The sensation was new and a bit disturbing, but I rode through the feelings as I watched the body form beside me, and Lily stepped inside the body. The connection stayed between us, swirling in the place where the abyss used to exist.

I could feel Lily's righteous anger in that spot, and I felt the sensations of our other form as it stepped away and separated from the main body, my body, the body I stood in now alone.

Henry's eyes were wild with fury, but the wrath melted away to be replaced with wide-eyed astonishment as our ghost body stepped away from our main body and became visible.

I was smiling victoriously, but I could feel Lucy's malicious, wicked smile that promised a world of hurt if Henry tried to mess with us again.

"You should learn to be careful whose mind you try to control in the future," Lily's voice rang out in warning.

"Holy shit!" Henry exclaimed, but his tone was filled with excitement instead of the fear I had expected. I frowned in confusion at his tone.

He laughed and clapped his hands together, and he looked and sounded even more kid-like as he squealed delightedly, "I cannot believe this! I was told no one like me existed, but here you are!"

"Huh?" I asked in complete confusion.

"What do you mean like you?" Lily asked suspiciously.

"No time to explain," Henry said excitedly as he stood from the rocking chair.

I had begun to believe that he was tied to the chair in some way as he had sat motionless, except for when he had saved himself from falling backward. Even then, however, his body had not moved from the chair.

Now, he had practically jumped from the chair excitedly and was standing in front of me, bouncing from one foot to the other as if doing some weird dance. He reached his hand out to me in invitation.

Waller moved quickly, pulling me from Henry's reach and shoving me behind him. Lily's ethereal form followed mine, still attached to my body by that connected spot inside my mind that was formerly known as the abyss.

I felt it pull suddenly as I was dragged behind Waller, and then a snapping sensation like a rubber band being stretched and then let loose suddenly filled that spot. The connection was snatched away with the snapping feeling, and I was suddenly alone inside my mind as Lily floated free and away. She joined Waller, standing like a physical shield in front of me, and stared down at the kid with a look of rage.

"You do not get to touch her," Lily seethed wrathfully.

I was stunned. The strange sensations had left my mind reeling with confusion. It felt the same as when I had awoken after being shot. Lily was nowhere inside my mind. The spot where the abyss had been lay empty, and I was completely alone in my body.

The only thing that kept me from panicking was the sight of Lily standing in front of me. Even though I could not feel her with me, I knew she was there because I could see her.

I turned my attention back to the kid standing before Waller. He was still excitedly bouncing on his feet and did not seem intimidated by Waller and Lily's icy gazes.

He bent and gazed at me around their bodies, waggling his eyebrows suggestively as he said, "So, you do not want to know how to control your abilities?"

I frowned, leaning around Waller and Lucy, even though Lucy put out an arm to try and stop me. I walked through her, shivering at the sensation of cold that drifted through me as I passed.

"What would you know about my abilities?" I asked suspiciously.

"Give me your hand and let me show you," he said as his excitement calmed a bit, and he reached out to me once more.

I looked at Lily, who was shaking her head. "I do not trust him," she said sharply.

I looked back to the kid as I said, "Neither do I."

Henry's excitement drained away, and his visage melted into a serious look that made him look years older than he had looked when he had been bouncing around excitedly.

"Look, I know you have no reason to trust me, but this is important, and we have no time," Henry said, and his tone had changed from excitement to seriousness.

"What are you talking about, kid?" Lily asked him in an exasperated voice.

"I am talking about WAMB," he answered Lily, but his eyes never left mine.

I did not respond, and neither did Waller or Lily. We just stood and looked at him inquisitively, waiting for him to elaborate. Finally, after a few moments of tense silence, Henry huffed impatiently and spoke.

"I am not trying to leach thoughts from your head. I am trying to let you into my head. You need to know what I know," he said, and I could hear the urgency in his tone.

When we did not respond, he sighed in exasperation and said, "Alright, I know that Waller probably told you that I was sent here to get information about you, and that is true, but after being here a few days, I have decided that I want to be here and be free. You can believe me or not, but what I have to show you is truly important."

He paused for a moment and then drew an imaginary 'x' on his chest as he said, "Cross my heart; you will want to know this."

Curiosity took over cautiousness. I raised my eyebrows at the kid as he stood, trying not to be intimidating. He simply stood silent and motionless with a calm expression on his young features. He smiled, still holding his hand out warily to me.

"Take my hand and see what I know," he said softly.

Lily was shaking her head as I moved to grasp his hand, but my curiosity had won out. There was something about this kid that I could not put my finger on, but I was about to find out what it was.

Lily blew out an exasperated breath and said firmly, "Hold on. If you are going to try to probe his mind before he can get to yours, then let me in as well. I will protect you if he tries anything funny."

I paused with my hand halfway to his. If he had wanted to, he could have grabbed my hand quickly enough before Lily could have gotten back in my head, but he did not.

He simply stood and waited patiently for Lily to step back into our body, and when I had felt her finally settle into my mind and the other body had disappeared into the back of my brain, I closed the distance and grasped Henry's hand.

I was instantly swept away into a whirlwind storm of emotions, memories, and thoughts that I could not be sure were my own or his, and I wondered if I had made a mistake in trusting him.

Lily was suddenly there, mentally grasping my hand and trying hard to pull me up from the tide. I held her hand firmly as fear gripped my soul, and I struggled not to be pulled under the overwhelming force of energy.

"Just let go," I heard Henry say softly. "Trust me, please."

The pleading tone pulled at my heartstrings. He was just a kid. How could I not trust him?

Taking a deep breath, I tightened my grip on Lily's hand and implored her to go with me. I felt her hesitation, but something inside me wanted to go into that whirlwind and find what it held.

My instincts were screaming at me that it would be okay. We were being pulled into Henry's mind, and everything inside me wanted to find out everything he knew.

"It will be okay," I said comfortingly to Lily. "We have to see what he needs to show us."

"How do you know it will be alright?" I heard Lily scream at me over the maelstrom of emotions swirling around us, and I could hear the fear in her tone.

"I don't know how I know. I just know. You may not trust him, but you can trust me." I filled my mind with the certainty that I felt deep in my soul, projecting that emotion out toward Lily, who still held onto my hand.

I felt her give in, felt her let go of the hold on our consciousness and slip away with me into the whirlwind that was Henry's mind.

Waller grabbed onto Lucy and Henry, as they both fell over before they could hit the floor. Careful not to pull them apart, he gently lowered them to the floor and stood guard over them. A wide smile spread across his face. This could be the salvation to all of their problems if Lucy could win this kid over.

He knew the boy held a similar ability as Lucy, which could greatly help their cause.

If only he had known how similar it was.

CHAPTER 37: Lost Boys

*** INSIDE HENRY'S MIND ***

Images, sounds, and emotions flew through me too rapidly to process anything. I held onto Lily, concentrating on the sensation of her hand in mine that my mind had conjured. I held onto her as I twirled around in a miasma of dizzying thoughts and memories.

"Concentrate," I heard Henry whisper, and his whisper carried through the whirring sounds in my mind. "You are trying to take everything in at once. Slow down and take it one thought at a time."

I closed my eyes and tried to do what he said, but the sensation of being thrown around the tide of Henry's mind made it hard.

"I can't," I cried out. "Everything is moving too fast."

"Just stop," Henry said. "Put down your feet and find solid ground."

I took a deep breath and thought about standing on solid ground, and suddenly I was. I held onto that sensation, ignoring the beckoning whirlwind that flowed around me. I still had a grip on Lily, so I concentrated on her being by my side, and she was.

"See, it is easy right?" I heard Henry, and he was there standing on my other side.

I turned to him and asked curiously, "How do you know so much about this?"

He did not have to answer. As if I had conjured the thoughts into being, the answer to my question came to me from his mind.

He had been a child when he was brought to WAMB. His parents had put him up for adoption at the tender age of three, the same age I had been when Waller had come for me.

He was raised in the facility where I had lived until I had escaped and had been put through many of the same tests and experiments.

He had learned to control his abilities over the years since he had had more practice than I had, and he had not had his twin taken away from him.

His twin?

He had a twin!

He and his twin had a traveling body similar to Lily's and mine. The abyss where his twin had been absorbed into him when they had been in the womb had formed into the body that they used for the other twin. The other twin rode the astral body when they were not resting in the main body.

Astral body!

That was a much better name than I had called it.

Now I knew how our astral body had been formed and why the abyss was gone. It developed into our astral body when we began to practice using it.

The difference was that they had had more time to practice with the astral body, so their astral body was more substantial than ours was. The twin riding the astral body could appear or disappear at will, and it could become solid when they wished. However, it took a tremendous amount of energy, so it wasn't something they often did. It was easier to ride the form while it was insubstantial and invisible, which is how Henry's twin rode it most of the time.

The mechanics of how they did this flowed into my mind, and I felt a rush of happiness that Lily and I finally knew how to do this and could begin to practice it. So much more information flowed through me, and I grasped each piece of information, wanting to learn as much as possible before this experience ended.

My power was not limitless. If I ran out of energy, this mental plane would shatter, and I would sleep until I was restored. If I pushed it and forced myself to stay awake, it could send me into a comatose state with Lily trapped inside.

I hurried to delve into more information, learning all I could about our abilities before it was too late, and then I remembered what else I was here to do.

I had to learn what Henry knew about WAMB, why they had come for us, and how they had found us. Stopping my search for information on our abilities, I switched focus to what Henry knew about WAMB's mission.

Henry had come with the troops that attacked us because he had been ordered to control the troops and get information from us. WAMB had found us through the help of a traitor, but I could not see a name or a face in Henry's mind. The traitor had assured WAMB that we would be caught unaware, but Henry had also been surprised.

Henry had been so stunned and distracted when another force had taken over the troops that Lily had been able to take him without a fight. He had not been prepared for an invasion of his mind since he thought he was the only one of his kind.

He had witnessed Lily force the soldiers to heal instead of kill and saw her stretch herself to her limit to protect us all. He felt her dominion over him slip when her energy ran low, but not before he had taken some information from her mind.

He knew about MDRT and their downfall, Blake's discovery of his traitorous father, and our plans to weaken WAMB by recruiting their members to join our mission to rebuild and create Liberty City.

During his two-day imprisonment in the basement, Henry had sat and contemplated on everything he had absorbed and learned, and he had decided that he wanted to join our cause, just as the healer and two nurses had.

He would have to find a way to consult with Hiram, his twin.

When this information hit my mind, I looked around at our mental dreamscape for the other side of Henry's mind, but there was nothing or no one to be found.

"Where is your twin?" I asked, turning my head to Henry.

"That was the overwhelming emotions and sensations you felt when you first delved into my thoughts," Henry said sadly. "My brother knows I have been captured, and he has shut himself off from me so that he can focus on saving me."

"So, you can communicate with him over that great distance?" I asked in amazement.

"As long as both of us live, we are still connected to this main body and thus can communicate with the other body no matter how far apart we are," he answered.

"But you cannot open the connection back up?" I asked sympathetically.

He shook his head. "No. He is withholding from me for some reason."

"So, one twin can hold back from the other if they choose?" My mind whirled with all of this new information.

"Well, yes. Have you not ever ignored your twin when you were angry with her?"

"I guess I have in a way, but only because we were forced to by WAMB's chip in our brain," I growled.

As he continued to speak, I watched as his face dropped into a scowl of anger and sadness. "They lied to us about your group. We were told that you were dangerous and that you planned on destroying all of us. We know WAMB is in no way innocent, but none of us mutants want to die because of them either."

My eyes softened as I gazed at him in sympathy. I knew this was not real. I knew that my mind had created this dreamscape world where our minds were merged and we were not standing here in our physical bodies, but that did not stop me from taking his hand in mine.

He looked into my eyes, and I smiled tenderly as I said, "you are an extraordinary boy, Henry. I would be proud to have you and your brother join our cause."

His face softened into a return smile as he squeezed my hand and replied, "knowing what I know now, what you know, I am glad that they made me go after your group."

"Me too," I said, still smiling, and then I frowned as a disturbing thought entered my mind.

"Did you never read any of their minds and discover their true intentions before doing what they told you to do?" I asked. "You certainly had no qualms about digging around in my mind."

Henry chuckled. "First of all, I did not dig into your mind. You stopped me but then gave it freely, just as I gave you all my thoughts. Secondly, I did not read their minds or control anyone unless told to because I did not want to be decommissioned for disobeying orders."

"What about when they forced you to do things you did not want to do…like…well…kill people?"

Henry's face fell, and his visage turned sour. He took a deep breath and said, "did you not get any of that when I let you in?"

I shook my head. "No, I could not absorb everything. There was too much information."

"Well, we are still here. Look for the answer. It is hard for me to talk about it, so it would be easier if you just pulled it from my memories. You still have enough energy for this last piece of information."

Henry fell silent.

I looked up at the whirling mass of memories, thoughts, and emotions that swirled above our heads like an angry storm. Pulling from the information I had gained from Henry's mind, I searched for how to read only certain information without getting overwhelmed with the rest of the churning miasma.

I took a deep breath and focused on the question blazing in my mind. I said it aloud just for emphasis. "Why did Henry not read the minds of the people that forced him to do things he did not want to do?"

I reached up and touched the mass of stormy memories and saw Henry shudder as if I had touched a part of him. I guess, in a way, I had. I was touching his mind, thoughts, and memories, but not physically. In any case, I could feel my hand reaching and searching for the specific memories and emotions I wanted. I could physically feel the coldness of the swirling miasma spinning around my hand as I touched it.

It was my brain's way of showing me my ability on a physical level, which made it easier for me to understand and maneuver someone else's mind to find what I needed.

I grasped at the cloud of thoughts, imagining that I was grabbing the one I needed, and let the images fill me as I closed my fist over it. I closed my eyes to see the thoughts more clearly and concentrate on what I had pulled from Henry's mind.

I saw Henry, only it wasn't Henry. This version of Henry was heftier in build and had darker skin. The freckles were the same, but the eyes were darker brown, and the hair was more of a true red. I was startled when I realized this must be Hiram, Henry's twin.

Hiram was standing in some sort of contraption enclosed in glass with wires and tubes coming out of it. I could tell it was causing him pain, and his image flickered in and out of invisibility.

It was the twin's astral body, and Hiram was riding it. But for some reason, he was trapped inside this contraption. A man in a lab coat paced in front of the cylindrical prison, and I could see Hiram's dark brown eyes fill with fury as they followed the man.

"Just listen and do what they tell you to do," the man said. "When you return successfully, I will let your brother out of the holding cell."

Holding cell? What…and then the knowledge came to me from Henry's mind even as I watched the vision of his memory unfold.

The holding cell was a specially constructed contraption designed to hold the astral body away from its original housing and drain it of its energy. Eventually, the astral body could die unless it was allowed to return to the body to be recharged.

My focus turned back to the vision of Henry's memory, and I saw him emerge from the back of the contraption, combing his hands through his red hair as he faced the man in the lab coat.

"I do not understand why they keep putting Hiram in that thing. I have learned not to refuse an order any longer, and I have no intention of doing so now."

The man pushed his wire-rimmed glasses up on his nose and replied, "This is only precautionary. When you return from your task, Hiram will be set free. The energy drain is turned off now, so you have plenty of time."

"When we find that damn chip that they implanted in our brain, we will have it yanked out and leave this place," Hiram's voice said through Henry's mind.

Henry remained silent in his head, but aloud he said, "Alright, I will do it. When I return, though, you must let him out. He needs to rest and recharge."

The man nodded and said, "you have my word."

The image drifted away as I opened my fist and let go of the memory, and then I paused when the words sank into my brain.

The chip…

Henry had had a chip implanted inside his mind, much as I had when I had first arrived at WAMB. It had taken Lily away from me, or at least I had thought it had, and now I realized what the chip had truly been implanted there for.

The chip was implanted not to hide the abyss…or rather the developing astral body…from my mind, but to extract it from me. They had planned to use me just as they were using Henry now, using Lily to control me by removing her and holding her prisoner as they had done to Hiram.

At that moment, I was so thankful to Greg for zapping it and rendering it useless. Even if the worst happened and I was taken back to WAMB, they would not be able to take Lily from me and use me as they were using Henry.

Rage and fury at what they were doing to this kid filled my soul as the place my mind had created began to break apart. As my energy drained, I felt myself being pulled from Henry's mind, but the anger gave me fuel.

I reached for one more answer to one more question as I drifted close to the exit of his mind, and the answer came to me instantly.

"Is Hiram being held at WAMB right now?"

"Yes…yes he is, and he knows that I have been captured, and he knows about you too now." I felt the surety of Henry's words as they floated to me, and just before I drifted out of his brain, I heard another voice calling to him.

It echoed in low tones as if it was calling to Henry from a distance, filled with panic and urgency. "Brother, I do not know how, but they know you have met someone like you. They are bringing the entire WAMB army after you and the other one. I am afraid, dear brother, that we may be in big trouble."

I was sucked suddenly from his mind and thrown into the distance between his mind and mine. Fear coursed through my thoughts as the implications of what Hiram had said sank in.

The entire WAMB army was coming here, and they were coming for us.

CHAPTER 38: Coming Together

The fear was a physical force that filled my body as I slammed back into my own mind, and I came up from the floor into a sitting position gasping in short, shallow breaths.

Sweat beaded up on my forehead, cold and clammy, and my hands trembled as they ran across my head to wipe it away. I heard Henry draw in a long, deep breath as he, too, sat up from his place on the floor beside me.

My hand had fallen from his when I had sat up, but I could see him come into view in my periphery. I turned my head towards him, and his eyes mirrored my horror.

"What are we going to do?" I whispered, and my voice trembled as violently as my hands.

"What happened?" Waller's deep, commanding tone boomed at us as we sat on the floor and tried to collect ourselves.

Lily was instantly awake, shooting into the place where our astral body…now I knew the right name for it…rested and bounding into the body with the force of a speeding bullet.

She rocketed out of me so forcefully that my body shot forward, and pain ricocheted through my head when I felt the body snap out of my mind.

"Oww, Lily, that hurt!" I groaned as she tumbled out onto the floor beside me in the astral body.

She sat up and looked up at Waller. Her voice was urgent as she said, "We need to gather everyone together… now."

Waller's brows rose questioningly. "What did you find out from Henry that is so important?"

Henry huffed as he pushed himself from the floor and rose to a standing position. "Nothing that I have not already told you. I told you they would be coming for me, and now they are coming for Lucy too."

Waller moved so quickly for such a big man. He had Henry in his grasp, holding him by his neck as his feet dangled in the air so fast that Lucy had no time to respond.

"Waller put him down! He is not threatening us; he is warning us!" Lily's voice rang out through the tiny room.

Waller stiffened at the sound of Lily's voice and slowly lowered Henry to the ground. He did not let go of his neck, though he did loosen his hold and allow Henry to breathe in a raspy breath to feed his oxygen-starved lungs.

"Explain," Waller said in his deep, booming voice.

"There is too much to explain and no time. Just get everyone together," I said calmly, but the tone of my voice belied the terror crawling its way up my spine.

I lifted myself from the floor slowly, steadying myself before trying to walk over to Waller. I laid my hand on his arm gently. "Let him go, Waller. He is on our side, and we must help him save his brother."

I gave Waller a knowing look as I added, "his twin brother."

Waller's eyes widened in astonishment as he slowly let go of Henry's neck. Henry crumpled to the floor, coughing and rubbing his neck as he tried to regain his breath.

"You mean…?" Waller did not finish the question before my head nodded furiously.

"Yes. WAMB has him contained in some kind of machine. He is in an astral body like Lily is right now. They have a spy that knows where we are, but I could not see who it was. The entire WAMB army is on its way here to recover Henry and try to capture me. They are bringing his brother with him for insurance." My voice stayed calm as I spoke, but my body began to tremble again.

Waller's eyes grew dark with fury as he rounded toward the door to the small room. "Come, all of you. We must prepare."

"Prepare for what?" I asked. "Do you have a plan?"

"Plan?" Waller spat with his hand on the doorknob. "The plan is to gather everyone together and leave. Project Liberty City is canceled."

"Leave? We can't just leave. They will kill my brother," Henry cried.

"We can't run from them forever," I said in a whispered tone.

"We need time to prepare if we want to fight," Waller retorted. "We have no time...."

Waller's words were cut off by Henry's choked tone.

"We have three days," Henry rasped, where he still sat crumpled on the floor. "They will prepare the army and begin the trip here in two days. It will take them another day to get to Daisville, but they will rest somewhere before coming here."

Waller jerked back around. "There will never be enough time to prepare for the entire WAMB army, boy. Do you not understand that? Ten of them almost killed us all. How are we going to fight off hundreds of them?"

Henry was still rubbing his neck as he sat on the floor. His pale skin grew even paler as he looked up into Waller's eyes with a helpless look.

The look belied his determined tone as he shot back, "I don't know, but we better think of something. I am not leaving my brother."

"Then you can stay here and die," Waller spat as he turned back to the door.

"And me," Lily said.

I stepped up beside her. "And me too, which probably means Blake and your son since they would not leave us here."

I watched as Waller's shoulders slumped in defeat, and he turned slowly to me. His stormy eyes locked on mine.

I gave him a small, sad smile and spoke in a low tone as I said, "Look, Waller, they caught us by surprise before. Had we been prepared, we would have defeated that tiny army easily. We were surprised on the road as well. Both times we were surprised and still won. Think of what we could do if we could prepare."

Waller's eyes narrowed in thought. "I would agree with you, Lucy, if it were a single troop or even a couple. But the entire army?"

I shrugged as if it were no big deal, even as my insides were churning with anxiety. "We wanted to dwindle their numbers. How better to do that than to take out the entire army."

Waller shook his head in frustration. "Let's just get everyone together in the dining room."

He turned once more to the door and left the room. Lily held a hand down to Henry, and he looked up at her questioningly.

"I want to practice becoming solid," she said with a shrug. "See if you can grab my hand."

"You know you have maybe two hours tops in the astral body solid, and that is if you are practiced at it," Henry said as he reached for her hand.

Lily hesitated, taking her hand back for just an instant before reaching down again with a look of determination. "That would be all the time I need. I did it yesterday without thinking about it when everyone was in trouble, and I held it for quite a while, even while holding ten minds under my control."

Henry's eyes widened. "You mean you held the form and used your ability simultaneously?"

Lily responded sarcastically, "I pulled you into the house, didn't I?"

"That was you?" Henry said.

"Since your fucking troops had shot Lucy, yes, it was me." Lily's eyes held anger for a moment, but she quickly regained control.

Henry looked ashamed as he said, "Sorry. I was only following orders." Then, his face and tone changed suddenly when he added, "Not even Hiram or I can do that. Usually, we can only use our ability in the physical body."

"Maybe it is because our astral body had more time to develop before we used it," I suggested. "Our astral body kind of stayed in the back of my mind until recently. Even when I gained back my memories and realized I had these gifts, I did not know that the abyss in the back of my mind was another form."

"The abyss?" Henry asked in confusion as Lily pulled him up from the floor.

"Yeah, you know that spot in the back of your mind where the astral body rests and recharges," I explained as I watched Henry physically touching Lily in wonder.

Henry frowned. "Mine is more of a cave, not an abyss."

"Maybe the size of the body's resting place determines how powerful the body is and how much energy it can hold," suggested Lily as she turned to me, smiling.

Henry and I both looked at her with questioning looks on our faces. She sighed and placed her hands on her hips.

"Look, that space in the back of your head is not a physical space. It is just your brain's way of helping you understand. By showing you a physical space in your mind's eye, you can better understand how much energy that space can hold. So, the bigger the space your mind creates for you, the more powerful the being inside you is. Your brain is translating power into size."

Lily paused for a moment as Henry and I processed what she said.

"Do you get it now?" she asked.

I nodded slowly. "I think I understand what you are trying to say."

Henry also nodded. "The cave does tend to grow bigger the older I get. Maybe mine will be an abyss by the time I am your age."

"Yes, maybe," Lily said as she turned for the door. "Come on. We need to get to the dining room and devise a plan to take down this army that is coming for us."

"Yeah," Henry said. "Take them down and save my brother."

"We are not going to take them all down," I said firmly as I moved toward the door where Lily held the door open for us. "Some of them will join us. Most of them, I hope."

Henry stepped through the door, and Lily held her arm up, stopping me from following Henry. Her eyes were serious as she caught my gaze.

"After the meeting, I would like to rest, and I think you should too. You should sleep while I sleep inside our body so that we can be at full strength." Her tone matched the expression in her eyes.

I frowned. "Lily, we are both fully healed. We will be fine."

The corners of her lips quirked up in a mischievous smile, softening the frown on her face. "Oh, I know, but I need lots and lots of energy."

I quirked one eyebrow. "Why?"

"Because Greg will be fully healed today," she said with a smile. Complete understanding hit my mind, and I felt the blush creep up my cheeks.

"Oh," was all I said as Lily dropped her arm, and I hurried out the door and after Henry.

We walked silently through the basement as we hurried to catch up with Waller and Henry. I was glad that Lily now had her own body due to our growing abilities and could interact with Greg without borrowing mine. It would save my body much pain.

My cheeks flamed again at the thought, and I cast it away quickly. I certainly did not want to walk into the dining room in front of everyone with flushed cheeks and have to avoid all of their questions about why I was so embarrassed. I only hoped the flaming blush in my cheeks would disappear before we got there.

The living room, dining room, and kitchen were one large open floor plan, so everyone standing around all three rooms could see when Waller stepped into the living room. He must have held a stern expression on his features because the cacophony of voices drifting down the basement steps toward us stopped abruptly.

I heard gasps around the room as Henry followed him out, and I heard a happy greeting from Greg when Lily stepped out.

I paused at the alcove leading into the living room when we walked up the stairs. I took a deep breath as I followed Lily into the room, and instantly Blake's eyes met mine from where he stood across the living room, waiting expectantly.

He was smiling an erotic smile that had me going weak in the knees. The sensuality of his dark brown gaze made my heart patter with longing as he strode toward me with the lithe gracefulness that his wonderfully muscled body held.

My mouth watered at the memory of his delicious kisses, and my skin danced with desire at the memory of his hands on my body. The walls of my sex pulsed with the need to be filled and stretched by him, and I had to lean against the wall to keep from sinking to the ground. I did not know whether my quivering legs could hold me up.

Blake had always affected me, but this was insane. I had never felt the desire for him so strongly before, and it made me wonder what had changed that had made my want for him so intense.

"You are alone inside your head now," Lily whispered as I stood, leaning against the wall. "Your emotions will be intensified because you do not have me as a buffer. I am not there to take some of your sensations, so you will experience everything fully."

"I had no clue that my feelings for Blake were that intense," I whispered to Lily just before Blake reached my side.

Lily snickered and said, "Yeah, good luck with that," Then she sauntered off toward where Greg stood smiling wickedly at her.

I watched her walk away with a smirk. I had received some of the emotion she had with Greg while I had been asleep and she had been in charge. Add that to what she already felt for Greg, and I had a feeling that my sister was about to get a dose of her own medicine.

"Good luck with what?" Blake's sultry voice asked, pulling me from my thoughts.

I cleared my throat.

"Oh, nothing important," I said, trying to sound nonchalant. "We are just trying to cope with our new abilities."

"How is that going?" he asked as he leaned against the wall beside me and drew me into his arms.

I swallowed as the sensations swirling through me became stronger, causing my heart to pound against my chest and my breathing to quicken.

"It is…" I said breathlessly, pausing to search for the right word. "It is intense."

Blake kissed the top of my head and took a huge breath as if drawing in my scent. He exhaled with a soft 'Mmmm' sound that had me practically drooling.

"Intense, huh?" he whispered against my hair as his lips drew down toward my ear.

The whole world fell away at Blake's touch. It was only him and me standing in a world burning with need and longing. His breath caressed my scalp through the covering of my black locks, and when his warm breath hit the bare skin of the top of my ear, I practically melted.

"I can give you intense, baby," Blake whispered huskily, then sucked my earlobe into his mouth.

I gasped. I experienced a moment of sensory overload as waves of crashing desire spread through my entire body, the body where I stood alone and was surrounded by those crashing waves.

A soft moan escaped my open lips, and my eyes fluttered closed. Blake's arms around me kept me upright as my knees went out from under me, and I sank fully into his embrace.

I heard his victorious chuckle as my body melted into him, and he held me tight and close to keep me from falling to the ground. Melting to the ground was a better word because I could feel the heat in my body rise to a towering inferno as he released my lobe and softly kissed the underside of my jawline and then trailed kisses across my cheeks and to the side of my mouth.

His lips captured mine in a soft, passionate kiss that had me wondering if I would pass out from the rising pleasure that coursed through my heated body.

"Ahem"

Someone cleared their throat loudly, and Blake broke the kiss. He did not let me go, and I was glad for that since I did not know if I could stand on my own. Waller stood in front of us with his hands on his hips and an exasperated look on his features.

His stormy eyes met mine as he said, "Lucy, you know how important this meeting is. You can play with Blake later."

"I will be happy to let her play with me later," Blake said as he nipped my ear lightly.

I gasped and swallowed, trying to keep at least a bit of my dignity under Waller's piercing gaze.

"I know, Waller. We will be right over," I said, and I hated how breathy my voice was.

His eyes narrowed slightly, and he stared at me a moment longer before turning and joining everyone else at the table.

Blake started to let me go, but I sagged against him and gripped his arm for support. He caught me quickly, wrapping his arm around my waist to steady me.

"Are you okay, Lucy?" he asked worriedly.

A soft, nervous chuckle escaped me as I answered, "Umm…well…it is hard to explain. Let's just say that everything is intensified since I am riding my body solo."

Blake's eyebrows rose, and then understanding crossed his face. He laughed delightedly and said, "So, that is what you meant by 'things were intense' with you and Lily."

I felt the flaming blush creep up my neck as I nodded and choked out a quick "uh huh."

"So, you could say I literally swept you off your feet," Blake said as he waggled his eyebrows.

"Don't get cute," I said sternly as I gave him a playful punch in the ribs.

He let out a soft 'oomph', which only made him laugh again.

I huffed and rolled my eyes as I carefully tried to stand alone. My legs were slightly shaky, but they held my weight as I walked carefully across the living room toward the dining room.

As I approached the table full of people, I glanced around quickly to see all the faces. It was good that the dining room table was so large because it was filled to capacity and then some.

Waller sat at the head of the table with his back to the window. The two nurses who had helped Megan tend the wounded leaned against the windowsill behind Waller since there was no room for them at the table. Five chairs were squeezed in on either side of the large oval table, which was initially only meant to hold four chairs on either side.

To the left of Waller sat Megan with Greg on her other side and Lily on the other side of Greg. Tyrone was on the other side of Lily, with Henry squeezed in on Tyrone's other side, and then finally Bonnie, who sat at the other end of the table.

Moving around the table, Darius sat close to Bonnie's right with two empty chairs next to him that I assumed were meant for Blake and me. Chris sat next to the empty chairs with Dianna between him and Waller.

As my eyes drifted back around the table, they flew automatically to Lily's. She looked up at me with wide eyes, and I noticed how they sparkled a bit too brightly. Her cheeks were flushed, and her mouth hung slightly open. She looked like she wanted to bolt from the table and hide somewhere.

I also noticed that Greg had scooted as far from her as possible in the small space around the table and had his arms folded on the tabletop. I frowned in confusion.

I tuned in to the spot in my mind where Lily and I were still connected even though she rode a different body, and I felt a radiating shadow of the emotions I had just experienced with Blake.

I turned to Greg, who held a satisfied smile as he gazed at her with lust-filled eyes. He still held his body away from hers. I snickered as I assumed Greg had gotten to her just as powerfully as Blake had gotten to me without touching her.

Could he touch her? Did he know he could touch her? Greg would be in for a real surprise when he discovered that he could touch her now.

I met her gaze again and gave her a knowing smile and a wink. She did not return my smile and only narrowed her eyes at me angrily. That only made me laugh as I sat at the table across from her. Blake sat beside me and placed his hand on my thigh under the table. We settled into our seats as Waller stood and prepared to speak.

I glanced around the table one last time. Fifteen. There were fifteen of us sitting and standing around the table, speaking of going to war against the entire WAMB army, which consisted of hundreds of warriors.

I had no clue what we would do, but we had better come up with something fast. Short of running, I could not think of a single thing, but running would not be an option unless we planned to leave Henry here alone because he would not leave without his brother.

I was not willing to leave Henry here. I had just met him, but I felt a kinship with him that I could not ignore, especially since my mind had melded with his. It was not only that, however. It was the sense that I had something in common with him.

Never in my life had I met anyone like me. Even before I had regained my memories, I had always felt different and apart from my friends and family. I had never felt a kinship with someone as I did with Henry. He was like the little brother I never had.

I turned my attention to Waller as he began to speak, catching everyone at the table up on everything. Not everyone had been present for our plans for Liberty City, so he started with that.

Blake passed out the packets to those that did not have them, mainly Darius, the two nurses, and Henry. After that, Waller told everyone about my interaction with Henry and what Henry and I had told him. A series of gasps, whispers, and extremities were spoken around the table as everyone soaked in this information. Waller held his arms up and silenced everyone.

"I am sure we can devise a plan," he said commandingly. "We have two powerful mentals, not to mention Chris, who can do crazy things with metal."

"The last troop they sent had ghost guns, dad. They were completely made of plastic," Greg said in frustration.

"I know, son, but you and I both know those guns never last long. They may send out a troop or two with those guns, but they would never arm the entire army with them."

Chris blew out a breath and nodded. "Waller is right. I will try to melt as many guns as I can as soon as I can."

Greg did not respond to Chris but instead turned back to his father. "Also, what about this supposed traitor? How are we going to find out who that is?"

Waller's eyes flicked between Lily and me as he spoke his next words. "Our two mentals can take over minds and steer them in another direction, as our wonderful new healer Darius and his two nurses can attest. Most of the army may decide to turn away and join us if we can manage that, and we might be able to find the identity of our traitor while they are at it."

"There are only a certain number of minds that can be taken this way before we are drained of all of our energy," Henry said. "Add that to trying to read minds and find the traitor, and you could be looking at comatose mentals."

"He is right," I agreed.

Waller sighed. "Alright, how about we take a break so everyone can brainstorm about what you can do to help? Focus on your abilities and how you can insert that into our mission. We will meet back here in an hour."

Everyone nodded their agreement and rose from the table. Lily came around the table toward me, so I stood where I was and waited for her. Her eyes looked miserable as she came up and gazed at me forlornly.

"Waller told you about the other soldiers, didn't he?" she asked softly.

I nodded. "Yes, he did, and I told him that I am not mad at either of you. You both did what you had to do to protect our family. I would have been mad had you not done anything."

Lily's eyes sparkled with the beginnings of tears as her sad look became one of surprise. She held that look for a moment before a smile spread across her face.

"Dammit, I guess this stupid astral body can fucking cry," she said in a shaky whisper as she wiped at her eyes.

I laughed and responded, "I hope they are happy tears."

Lily moved toward me and threw out her arms. She paused for a split second before wrapping them around my shoulders and pulling me toward her. I gasped in disbelief as I felt her. She had made the astral body substantial, and I could feel her body pressed against mine.

I smiled as I wrapped my arms around her waist and hugged my sister for the first time in our lives.

CHAPTER 39: Free Time

*** LIBERTY CITY HEADQUARTERS, LILY ***

"So, where is that sister of yours?" Greg asked Lily as he sauntered into the room.

She had been sitting on her sister's bed, running her hands over the silken comforter, still in a state of wonderment over the fact that she could feel the softness of the silk in this body.

She had been in this form since she had left the dining room after hugging her sister for the first time in their lives. The memory made her smile softly. It had felt good to finally touch her sister physically, and the bond they had formed made it all that much better.

She was distracted by Greg's voice when he entered the room, and her eyes jerked up from where she had been staring at the red silk comforter.

She met Greg's hazel eyes and smiled. "She's out back with Blake. She said something about wanting to sit on a log."

Lily waggled her eyes suggestively at him, and he barked a humorous laugh. "Nah, that log is too rough for your sis, and Blake's pansy ass would never be that rough with Lucy."

Lily's heart fluttered as Greg came further into the room, striding closer to the bed where Lily sat. His smoldering gaze made her gasp as he stopped inches away and knelt in front of her.

"I saw you hug her just before you turned and disappeared down the hall," Greg said, lifting an eyebrow questioningly.

Lily smiled and nodded. "Yes, I did."

"So, can you touch anyone, or is that just for your sister, like when only she could see you?" Greg asked

Lily's smile widened as she caught hope in his amber gaze. "I can touch anyone I like, and they can touch me as well."

Greg smiled slyly as he asked, "If I can touch you, does that mean I can fuck you?"

Lily's smile matched his as she replied, "If you can touch it, then you can fuck it."

Greg reached out to her tentatively and touched her hand, where it still stroked the softness of the silk comforter. His eyes held delight as his fingertips touched the back of her hand. He closed his hand over hers and grasped it, slowly drawing her hand to his lips.

He closed his eyes and shuttered as her hand touched his lips. He kissed her hand softly and sighed, his warm breath brushing against the skin of her astral body and eliciting a shudder of her own.

Lily closed her eyes and thanked whatever Gods or Goddesses made it possible for this astral body to feel sensation, especially since the delicious, sultry sensations pumping through her body from Greg's touch were so delightful.

Greg stood from his crouch and pulled Lily up with him. He wrapped his arms around her waist and jerked her to him with a sensual smile. He nuzzled the top of her head with a happy little sigh.

"I can finally touch you," he breathed against her hair.

"You could touch me before," Lily said. "I was just in a different body, is all."

"It isn't the same," he said, luxuriating in the feel of her soft silken hair against his cheek. "This is you; I mean, it is really you. Your own body and everything."

"Well, technically, Lucy can travel in this body as well as I can. We share both bodies."

"Yes, but who will ride this body most of the time?" Greg asked.

"Probably me," Lily answered with a smile.

"That is my point. Lucy controls your physical body most of the time, so everyone associates that body with Lucy. Everyone will eventually associate this body with you since you will be in control most of the time."

Lily nodded against Greg's cheek as she cuddled into him and responded, "I see your point."

Greg pulled away to look down into her eyes and said, "We have an entire hour to kill. What do you say we take this new body for a spin."

He waggled his eyebrows suggestively, causing Lily to laugh, but the laughter died in her throat when Greg's playful look turned dangerously sensual, and he leaned toward her to capture her lips with his.

She gasped as the electric touch of his lips pressed against hers sent a tsunami of sensations crashing through the astral body. Obviously, this body was equipped with the same parts as a physical body because she could feel the pulsing of vaginal walls in the center of her groin.

The pleasure that Greg had made her feel in the past was nothing compared to this. With one simple touch and one kiss, he had her panting and almost climaxing. When she had explained to Lucy about the bodies' experiences being heightened due to being alone in the body, she was sorely understating.

His lips trailed around her cheek and caressed her earlobe as his hands moved down to grasp her ass. He whispered into her ear, sending a shiver through her that made a small sigh escape her throat.

"I cannot fuck you like I want to," he said.

Lily's eyes flew open, and she pulled away from him to look into his eyes. His hands stayed where they were, grasping her butt cheeks and squeezing softly, and she placed her hands on his muscled chest for support.

"Why can't you?" Lily asked, her voice rough with unfulfilled desire.

He let go of one cheek to bring his hand up to her face. He cupped the side of her face in his palm as he smiled down at her with his hazel eyes. His visage was soft and tender, filled with emotion so intense that it made Lily shudder in his arms.

"Because, love, this body has not experienced intimacy yet, so you are essentially a virgin."

Lily's eyes widened in shock, causing Greg to chuckle as he kissed the tip of her nose.

"You are adorable when you are shocked," he said humorously.

Lily swallowed hard, not finding any of this funny, and said, "Alright, I am a virgin again." She paused for a moment and took a breath, and then asked, "So, what does that have to do with you not being able to fuck me?"

Greg sighed and said, "It is not as if I do not want to, but I will need to be gentle with you at first. We can work our way up to the rough stuff gradually. I do not want to do anything that may permanently harm this body."

Lily nodded her head slowly as she choked out, "Okay. That makes sense."

Greg looked deeply into her eyes, his hazel depths almost hypnotic as he whispered, "I will need to make love to you before I can fuck you, but there are other things I can do to give you a bit of pain."

Lily's heart pattered nervously. She did not think she was ready for this type of sensual overload. She had always viewed sex as what it was…sex…and maybe a bit of rough play thrown in. She had never experienced gentleness or had anyone 'make love' to her. Hell, she had never had any sexual experience at all before Greg.

Greg must have seen the nervous expression on Lily's face because he pulled her back to him and, grasping the back of her head, pushed her head against his chest, cradling her to him.

He spoke in low, deep tones, saying, "Relax, love. I got you."

"I don't know how to do this," Lily said, her voice breaking as she felt her eyes tear up.

"Why the hell am I crying?" Lily asked herself.

She heard her sister's whispering answer in her head. *"Because you are afraid. You are afraid of being loved."*

"Get out of my head," Lily snapped, sounding angrier than she had intended.

She felt a caress of understanding brush against her mind, and then she felt the connection between her and Lucy snap. Lucy had let her astral body go free from the link in the back of her mind, and Lily was now truly alone in the astral body.

"You don't know how to do what?" Greg asked, and Lily could hear the confusion in his tone.

"I don't know how to be loved," Lily choked out. "Pain and anger are all I have ever known."

Greg tightened his hold on her and sighed against the top of her head. "Lily, I promise it will be okay. I am no expert on love, but I know I love you."

Lily's heart pounded so hard against her chest that she was sure that Greg could feel it against his chest. She took a deep breath and blew it out slowly to calm her frazzled nerves.

"I love you too," she squeaked out as her throat closed and her chest tightened with apprehension.

Greg slid his arms to her shoulders and drew her back so that he could look down into her eyes. The seduction in their hazel depths had Lily's anxiety draining away, to be replaced with something else that lit her nerves on fire in a good way.

Wanton desire coursed through her veins as Greg leaned down and kissed her softly. This time she embraced it, soaking in the intense sensations that flowed through her. She rode the pleasure of his kiss as he backed her up until the backs of her knees hit the bed.

He pushed her gently down to sitting and then leaned her back further until she was lying on the bed with her legs hanging over the side, and he never broke the passionate kiss that had her panting with need.

Her walls pulsed with the desire to have him inside her, and the delicious pressure began to build in her groin. She moaned softly as Greg covered her body with his, propping himself on one arm as he used the other arm to run down her side and grasp her hip.

He continued the kiss until Lily thought the pressure would spill over just from the touch of their lips and the feel of his body pressed against hers.

Suddenly, he broke the kiss. He pulled Lily up to a sitting position and, in a voice broken with longing and need, said gruffly, "Take off your clothes and lie back on the bed."

Greg got up from the bed to close and lock the bedroom door, then came back to stand by the bed as he took off his clothes. Lily climbed onto the bed naked and exposed to Greg's rakish eyes. With a seductive growl, he looked her up and down, climbed on top of her, and began lavishing her with his touch, tongue, and mouth.

He explored every inch of her body, including the sensitive area where her walls pulsed and shot electric sensations through her as Greg's tongue and lips made love to her sex.

With every touch, lick, suck, and kiss, Lily moaned in ecstasy as he brought her almost to the edge before stopping his torturous assault on her sex and climbing back up to cover her body with his once more.

He positioned himself between her legs, holding his upper body off of her with his arms. The head of his massive erection touched her tight opening, and she gasped at the sensation that it shot through her core.

"Do you still want pain with your pleasure?" he asked in a husky whisper as he held himself poised against her opening.

Lily swallowed hard as she nodded her head.

Greg's seductive smile grew as he gazed deeply into her eyes, and his eyes began to glow. Then, he pushed himself inside her slowly, stretching and filling her up with every exquisite inch that went inside her.

She cried out in delightful pain as his head pierced the newness of the astral body, breaking through the virginal barrier. That pain only lasted a second before he pushed himself into her more deeply, and then she felt different pain.

Tiny sparks of electricity pulsed into her vaginal walls from Greg's deeply buried member, shooting into every nerve ending in her body and freezing her muscles.

The sensation was painful and exquisite and just what Lily needed. Her world exploded with lustful pleasure as the electricity coursed through her body, with every inch of his shaft delving into her core. He pushed himself into her depths ever so slowly as he pulsed his electric pleasure into her, and the pressure inside her almost spilled over when he came to the end of her.

He froze inside her and carefully leaned his upper body down to her, propping himself with his elbows on either side of her head to keep her from taking all his weight. He kissed her passionately with all of him buried inside her, and then he stopped pulsing his electricity through her.

Her muscles quivered with the release of the electricity and pain, and her walls pulsed with the need to release that tide of pleasure into her body. Without breaking the kiss, he pulled himself out of her as slowly as he had entered her. He stopped just before he was completely out, then began to slowly enter her and pulse his power into her again.

This time when he was buried all of the way inside her, he rotated his hips and ground into her, brushing his body against that sensitive spot as his sparks danced along her nerve endings.

Her muscles clenched with the release of electricity this time, and she cried out in pain and pleasure against his lips as he rocked his hips and ground against her sensitive bud. Through it all, he never broke the kiss. The pressure built even higher as he pulled out and repeated the process one more time, and then he broke the kiss.

"Have you had enough pain?" Greg asked in a rasping, breathless tone.

Lily could not answer as she lay quivering with the release of his electricity and the swirling sensations of blissful pleasure that curled through her body.

"If you cannot speak, then you have had enough," he said with a seductive chuckle. "Now, we can make love."

He pushed into her again, but this time there was no electricity. This time, it was only him and the sensation of his slow, steady rhythm out and in, grind, and then out and in again. She cried out in pleasure as the pressure in her groin grew with every dance of his body in hers, and her hips began to match his movements in a slow, delicious dance of torturous, sensual sensations.

Just as the pressure began to spill over, Greg's lips crashed into hers in a heated kiss that had them both crying out against each other's mouths with the pleasure of their lovemaking.

The powerful crescendo of her orgasm crashing through her had her digging her nails into his back and raking them down his body, which sent him over the edge with her. He broke the kiss to throw his head back and cry out as her nails ran down his back.

Their combined cries of passionate pleasure rang through the room as their powerful climax ran through them with every pulse of her vaginal walls against his throbbing member, leaving them weak and trembling as the long orgasm ended.

He pulled out of her gently, then collapsed to the bed beside her and pulled her into his arms.

When Greg's breathing had calmed to a tolerable level, he drew her to him even tighter with a chuckle as he said, "That was not so bad now, was it?"

Lily laughed aloud breathlessly as she replied, "No, it was wonderful. I will never look at electricity the same again."

Greg laughed aloud and said, "That was only small flicks of my power. Real electricity would only hurt."

"Whatever it was, I loved it," Lily sighed happily.

She closed her eyes with a contentment that she had never felt before, and then she felt something else invade her pleasurable thoughts.

There was a pull in the pit of her stomach that made it roil with momentary nausea. Her eyes flew open, and she hissed in a breath as she realized what was happening. She had run out of energy. The connection with the physical body snapped back into place, and she began to be pulled to it like a fish on a line.

Greg lifted his head warily to look at her. "What's wrong, love?"

"I am fading," she whispered to him. "I have used up all of this body's energy. I must return to the physical body to recharge."

A look of hurt flitted through Greg's eyes, but it faded away with his understanding smile.

His voice was humorous as he said, "I wore you out that much?"

Lily laughed as she answered, "Yes, you did. Without you feeding me power, I probably would not have lasted as long as I did."

"So, the little pulses I gave you was a good thing?" he asked humorously.

"It was the best thing." She felt herself fading and smiled sadly as she whispered, "I will see you soon, babe."

She saw Greg's visage fall as she reached out to touch the side of his face, and her hand went right through him.

Greg's sad smile matched her own as he watched her flicker and fade away.

"See you soon, love," he whispered to the empty air.

I got up from the table and headed out the kitchen's back door. I could feel Blake at my back as he followed me, and I smiled. We had an hour, and I intended to make the most of it now that we were both completely healed.

I knew Lily had gone to our room, and Greg was planning on following her in there after speaking with his father, so I opted for an alternate setting.

No, I was not going to sit on that damn log.

I was going out into the field on the other side of the tiny forest, where the tall grass flowed gently on a warm, soft breeze. It looked lovely and smelled sweet, and I thought it would be wildly romantic to make love out there, hidden by the grass and warmed by the sun. I smiled at the thought as I continued to walk, and Blake came to my side and took my hand.

"Where are we going?" he asked curiously.

I looked into his eyes with a heated look that had him raising his eyebrows questioningly. A slow, sensual smile spread across his face at my answer.

"I am going to take you out into this field and ravish you," I said huskily.

"That is the best idea I think you have ever had," he said.

He pulled at my hand and pulled me to his side, wrapping his arm around my shoulders as we passed the tiny forested area where the log sat. I glanced sideways at it and tried to ignore the sick feelings it brought into my stomach.

Suddenly, I felt a confused helplessness enter my mind through the connection I still carried to the astral body. Frowning, I stopped walking and pulled myself away from Blake's hold.

"Give me a minute," I said to him. "I think something is wrong with Lily." Blake stepped back, giving me an understanding, knowing look, and I closed my eyes in concentration.

Lily was scared. What was she scared of? I pulled on the thoughts lingering in the astral body's brain, and the revelation of what was causing Lily's fears made me smile softly.

"Why the hell am I crying?" Lily's voice asked herself in my mind.

I answered, *"Because you are afraid. You are afraid of being loved."*

I felt her indignation, but I also felt her acceptance of my answer, which made her angry.

"Get out of my head," Lily snapped furiously, but I did not take offense. I knew that she was angry at herself and not me.

I gave her what she wanted.

Concentrating on the bond in the back of my mind where the astral body's resting place lay empty, I imagined a shiny thread that bound my mind to that body. I pictured a pair of scissors cutting the cord in half. It snapped away, and just like that, the connection was broken between me and the astral body.

I was glad that I had gleaned that knowledge from Henry's mind. It gave us both some privacy with the men we loved. I opened my eyes to see Blake watching me with interest, and I smiled at him.

"You look beautiful when you are concentrating," he whispered as he came close to me. "Your eyes look like sapphires when they glow."

I looked at our surroundings and realized I had stopped at the edge of the field on the other side of the mini forest. I locked gazes with Blake and gave him a steamily sultry look, turned away from him, and fled into the field's tall grass. I heard his gasp of surprise and then his whoop of joy as he chased me into the tall grass, and I laughed in delight as the thrill of knowing he was chasing me ran through my body.

I heard him getting closer as I ran, and I purposefully slowed and let him catch me, grabbing me around my waist and pulling me to the ground in his arms. We were laughing and breathless as we rolled around in the grass, and we ended with me on top of him, straddling his body.

"Gotcha," I said victoriously as I smiled down at him.

His look burned with seduction, making my groin pulse with desire. His voice sent delicious little sparks of ecstasy shooting through me as he spoke.

"You can take me anytime you want, babe."

My heart lurched with need so intense that I had to take in a few quick breaths to keep from climaxing right where I sat.

Then I thought about where I sat.

The position had possibilities if only our clothes were not in the way. My smile faded to be replaced with a lustful grin as I pulled my shirt off and took off my bra. The heat in Blake's eyes as he watched me take off my clothes sent tremors through me, and when his hands came up to cup my breasts, the electric sensation of his touch had me throwing my head back with a gasp of pleasure.

Blake raised his upper body from the ground, sitting up with his legs straight out and me still straddling his lap. He wrapped his arms around me and pulled me to him, capturing my mouth with his and kissing me deeply and passionately.

His hands ran up and down my back, eliciting happy little sighs from me at the feel of his hands on my naked skin. He broke the kiss momentarily to take off his shirt, and when he pulled me back to him once more, the sensation of our naked upper bodies pressed together had me panting with a need so intense that I wanted to scream in frustration.

We still had the barrier of our pants in the way, and I wished my magic could make clothing disappear. I reached down between our bodies as the kiss became urgent, scooting my hips back so I could reach Blake's button and zipper. Frantically, I wrestled with the fastening of his jeans with a growl of frustration against our still-joined lips. Blake broke the kiss with a growl of his own. He placed his hands on my hips and set me off him so he could stand up and take off his jeans.

He spread our shirts and his jeans on the ground and sat down on them. I had already taken my pants off while he had been busy arranging the clothes on the ground, and when he sat back down, he pulled me down with him. I was on my knees above him. With his gaze locked on mine, he grasped my hips and positioned me on top of his massive hardness. He slowly guided me down onto him as he pressed his hips up to meet mine.

I went down on him slowly, relishing the feel of him filling me up and stretching me. I gasped as he hit the end of me when our bodies finally melded together, and he was fully inside of me. He ran his hands up my body and cupped my breasts, pinching and rolling my nipples with his fingers as I cried out over him. I began rocking my hips back and forth with him buried inside me, and the sensation was exquisite.

I placed my hands on his muscular chest for support so I could raise my hips up and come up from him a bit. I did not let his shaft come out of me but instead began to lower myself slowly onto him until our bodies were melded together once more.

I rocked forward once and then came back up again.

Blake's eyes were shuttered with pleasure as I found my rhythm and began to ride him slowly. The sensation of being in control of my own pleasure was powerfully seductive as I rode him and stared down into his deep brown eyes.

He continued to play and stroke my breasts and nipples as I rode his massive hardness, building my pleasure deep inside with the tip of his shaft hitting me over and over with my strokes and his body brushing against my sensitive bud with every grind.

Moans of pleasure left his slightly parted lips as I began to pump my hips faster. He began to rock his hips upward to match my rhythm, and his hands fell from my breasts to grasp my hips in both of his large hands. He held on as I rode him, and I could feel his shaft pulsing inside me as he came close to the edge.

His breath shuddered in a deep moan as my walls began pulsing around his member, and my nails dug into his skin as the pressure came over the edge and spilled into me with an intensity that had me throwing my head back and screaming my pleasure into the sky.

Blake grasped my hips tighter and pulled me to him in a desperate motion, marrying our bodies together firmly, and I felt his warm liquid pour into me as my walls pulsed around him and his cries mingled in the air with my screams.

I sat there for a moment, our bodies wedded tightly together, as delicious aftershocks flowed through me, and then I collapsed on top of him, breathless and spent. I pushed up and gently pulled him out of me and then rolled off him and into his waiting arm, laying my head on his shoulder with a contented sigh.

We lay there for a long moment relearning how to breathe, staring up at the beautiful cloud-filled sky in silence. As I lay there, I felt the astral body reconnect with my mind, pulling sharply and dragging it back into its resting place. I smiled as I felt it settle in for a long, recharging rest.

"Did you have a good time?" I asked Lily as I felt her presence return to me with the body.

"I had just as good of a time as I imagine you did," she replied sarcastically.

I laughed silently as I rested in Blake's arms and wished we did not have hell's army coming after us.

If we could only stay this way forever, life would be perfect.

Then again, when had my life ever been perfect?

CHAPTER 40: Preparations

Everyone was back at the table in the same seats they had been in before, as if they had been assigned. The only seat that remained empty was Lily's. I had assumed that Henry would have filled that spot since he had decided to join us, but he was not there.

I guess he had decided to stay down in his basement.

I gave Greg a knowing look as I sat down and noticed the sadness at the corners of his eyes. I frowned a question at him, but he only shook his head and looked away from me.

When he looked back my way, I gave him a comforting smile and mouthed, 'she will be back' at him. He returned my smile with a slight nod, but the sadness remained in his hazel eyes.

I was distracted by Waller standing from his seat, looking at all of us expectantly. He met each of our eyes in turn, and his sharp, stony gaze finally rested on mine.

"Did anyone think of anything?" he asked.

I gulped guiltily and averted my eyes, feeling the heated blush that crept into my cheeks. Blake stood, pulling Waller's attention from me, and I did not think I could love Blake more at that moment.

"I…um…we….er, that is Lucy, and I think someone should go back to Pikesburg and recruit Joseph's family. Bonnie said they may be willing. Also, whoever goes can stop and recruit on the way if you would be willing to share the location of some of your protected mutants."

Blake sat back down, and I leaned into him as Waller turned away in thought.

"I could kiss you right now," I whispered.

Blake chuckled and whispered, "I will hold you to that and more later."

My blush returned at his statement, but everyone was paying attention to Waller.

"Tyrone, do you think you could round up the troops?" Waller asked. "I have a few places you could stop at along the way. I have many that may be willing to help."

Tyrone stood and gave Waller a wide smile. "If they are willing to help for the same reason as I am, you must have saved many babies."

Waller waved his hand in the air dismissively. "It was not just the babies. There are others to whom I gave new identities and lives to avoid taking them back there. Scientists, doctors, escapees, the list goes on."

Waller's eyes flashed with a momentary look of sorrow as he added, "Unfortunately, I had to take some of them back, else WAMB would have gotten suspicious that I 'lost' them all."

"That must have been horrible for you," Megan said softly as she reached out and grasped his hand.

He squeezed her hand and smiled down at her. "You had it hard as well, my dear. We both did."

They stared at each other lovingly for a long moment as the rest of us at the table shifted uncomfortably in our seats. Finally, Waller turned his attention to those at the table.

"So, what do you think, Tyrone? Are you up for a little road trip?" Waller asked.

Tyrone nodded and was about to speak when a flurry of orange-red hair, freckles, running legs, and flailing arms came hurrying into the dining room.

"It's too late; they're coming!" Henry exclaimed as he ran into the room.

Everyone shot up from the table in alarm and began speaking at once. A chorus of voices shouted…

"What do you mean they are coming?"

"How? They had no time to get here."

And…

"What are we going to do?"

The voices blended together and rang out through the large room as I stayed in my seat and breathed in calmly and deeply. I stood calmly, trying to keep hold of my quivering nerves, and shouted, "Everyone, calm down!"

Silence filled the room. Everyone was looking at me, but I did not care. I ignored everyone else and caught Henry's gaze, motioning him over to me with a gesture.

"Lucy, we have to leave," he said as he walked around the table to me. "Hiram says they are almost here."

"I thought you said they were going to wait a couple of days," I said urgently.

"They were, but the commander ordered them to go sooner," he responded.

"You also said that you were not going to leave without your brother," I said firmly.

Henry's face dropped as he shot back, "Well, I won't be any good to him dead now, will I?"

"He told you they are on their way?"

Henry nodded but did not respond, so I asked, "So, you are in contact with Hiram right now?

He silently nodded once more.

Taking a deep, calming breath, I said, "that is good. Let's not panic, alright? Ask him how many are with him."

Henry glanced at me questioningly, but he did as I said. He closed his eyes, concentrated for a moment, then opened his eyes.

"He said there are around fifty," Henry said with a frown. "I thought they were bringing the entire army."

I shrugged. "Maybe their army has shrunk since Waller left. He was rather respected."

Henry's frown deepened as he responded, "Yeah, maybe. I don't know; something just doesn't seem right. Hiram sounds…I don't know…funny."

"How far away are they?" I asked.

"They will be here in about three hours," Henry said. "They left late in the night and traveled all the way through. They are not even going to stop before they come here."

"Well, that is just stupid," I said. "They will be tired and not in any shape to fight."

"Maybe that's why Hiram sounds funny," Henry said. "Maybe he is tired. That cannot be good. He needs to recharge soon, or I will lose him, and I may not be able to get him back."

I shivered, thinking how I would feel if it were Lily imprisoned in some glass cylinder thingy, and I could not bring her back to me. We had to come up with a plan. We had to save Henry's brother. I glanced up to tell Waller this, only to find everyone staring at Henry and me. I quirked an eyebrow questioningly.

"What?" I said, shrugging.

Henry leaned into me and whispered, "They don't know about me yet. I did not tell anyone except you and Waller."

"Oh," I said in understanding, and then louder for everyone in the room, I added, "Henry is like me. His brother is with WAMB as their prisoner, contained in some kind of cylindrical gadget, and Henry is communicating with him. His brother, Hiram, is riding the astral body."

That was the best way I could sum it up, and I just hoped everyone understood. The cacophony of voices started up again, but this time it was excited whispers about Henry. However, No one seemed to be asking any questions, so I did not explain further. I simply stood beside Henry and contemplated our next move.

There were only a little over fifty, he had said. If we split the numbers and combine our powers, we may be able to overtake all of their minds. I ignored everyone else and turned to Henry. I told Henry of my theory of him taking half the army and me taking the other half, and I thought his eyes would pop out of his skull.

"You can take that many minds at a time?" he asked astoundedly.

"I believe the most Lily has taken was twenty, but we may be able to take on more if we merge. We have been practicing that."

"What do you mean merge?" Henry asked, and it stunned me for a moment.

I thought back to the information I had gained from Henry during our merging, and then I realized that he and his brother had always done things separately. I had not paid attention to that information until now.

How could Henry be so much more experienced in all of this than I and yet know less? It was true that I had learned much from him about our other form, the astral body, but had he paid attention to the information he had gotten from me?

The melding was supposed to have gone both ways.

"Henry, did you pay attention to what you got from my head when we connected?" I asked.

He bowed his head shamefully as if I were his parent and had just reprimanded him. "No, I just kind of stored it away for later."

"I suggest you look at it now," I said sternly.

I did not want to be too hard on the kid, but he needed to understand this and understand it quickly. He closed his eyes tightly, and I could see his eyelids flutter as he concentrated. I knew by the fluttering that he was searching through his mind, honing in on the needed information. I knew this because it is how I processed the vast amounts of data in my own head.

After a few moments, Henry's eyes flew open wide, and he gasped. "I never thought to merge with him. I always considered him separate from me."

I frowned, trying to decide how best to explain. "He is separate, but he is also a part of you, part of your mind, and can be connected with you if you let him."

"He is connected to me," Henry said, his brows furrowing in confusion. "We have a connection in that spot where the astral body rests. That is how we communicate."

I sighed in frustration and tried again. "Yes, but this connection is deeper than that. It is soul level. You two would share the body, as in both being in the front instead of one hanging in the back out of the action or hovering around in an astral body. I am not sure because Lily and I have not tried it yet, but I am confident we could combine our powers and make them doubly stronger this way."

"That could come in handy right now," he said.

I smiled and nodded. "Yes! Now you get it."

"Well, we must break him out of that cage first. There is magic dampening built into his prison, so we would not be able to merge while he is still in there."

It was my turn to frown. "How is he even able to stay in contact with you?"

Henry chuckled and shook his head at me as if I were a small, unknowing child. I started to get angry but then realized that, in a way, I was unknowing, though I was definitely not a child.

"The connection is not part of our magic. The connection exists because we were born that way, two beings in one body. Our ability is over minds."

I frowned even more as I said, "I don't understand."

Henry huffed impatiently and ran his hand through his fiery tresses, and then his eyes brightened in revelation. "Think of it this way. Think back to when you have used your ability in the past. You always feel the energy building inside you when you use your magic. Now, think of the times when you communicate or connect with Lily inside of your mind. There is no building of energy, right?

That is because the ability to communicate is innate. It is a natural ability, so you do not need to build energy to wield it. Therefore, it cannot count as magic."

Understanding dawned inside of me. Henry was right! I had always felt the tingling in my fingertips and up my arms when I had used my ability; hell, I felt it even when Lily was wielding the magic.

Communication with her was different. There was no building of power or anything. It just came naturally to me. Then I thought about when she left the body and rode the astral body and when I had done that. There was always dizziness accompanying the transition, as if a bit of energy was zapped from me. So, riding the astral body, entering and leaving the physical body, had to be a form of magic.

Hiram could not re-enter Henry's body because the magic-dampening prison prevented it. If Hiram could not re-enter the physical body, then he would not be able to truly merge with Henry.

Henry must have seen the understanding dawning in my eyes. Smiling proudly, he said, "You get it now, don't you?"

I smiled and nodded, but my smile quickly faded. "So, we must figure out how to get Hiram out of that prison first."

"Yes, and then we only have the slight hope that Hiram and I will be able to figure out this merging technique fast enough to take our half of the army if he even has enough energy left," he said sullenly.

"What you need is a distraction," Blake said beside me.

I startled. I had forgotten about everyone else in the room while I had been in conversation with Henry, and I certainly had not noticed that everyone had stopped talking and was paying attention to us.

I turned to look at Blake, and his dark brown eyes looked more serious than I had ever seen before. It sent chills up my spine, and fear squeezed my heart in my chest. Blake had always been brooding and angry, although he had been happier since we had been officially together, but I had never seen him look this serious. It scared me.

Swallowing the baseball-sized lump that had formed in the back of my throat, I asked, "How do you propose we create a distraction?"

"We were all on defense the last time," Greg said from across the table where he stood next to his father. "We were surprised and had no chance to act or react, for that matter. This time, we will not be surprised. We can start offensively instead."

"What did you have in mind, son?" Waller asked.

"We all have our own abilities, but some of us could not use them because we were gunned down immediately. If we are shielded from the bullets, we can use our abilities to fight. While the soldiers are trying to find a way to stop us, kill us, or do whatever they plan to do to us…," Greg paused and took a deep breath. His eyes were tortured as he looked at me and added, "Lily can use her astral body to sneak in invisibly and free Hiram from the cage."

I knew what the tortured look meant. He hated putting Lily in harm's way. It was endearing that he had enough confidence in Lily to do the job and take care of herself, though.

I smiled encouragingly at him and said, "It is a good plan."

"Who is watching the cameras?" Waller asked suddenly, glancing around the table at all of us.

My heart leaped into my throat. This was exactly how we had been taken by surprise the last time. I turned wide, frightened eyes toward the window, expecting to see the black SUVs barreling up the gravel driveway to the house, but nothing was there.

"Take it easy," Henry said, touching my arm lightly in comfort. "They still have time before they get here."

"Well, then I suggest we all coordinate our attacks and get prepared, and for shit's sake, someone has to man the cameras!" Waller exclaimed.

He began barking orders, turning to each person in turn as he gave everyone their assignments.

"Blake, you and Greg are in charge of planning the attack. Use every resource we have, including everyone's abilities.

Megan, take Darius and the two nurses down to the basement and turn it into the infirmary. That is the safest place.

Henry, you and Lucy will watch the cameras, and while you watch, practice with Lily on this merging thing and show Henry how to do it so that he won't be scrambling to do it while we are in the middle of battle.

Alright, you all have your assignments, so go now!"

Everyone scrambled to do as they were told. Blake grabbed me and gave me a heated kiss before jogging after Greg. Greg would not meet my eyes as he turned and headed for the front door, but I saw the sadness before he turned away.

I sighed and shook my head.

Maybe someday, after she had gotten in some practice, Lily could ride the body longer and spend some time with Greg. Until then, he would have to deal.

I turned and followed Henry down the hallway to the master bedroom, where Waller had set up the surveillance cameras. He held the door open and allowed me to enter before coming in behind me and shutting the door.

The monitors for the cameras sat on a large desk in the corner of the room. I walked over to the desk and sat in the plush, vinyl desk chair in front of the four monitors. I looked at the pictures on the screens and wanted a hole to open up and swallow me.

One of the cameras was positioned in the small wooded area at the back of the property, and you could see the edge of the log in the picture. Had someone been watching when Greg and Lily had…oh God…had someone seen them? Seen me since she had been riding my body at the time?

I looked closely at the screen, trying to determine if someone had even been able to see anything. The camera was focused more on the field behind the wooded area than anything, and only the edge of the log was visible. Greg and Lily had been in the middle of the log, hadn't they? I had no way of knowing, and I sure was not going to ask. I just hoped that no one had seen anything.

"Is something wrong?" Henry asked, coming up beside me.

I guiltily jerked my gaze away from that particular screen as I shook my head. "No, nothing. Everything seems fine."

"Is Lily ready to wake up yet?" he asked, and I was glad that he did not push me to say anything else.

I was sure he had seen my face flaming with embarrassment as I stared at the screen, but he was too polite to say anything. It endeared me to the kid, and I decided I liked him very much.

"She might be, but I want to conserve her energy. It would not end well if we use up our energy before they get here."

Henry shrugged, "Yeah, but it doesn't take that much energy to ride the astral body invisible. She could practice that while we wait."

"I think she has that part down. It is the merging part that I am worried about, and that does take energy," I said.

"I would not know about that since I just learned it from you." He looked chagrined, so I touched his arm gently. He looked at me with a sad smile.

"Don't be so hard on yourself. You had no one to talk to about it. Until I met you, I didn't either, and look how inexperienced I am compared to you."

The sadness left his smile as he said, "Yeah, and you are much older than me too."

I rolled my eyes and gave him an indignant look. "I am not that much older than you."

"Oh, come on. You are ancient," he said, but he was smiling humorously when he said it.

I gave him a playful punch on the shoulder and said, "Shut up you."

His smile disappeared. "Seriously, though, we really should practice. I cannot practice, but maybe I can ride your brain while you do so I can see how it is done."

"Alright. Let me see if Lily will wake up, and then we can try."

"Do not bother trying to wake me," Lily's voice called out from the back of my mind. *"I am already awake."*

"How long have you been listening?" I asked, trying to decipher how much she had heard and how much I would need to show her.

"Long enough, and you don't have to show me. I can search it out when I need to," she replied.

"Do you have any idea how to do this?" I asked.

"Maybe, but you have to trust me."

My stomach did a nervous roil. I had lost trust in Lily long ago when she had tried to force Blake and me to have sex before we were together. However, she had since been building that trust back. She had done much to show me that she had changed and cared for me. Because of that, I was learning to trust her more and more.

But did I fully trust her yet?

If I was honest, the answer would be no, but we had no choice right now. I would have to trust her if we wanted to help Henry save his brother and survive.

"You do not have to answer. I can read your thoughts. I am not offended, sister; you are right. I still have a lot of work to do to earn back your trust, but maybe this could help."

I took a deep, calming breath and said, *"Alright, Lily. How do we do this?"*

"Just close your eyes and concentrate on the sensation. Feel me come to you and accept my presence. Imagine that you are a sponge, and you will absorb my essence."

I nodded as she spoke to me in my head. I reached out my hand to Henry, and he took it. Instantly, I could feel him enter my mind into that dreamscape where we had merged before, but I did not follow.

Instead, I closed my eyes and concentrated on Lily, on that spot in the back of my mind where she lived. I could feel Henry in the middle, watching with interest as Lily came closer to the front where I waited.

I felt her approach cautiously, but I opened myself to her trustingly, and I felt her happiness at my acceptance. She filled me, coming to the front with me as if she were going to take control of the body. Instead, she hovered just on the edge of taking control, and her voice was so loud in my head that it made me jump.

"Now, Lucy. Take me in now. Merge us."

Concentrating harder than ever, I imagined I was a sponge and Lily was water. I let all of the air out of my lungs, and as I breathed deeply in, I soaked her up into me.

The sensation was stranger than anything I had ever felt. It was as if she was water, flowing through me, over me, on me, touching me everywhere she could possibly touch. I imagined her cold wateriness soaking my skin, my hair, entering my orifices, and filling me completely. My physical body shuddered all over at the sensation, and when the merge was complete, 'I' became 'we'.

We were one being, one mind, one soul. We were merged more completely than ever before, and when we began to call our power, the tingling sensation became more of a powerful burning that filled us and swirled within us. We could feel the intensity of this power, and we knew beyond a shadow of a doubt that we could take the entire army by ourselves if we could gather enough energy.

We felt a lurch of surprised horror within us and remembered Henry still riding our mind. He was astonished at our tremendous power and was wondering how we had not known before just how outrageously powerful we were. He pulled himself from our mind, snapping himself back into reality, and stood beside us at the desk and monitors again.

"This is the first time we have ever done this," we said aloud, and we marveled at how wondrous our combined voice sounded. It was musical, beautiful, and flowed like a song through the room. "We would have done this much sooner had we known how strong we could be."

Henry gaped at us as if we had grown two heads. We turned our gaze to the big mirror on the dresser in the bedroom, and our gasp was louder than Henry's.

Our eyes glowed with a bright blue light. Our blond streaked black hair swayed in an invisible wind. We looked almost ethereal and felt great! We felt as if we could take on the world!

Suddenly, a feeling of nausea flowed through us, and part of us began to slip away and flow into the back of our mind. The merge started to break apart as if flakes of the sponge I had imagined myself to be were flaking away.

Lily slid back into her resting spot, and I could tell that the merge had zapped much of her energy in just the few minutes we had joined.

"Sorry, sis. We will have to practice that more before we can hold it for long," she said regrettably.

Dammit! We had done it, but it had slipped away.

Sighing, I answered Lily in a resigned tone. *"Don't beat yourself up about it. We cannot expect to be perfect right away. Maybe we can hold it longer if you rest until they get here. We only need enough time to convince them to join us and leave WAMB."*

"After I have freed Hiram, you mean," she said.

"Yes, after that. Just rest for now. We will do what we can when the time comes."

I felt Lily slip away into her resting spot, and I turned my attention back to the outside of my body. Henry was still gaping at me as if I were some kind of circus attraction.

"What?" I asked, quirking an eyebrow at him.

"You used up all your energy at once," he answered. "Why did you do that?"

"I did not mean to. Lily and I were merged, and we called energy to us to see how strong we could be together, but we did not mean to use up our energy," I said irritably.

"I am willing to bet that that is why the merge did not last long," he said, seemingly unaffected by my petulance. "You pulled so much magic in that it zapped you. You should have been careful how much you pulled."

"How am I supposed to control that?" I asked.

"Concentrate on the tingling. Do not let it grow to a burn; that is when you know you are pulling too much," he said.

"Yeah, it did burn," I said, and the crankiness was gone. "It burned right away, though."

"You pulled too hard," he said. "Do not pull that hard. Just pull lightly."

I huffed in frustration. "Alright. Next time, I…we…will try to pull lightly."

I turned my attention to the monitors, resting my chin in my hand. I glanced at each of the four screens, glancing over the one with the log rapidly with a cringe. Something caught my attention, a flick of one of the screens out of the corner of my eye.

I turned my eyes to the screen to see what had caught my attention, and my heart began to pound furiously in my chest. I turned to Henry with wide eyes as my hands began to tremble, and my breathing became quick and shallow.

He frowned and looked at the screen I had just turned from, and then his eyes went wide as he turned to me.

"Go," Henry said, pulling on my shoulder as if trying to pull me to my feet. "Go get someone, hurry!"

I stared back at the screen for another moment and then stood on wobbly legs. I had to pull myself together. I had to get Blake. I turned for the door and hurried across the room. I jogged down the hallway and into the great room, turning my head this way and that.

He was nowhere to be found in the living room, dining room, or kitchen. I wondered where he could be. I had to find him quickly. Then I remembered that he and Greg had been assigned to strategize with the others, so I ran to the front door and threw it open.

Sticking my head out the door, I called, "Blake, where are you!?"

Thankfully, I heard an answering cry, but it came from behind me inside the house.

"I'm down here. I am coming back up now," Waller's voice said from the open basement door.

I hurried to the basement door, fidgeting impatiently as I waited for him to climb the stairs. He was frowning, and his stormy eyes were worried as he glanced up the stairs at me. He reached the top of the stairs, and I did something I had not done since I was four years old. I threw myself into his arms, trembling and scared and feeling like I was that little girl again.

I was that little girl again.

I was suddenly thrown back into the past as I felt Waller's arms tighten around me, and memories long forgotten, and newly restored, came swirling back into my mind.

I was four years old again, and the big scary bad man with the bald head and the cool snake tattoo was my only safe haven when I was scared. He had been the one that had come to take me to the special school. He was the one that helped me exercise and become stronger. He was the one that comforted me when I realized that I had lost Lily.

He was the one that told me to come to him if anyone tried to hurt me, and so I did. Whenever I was scared, I ran to him because Lily was no longer there to come and save me. They had taken her away from me.

He was always there, standing in the training room with his stormy eyes that always looked at me with kindness. The other kids were scared of him, but I wasn't. He was the big, evil, scary man to everyone else but me.

He could not stop the tests and the doctors from giving me shots, but he could comfort me in his big, giant arms. I felt safe there.

I felt safe.

I shuddered at the memories that being in Waller's arms again had invoked. I had forgotten all those times when he had comforted me, but I remembered them now. He had never refused me in the past because that piece of his heart that I had not even known I had captured would not allow him to, and he did not refuse me now.

"Lucy?" His voice made me jump even though it was soft and comforting. I trembled more violently, even as he held me tightly.

"Lucy, what has happened?" Waller asked gently as he held onto me, swaying side to side with me just as he used to when I was small.

"Th…th…there is a car com…coming up the driveway."

"Lucy, why would a car coming up the driveway scare you so badly?" Waller asked. "It is too early for it to be the WAMB army, and even so, you were not that scared earlier when we were planning our attack."

I cuddled tighter into him as my heart raced and my breathing became shallow. "Not WAMB," I whispered hoarsely through the lump that had formed in my throat. "It…it…red sports car…Blake…oh, God, poor Blake."

"Lucy, calm down, sweetie. Remember, like we used to? Take a deep breath…now let it out slowly…now find a happy song…close your eyes and listen."

I did as he said almost methodically as I tried to calm my racing heart and trembling nerves. What would Blake think when he saw the little red car coming up the driveway? It would be here any second. Once a vehicle turned into the long, winding driveway, it only took three minutes to get to the house.

"We have to get Blake," I said urgently.

"Lucy, tell me who you think is in the car," Waller said calmly but firmly.

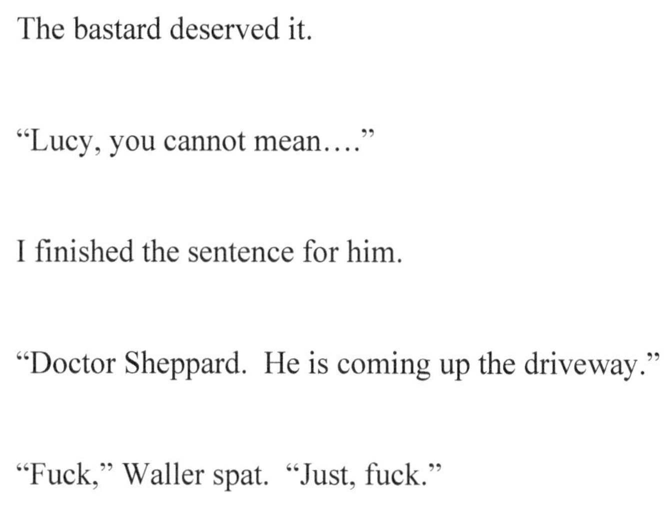

I swallowed hard and pulled away from Waller to look him in the face. I knew my face was tortured and twisted with fear as I tried to find my tongue. "I know that car, but the last time I saw it, it was through Lily's eyes, flipped up on its side on the side of the interstate."

Waller's eyes grew disbelieving as he began putting the scrambled pieces I had given him together. I could feel Lily coming, and I knew she would be royally pissed and ready to draw blood, which gave me a bit of satisfaction.

The bastard deserved it.

"Lucy, you cannot mean…."

I finished the sentence for him.

"Doctor Sheppard. He is coming up the driveway."

"Fuck," Waller spat. "Just, fuck."

PART NINE

SHOWDOWN

CHAPTER 41: Doctor Sheppard

"What in bloody hell…What is going on?" Blake came storming in the front door, making us recoil and flinch.

"I heard you call for me…," he said urgently, and then he froze. His dark eyes slanted worriedly as he saw me in Waller's embrace, crying as if my world had just ended.

"Lucy, are you alright?" he asked in a low voice.

"Blake," I whispered weakly, knowing I needed to tell him but not knowing how to say it.

"She has suffered a horrendous shock," Waller said in his deep, calm voice.

I began walking unsteadily toward Blake as he stepped further into the room. He reached out and steadied me, pulling me into his arms and holding me tight against him. I stifled a sob.

"What got you so upset, baby?" Blake softly asked as I cuddled into him.

Before I could answer, the sound of a car pulling into the gravel lot in front of the house rang through the still-open front door. Waller moved quicker than a man of his size should have been able to as he hurried to push past us and beat Blake out of the door. Blake started to turn, but I clung to his shirt and pulled him back to me.

"No," I said urgently. "Do not go out there, please."

Blake frowned down at me. "Who's out there?"

"It…it's…," I choked on a sob and could not say the words.

I did not have to, however.

"I was hoping you would be home." Doc's sarcastically sing-song voice came floating through the open door, and I felt Blake's body stiffen and heard his sharp intake of breath. I watched the emotions flick through his dark brown depths.

The pain of loss, confusion, the sting of betrayal, and finally, a burning fury that lit the color of his eyes to a deep, molten gold flowed through his visage as I watched.

"How the fuck are you still alive?" Waller asked as he stepped out onto the porch.

"Did you think you could have gotten rid of me that easily?" Doc asked menacingly.

"We were hoping," Waller answered nonchalantly as if unbothered by the dangerous fury in Doc's tone.

"You have a lot to learn," Doc responded.

Blake started to move, but I held firm to his shirt. Finally, he covered my hands with his and pried them from his shirt gently.

"Lucy, let me go," he said gently, but I could hear the livid undertones.

"Please, Blake, do not go out there," I begged, but I knew it would not help.

"I have to," he said as he looked resolutely into my eyes.

I sighed in defeat and let him go. He moved around me, and I turned to follow. I could not stop him from confronting his thought-to-be-dead father, but I could follow and watch to ensure that Doc did not hurt Blake more than he already had.

At least I could try.

Blake stepped into the doorway, but I could not see around him, which meant that Doc could not see me yet. I did not bother to peer around Blake. Instead, I stayed in his shadow and listened.

"Ah, Blake, my son. There you are. I have come to take you and Lucy home," Doc said, and his tone had changed to that friendly tone that Doc had always had before we had all discovered that he had gone rogue.

"I am no longer your son," Blake ground out furiously. "You are not my father. My father is dead to me."

"Come on, Blake. Do not be this way," Doc said in a mock pleading voice. "These people have messed with your mind. Come back with me, and we can fix you and Lucy."

"Go away and leave us alone, or I will kill you, and you will not come back from the dead this time." Blake's voice held a finality that made me shudder, but Doc did not seem affected by it.

He laughed humorously, but I could hear the pretense in his tone as he said, "Come now, Blake. It is impossible to come back from the dead. I was still alive when you left me. Even the car lived through the crash."

"I checked," Blake said tightly. "There was no heartbeat, and you were not breathing."

Doc's voice did change then. His tone was dark and ominous, sending shivers up and down my spine. However, his words had my heart freezing in my chest.

"I never said the body did not die. I said that I did not die."

I sucked in a breath and held it. The implications of what Doctor Sheppard was saying had me suspended as if time had ceased to exist and I was standing in a haze of nothingness.

The only way a body could die and let the inhabitant live was if…

No…

That was insane.

I had known this man practically my entire life. How could he have kept this hidden from me?

"He is a null," Lily's voice answered my thoughts. *"He can keep anything from anyone, even the strongest mental…or…."*

"Or, he can absorb the power," I finished for her. *"He can absorb the power of any mutant and use it."*

"Yes, and he had on the cuffs so no one would be the wiser, but…" she paused, urging me to think out the problem on my own.

"The cuffs do not work on nulls," I finished her again and wondered why I had not thought of it before.

Stepping around Blake, I came into view of Doctor Sheppard and stared into his evil, faded blue eyes.

"You absorbed my powers," I said matter-of-factly. "When Lily grabbed your arm back at the lab, you created a temporary twin inside your mind and allowed it to take over your body right before death.

When your body died, you were safely tucked away in the back of your brain. Then, after you were sure no one would see, you took back control which reanimated the body, and the twin faded away since it was only temporary."

Blake and Waller were staring at me in open-mouthed shock. Doc stared at me with deadly fury.

I ignored them as I listened to my sister's voice inside my mind. *"The question is, why did he let himself be captured in the first place?"*

"Why did you let yourself be captured in the first place?"

I asked Lily's question aloud as I stepped further onto the porch.

"You think I let you capture me?" Doc asked, and I scoffed at his mock surprise.

"You could have gotten away if you had wanted to. The cuffs do not work on nulls."

"You were always too smart for your own good," Doc said with a huff. "You never knew everything your abilities could do, much less what others could do. So how did you figure all of this out?"

"She had help," A voice said from the still-open doorway.

I turned to see Henry step out onto the porch and glare menacingly at Doc, and then he turned that anger toward me.

I raised an eyebrow at him, but before I could say anything, he spat his words at me in a furious tone. "I knew I should not have trusted you. I gave you all my knowledge and secrets, so you could give it all to him."

He gestured angrily toward Doc as I stared at him in confusion.

"Do you know this man?" I asked quietly.

Henry frowned in annoyance, but he lowered his voice as well as he answered, "of course I do, but I had no idea that Blake was his son or that you were his son's girlfriend."

Blake did not return Henry's glare. Instead, he narrowed his eyes toward Doc as he said through clenched teeth, "I did not know he was an evil asshole until recently. My father is dead, and this man is no longer my father."

Henry laughed sarcastically. "Do you expect me to believe that? I may be young, but I am not stupid."

"Henry, my boy," Doc said, unaware of our silent conversation on the porch. "I did not know you were here with these traitors."

Henry's head snapped toward Doc.

"Did you say they are traitors?" he asked in a louder tone.

"Yes, son, they are traitors. So what are you doing here with them?" Doc asked in a mock innocent tone. "I'll make you a deal. You get them to come back with us so I can fix them, and I will let Hiram out of the cage. What do you say?"

Henry did not answer Doc. Instead, He turned back to Blake in surprise. "You betrayed your father?"

Blake's glare had stayed locked on Doc during the entire conversation as if he feared that Doc would disappear if he looked away.

"As I said," Blake responded to Henry as he continued to stare at Doc. "I did not know my father was evil."

"How could you not know?" Henry asked in disbelief. "How could the creator and leader of WAMB not be evil?"

Blake did look away from his father then. His head whipped around suddenly and pierced Henry with a look of disbelief, despair, and shock.

"WHAT?!" Waller's cry of disbelief rang through the air that had suddenly turned silent and thick with tension. Henry backed away from him where Waller had stood silently watching the exchange.

Waller's gaze alternated between Henry and Doc as he strode toward the steps leading down into the yard and said, "Did that boy just call you the leader of WAMB?"

Lily lurched from my mind so suddenly that my head reeled with dizziness and confusion. I stumbled forward and almost fell, but Blake shot forward and caught me, even as he flinched away from the sudden appearance of Lily beside me. Henry let out a surprised squeal and jumped back as Lily whipped around and glared at Doc, much as Waller was doing. She said nothing and only stood glaring at Doc, who was laughing maniacally at the entire scene.

"Yes, I do believe he did," Doc answered. "I am surprised that none of you have figured it out before now."

"You cannot be the leader of WAMB," Waller said. "It makes absolutely no sense."

"It makes perfect sense," Lily said, and I shuddered at the sensation of the astral body snapping from my mind as she stepped out of range, causing the astral body to separate from the physical body.

I would never get used to that sensation.

Doc's wicked gaze snapped to Lily as she came to the edge of the porch and stood beside Waller. She turned sideways so we would be in her sights as she spoke.

"I could not figure it out before. I could not figure out how Doctor Waller had hidden all of us away for years, allowing us to grow up with fake families with WAMB none the wiser.

You all thought that you were hidden and safe from Waller because you did not use your abilities, and you thought you were safe from WAMB because Doctor Sheppard hid us.

Did no one find it suspicious? Did none of you so-called intelligent people ever wonder how WAMB could not find us even though they are this big corporation with government funding and brilliant scientists under its employ?"

"You did not think of it either," I shot back at her.

She fisted her hands on her hips. "I was asleep because of that damn medicine that your fake mother kept feeding us, remember?"

She was right. She had figured it out quickly, and my brain made the connection as soon as Lily's had. But Lily had bounded out of me so fast that my awareness had not caught up with my brain. Had I been able to keep my memories and Lily, she may have helped me figure it out sooner.

"Stop getting us distracted or release the connection and let me think on my own," Lily snapped, and I focused my thoughts on her once more.

"Sorry," I mumbled.

She waved away my apology as she continued, "anyway, when Lucy came of age and began to regain her memories, WAMB was coming to collect us, but then Waller tried to take us away. Waller, of course, had no idea that WAMB had been watching us all along and that we had never really escaped.

When Waller interfered and tried to take us, Doctor Sheppard used that to his advantage. He knew we would come to him for help, and then he could gain my trust and use me for his experiments. However, Waller refused to give up and kept trying to rescue me from Doc, which he finally did through his son."

"If I had known that you had that information against me before, I would have never let you or your family live," Doctor Sheppard spat. "I knew you had begun to suspect me of something, which is why I created the ruse of having my wife taken from me because I refused an order…."

Blake cut him off, his fury and sadness filling the air around us as if it were a living thing and Blake was its controller. His tone was filled with that living anger as he said, "You killed my mother to keep your cover?"

"She was beginning to suspect something as well," Doc spat. "I had to stop them all from finding out. I should have killed them all, especially that damn son of his."

He pointed at Waller, who took another menacing step forward, but Lily reached out and grabbed his arm, stopping his advance.

Lily laughed. "Yeah, that boy threw all your plans out the window when he zapped the chip and took away your ability to take me from Lucy as you took Hiram from Henry."

She paused and turned to Henry, who had stood silently listening.

"What do Hiram and I have to do with all of this?" He asked.

"Doc is not using Hiram to control you, Henry," she answered. "He is using Hiram the same way he wants to use me. He is using us because we are the parts of you and Lucy that makes you immortal."

Henry looked at her in disbelief, and so did I. I was not immortal. That could not be true…

Could it?

Lily put her hands on her hips and scoffed as she said, "Do you believe that we would die if we took over the body while it was passing? The only reason Doc here lost his twin was that it was not real. We are part of your souls, which means we live as long as your souls live. So if we take a death for you, your soul still lives, and after we have regained energy from taking a death, we will come back.

That is why he has been using Hiram. He wants to learn how to wrench us from our physical bodies and make our astral bodies permanent and subservient to him. After that, you and Lucy will be the parents of the first set of genetically controlled and created mutant twins, using Lucy's uterus to grow it and your sperm to create it. Then, he can continue the process until he has an army of the twins.

He will keep the physical-bodied breeding twins in stasis, like a herd of breeding cattle, and use the astral bodies as the actual army. Imagine how powerful an entire army of astral bodies can become invisible and take over minds would be, especially since they cannot die. And imagine how powerful the person that controlled that army would be."

She turned back to Doc with a triumphant smile and drawled out, "Isn't that right, dear Doctor Sheppard?"

Doc's eyes narrowed at Lily in a heated fury that scared me. "You think you know everything? Then tell me why would I send Henry here to kill you if I needed you and him alive, and why would I send my own agents to shoot us down on the highway?"

Lily turned back to Doc and scoffed. "Oh, please. That was just another one of your plots to make you seem innocent. It was easy for you to send out mental messages to your soldiers with my power running through you.

You risked your own son's life to have your WAMB agents save you by shooting your car off the road, knowing that if you did not make it, you had the temporary twin inside your head to take the fall for yourself."

I heard Blake's gulp as he swallowed hard, and I turned to look at him. The sadness I saw in his eyes almost brought me to my knees. I put my arms around his waist and squeezed tightly as if I could hug his pain away. I turned my attention back to Lily as she continued.

"You had no idea that Waller had already told us of your schemes until we confronted you about it, so when you found out we knew, you sent Henry and the agents here to kill us all, but you figured that I would save Lucy.

Henry would find us alive after the carnage, and you would order him to bring the poor girl to you so that you could heal her. It was a good plan, but you did not account for one thing."

"And what was that?" Doc rasped in a sinister tone.

"You did not account for the fact that I have changed, and I helped her friends instead of saving myself as I would have in the past," Lily said, turning her head to smile at me.

"Yes, you are right. I did not account for that fact, but it is a fact that I will not forget this time." Doc smiled maliciously, causing the hairs on the back of my neck to stand at attention.

Chills ran up my spine at the sounds of many vehicles coming up the gravel road toward the house.

"Fuck me," Waller said in a hoarse whisper. "The slimy son of a bitch set us up. He showed up here first and outed himself as a diversion, and now we have lost our element of surprise."

CHAPTER 42: The Rescue

Lily growled in anger, narrowing her eyes at Doc as she grabbed Waller's arm and backed them both up, joining Blake, Henry, and me next to the house's open door.

"How are we going to save Hiram now?" she whispered urgently.

I started to answer and opened my mouth to say that we would figure something out when the ground around us shook violently. It shook so hard that it almost knocked us off our feet, but we recovered and held onto the doorway and each other for support.

Doc leaned against his car, searching the area with wide eyes as a large crack began forming in the earth behind the back tires.

"What is going on?" Doc screamed, and I heard a touch of fear in his tone. "Who is doing this? Blake's affinity for the earth was never this strong!"

"Mine is," came a deep, booming voice from around the side of the house.

Tyrone stepped out with golden glowing eyes, holding his hands out toward the ground as the trembling became stronger and the crack opened longer and wider. Doc fell to the ground as his car slid into the large aperture, and we all heard the crash as it landed far, far down in the earth.

Apparently, it was deep too.

The crack continued to grow until it stretched across the ground, blocking anyone that came up the driveway from reaching the house. Unless someone had the ability to make a bridge appear out of thin air, the soldiers would not be able to get to us when they arrived.

The black WAMB SUVs speeding up the driveway did not expect a large hole in the ground, so the first two that came up side-by-side slammed on their brakes quickly. But, unfortunately, they were too late to stop.

I cringed as I heard the two cars crash deep down in the long pit, and I hoped that Henry's brother was not in one of them. But then again, how would they have fit a big cylindrical prison in the back of an SUV?

The answer came as the rest of the vehicles came to a screeching halt behind the crack. One of the vehicles was a truck with an open bed, and strapped into the bed of the truck was a large, glass cylinder with tubes coming out of it and lights strobing all around it.

I gasped when I saw it, and Henry tried to lurch himself forward and run out into the yard toward his brother, who stood inside the cylinder with his hands pressed to the glass, staring at us all with a helpless look of surrender.

Blake grabbed his arm and pulled him back, preventing him from stepping off the porch. Soldiers began to pile out of the vehicles with guns drawn as Doctor Sheppard pulled himself from the ground and began barking orders for them to start shooting.

Tyrone moved quickly to the porch and was almost to us when the first hail of gunfire came, sending us all to the ground in an attempt to take cover. Tyrone fell to the ground just below the porch steps with his hand still flung out toward the crack in the earth, and the ground began to tremble again.

It sent the soldiers scrambling to hold their footing, temporarily ceasing the gunfire long enough for us to pull ourselves to our feet and escape into the house with Tyrone close on our heels.

"My brother," Henry cried as we all scrambled into the house, and we had to pull him with us forcibly. "Please don't send more of them into the ground until we rescue my brother."

"I dare not use my abilities more than I have to with that null out there," Tyrone said. "I caught him off guard this time, but if I continue to use my ability, he could absorb it and use it against us."

"That null is Doctor Sheppard, the leader of WAMB, and he is coming toward the house now," Waller said as he stared out the window.

"Dad, take cover before they start shooting again," Greg said, startling us as the others came piling into the living room from the back door.

"Gene, please do not get shot again," Megan said, making Waller move away from the window.

Megan went to him at the same time that Lily ran over to Greg, and the men wrapped their ladies up in their arms.

"Do not stay in this form long, love, or you will run out of energy again. You have barely had time to rest from the last time," Greg whispered into Lily's hair.

She nodded as she stepped back, and Greg kissed the top of her head before releasing her. Then, she turned back to me, and I heard the collective gasps as she disappeared before everyone's eyes. I could still see her, smiling wickedly at the fact that she had shocked everyone. I smiled and shook my head at her.

"We will have to be careful with our abilities," Bonnie said as she entered the room behind Greg. "We do not want him absorbing them and using our own magic against us."

Waller locked the front door and moved toward the dining room, where we were all standing. "Agreed, but we need to find a way to get Henry's brother out of that glass cage," he said.

The pounding on the door made us all flinch violently. "Little pigs, little pigs let me in," came an evil whine from the other side of the door. "Or I'll huff and puff and kill your brother."

Henry tried to reach the door again, but Blake held him firmly.

"You would not kill him," I yelled out. "You need him for your research."

I heard Doc's maniacal laugh from the other side of the door before he said, "Do you think you and Henry are my only sets of twins?"

"Then why don't you just leave us alone and use them," Henry called out, still struggling against Blake's hold.

"Fine, have it your way," Doc called out. "I will order it done now."

"Nooo!" Henry called out, then doubled over as if in pain.

I knew that pain. It was how I felt when Lily had been ripped away from me the first time I had woken up to find the chip in my head and Lily gone.

"Henry, what's happening?" I asked urgently as I came to stand by him.

"I can feel it," he said in a strained whisper. "I can feel his energy being sapped away, like a piece of my soul is dying."

"It is," Lily said, piercing me with a knowing look, but I was the only one that could hear her.

"Everyone, to the basement!" Waller called out. "We need to regroup and come up with a plan."

"Darius and the nurses are down there now, setting up the infirmary as you asked them to," Megan said as she moved with Waller toward the basement door.

We had almost reached the basement door when the gunfire began again. We were close enough to get there this time without anyone getting shot. We clambered down the steps with Waller in the lead and Tyrone at our rear. When Tyrone came down the final step, he stopped in front of me with a determined look.

Dianna and Chris were in front of Tyrone, and Dianna stopped to count heads and ensure everyone was there.

Henry had crumpled to the floor at Blake's feet, and a cold sweat had broken out over his face. He moaned in pain as he curled into a fetal position on the floor.

"Come with me," Tyrone said urgently, grabbing my upper arm and moving toward the back of the basement. "I have a plan."

Blake, Waller, and Lily followed on our heels as Tyrone pulled me toward the end of the basement hallway where the bedrooms were. He pulled me into Henry's bedroom, releasing me so he could pull the bed from the wall and scoot it out of the way.

He whirled around to face us as he pointed at the wall and said, "There is a weak spot here in the wall. I can feel the earth digging into that spot from the outside. It was pushed into that spot by a tree root, and the spot is now weak enough for the earth to break the concrete."

"The house is old, so there are bound to be foundational and other problems with it. So what's your point?" Waller asked.

"My point is that the problem works to our advantage. The weak spot allows me access to the earth even through the synthetic material of the wall. I can call the earth to break through the wall and open a tunnel. We can travel underground to the truck, rescue Hiram, and get back here before Doc knows what happened. We only need a distraction so that no one sees us pass by the ravine I created."

"And we need to do all that before Hiram dies," I added. "We don't have much time."

"I can go," Greg said as he walked up the hallway. "I can zap the cage with just enough juice to short it out so that Hiram can simply snap back into Henry as Lily snaps back into Lucy."

Everyone looked at me. "Greg is right. When I need Lily to return quickly, I imagine snapping her back into my body like a rubber band. It hurts a bit, but it works."

"Fine," Tyrone said. "Let's get it done quickly, then. Greg, stay with me. Lucy, tell Henry what we are doing so he can prepare to snap Hiram back the moment he is free."

"I'm on it," I said and turned back down the hallway.

Lily whispered to me quickly, halting my steps before I could get too far. "Tell Greg I said to be careful, please."

I turned and said, "Lily says to be careful, Greg."

"I'll be fine," he shouted with a cocky smile. "Tell her to get her rest. She will need to be at full strength for me when this is all over."

I rolled my eyes at him as Tyrone's eyes began to glow. He pointed toward the wall, and then I turned and started back toward Henry. I heard Waller's booming tone as I walked away.

"Blake, take the others and see if you can get back upstairs somehow to create that distraction, but don't get shot," Waller said.

"We will figure it out," Blake said.

I heard Blake's footsteps coming toward me, but I kept my pace as I hurried to the fallen boy on the floor. I knelt beside him and gently touched his back as I spoke to him.

"Henry, listen to me. Tyrone and Greg are going to get Hiram out of that cage. As soon as you feel that he is free, you will have to snap him back to you. Can you do that?"

Henry lifted his tear and sweat-stained face to me and nodded weakly.

"I will stay right here with you. I won't leave you until I know Hiram is safe."

Henry nodded once more, and then his head slumped back to the ground as if Henry did not have the strength to keep it up. I sat down next to him and rubbed comforting circles around his back.

"I will go out with the others," Lily said as she stood over me. "I may be able to help."

"Just be careful and don't use up your energy," I told her.

She nodded and turned as Blake, Chris, Megan, and Dianna hurried toward the stairs leading back into the central part of the house. Blake's eyes met mine just before he started up the stairs.

He paused and mouthed 'I love you' at me before turning and following the others up the stairs. My heart lurched as a horrid feeling of apprehension flowed through me.

"I will keep him safe," Lily said as she followed him up the stairs, and I knew that she had probably gotten the backlash of the worry that had surged through me.

I turned my attention inward as I watched through Lily's eyes while I continued to rub Henry's back. I noticed the trembling in his body and prayed that Tyrone and Greg hurried.

*** TYRONE'S TUNNEL, GREG ***

Greg followed behind Tyrone as he fascinatingly watched the earth obey Tyrone's commands. The earth had opened up after tumbling free into the weak spot in the hallway wall. After that, it had formed into a perfectly round tunnel large enough for them to walk through without stooping over.

It was super dark, though, and Greg found it more difficult to see as they traversed through the ground. It was also silent, the only sounds coming from the rumbling of the earth as it turned and shaped itself around them.

Greg's vision was almost void when a bright light finally pierced the darkness in front of them. Greg could see around Tyrone's body suddenly, and what he saw had him pausing in his tracks.

They had arrived at the open crack Tyrone had made to prevent the soldiers from reaching the house. The two vehicles that had crashed into the pit and Doctor Sheppard's car became visible as the mouth of the tunnel formed.

Doc's red car had been smashed to oblivion under the weight of the two larger vehicles that had landed nose-down in the crevice, side-by-side. One soldier's body hung from one of the windshields, and blood had pooled on the ground below. The other SUV had completely lost its windshield, and five bodies were piled on the ground amid the broken glass.

"Be careful," Greg whispered up to Tyrone. "We cannot be sure that all of them are dead."

"You watch my back. I must concentrate on building the next tunnel," Tyrone whispered back.

"I got you," Greg said. "You did calculate the distance between the crevice and the truck, right?"

Tyrone looked back over his shoulder. "Of course I did. Just watch my back."

"I'm watching," Greg said as they crept toward the wreckage.

Nothing moved, and no sound came from either vehicle as they crept out of the cave and into the crevice. Instead, the sounds of screaming, gunfire, and chaos came from above their heads, and Greg smiled at the sound.

His friends and family were up there, creating havoc and doing a damn good job at it, judging from the sounds.

*** THE BASEMENT DOOR, BLAKE ***

"Stay back and wait for my signal," Megan whispered down from the top of the stairs.

Blake was at the back of the line, staring up at Megan across the bodies of Chris and Dianna. His head was still reeling from the realization that his father was the leader of the organization that he had run from for his entire life.

How had he not known? How had his father kept it hidden from him for so long?

Because he had not paid attention, that was why. Instead, he had been living his fantasy life, falling for Lucy, and only speaking with his father during occasional visits. In hindsight, Blake should have begun to suspect his father of foul play much sooner than he did. His father had never failed to ask about Lucy, but Blake had attributed it to his father caring for her.

He should never have taken her back to MDRT, his father's phony side organization that he had started to make himself look innocent. Blake knew that now. He had always been wary of MDRT and taking Lucy there, and now he knew why. He should have listened to his instincts. It was too late to worry about it now, however. Instead, he needed to focus on creating a distraction so that Tyrone and Greg could rescue Hiram.

"Chris, do your thing," Megan whispered loudly from the top of the stairs, cutting into Blake's thoughts.

He turned his attention to Chris, who pushed past Megan and cracked open the door. The gunfire had ceased temporarily, and Chris peeped his head through the crack.

"Is anyone left alive in there?" Doctor Sheppard's voice came from outside.

Chris did not answer. Instead, he closed his eyes in concentration, hiding his eye's glow, and after a few moments, they could hear confused shouting coming from outside.

"What the fuck is going on over there," Doctor Sheppard screamed, and they could hear his commanding voice fading as he stepped away from the house.

"Dianna, your turn," Megan whispered, and Chris and Dianna switched places quickly.

Dianna closed her eyes with her fingers to her temples, and the sound of bobcat screams filled the air, mingling with the screams and terror-filled shouts of the soldiers as Dianna's cats attacked.

Blake came up the stairs but paused when he heard his former father's angry shouts.

"Dianna, stop before he absorbs your magic," Blake hissed at her as he came to the top of the stairs, squeezing past Chris and huddling up beside Dianna. "We can't afford to fight off a herd of angry bobcats."

Dianna opened her eyes and dropped her hands back to her lap, shaking her head as if to clear it.

"Blake, go see if you can find out what is happening," Megan said. "I will shield you just in case Doc has absorbed any magic."

"No need," Blake whispered. "I won't be out there long enough for him to notice. Besides, your shields won't hold out a bobcat."

Blake chuckled humorously, but his heart pattered with fear as he carefully opened the door and stepped silently out of the basement. He closed the door behind him, turned out of the small alcove that hid the door, and into the ravished living room.

He stopped just inside the living room, hunkered down stealthily and listening for any sounds of gunfire coming from outside, but the only sounds he could hear were the sounds of angry confusion as the troops tried to fight off melting guns and angry wildlife. That was good. They had caused enough chaos to divert attention away from the cage and the crevice where Greg and Tyrone were.

So far, their plan was working.

Blake turned to go back to the basement when something caught his attention. Someone, or something, was moving around in the far corner of the living room, moving through the shadow that the billowing curtains of the shot-out windows had created.

He squinted his eyes and peered into the shadow, trying to see more clearly into that spot of darkness across the room. The darkness roiled as if alive, and Blake's nerves stood on end as his brain let him know that something was not right.

He stood straight and started backing slowly away from the sight as the tingling of his building power swirled through his fingertips. Whoever, or whatever it was, was now moving toward him, coming closer to the light streaming through the glassless window.

Blake's back touched the side of the alcove that hid the basement door, and he meant to turn and run and flee into the basement, but before he could, the figure's face touched the light and became visible.

Blake's heart hammered in his chest, his glowing eyes went wide, and every hair on his body stood on end. His brain screamed at him to run or fight, but his muscles remained frozen where he stood.

His magic would not work on this one, and it was too late to run. Cold fear radiated through his body, sizzling out the heat of the flame he had been about to throw.

He closed his eyes in defeat as an image of Lucy floated into his vision. His heart filled with sorrow as he mentally gazed upon the last picture of her he would ever see.

Blake knew in his heart that he was about to die.

*** THE CREVICE, TYRONE ***

Tyrone carefully picked his way around the trashed SUVs and the crushed red sports car. Shards of broken glass, twisted metal, and broken bodies littered the ground, and the blood pooling around it all made the earth under their feet slick and treacherous. He almost tripped over a hand sticking out from under a big metal sheet and flung out his arm to catch himself.

He hit the side of the crushed car, and the sound of his hand hitting metal rang through the chasm. He cringed and waited, expecting to hear people shouting to look down and see what had made that noise, but the sound of chaos above ensued, and he sighed in relief.

"Stop making so much noise," Greg whispered from behind him.

Tyrone whipped around and quietly spat back, "I didn't do it on purpose, you nitwit."

"I could turn back and get Chris to have him melt all this scrap and make it easier," Greg suggested.

"No," Tyrone said. "He might be busy with the chaos up there. Do not distract him."

Tyrone turned and began traversing his way to the other side of the fissure once more, and this time he did not slip or trip again. He reached the other side of the gorge and concentrated his magic on creating another tunnel on this side that would lead to the truck that held the glass cage.

His affinity for earth filled him as his eyes glowed brightly, and he aimed his power at the raw dirt on the side of the crevice. He took in a breath and envisioned what he wanted in his mind.

Messages and emotions filtered through his connection to the ground since his connection to the earth worked both ways, and sometimes it was a double-edged sword. Sometimes, he got messages from the earth on what IT wanted HIM to do, and he got one of those now.

Blake had a slight affinity for the earth, but since he had a relationship with all of the elements, his affinities were not as strong as they would be if he had only held one. Despite this, the earth held a deep respect for Blake, just as it had for Tyrone. For this reason, the earth made Tyrone aware that Blake was in trouble.

The earth sent Tyrone a vision of a dark, shadowy figure that held Blake in its arms. It had Blake's back to its front, holding a sharp, shining blade at Blake's neck and whispering evil intent into his ear. The earth radiated emotions through the connection, and Tyrone went to his knees as terror, regret, and helplessness flowed through the link. He had the sudden urge to get up and run, run back through the tunnel, down the hall, up the stairs, and save Blake.

But he could not.

He sent this out to the earth, explaining that they had to save the boy Hiram or they would all be lost. He promised to turn and run back as soon as Hiram was free. He only hoped he would not be too late.

"Tyrone, we have to get going. The screams from above are quieting," Greg's voice tore Tyrone from his communion.

"Sorry, the earth sent me a message," Tyrone said in a shaky voice. "Blake is in trouble."

"Fuck," Greg spat almost too loudly. "Dammit, what has sissy boy gotten into now?"

"Someone has a knife held to his throat. We may already be too late," Tyrone answered.

"Double fuck," Greg said in a lower tone this time. "We gotta go back."

"No," Tyrone said forcefully, grabbing Greg's arm urgently. "If we don't save the boy, we are all doomed."

"First, let go of my arm and never grab me like that again," Greg seethed in quiet fury, glancing down to where Tyrone had his hand wrapped around Greg's arm.

When Tyrone did not let go, he moved his gaze back up to Tyrone's face and glared. "Second, Lucy would never forgive me if something happened to Blake when I could have done something about it."

"Lucy would never forgive you if you let the boy die either," Tyrone said, but he did not let go of Greg's arm.

Tyrone was not afraid of anything when his element surrounded him, and right now they were both surrounded by his earth's protective embrace. Greg's intimidating gazes did nothing to Tyrone's resolve.

Greg took a long breath and closed his eyes as if he were centering himself. Then, he opened his eyes and stared into the glowing topaz depths of Tyrone's eyes.

"Fine, let's hurry so we can get back there and figure out what is going on," Greg said in a calmer tone.

Tyrone did not respond. He let go of Greg, turned back to his earth, and opened another tunnel. The tunnel opened more smoothly and faster than the last one as if the earth were hurrying the mission along so they could get back to Blake.

It probably was.

They reached their destination quickly, thanks to the earth's urgency, and finally, the ground opened upward instead of forward. Tyrone opened the top layer carefully, making sure that the hole in the ground opened up underneath the truck. It would hinder things if the soldiers began falling into a random hole in the ground.

When Tyrone had removed the top layer of earth and could see the underside of a vehicle, he breathed a sigh of relief. It was not over yet, however. Greg still had to climb up and get close enough to zap the cage without being seen.

"You're up, electric boy," Tyrone said, turning to Greg and motioning toward the hole above their heads.

Greg quirked one eyebrow. "Electric boy?"

Tyrone just shook his head and motioned once again toward the hole.

Greg smirked and mumbled, 'electric boy' under his breath as he climbed toward the hole. Tyrone had left handy little handholds and footholds in the earth, making climbing easier.

"Electric boy," Greg whispered more firmly as he reached the hole's edge and peered out under the truck. He could see feet running to and fro around the truck and one set of feet standing firm at the back of the truck. So that must be the guard.

Still smirking, Greg slithered out of the hole and kept to the ground under the truck. "Electric boy. I like it," he whispered to himself as he crawled across the ground on his belly, using his elbows and legs to propel him forward.

Thankfully, he had trained with his father more than any other mutant, so his military skills were top-notch. Unfortunately for the guard, one of those skills allowed him to cut just the right spot on the guard's heel, and the guard instantly went down screaming.

No one noticed through the chaos of attacking bobcats and melting guns as the guard's screams mingled with the other cries rending through the dusky air.

Greg noticed the dimming of the day and realized it was almost nighttime. They had to gain some advantage before darkness fell over the earth and rendered their sight useless. They would not be able to keep an eye on the army in the dark.

He slithered out from under the truck stealthily. Once more, he silently thanked his father for his military training since he had had the hindsight to don the proper clothing, causing him to blend in with the other soldiers running amok around the truck.

He worked quickly, sending a small zap of energy toward the top of the cage where he could see most of the wires sticking out. Then, he ducked back under the underside of the truck when he heard the little electrical 'zaps' that signified the shorting out of electrical circuits.

There were a few loud pops, more soldiers screaming as flames shot from the contraption, and then the cage glass shattered as it could no longer contain the building pressure of smoke and flames building up under the glass.

Satisfied that Hiram had escaped with the cage breaking, Greg slipped back into the hole, turned, and ran back toward the house as fast as he could. He hoped he was not too late to save Blake.

CHAPTER 43: Hiram

*** THE BASEMENT FLOOR ***

Henry's clammy skin grew paler as my worry for him became almost unbearable. Nevertheless, I still sat on the floor by him, rubbing circles on his back for comfort, even though I was sure it was doing nothing to comfort him.

Darius could do nothing except take him into the infirmary that he and the two nurses had set up on the fly to make him more comfortable, but Henry had not wanted to move.

The two nurses hovering around us seemed to be at a loss as they paced around, getting water and putting cold rags on Henry's head. His body trembled when they would replace the rag, as if the coldness were soaking into his soul.

The only other medical personnel in the house was Megan, who was upstairs. Not that she could do anything anyway. He needed his brother, and nothing I said or did would make it better until Hiram returned.

They should have succeeded by now, and Hiram should have been back in the body. Blake and the others should have been back by now as well. Where was Waller? What was he doing?

"Oh, for shit's sake, would you calm down or release me already? You are making me crazy!" Lily admonished me in my head. *"We are all still at the top of the steps waiting for Blake to come back."*

"I can't help it, Lily. I feel so useless right now," I said helplessly, realizing I had said it aloud.

"You are not useless," Henry said through his chattering teeth. "Believe it or not, your presence is helping me hold myself together."

"Oh. I didn't think you even noticed anyone right now," I said as I continued to rub his back comfortingly. It made me feel better to know that he appreciated my presence.

"I know you are there, and the back rub is nice," he said and tried to smile, but the chattering would not let him.

I smiled enough for the both of us.

"How is he?" Waller asked as he came into the rec room from the hallway.

"The same," I answered before asking, "Where the hell have you been?"

"I was guarding the tunnel and waiting for Greg and Tyrone to return," Waller said as he knelt beside us and gently placed a hand on Henry's head.

I looked at the big man with new eyes. The smooth skin of his bald head shone in the overhead lights of the basement, and the lights reflected off the snake tattoo that curled around his neck. The snake's head, with its flickering tongue, sat under his ear. Its body wound around his neck and up the back of his head, and the tip of its tail touched the top of his spine.

He looked intimidating, but he no longer scared me as he had before. Instead, with my memories of him intact, I could see him as nothing more than my childhood comfort zone. How often had I thrown myself at him as I had done earlier? How many times had I cried in his arms?

Many times.

Now I looked at the hugely muscled man and wondered how I had ever gotten through life without the feeling of safety he invoked in me. The answer? I had not. He had always been there; I just had not known it.

Waller's big, stormy gaze landed on me, and he quirked an eyebrow. "Why are you looking at me like that?"

I shrugged as I smiled and said, "I was just playing through my newly recovered childhood memories and realized how much I actually cared for you...care for you."

Waller's eyes softened, and he looked embarrassed! I had never seen him embarrassed before.

"You shouldn't dwell on the past," he said softly.

"Why did you not out yourself before? Why did you continue to play the villain?" I asked curiously.

"I thought I was protecting you. But, if I had known then…well, you know the old adage. I would have told you sooner had I known who Doc was."

I nodded and opened my mouth to respond, but then a feeling of dread and fear washed over me. I froze, tuning my attention inside where my connection to Lily was, and I remembered what she had said to me before I had gotten distracted by Henry.

She had let Blake go outside the basement alone.

"Lily?" I called aloud, yelling up the stairs even though I knew we were supposed to remain silent.

I could not help it. The trepidation and fright grew inside me as if an ocean of horror had opened up inside my soul. I scrambled up from the floor and started for the stairs, but Waller's hand on my arm stopped me.

He had risen from his kneeling position and was standing beside me now, holding my arm and keeping me from running up the stairs.

"Lucy, what is it?" he asked urgently.

I started to struggle, but suddenly Henry shot up from the floor into a sitting position, taking in a deep, loud lung full of air as he did. He looked around wide-eyed for a moment as if he did not remember where he was or what was happening.

"Henry!" I cried and knelt back down to the ground beside him, pulling away from Waller's arm. "What happened? Is it Hiram?"

He turned to look at me, and I flinched back away from him at the strange look in his eyes. They were even a different color now. His ordinarily light brown eyes had turned to more of a hazel color, with the green sparkling in strips around his irises.

"I am back," Henry responded cryptically.

"Huh?" I responded and realized I sounded like a moron. I felt like one, too, because I realized what was happening when I should have picked up on it immediately.

"Hiram," I said, and it was not a question.

He nodded in confirmation, and I blew out a relieved breath. Greg and Tyrone had done it. They had saved Hiram.

"Thank goodness," I whispered, and then I looked into Hiram's hazel eyes and said aloud, "Nice to meet you, Hiram. I am Lucy."

Hiram smiled, and it made his entire face light up. And it was his face. Henry was no longer there. Hiram's face looked older, his lips thicker, his cheeks fuller, and his freckles were not as prominent. His red hair was more of a deep, richer red rather than the lighter orangey red of Henry's, and even his body was more filled out than his twin counterpart.

His entire body had changed!

I wonder if my body changed when Lily was in control. I knew that her astral body had more voluptuous hips and breasts than I had…enviously so… and I wondered if the physical body changed as the astral body did.

I started to ask when that terrible dread washed over me again. Dammit, why was I so easily distracted right now? I was usually more focused than this.

"Lily," I said. "Something is wrong with Lily, and I keep getting distracted."

Hiram got up from the floor, and I stood up straight. Waller hovered as if he were going to grab me again, but I shot him a 'don't-you-dare' look, and he dropped his arm. I started toward the stairway, and Waller followed, still hovering but making no move to grab.

"Lily is your twin," Hiram said as he followed me to the foot of the stairs.

It was not a question, but I answered it anyway. "Yes, she is."

"I am getting information from Henry. I have been apart from him for a long time."

I jerked my gaze around before stepping onto the stairs. "How long have you been apart?"

"Doctor Sheppard has kept me in that cage for months now. He re-energizes me and then zaps my energy to threaten Henry. I am more grateful to your group than you could ever know."

I shook my head, disappointed at what they had done to these boys, and turned back to the stairs. I walked up the stairs, careful not to make too much noise, and frowned in confusion as I saw Megan, Chris, and Dianna hovering at the top.

"Why are you all sitting around here?" I asked.

They looked down at me with worry in their eyes, but it was Dianna that answered me.

"Blake has not come back yet, and everything has fallen deathly quiet. We were trying to decide what to do," she said worriedly.

"Lucy, Blake is in trouble," Lily screamed in my head, and I suddenly only had one mission.

I had to get to Blake.

*** THE TUNNEL, GREG ***

The trip back through the tunnel and into the aperture went smoothly. It was easier to scale the crevice floor this time since Greg and Tyrone knew where the danger lay and was better prepared. Tyrone was closing the tunnel behind them as they went, so by the time they got back into the house, the tunnel was gone as if it had never existed.

That was when the trouble started.

Darius and the two nurses came scurrying around the corner and into the hall, heading for the largest bedroom in the basement where Darius had set up the infirmary.

Darius froze when he saw the two men. "You both need to get topside at once."

Greg stepped forward, fear causing his heart to lurch inside his chest. "Is it Blake? Are we too late?"

"Blake?" Darius asked in confusion. "I don't know about Blake, but a commotion came from upstairs. Waller, Lucy, and that new kid ran up to check it out. We are getting the infirmary ready just in case."

Greg did not ask any more questions or turn to see if Tyrone was following. Instead, he ran down the hallway toward the stairs, took the stairs two at a time, and burst through the door.

The first thing he noticed was darkness. The alcove light was not on, and the dusky night had turned dark while they had been in the tunnels. He paused for a moment to let his eyes adjust, and that was when Tyrone crashed into Greg's back in his rush to get up the stairs.

Greg did not go down but stumbled forward out of the alcove, and when he turned around, the living room was visible. It was washed in the moonlight that streamed in from the glassless windows, and the sight had Greg wanting to crumple to his knees.

Glass, broken wood from the tattered window panes, and stuffing from the shot-up sofas littered the floor. The coffee table in the middle of the room had been thrown aside and riddled with bullet holes. One sofa was tipped backward, while the other was askew from its place against the far wall.

The silence in the room was deafening.

Greg swallowed hard and breathed against the fear that threatened to climb into his throat and smother him. His head swam with icy waves of fear that crashed through his body, and if not for Tyrone's presence and worry for his friends, he would have run back down into the safety of the basement.

"Something is not right here," Tyrone whispered into the silence.

"You can say that again," Greg responded. "Where is everyone?"

A cry of pain rang out down the hallway, and Greg did not hesitate. He bolted away, heading for the hallway and the sound of the scream. He knew that cry. It was Lily's cry when she was in pain, and it was pain without pleasure.

He felt Tyrone hot on his heels as he crashed into the room where the sound had come from, and his body froze in the doorway when he came face-to-face with Doctor Sheppard. He glanced around Doc's body, and the fury that burned inside him raged into an inferno of white-hot wrath.

While the sight of Lily tied to a bed, helpless and nearly naked, lit a burning desire deep in his soul, the thought that it was Doc that had bound her there, and made the cuts on her legs and arms, burned away the desire.

No one treated Lily this way except for him, and only if she wanted it. Lily did not look as if she wanted this now, and Greg was going to tear Doctor Sheppard apart with his bare hands for touching his woman.

*** THE UPSTAIRS BEDROOM, LILY ***

"I should not have gone upstairs alone," Lily told herself as she lay stretched out on the bed, tied to the posts by her wrists and ankles.

"I should have gotten back into the body with Lucy and merged with her to save Blake, but I had let my heart overrule my head."

She laughed silently to herself at this thought. The one time she had decided to be soft and stupid instead of ruthless and calculating, she had gotten into trouble. She would not make that mistake again.

She had darted up the stairs when the others had begun to worry that Blake had not returned, and when she saw Blake trapped in the hold with the knife to his throat, she had appeared and screamed at the figure that held him. Doctor Sheppard froze with the blade to Blake's throat, and his sinister smile spread across his face at the sight of Lily appearing before him.

"Hello, dear Lily. I was hoping you would join the party."

"What do you want?" Lily hissed. She narrowed her eyes hatefully at him as she spoke.

"I was admonishing my son. He has been very naughty as of late," Doc said in his evil, sly tone.

"I am not your son," Blake ground out between clenched teeth.

"Then I will not feel so guilty when I slit your throat," Doc spat back, pressing the blade deeper into the skin of Blake's neck.

"No!" Lily cried out and then cursed herself for dropping her angry demeanor.

She knew from the evil, knowing gleam in Doc's icy blue eyes that she had lost her advantage over the situation. Doc knew she cared, which was not typical for Lily.

"So, my son got to you as he got to Lucy," he said mockingly.

"Actually, I prefer fucking Waller's son. You know, the one that let me out?" Lily purred, hoping to recover a bit of advantage by pissing him off.

If she could piss him off enough, maybe she could get Blake and her both out of this situation. Angry people always make mistakes. Doc's face darkened with fury, and his hold on Blake faltered slightly, but it was enough.

Quicker than Lily had ever seen him move, Blake slammed his foot down on Doc's instep and elbowed him in the gut. The knife slid across Blake's skin on the side of his neck as Doc doubled over, and Lily screamed.

Blake did not seem to notice the blade slashing his skin, however. Instead, he used the seconds he had to react to his advantage by grabbing the wrist of the hand that had slid from around his shoulders and twisting Doc's arm up and around while using his other hand to place it on the back of Doc's shoulder and push down, holding Doc in a bent over position.

Blake pushed his fingers into Doc's wrist, pushing down on the pressure point until Doc released the knife. Then, with Doc disarmed, Blake twisted the arm again and bore down on the same shoulder, forcing Doc to the floor.

The entire thing was over in an instant, and Lily breathed a sigh of relief as Doc's face hit the floor, but her relief was short-lived. Before Lily could even shout a warning, another figure flew through the window and tackled Blake to the ground.

Lily's eyes widened in disbelief as she turned to the window, as if in a horror movie when the person knew the killer was behind them. The troops had rallied, throwing ropes across the aperture and traversing the crack in the ground. Many of them had already made it to the other side, and one of them now had Blake held to the ground.

"Do not kill him," Doc said as he gathered himself off the floor. "He is my son. I will take care of him."

"I am not your son!" Blake shouted as he struggled with the soldier.

Two more came in from the window and came for Lily, but before she could turn and run or disappear, Doc's voice rang through her ears and shattered her resolve.

"You will stay and do as you are told, or Blake will die. What will Lucy think of you if you let her lover die?"

Lily turned and stared into his evil icy eyes. "You would really kill your own son?"

"You heard him. He is not my son."

Doc moved forward and grabbed Lily's arm, and Lily let herself be taken. Doc ordered the soldiers to watch the basement door, then took Lily and Blake into the smaller bedroom down the hallway. That was how she had ended up chained to this damn bed and Blake tied to a chair in the corner of the room.

They could not use their powers to escape because of the null in the room, but if it came down to it, Lily would not hesitate. For now, the only thing Doc had done was talk a lot and cut her legs and arms for emphasis.

That was okay. She had taken worse for Lucy.

Doc had practically ignored Blake since his focus had been on trying to tame Lily, which was a mistake. Lily could tell by the quick glances she sneaked Blake's way that he was slowly and methodically slipping through his ropes.

Doc was pacing at the foot of the bed. He had cut through her top so that it hung open, exposing her bra and bare stomach to the room. Lily did not mind that. The clothes were not real. They were as real as the body was real. If she was corporeal, then so were the clothes. They could easily be replaced with a thought, but Lily was unwilling to risk Doc absorbing anything from her.

"I will ask you once more, Lily. Tell me what you know of the new mutants in your group, especially the one that makes the earth tremble." Doc turned and looked at her with his evil glare.

Through gritted teeth, Lily narrowed her eyes and said, "And I will tell you one more time to go to hell."

Doc lifted the knife and slashed through the bare skin of Lily's leg. She tried not to scream, she did, but the cut was deep, and this body felt sensations much stronger than the physical body.

She cried out in pain, and suddenly, she heard footsteps thundering up the hallway toward the room. Doc moved quickly to the doorway, standing just out of reach of the door when it crashed inwards, revealing the sweetest sight Lily had seen all day.

Greg stood in the doorway, his face heated with a blinding fury that had Lily's heart pounding with passion. Greg was about to hurt someone, and the promise of violence, especially since it was her man about to dish it out, had her insides quivering with need. Lily would love this fight, and judging from the golden glow of her lover's eyes, they would win.

I scrambled up the steps toward the worried trio, admonishing them as I went. "If you thought there might be trouble, why are you cowering here? We need to go find Blake."

Megan put her arm out to stop me, but I brushed it aside even as she spoke, "Lucy, be sensible. Blake told us to wait until he came back. If he hasn't come back, then there must be trouble."

"Exactly," I said. "We have to go help him!"

I heard other footsteps coming up the stairs behind me, and suddenly, the staircase was getting overcrowded with so many bodies. I looked behind me and saw Waller and Hiram coming up the stairs.

"Blake is missing," I said, and I saw the determination in Waller's eyes.

"Well, then, what are you waiting for? Get out that door and find him," Waller said.

I nodded determinedly and turned to the others. "You heard him. Let's go."

They scrambled up from where they sat, and Megan carefully opened the basement door.

The sound of cocking guns had everyone freezing on the stairs. Megan gazed up into the barrels of seven guns and the men holding them.

"All of you come out with your hands up and come with us," one of the soldiers said.

"Just do as they say," I whispered to her. "I got this."

And I did.

I had felt their presence before Megan opened the door, and I had already taken their minds. If Doc saw us, I would close my eyes, and he would be none the wiser, thinking that his soldiers had captured us.

There would be no reason for him to think that I was using my gifts to control the men, so he would not believe that he could siphon power from me.

Megan glanced over her shoulder at me, and I could see the fear in her eyes. I gave her a comforting smile and the full weight of my stare. I could tell from the widening of her eyes that she saw my eye's glow which nudged her forward. She raised her hands over her head and climbed into the alcove, and the rest of us followed.

"You have them, don't you?" Hiram whispered as he passed me.

I nodded.

He paused and leaned into me closely, whispering for my ears only, "There are too many. You will run out of energy without Lily. Let me have five of them, leaving you only two."

I nodded again, and suddenly the weight in my mind was lessened. I could feel the three minds slip from me, but I knew it was because of Hiram. I turned to see the green glow of his eyes, and I smiled my thanks as he passed me and followed the others up the stairs, and I followed behind him.

I had the soldiers lead us toward the master bedroom at the end of the hallway. I planned to search the house from one end to the other, starting with the master suite on that end of the house. We had just entered the large bedroom when the feeling hit me, and I went down to the floor, groaning in pain.

Lily had been hurt, and I could feel her energy slipping away even as the bond pulled her back toward me. I was about to call her back, about to snap that band that would instantly place her back into her resting spot, when one of the soldiers that Hiram had taken from me stepped into my view.

He pulled something from one of his side pockets, and my eyes widened as I stared into the large, luminous crystal he held in front of me.

It was beautiful.

It was dangerous.

It was my downfall.

I could feel the energy-draining powers of the stone as the soldier reached out to touch it to my head. I glanced toward the others out of my periphery and saw that the other two guards that Hiram was controlling had everyone backed against the wall between the large bed and the dresser with guns pointed at their faces.

I struggled with myself in that split second of a moment before the crystal touched my forehead as if time stood still and I had an eternity to decide what to do.

Could I do it without Lily's influence? Could I make the guards that I controlled shoot the other three?

No. It was too risky. One of them might hit one of my friends.

Could I get Lily back inside of me before that rock zapped all of my energy, and if I did, what would it do to her?

No, I could not do that either.

Before the rock touched me, I felt the other two soldiers slip from my hold and point their guns toward my friends. Hiram's glowing eyes held victory as he looked down at me in triumph.

I looked up into Hiram's gaze and whispered shakily, "Why?"

"You are very powerful, Lucy. However, I believe you are too kind-hearted to play as I would like you to, and I cannot have you as an enemy since I cannot control you," he said arrogantly.

"But we saved you," I said. "Henry said…"

Hiram scoffed, interrupting me, and responded, "you saved Henry, you mean. He would have died without me. I own this body, not him, and now I will own and control all this power, including your friends."

The crystal touched my forehead, and all sensations slipped away along with the world. I heard screaming and wondered who was in pain, and then I realized that the screaming was me. Darkness engulfed my soul as I heard Lily screaming with me, and the connection I held with her in the back of my mind stretched and started to snap.

I was going to lose her, but not before I lost myself. I could feel my energy being drained by the crystal, and I would be gone into the oblivion swirling around in my mind before that band broke.

The miasma of darkness drew closer, and I felt myself being pulled into it. I reached out, trying to hold onto my sanity even as I felt it slip away into the void. One name rang true through everything.

Blake.

The last thought that rolled through my mind was that if Blake died because I failed to save him, I hoped I would never wake up.

CHAPTER 44: Hell's Bells

*** THE UPSTAIRS BEDROOM, GREG ***

Greg's voice was low, husky, and dangerously furious as he stared directly into Doc's icy blues and said, "What the fuck have you done to Lily?"

The ferocity in Greg's glowing golden depths had Doc taking a step back, even as it had Lily writhing against the chains on the bed. He glanced her way and gave her a wicked smile as if he knew how his anger was affecting her, and then his terrible gaze moved back to Doctor Sheppard.

Blake made a sound deep in his throat, which drew Greg's attention to the corner of the room where Blake sat tied and gagged. Blake's eyes darted toward Doc, and he was motioning furiously with his head. He kept making urgent little 'mm... mm... mm' sounds.

Greg frowned in confusion and looked back at Doc more probingly, and that was when he noticed Doc had his hands hidden behind his back.

"What are you hiding behind your back, you fucking coward," Greg spat viciously and smiled when he saw the tell-tale sign of anger spread across Doc's face.

Doc's cheeks reddened, and his eyes narrowed behind his wire-rimmed glasses. "I am no coward."

"Yes, you are," Greg said as he stepped into the room, crowding Doc and forcing him to either step back or be shoved by the bigger man.

"Any man who has to tie people up and bully them into doing what they want is a coward. Why don't you fight like a man?" Greg's tone had grown icier as he stalked further and further into the room until he had Doc backed up to the bedpost.

Greg had forgotten about Tyrone at his back. As Greg moved further into the room, Tyrone entered and slowly began to inch toward Blake.

"Touch me, and I will absorb all of your energy and use it against you," Doc said to Greg threateningly.

Greg only smiled, but it was an evil, menacing smile that put Doc's malicious smile to shame. He invaded Doc's personal space, stepping so close to him that their chests touched as he peered straight ahead into Doc's eyes.

"I guess Lucy never told you about my other ability, did she?" Greg seethed, but he did not wait for an answer before continuing. "You can push your puny mental powers into me all you want, and I can give them right back to you, along with a little shock. However, for you, I will make an exception."

Greg could see the start of the fear that began to spread through Doc's baby blues, which made Greg's smile grow even wider as he added, "For you, Doc, I will give you a big shock."

Greg reached up to grab Doc by the shoulders, but suddenly, Doc pulled one hand out from behind his back.

Lily screamed, "No! Greg!"

Greg jumped back, but it was too late. The knife that Doc had hidden behind his back sliced across Greg's stomach, slicing through his thick army jacket and into his skin.

That pissed Greg off.

He felt no pain from the blood soaking the front of his jacket as he grabbed Doc's wrist that held the knife and twisted it viciously. Doc screamed. Greg heard a satisfying pop sound as Doc's wrist was dislocated, and then the knife fell to the floor. Greg had felt the sucking drain of Doc's magic as soon as he had touched Doc's wrist, but he pushed it away effortlessly, much like brushing away an annoying insect.

Greg grabbed Doc's shoulders and watched his eyes fill with terror as Greg threw Doc's power back at him along with his own. He held back at first, letting his power build inside him and only giving Doc a small taste of his true nature. It made Greg dizzy, and black spots began to fill the corners of his vision, but he forced himself to remain upright and gripped Doc's shoulders tighter.

The power built and built until Greg felt as if his entire body was made of pure electricity. Doc's eyes grew wide with horrified terror as Greg's whole body began to crackle, and tendrils of electric lightning started to snake around him. Greg's eyes glowed even brighter as tiny wisps of electricity danced around them. Doc began to struggle violently as much as he could with Greg's electricity running through his body and seizing his muscles.

Then, Greg's smile grew even more malicious as he felt his voltage charge to the max.

Calmly, through gritted teeth and with a furious growl, Greg stared straight into Doc's terror-filled eyes and said, "Absorb this, bitch,"

He let it all go, his entire voltage, higher than anything he had ever released. With the fury of an F5 tornado, Greg let it all go.

*** THE LIVING ROOM, BONNIE ***

Bonnie watched from down the hallway as electric sparks of light danced out of the room, casting shadows along the wall of the hall. She knew it was Greg, but she wondered who he was zapping.

So far, she had frozen at least a dozen soldiers who had tried to make it into the house. They stood like icy statues all along the grass in the yard, frozen in time before reaching the house.

She knew they would live encased in magic ice until she decided to release them or until someone with fire ability melted them, but she was hoping to find Lucy to take their minds. She did not relish the idea of killing, so if Lucy could convince them to join, she would not have to kill anyone.

She wondered if she should sneak down the hallway and meet up with Greg and whoever was with him or keep looking for the others. She had been separated from everyone when they ran into the basement. She had run back toward the back door and had hidden in the wooded area outside. She remembered being trapped in the house the last time WAMB had come shooting, and she was not about to be put in that situation again.

She had heard the animals attacking the soldiers and knew her friends were fighting back. So she had stayed hidden until darkness fell and the night became silent, and then she had left her hiding place and sneaked back into the house to look for everyone.

So, here she was now, wondering where everyone was. She knew the bedroom she had seen the sparks come from was not big enough to hold everyone, but the master suite was.

She turned away from the bedroom when the sparks fell silent, and the hallway darkened. She turned, walked across the great room, and started down the other hallway toward the master suite but paused when she heard a strange voice coming from the room.

"I own this body, not him, and now I will own all of the power, including yours."

"Who was that?" Bonnie asked herself.

It sounded a bit like Henry, that new twin boy, but this one's voice was not adolescently stuck between childlike and manhood. Instead, this person's voice had moved fully into manhood and sounded malicious.

Henry was a sweet boy. Whoever was talking was not Henry, even though he did sound like him. Bonnie knew Henry better than anyone else. Henry had come at Waller's call back at the old farmhouse, but he had been turned away because he had not been old enough, according to Lily.

Henry had approached her before leaving the farmhouse, told her he was disappointed that he had not gotten to join, given her his phone number, and begged her to keep in touch.

Bonnie had done just that. What could it hurt? When they found this place, Bonnie called him and asked him to come and try to join again despite his age. She was sure that Lucy would not turn him down since they needed all the help that they could get.

Bonnie had been surprised when Henry had shown up with WAMB and had been captured by Lily, and Lily had not even recognized him. When Bonnie asked Henry how he had ended up with WAMB, he told her about his brother and swore Bonnie to secrecy about his being at the farmhouse and his and Bonnie's friendship.

Bonnie had agreed, but only with Henry's promise that he would tell someone eventually, and he had. He had told Lucy, and Bonnie felt sure that Lucy would help him.

Frowning in confusion, Bonnie moved further down the hallway and froze midway when she heard Lucy scream. There was no more time for hiding and hesitation. She shot down the hallway and into the room, but her confusion only grew when she took in the scene.

Her new friends, who had offered her a city of freedom and comfort, were being held at gunpoint by a group of soldiers. At the same time, Lucy knelt on the floor in front of another soldier, who was holding some weird, lighted crystal to her forehead. And finally, someone who looked like Henry but was not Henry, was pacing around the floor, cackling with evil laughter.

What the hell was this?

All eyes turned as she burst into the room, and she looked up from her confused state to find everyone staring at her, and two guards had turned their guns on her.

She looked over to Lucy's now unconscious body lying on the floor. She must have fallen over after Bonnie had come into the room. She then turned to Waller's helpless, worried expression as he fidgeted to go to Lucy, then turned to the malevolent, piercing gaze of the person who looked like Henry.

"What the hell is going on?" Bonnie asked.

"Who the hell are you is a better question," the Henry look-alike said.

She frowned at him. "It's me, Henry. It's Bonnie; you know the girl you befriended back at the farmhouse? Why are you hurting our friends?"

He wrinkled his nose in disgust. "You are the little farm girl from whom Henry was leaching information?"

Cold dread slithered through her soul at his words, and finally, Bonnie realized who this must be. From the looks of things, he must be the twin, the evil twin, and Bonnie had played right into his hands. Unknowingly, Bonnie had been the spy that had outed them all to WAMB all along. The thought made Bonnie want to hurl herself from the highest window, but first, she would fix this.

 "You are not Henry," Bonnie spat.

"Heh, smart too, I see," he said sarcastically. "So, what is your superpower, little girl?"

Bonnie narrowed her eyes and started to raise her hands, but Waller's furiously shaking head gave her pause. She glanced from him to the soldiers, to her other friends, who were staring at her worriedly.

She smiled at them all. She was at peace. She knew what would happen to her the moment her ice shot from her hands, but that was okay. She deserved it. She had been Doc's unwitting spy through Henry and had not been smart enough to figure it out and stop it.

It was her fault that WAMB was here. It was her fault that her friends were in danger, so it was her responsibility to fix the situation.

Taking a deep, preparing breath, Bonnie lifted her arms and flung ice from her hands, encasing her target in a solid sheet of ice right before the bullets riddled her chest, and she went down. Her eyes had not even had a chance to glow.

It only hurt for a second, and then the void claimed her soul, and she stepped into a different kind of light where all was peace and love.

*** THE UPSTAIRS BEDROOM ***

No, no, no. This could not be happening. Doc had been so severely electrocuted that he had burned up and flaked away into pieces. It had fried him to a crispy black mess, and Doc's blackened ashes lay next to Greg, who had collapsed onto the floor.

Tyrone had helped Blake out of the ropes, but it had been too late to save Greg. Lily had altered her astral body into etherealness while Doc had been distracted, and the chains had fallen through her. Then, she flung herself off the bed and stood beside Blake and Tyrone solid again, but it was too late.

They could do nothing without being electrocuted themselves, and no matter how much Blake, Tyrone, and Lily screamed, he continued to pour his magic into Doc and would not let go.

He had used up all of his energy—every last drop.

Now he lay in a crumpled heap, and he was not breathing, nor was his heart beating. Tyrone had run to get Darius. Blake was performing CPR on his fallen frenemy, but Greg was not responding, and Blake was getting tired.

She knelt beside Blake and said, "Let me take over. You are getting tired."

Blake was performing chest compressions, counting each one as he pushed down on Greg's chest, and when he got to thirty, he bent over and breathed into Greg's open mouth.

"Wake up, dammit," he muttered at Greg's nonresponsive body after breathing into his mouth, and then he started the compressions again, counting methodically like before.

"Blake!" Lily yelled more firmly. "Let me take over. Find Tyrone, Darius, and the nurses! Get them here faster!"

Blake finally looked up at her, and the tortured look on his face made her heart sink. Blake stopped the compressions and shook his head, gesturing for Lily to take over as he rose from the floor.

Lily could tell he was having difficulty standing, but he did it. She immediately took Blake's place, giving Greg a breath before starting her own methodical chest compressions.

"Please, please let him wake up," she thought to herself as she continued to push and count, breathe, and then push and count.

She had no concept of time or how long Greg had been…no, she would not say the word. Instead, she kept up her work and concentrated on counting and watching his chest rise and fall every time she gave him a breath.

She was not paying attention to her energy levels, so she was unpleasantly surprised when she felt the pull in her gut that signified she was being pulled back into the physical body.

No! She could not go yet! Greg had not woken up yet, and she refused to give up on him now! She gave him one more breath of life and then returned to the compressions.

Her hands went right through him. She was no longer solid and could no longer touch him, much less give him any more CPR, and yet he still seemed lifeless.

The helpless, sorrowful cry she released from her chest as she was pulled back into the physical body echoed in the room long after Lily's form was gone.

*** THE MASTER SUITE ***

I thought it was my imagination at first. My breath came out of my open mouth, and puffs of mist rose in the air. My body trembled with frigid cold, and then I realized I was lying on a sheet of ice.

My vision was fuzzy as I opened my eyes, but I could hear sobbing and keening from somewhere in the icy room. My vision cleared slowly, and I looked up to see a frozen body standing over me, holding something in his hand.

Memory came rushing back as I pulled a painful breath into my frozen lungs. The crystal! It had been draining my powers, but now it sat frozen in the icy man's hand.

I turned my head and saw another body lying on the floor across from me. She was on her back, her red hair strewn around her head as if she had on a red halo. Blood pooled around her body, slithering around as if reaching out to mingle with the red of her hair.

It was Bonnie.

She lay so still and lifeless. Her chest did not rise and fall; I knew she was dead judging by this and the blood slinking around her on the floor.

I felt numb and frozen and wondered if I were dead too. Was I dead or dreaming? This had to be a horrid nightmare. This could not be happening.

I focused on my body and energy, hoping that I would find that I was dreaming and wake up safe and warm in my bed. But it was not a dream. I was very much awake and very much alive. I could feel the buzzing of my magic curling through me, so the crystal had not drained me of my energy. Bonnie must have frozen the man before the crystal drained me and died shortly after.

How had she died?

I was about to try to get up from the floor, but then I felt Lily snap back into her resting place in the back of my mind, and I felt her intense agony and grief at having been pulled back into our body.

Pictures, images, and memories of what had happened to her filled my brain, and the sound of the awful scream she had emitted right before being pulled back into our body because she could not save Greg filled my brain.

Greg!

My pain and sorrow filled my chest, mixing and mingling with Lily's until it became a vast tidal wave of anguish and loss. I wailed, the sound filling the room and coalescing with the sorrowful moans already in the air.

"Lucy!" someone shouted upon hearing my cries, and suddenly I was scooped up from the floor by a hand on my arm. They pulled me up roughly, shoved me against the wall where my friends stood, and then released me to fall to the floor.

A pair of strong arms encircled me and kept me from falling, and I turned into those arms and buried my face into a muscled chest.

"Greg is dead," I wailed miserably, and the body that held me stiffened.

"How do you know that?" Waller's deep, trembling voice said.

I began to tremble violently as the sobs wracked my body, and I could feel Lily inside, crying with me. It made me cry harder. Lily never cried.

"L…Lily…Lily told…me," I managed to say between sobs.

"God, no," I heard Waller say softly, and then his arms tightened around me, and he laid his cheek on the top of my head.

"Everyone shut up and stay still!" one of the soldiers yelled. "You will stay here until we hear from the boss!"

"Your boss is frozen in fucking ice!" I heard Chris yell back defiantly.

"He is not our boss," said one of the other soldiers.

I heard Waller let out a choked sob and say, "My son."

He buried his face into the hair on the top of my head, and then I felt another pair of arms wrap around me.

"No, no, no," Megan choked out as she laid her head on my shoulder and began to weep.

The sobs, wails, and keening filled the room, even as the guards yelled at us to keep quiet. I knew we should not ignore them, but at that moment, I would not have cared if they had shot me.

Greg was gone, and I did not know where Blake was. Bonnie was dead, too. We were losing this fight, and I did not know if I could bear the loss. I felt the courage slip from me as Lily cried inside me, and I cried aloud in Waller and Megan's arms.

Everything was falling apart, but at least I knew that Doctor Sheppard was finally dead.

I hoped he was suffering in death.

I hoped he liked the sounds of Hell's bells.

CHAPTER 45: Hell Hath No Fury

*** THE LIVING ROOM, BLAKE ***

Blake stumbled from the bedroom and walked shakily down the hallway toward the living room. His limbs were weak and shaky, and he did not know how long his legs would hold him. Everything seemed unreal, like he was walking through a nightmare, and his emotions seemed detached from reality. He was cold, but not the kind of cold that his fire could fix.

Blake knew he was probably in shock but could not let himself fall apart. He had seen Lily begin to flicker as he had run from the room, which meant she was on the verge of snapping back into Lucy's body.

Lucy.

The thought of her made him move forward and kept him going even in the face of the cold numbness coursing through his soul. He had to keep going for her. He had to get to the infirmary. He had just made it halfway to the alcove that hid the small basement door when he heard it.

The sound sent chills through him and awoke the numb emotions that had frozen inside him. His breath caught in his throat, and his heart thumped painfully against his chest. The awful, grief-stricken, desolate sound of Lucy screaming filled his ears and consumed his soul. Adrenaline coursed through his body, awakening his shaking limbs and giving him strength.

The sound had come down the hallway that led to the master suite. Blake turned and fled down the hallway toward the sound of his beloved Lucy's keening cries.

*** THE INFIRMARY, DARIUS ***

"We need you upstairs, now!" Tyrone's deep, booming voice called out as he burst into the infirmary. "Greg is down, and they are performing CPR on him now."

Darius did not hesitate. He ran from the room, following Tyrone down the hallway to the stairs with the two nurses following on his heels.

"What happened?" Darius asked breathlessly as he kept up with Tyrone.

"He drained himself," Tyrone answered as he took the steps two at a time.

Darius followed, but Tyrone's answer filled him with doubt. Unfortunately, there was not much he could do about that. His magic focused on physical wounds, not metaphysical ones. Darius's healing abilities could not fix Greg's draining his energy by using his magic.

It was good that they were giving him CPR. That may get his heart and breathing back up, and Greg could naturally build his energy back on his own. It may be hopeless if they could not get his heart beating again. He released that thought as he ran down the hallway behind Tyrone.

A long, sorrowful scream came from the other hallway across the living room, and Darius almost hesitated. Tyrone's voice came at him, though, and he ignored the cry and kept moving toward the bedroom door.

"He is in here!" Tyrone called.

Darius ran into the room to find Tyrone kneeling beside Greg's lifeless form, lying on the floor at the foot of the bed. There was a pile of blackened, charred ashes by Greg's feet, and Darius wondered what had caused that.

Frowning, he knelt beside Tyrone and said, "I thought you said someone was giving him CPR."

Tyrone was frowning, too, as he responded, "They were. Blake and Lily were here. Lily might have used up her energy and had to return to Lucy, but I don't know where Blake has gone."

Darius was only half listening. He had placed his fingers against Greg's neck to check for a pulse. Greg's skin was pale, paler than he had ever seen it, and his eyes were closed and sunken. However, his lips still had a pinkish color, which gave Darius a bit of hope.

Greg's skin was cold against his fingers, and Darius's hope vanished. Fearing the worst, he pressed his fingers deeper into the spot on Greg's neck where his pulse should be and concentrated.

There, just barely, Darius thought he felt a slight pulse. He held his breath, hoping for another beat, and felt another small jump under his fingers. It was weak and slow, but it was there.

Hope flared in his chest again as he removed his fingers and bent down over Greg's body. He held his cheek against Greg's opened mouth as he gazed down the length of Greg's chest, searching for the rise and fall of Greg's chest or the slightest whisper of breath against his cheek.

Greg's chest barely moved, but it moved, and Darius could feel a faint brush of air against his cheek. He placed his hand over Greg's chest and concentrated on his magic. Darius knew that the bone that protected his heart was probably broken if Blake had done his CPR correctly.

Sure enough, Darius's gift let him feel the brokenness of Greg's chest bone. Darius sent his healing energies into the bone, setting it back in place and mending it.

Greg sucked in a gasping breath as the bone mended, and Darius let out a relieved breath. Greg was alive.

"Let's get him down to the infirmary. He is still alive," Darius said.

He watched Tyrone's eyes fill with relief as the big man picked Greg off the floor and followed Tyrone and the nurses back toward the basement stairs.

*** THE MASTER SUITE ***

I did not know how much time had passed as we all stood and mourned the loss of Greg, Bonnie, and Henry. Yet, it seemed like an eternity as the six guards held their guns on us and waited for a master I knew would never come.

He was dead.

My sobs had quieted, as had everyone else's, and soft little hiccups escaped my throat as my trembling body tried to recover from the shock and pain.

"We have to do something," Waller whispered into my hair so low that I had to strain to hear. "We cannot just stand here and do nothing."

I tilted my head and buried my face in his neck, making it appear as if I was nuzzling into him for comfort.

I made my voice as low as possible as I said, "if any of us try anything, they will shoot us. Enough people have already died."

Megan, who was still pressed close to me and cuddled into my side, whispered, "What are we going to do?"

Before I could answer or think of anything, the sound of a voice calling my name had my heart lifting inside my chest.

"Lucy!" Blake's voice called from down the hallway.

Two of the six soldiers instantly trained their guns on the door.

"No! Blake, do not come in here! They will shoot you!" I cried in panic.

"I told you to shut up!" The guard closest to me said, and he reached out for me.

Waller tried to keep me from the soldier's grip, but the soldier grabbed my arm that was wrapped around Waller's waist and pulled hard. I stumbled sideways out of Waller's grasp, and the soldier that had ripped me away from Waller hit me in the head with the butt of the gun he held in his other hand.

Pain exploded in my head, and even Lily screamed as the pain ripped through us. Starbursts of light danced in my vision, and I felt a trickle of something wet slide down the side of my face. For a moment, I was disoriented as I swayed in place, and then the guard shoved me back in the line of my friends against the wall.

My stomach roiled with nausea as I was propelled toward the wall, but Chris caught me before I could hit the wall. I stood there for a moment, woozy and unsettled, and tried to breathe through the pain in my skull. I closed my eyes against the flashing lights in my vision as I tried to keep from throwing up all over Chris.

I wondered if Blake had heeded my warning and not come into the room, but then I felt the heat at my back and heard men screaming. I opened my eyes, but my vision was fuzzy. Turning in Chris's arms, I squinted my eyes, straining to see what was happening.

I could hear Blake screaming as if he was belting out a war cry, and I smelled the acrid odor of burning flesh wafting through the room. My vision cleared, and I could see a wavering in the air in front of us. Then, finally, I realized what it was and glanced over to see Megan holding her hands out in front of her with the emerald glow coming from her eyes. She was shielding us from Blake's fire.

The only thing I could see through the shield was a blanket of fire filling the room, coating the soldiers and burning them alive as they screamed their pain. I squeezed my eyes shut and covered my ears. I could not watch it. I could not take the suffering, even though I knew that they would have killed us if they could.

I knew Blake did not have my qualms, especially concerning me. I had doubts about Blake in the past and insecurities about his feelings for me, but I knew now that I had been wrong.

Blake would burn the world to save me.

*** THE INFIRMARY, DARIUS ***

"Lay him down on the bed," Darius instructed Tyrone as they entered the makeshift infirmary he had set up. Greg was breathing steadier now, and his pulse was stronger. Darius was confident that he would make it, but he needed rest.

"He will have to get some rest and restore his energy," Darius said to Tyrone. "Sit with him and make sure he rests."

"Where are you going?" Tyrone asked Darius as he turned to leave the room.

"I heard screaming on our way down here. I need to check it out and see if anyone needs my help." Darius kept walking as he spoke, shouting the last of his statement down the hallway.

He did not wait to see if Tyrone would respond. Instead, he kept walking toward the stairs, up the stairs, and into the living room. He heard the shuffling of feet in the darkness and backed into a shadowed corner quickly, hoping that whoever was walking around was friendly or had not seen him.

He saw three soldiers methodically sweeping their rifles with attached flashlights back and forth across the kitchen, and Darius slipped into the hallway before the flashlight beams could land on him. He stood back against the wall, holding his breath and waiting. If he was caught now, he would be dead and unable to help anyone else.

He watched for the beams and breathed a sigh of relief as he saw them move down the other hallway opposite the living room. He waited for them to disappear into one of the rooms, then darted down the hallway and dipped into the bathroom across from the master bedroom. He could see into the room since the door hung open, and the first sight he saw had his heart jumping into his throat.

Bonnie lay lifeless on the floor as blood pooled and spread around her. The blood had soaked into her clothes and hair and had seeped around her hands and feet. He knew she was dead. Her skin was already turning blue. The blood was already coagulating on the floor.

Frowning, Darius noticed fresh blood flowing into the dried blood. Someone else was bleeding, and they had been hurt more recently than Bonnie had. The blood was fresher.

Darius knelt on the ground and peeped around the doorframe, looking for any sign of lights coming from the living room or the other hallway. He saw no lights, so he scurried across the hallway on hands and knees, slinking toward the bedroom stealthily and carefully crawling over the blood.

He could not avoid it all, so he crawled through the spots with the least amount of blood until he could see fully into the room.

The sight made his own blood run cold in his veins.

*** THE MASTER SUITE ***

The bank of fire lowered as the bodies fell to the floor and continued to burn. I could see over the fire now, and the sight of Blake standing there with his glowing eyes fixed on me had my heart singing with happy relief.

Blake waved his hand over the fire, and it died to small, flickering flames that I could easily leap over and avoid. Megan dropped the shields, and instantly the heat that had built in the room hit me. It stole my breath for a moment, but the vision of Blake coming toward me with relief shining in his dark brown eyes made me forget about the fire's heat. His eyes were no longer glowing.

I pulled away from Chris's hold and started to go to him, but a movement behind him gave me pause. I frowned at the wavering air straining to see what was moving toward Blake's back, but the smoke that had built up in the room ruined my vision.

I squinted as I looked over Blake's shoulder at the tall figure moving in the smoke, and then my eyes widened as recognition came to me. Lily awoke inside my mind and jolted to the front so intensely that I stumbled forward. I caught myself, reaching a hand out toward Blake as I opened my mouth to scream, but it was too late.

I watched in wide-eyed horror as the knife blade sliced across Blake's throat, slashing his neck open as blood poured down the front of him, and Lily watched with me. Blake's body fell to the floor, and Hiram's evil hazel eyes filled with triumph as his arrogant gaze locked with my horror-filled one.

Hiram stared into my eyes and watched the transformation of horror into a slow-burning white-hot rage. I could see crystal blue light in my periphery, and I knew my eyes were glowing brightly. Lily's pain and fury collided with mine as we joined and merged into one.

There would be no more practice. We were doing this now.

The rage filled us and overflowed, filling the air around us with an energy so intensely powerful that it lit our body with a bright white light and lifted us off the floor. We hovered there for a moment, soaking in the scene around us as our mind and heart shattered into pieces, and those pieces went out into the starless night.

*** THE HALLWAY FLOOR, DARIUS ***

Darius's breath caught in his throat as he watched Lily light up like the brightest of stars and float into the air. The looks on everyone's faces as they stared, huddled against the far wall of the bedroom, matched his own as he watched with horrified fascination.

The choking sound caught his attention.

He stayed hovered on the ground as he looked for the sound, but he did not have to look far. Blake lay on his side, just in front of Bonnie, and Darius could hear the choking, wheezing sound coming from Blake's body. However, Blake's back was to him, so he could not see what was causing Blake to make those sounds.

He surveyed his surroundings, making sure it was safe to approach the fallen man. Fortunately, the smoke that filled the room hovered over the floor, making it difficult to see anything above, but the floor was clear.

Darius crept forward, figuring no one could see him below if he could not see above. The only thing he could see above was Lucy hovering in the air, but that was because the light that filled her body cut through the smoke like a lighthouse cutting through the fog.

He reached Blake's legs and was careful to avoid them, just in case he was hurt too badly to move. He crawled to Blake's front and gasped in revulsion at the gaping hole in Blake's throat.

Who had done this to him?

He had lost so much blood that Darius feared healing him would not help. Blake needed blood, or at least a bag of lactose or saline to fill his veins until his body could make more blood. No matter what, Darius was willing to try anyway.

Darius held his palm to Blake's neck and released his energy, hoping that it was not too late to save him.

*** THE MASTER SUITE ***
*** LILY/LUCY ***

We could see all. The entirety of every emotion, thought, and knowledge of every inhabitant in the place was ours for the taking.

We saw the seven soldiers standing by the shattered remnants of the cage that had held Hiram in the truck's bed. They were still on duty, still guarding what was left, waiting on their instructions.

We should have left Hiram to rot in that cage. We no longer cared that Henry would have died. Maybe he deserved it, and perhaps he did not; we no longer cared.

The guards milled around impatiently, wondering what was happening inside the house as they waited for their master to return.

If they only knew.

They would never know. They would never know anything again. We sent piercing pain into their minds like no other they had felt before. It was cruel to kill someone with pain, but we did not care. They deserved it. They all deserved what was coming to them.

The shards of painful energy stole every thought from their brains as they crumpled to the ground, and we soaked it all in. Everything that made them who they were was pulled away from them as they writhed in agony on the cold, dark earth. We watched in detached fascination as their souls left their bodies and drifted away for unknown destinations.

We knew where those souls were headed.

Hell hath no fury.

We saw the three soldiers searching the house, their search coming up empty in the three bedrooms and single bath down the hallway. They had found nothing but a pile of ashes in one bedroom floor. Faintly, we thought something was missing from this scene, but the thought flitted away like the ashes that slithered around the room as they were disturbed by the soldier's footfalls.

The soldiers turned to leave the room, but they would not reach the end of the hall. The soldier in the front of the line turned suddenly and raised his shotgun to his shoulder. Our lips tipped up into a cruel smile as he blew away his two comrades and then turned the gun on himself. It was challenging to blow oneself away with a shotgun, but it could be done. We made sure it could be done.

Hell hath no fury.

We searched, spreading our awareness across the land to the end of the property. The dozen or so soldiers in the front yard were frozen into icy statues, but we could feel their minds still alive in their arctic prisons.

That would not do at all.

We forced our awareness into the ice, into their minds, and sent an overload of energetic force so powerful that their brains exploded inside their heads. The insides of the frozen figures rained red blood, sending melting pools of red water coursing down the sides of the ice.

Hell hath no fury.

We could feel our energy start to dwindle, but we were not done yet. There was still one more person we needed to take out, and they were right here in this room.

Hiram stood, staring up at us in wonder. We had been in that mind before when Henry had been the sole occupant, but it would not be hard to retake it even with Hiram behind the wheel. We shoved our awareness into him, hard and fast, causing him to stumble across the room. He almost fell over Blake's body, causing our rage to burn hotter.

He was not allowed to touch him ever again.

Our minds collided with theirs, and we got a momentary flash of Henry trapped deep within the confines of Hiram's control. We dove at him, slithering into the depths of his fear as he lay imprisoned in his own head. Henry screamed as we violated his mind, invading every thought, memory, and emotion he had. We laid it bare for us to see; everything he tried to keep hidden was ours. We left nothing behind.

Henry had not been innocent as we had thought him to be. He had known everything Hiram had planned, but he had kept the information hidden so deep inside that we had not gotten anything from him when we had melded our mind with his.

He had manipulated poor Bonnie into betraying us and giving away secrets and our location. He had followed along with everything his brother had planned like a good little soldier. Henry was not cruel or heartless like his brother. He had simply been scared of Hiram and what Hiram might have made him do had he not kept his mouth shut.

We could not tolerate that kind of bullying from anyone.

We knew that Henry probably would not survive the death of his twin, but we did not care. He had not been innocent. He had a choice, and he chose wrong.

We left Henry alone in his secret hiding place and pulled back into the front of his mind, where Hiram was still in control of Henry's body. Hiram was there, laughing and taunting, not believing that we could do anything to hurt him.

He did not believe we would be willing to risk Henry.

He was wrong.

We sent everything we had into that cruel mind, driving our energy deep into Hiram's soul. First, we heard him start to scream with rage, and then the scream turned to one of pain as we drove into him with all the fury of a woman scorned.

Because we were scorned.

He had killed our Blake, and had caused the death of our Greg and our beloved Doctor Sheppard because now we knew, because of our massive take-over of Henry's mind, that Hiram had been the true leader of WAMB.

Hiram had been controlling Doctor Sheppard's mind for years, and no one had ever known. Of course, Doc was a null, so why would anyone suspect that another mental could control him? But Hiram had been able to. Hiram was so good at controlling minds that he could own multiple minds from far distances and control other mentals and nulls.

He was even now trying to control us, but it would never work. We were far too powerful for Hiram because we could do something that he could not. We could merge and become one because Lily and I were ultimately one. We worked together, unlike Hiram and his brow-beaten twin.

It made us far more powerful.

We knew that when Hiram was gone, WAMB would fall because no one was left to control their minds anymore. The people of WAMB would never know what had happened to them, and some would never recover their memories or sanity. Most would go back to their everyday lives with absolutely no recollection of WAMB or anyone associated with it.

Hiram deserved to die, and we were going to kill him.

We poured our fury and agony into him, driving it deeper and deeper into his mind until his entire body was riddled with it. Then, finally, we forced it through him with an intensity so deep that his whole body shuttered violently.

We felt his puny little attempt at pushing our energy out of him, and we swatted it away as if it were nothing but an annoying insect buzzing around our face. His eyes widened with terror when he realized what we were about to do.

Distantly, we could hear voices calling our names, begging us to stop before it was too late. One voice stood out above all the others, but that voice could not be calling to us. That voice no longer existed in the land of the living. It must have been a figment of our imagination, or maybe it was calling to us from the other side as if awaiting our arrival because that was surely where we were going after this.

We ignored the voices, refocusing our concentration on the task at hand. We gathered every last bit of energy in us, focusing it on that one thing that we wanted it to do. We flung our hands out, palms facing Hiram's cruel face, and the energy left us and crashed into his mind, where pieces of us were already coalescing through his brain.

It exploded into a burst of energy so intense that it sent blood and shards of skull and brain soaring through the room as Hiram's head exploded into a bloody, pulpy mass that fell from his shoulders, and his headless body fell to the floor with a satisfying thud.

As our energy left us, we felt ourselves fall from the air and crash to the floor beside his body. The light that had filled us dimmed and flickered out as our consciousness left us, and we closed our non-glowing eyes to darkness.

We were done. We had accomplished our goal. Every last person who hurt us and had taken away our loved ones were dead, and now we would die with them.

With the last of our energy dwindling, we smiled in satisfaction even as we lay dying. The world would be right without those bastards in it, and hell would have shiny new toys to play with.

Hell hath no fury as a woman scorned.

EPILOGUE

I was not supposed to wake up. I was supposed to be dead.
Maybe I was dead. Perhaps this was heaven, or maybe it was hell.

I probably deserved to be in hell.

I had not only killed, but I had been cruel about it. I had been
merged with Lily, so she could have influenced me. But, no, I could
not keep lying to myself. I could not keep blaming Lily for my cruel
tendencies.

They were there, buried deep inside, but they were there all the
same. It took an act of horrendous evil to bring them out, but that is
what had happened, had it not? My world had been shattered and
ripped apart by a cruel monster, and he had paid the price.

Unfortunately, so had the soldiers that had made the unfortunate
choice to come along with him, or maybe they had no choice.
Maybe they were innocents who Hiram had forced to come along.

That would undoubtedly earn me a ticket into hell.

Either way, it was over, and I would have to suffer the
consequences of my actions. That was okay. I would do it happily,
knowing that my friends who were still alive would no longer have
to be afraid of WAMB. They would be free to build their Liberty
City and live a life of safety, happiness, and freedom. That made
any divine punishment that I would suffer worth it.

Slowly, I opened my eyes, and the sight that met me had me wondering if I had gone to heaven after all. Two sets of eyes, one hazel and one deep, dark brown, met my eyes as they opened.

My heavy heart, fraught with the substantial weight of agony and loss, lifted as if its burden had been made of feathers. Lily's sluggish presence inside her hiding place perked up and curled to the surface with me, staring precariously out of our eyes. She thought that we might be hallucinating, or perhaps we were really and truly going crazy this time. She held her breath and waited, curious to see if the apparitions would speak.

I lifted my hands, both hands, one to each face. My hands both touched skin, and I gasped at the raw emotion in both sets of eyes. One hand touched the smooth planes of a newly shaved jawline, which made my heart swell with emotion. The other hand touched the roughness of a goatee, which made Lily stir with hope.

My voice was strained and hoarse when it came out, and it hurt my scratchy, raw throat. "Am I dreaming?"

Blake choked out a sob mixed with a chuckle and opened his mouth as if to answer but then only smiled and shook his head as a single tear trickled down his cheek. That was my Blake, so raw with the emotional overload that he could not speak.

My fingers tickled the side of his cheek and ran down his face to his neck. I had watched his throat be torn open by the blade of a knife. How was it possible that he was alive?

Then, I saw the tiny silver scar that traveled the length of his neck from one jawline to the other, and I shivered with the memory that had broken us and caused us to go on a rampage of mass destruction.

Well, that combined with the knowledge that Greg was dead. Or, at least, we thought Greg was dead.

I turned to my other hand that sat on the strong planes of his jaw, and his eyes were also moist. Lily came forward and looked out of our eyes. Our Greg did not have the same problem as our Blake. He was made of thicker stuff and could hold sensory overloads, but our Greg could still cry.

A tiny tear traveled down his face as he said, "you were supposed to stay on that bed for me, love. I was disappointed that I did not get to play with you while you were tied up."

I backed away to let Lily have her moment as she laughed at Greg's silly attempt at being sexy for her. I tensed as I waited for Blake's usual angry reaction.

Surprised delight had me returning to the surface again as Blake laughed, a full-bellied, choking laugh that was still thick and mixed with tears. Our eyes widened as we turned to Blake, and he was looking at Greg with affection!

What the hell was going on?

Blake finally found his voice, but it was to Greg that he spoke. "Judging by the look on her face when you walked in looking all kick-ass-angry, I am surprised she jump your bones then and there."

It was Greg's turn to laugh, and our attention turned to him. The icy disregard he usually held for Blake was gone, replaced by a look one would give a brother.

Now we knew we had to be either dreaming or dead.

Greg responded, "Yeah, Lily likes it when I'm in badass mode."

Yes. Yes, Lily did like it very much.

I shook my head as she stretched out inside me as if she were a muscle that had been still a long time and needed to be worked out. Then, I felt her go for the astral body and gasped at the sensation of it.

The body lay curled up in that spot that used to contain an empty abyss, which had been the astral body's resting place. The body had been tiny with tons of space around it because we had not used it enough to grow it, but now the body filled the area and then some. It curled into the space as a fetus curls inside the womb, and I could feel its awareness awaken as Lily entered it.

I had no idea how my brain would handle the massiveness of that now fully grown astral body if it uncurled from its space, but it did. My mind expanded beyond space as if my brain had no boundaries, and we had infinite room to accommodate the body when it unfurled.

The body stretched like a languid cat and filled out into Lily's voluptuous form. I felt her leave our physical body and shivered at the sensation. It was that chilling sensation one got as if someone had just stepped over their grave.

My hands dropped away from the men's faces, and I struggled to sit up. Blake was suddenly there, pulling me into a sitting position and laughing as he watched Greg flinch at Lily's sudden presence beside him.

"Stop doing that, woman. You will give me a heart attack one day," Greg said breathlessly.

"Dude, you gave yourself a heart attack, and yet you are still here," Blake said, chuckling.

Greg smiled at him and responded, "Yeah, thanks to you."

Blake returned his smile, gesturing to Lily as he said, "Lily helped."

"What the hell is going on?" I asked, finally finding my own voice now that Lily was riding her own body. "How are you two alive, and why are you two not killing each other? Not that I'm complaining, but...."

"That, my dear, is a long story," Blake said as he sat on the side of the bed. He pulled me into his arms, and Greg sat with Lily on the foot of the bed as Blake told me everything.

He told me of doing CPR on Greg, not realizing that he had kept his sluggish heart beating and had saved his life. He told me of Darius's brave search through the house despite being surrounded by danger and how he had crawled to Blake's rescue through fire, smoke, and blood.

Sadly, we thought of poor Bonnie, that had lost her life defending our group of friends, and we all had a moment of silence for her. I told them of Bonnie's unwitting betrayal, of how Henry had manipulated her into divulging our location, but they were not angry. We all forgave her and were thankful for her sacrifice.

"As far as Greg and I not killing each other," Blake said after finishing the story. "I decided it would be bad form to kill him after I worked so hard to save his life."

Greg chuckled. "And I decided it would be shitty of me to kill the person who saved my father and the woman I loved...oh, and saved me as well."

"And, just what did you do while I was running around saving everyone?" Blake asked humorously.

Greg quirked an eyebrow and answered, "killing the big bad guy and saving your sorry ass."

"Fair enough," Blake said, laughing, and we all joined in the laughter.

I thought for a moment about telling them about Doctor Sheppard, about how he had been innocent through it all because he was being controlled by Hiram, but I decided against it. If we told them now, it would only cause Blake more grief and make Greg feel guilty for killing Blake's father.

No, we would not tell them now.

We knew that we would probably begin to get visitors from WAMB now that Hiram's influence was gone from all of their minds, and Waller had already gone searching for the lost mutants.

We would have to tell them eventually before some of the people coming possibly knew about the Doctor Sheppard puppet. At least the ones who still had their memories. We also had to begin to work on building our city if we wanted room for everyone coming.

I pushed the thoughts aside as I cuddled into Blake, and I felt the sensations of Lily cuddling into Greg. The thrill of finding our men alive when we had lived through the agonizing hopelessness of their deaths was enough for us for now. We could deal with life later.

I was only glad we had a life to deal with, and I was thrilled that we had our men to live that life with us. No matter what problems arose, we would deal with them and have our men at our side.

It was hard to think that months ago, I had been a clueless adolescent girl crushing on two guys, with everyday adolescent problems such as what I would wear that day, how I wanted to do my hair, and which guy I was finally going to choose.

Now, I had this extraordinary adult life with both of my men, and I did not care what I was wearing or how my hair looked. The only thing I cared about was that they were all alive, and we would all spend the rest of our lives together.

At least, that was the plan.

FREE DOWNLOAD!

https://mymeshara.wixsite.com/nethersouls**/landing-page**

ABOUT THE AUTHOR

Rebecca Jose lives in a small town in the heart of Kentucky. She has three grown kids, a multitude of "adopted" kids, seven grandkids, four dogs, and a parrot. She enjoys her job at a local historical sight in Harrodsburg, Kentucky.

When she is not working at her job, or at home on the computer, she enjoys her time with her husband, grandkids, and the rest of her family. Her dream is to create many stories for many readers, and she hopes that people will enjoy her stories for years to come.

If you enjoyed this story, please write a review and post it to your favorite reading site. Tell others about Rebecca Jose and her stories, so that they may be able to enjoy them as well.

THANK YOU FOR READING AND FOR BEING A FAN...

**LOVE ALWAYS,
REBECCA JOSE XOXO**

Destiny Faith was destined to save the world from the demon dragons, leading them into the light and saving them, preventing them from destroying the dragon planet Mikka.

Ethan Tenebris was destined to destroy the world, purging the world of the angel dragons and giving way for the demon dragons to take over the planet.

When Faith and Ethan meet, will her love be bright enough to lead Ethan into the light, or will Ethan drag Faith down into his darkness?

FIND OUT IN THE FIRST BOOK OF THE DRAGONS OF DESTINY TRILOGY...